STACY M. JONES

# The Drowned Boys

*For J.S.*

# Acknowledgement

For some novels, I draw on my own investigative experience and The Drowned Boys is one of those stories. Thank you to Jamie for working on the case with me so many years ago. It was a hard case for both of us to let go. Thanks also to the many families who have lost a loved one to a suspicious drowning. They really are among the hardest homicide cases to prove. For many of you, your fight for justice continues. Thanks for sharing your stories and memories with me. I hope I conveyed your struggle with the respect it deserves.

Special thanks to 17 Studio Book Design for bringing my stories to life with amazing covers. Thank you to Dj Hendrickson for your insightful editing and Liza Wood for proofreading and revisions. Thanks to my family and friends who are always a source of support and encouragement. Thank you to my early readers whose feedback was invaluable.

# CHAPTER 1

At two in the morning, I slipped out of the bed I share with my husband, Det. Luke Morgan, pulled my robe from a nearby chair and headed for the living room. I'd had wine with dinner the night before and that always gave me insomnia. It was a lesson I had to learn the hard way, over and over again. I didn't want to wake Luke since Sunday was one of his only mornings to sleep in. He had developed a new habit of rising by five each morning to get in an early workout.

Once in the living room, I grabbed the television remote control from the coffee table and snuggled back into my favorite oversized chair, kicking my feet up on the ottoman. I turned on the television, flipping through the channels to find any nineties' sitcom rerun.

Instead, all the local stations were featuring late-breaking news.

A body had been found twisted in branches and caught near one of the pillars on the Little Rock side of the Main Street bridge, which connected downtown Little Rock to North Little Rock. I was so focused on the broadcast images of the Little Rock dive team retrieving the body that I missed the phone ringing and the water turning on as Luke prepared to leave.

When he reached the bottom step, I quieted the television and turned to him, surprised that he was already dressed. "Is the body in the river your case?"

He confirmed it was by grabbing a light jacket from the coat closet. "They don't know if it's a homicide yet. I'm sure they don't want to take any chances, given the recent drownings." Luke shrugged on the jacket and looked over at me with a lopsided grin. "Not able to sleep?"

I raised my shoulders to shrug but didn't even have the energy for that. "I woke up about thirty minutes ago and couldn't fall back to sleep. I didn't want to wake you."

Luke walked over and dropped a kiss on my forehead and then on my lips. "Never worry about waking me. Take one of those melatonin gummies I picked up at the pharmacy."

I wrinkled my nose. "You know I don't like taking drugs."

Luke laughed. "It's not drugs. They put you to sleep last time you took them." He tugged at my long auburn hair that had grown well past my shoulders in recent months.

"They gave me nightmares and then I was useless the next morning. I felt like my brain worked on overdrive all night." That was true. While I had felt rested, my dream activity had ramped up. "I hope it's not a homicide." The broadcaster was already speculating that it could be a homicide and that it was tied to the recent drowning cases across the south.

Luke glanced over his shoulder at the television. "We don't need all that craziness here." After he watched a snippet of the segment, he turned back to me and kissed me goodbye before heading out the front door.

Luke was right. We didn't need the craziness here in Little Rock. Over the last few months, there had been a rash of drowning cases of young college-age males in cities across the south – Virginia Beach, Charleston, Atlanta, Austin, New Orleans, Mobile, Nashville, and now Little Rock. Each one had been closed by law enforcement as either an accidental or undetermined drowning death. This would make eight in about ten weeks. The first happened in New Orleans in early

August.

There had been so many in such a short period that news pundits were speculating if they were part of what a retired detective had dubbed the Cross Killings. The detective, Ned Shaw, had connected something like sixty cases in all that he said fit a pattern. In truth, what he found wasn't much more than a bunch of speculation that hinged on graffiti of crosses found near where the bodies were found in the water or where he assumed the bodies went into the water. Some of the crosses were upright and others formed an X.

I had worked one of the Cross Killings years ago.

It had been the worst case of my private investigation career.

I hadn't been in business for more than a few months when I was hired to investigate one of the cases that happened in Troy, my hometown. I never did find out what happened to that young man and the case hung over me for years. The truth was by the time I got involved, the case had already been tainted by Shaw who had convinced the victim's father his son had been killed by a serial killer. No matter what evidence I showed him to the contrary, he didn't want to hear it. The local cops were so disgusted with it all that they had washed their hands of it.

Eventually, I washed my hands of it too and never looked back until Cooper Deagnan, my investigative partner, got a call back in the spring about looking into one of the cases in Chicago. I refused to get involved and he passed it off to a Chicago investigator he knew. He never brought it up again.

Then the drowning cases started in the south.

Shaw had a ragtag group of other retired detectives and a disgraced medical examiner working with him. One of the things they had never addressed in a way that made sense to me was the graffiti. For them, it was what connected all the cases. For me, it was innocuous graffiti that was too commonplace to mean anything. Besides, how would a killer know where a body would be found? How would Shaw know where the bodies went into the water? None of it made sense. I could walk the river any day of the week and find a cross in graffiti that meant nothing.

In my opinion, all Shaw did was ensure that no sensible police force or private investigator wanted to touch the cases again.

When no one initially picked up on Shaw's serial killer theory, he had postulated something even more nefarious. A group of roaming serial killers working together to one-up each other on the body count. I had never heard of such nonsense.

I watched the news a little while longer. When I felt my eyes closing and sleep taking over, I grabbed a throw blanket from the ottoman and wrapped it around me. I clicked off the news and fell asleep right there in the chair.

I woke in the later morning with the sun shining in the front window. I stretched my arms and legs and then pushed myself up off the chair. I folded the blanket and headed upstairs to find my phone. While I had been hoping for a text from Luke, all I had was a message from Cooper asking me to meet him for breakfast near his loft in downtown Little Rock. I texted back that I could meet him there at nine and then went about getting myself ready.

At five to nine, I strolled in and found a seat in the casual local breakfast shop where Cooper and I liked to meet. It was a block away from where he lived with his wife, Adele, who frequently stopped there for coffee on her way to her law office. She had made quite the name for herself in the short time she had been practicing in Little Rock. We handled many of her criminal defense cases. Our business had grown over the last year due in part to the work Adele gave us.

While I waited for Cooper, I ordered a coffee from our server and then scrolled through my phone, looking for any updates on the case. There weren't any that I could find. All the news outlets were saying what they had reported in the wee hours of the morning.

"What are you reading?" Cooper asked as he pulled out the chair across from me and sat. The server rushed over, gushed a hello, and then we ordered breakfast.

When she was gone, I raised my eyes to his. "Are you a local celebrity in here or what?"

Cooper's pale cheeks reddened. "I'm in here nearly every morning and leave a big tip. Adele does the same. You get to know people after a while." He pointed to my phone and asked his question again.

"News about the drowning case last night. Luke got called out and I haven't heard from him since," I explained. "I assume it's not an accident with him being gone this long."

Cooper waited until our server dropped off his coffee and warmed mine. Then he took a sip and eyed me over the rim of the mug. "That's what I want to talk to you about. Not this case but one of the others."

"A recent one or older case?"

"The case in New Orleans. Danny Thibodeaux was last seen at a bar in the French Quarter. He was found in the Mississippi River near where he was last seen. I spoke to his parents and they believe there are some anomalies in the case, which has been ruled an accident. The cops closed the case too quickly for the family's liking."

"Because it was ruled an accident. That's what happens." This was a familiar outcome in these cases and I understood why families were susceptible to the Cross Killers theory. It was something to go on, even if it was speculative and didn't make sense. "Are you going to take the case?"

Cooper cradled the coffee cup in his hands. "I don't need you to go to New Orleans with me. There's more though."

I was happy to hear he didn't need me on the case. I raised my eyebrows. "More than you going to New Orleans?"

Cooper nodded and tried not to smile. "It requires some travel on your part."

I sat back and folded my arms across my chest. "You know that I don't want to be involved in these cases. I'm not looking to dredge up the past. Besides, most of the cases are so old any evidence that might be there is long gone and the cops aren't cooperative."

"I heard you the first time," Cooper said, waving me off. "What if I told you there's one more case smack in the middle of the most recent in the south? This one happened in the northeast on Labor Day weekend."

"Where in the northeast?" I asked cautiously. Cooper knew how much I loved the fall back home in New York. It was easy to bribe me with pumpkins and fall leaves. The apple cider donuts got me every time.

"Troy."

I pulled back. "I didn't hear about any drowning in Troy."

"It's been fairly hush-hush," Cooper said, knowing he had me on the hook. "The medical examiner ruled it an accidental drowning and the Troy Police Department closed their investigation. I had an enlightening call with a bar owner who believes this was a homicide. He has been speaking with the family and they want a real investigation. If it was an accident, they will believe our findings. They want to know the truth and put it to rest. They have the money to pay well for your time. Enough that you could bring in someone else to help if you wanted."

Cooper was wearing me down. I hadn't been home since I got married and I had been itching to see my mother and sister. "What did you tell them? Do they know it would be me investigating without you?"

"They requested you. It seems you've made quite the name for yourself back home on the last few cases we had up there." Cooper took another sip of his coffee while I deliberated. Then he leaned into the table and locked his gaze on me. "What do you think? Want a free trip to Troy in the fall?"

It was like the apple cider donuts were calling my name. Even though I could tell by the look on his face he knew I was going to say yes, I made him wait a moment longer. "What about our cases here? We have several pending. It's not like we can shut down until those other two cases are solved."

Cooper agreed with me. "That's the other thing I wanted to discuss with you. I think it's time we grow our business and bring on a few other investigators. What do you think?"

I thought it was a great idea, but didn't know how we could pull it together that quickly. "Who would you find in time?"

"Leave it to me," he said with a wink. "So, what do I tell them in Troy? You in or not?"

I took a deep breath and let it out slowly, knowing I'd probably regret it. "I'm in."

My mother and sister would be happy to have me home.

# CHAPTER 2

Luke reached his hand to his desk phone and let it hover there before reconsidering. The last thing he should do was try to rush the medical examiner's office. Ed Purvis, the county's long-time medical examiner, was one of the best in the country. He spoke regularly at conferences and worked homicide cases with the police better than most. He'd get back to Luke as soon as he knew anything.

Luke drummed his fingers on the table as he considered his options. None of them were good. The victim, Rob Hall, had been a local college student who had gone out for a night of drinking with friends in the city's downtown River Market area. According to his friends, Rob left the bar on his own and wasn't seen again. One witness, a homeless man, recalled Rob walking alone on the path that ran adjacent to the Arkansas River. That was all the evidence Luke had been able to gather at three in the morning.

Once he finished at the scene, Luke and his partner, Det. Bill Tyler, made the death notification to Rob's parents. It was a knock on the door at five in the morning that no parent or spouse wanted. The parents were scheduled to come to the police station later that morning near ten so Luke could interview them more thoroughly. Rob's friends were expected at noon.

Tyler went home after that, but Luke was too keyed up to leave the police station. Instead, he hit the gym. After a solid workout and a hot shower and a change of clothes, Luke got down to work. Only there wasn't much for him to do – everything was contingent on something else. The crime scene techs were still processing the evidence found at the scene, not that there was much. Purvis was still completing the autopsy and no bars were open yet to pull surveillance footage.

All Luke could do was sit at his desk and stew over the evidence, and more importantly, the lack of evidence to indicate a homicide. He wasn't even sure it should be his case. All signs pointed to accidental drowning. Luke knew he had to have an airtight case before going public. The media scrutiny, not only local but national, would be intense.

Later, Captain Kurt Meadows shouted to Luke from his office as he flicked on the light. "Brief me when you get ready." Then he disappeared into his office and Luke was left in the quiet detective's bullpen on the second floor of the police station. It was Sunday and the staffing in the office would be limited. Most were running down leads in the field.

Luke didn't even have any files to gather to brief his captain. He headed for the office, knocked once, and then pushed open the door. "We can go over the limited information I have. I'm still waiting for an update from Purvis. Family and friends will be in for interviews later this morning. The middle of the night wasn't exactly a good time to gather information. Plus, most of the friends had been drinking."

Captain Meadows had a head of sparse white hair that most times couldn't be seen under his captain's hat. His hands were as sun spotted as his face, and his blue eyes were dulling with age. The man was nearing sixty-five and past retirement age, but he was holding strong. He raised his eyes and waved Luke in. "Understood but sit and let's talk. There are a few things I want to go over before we get too far down the road in this case. Is Tyler in yet?"

Luke sat in one of the two seats in front of Captain Meadows's desk. "Not yet. I told him to get a little sleep and come in when he was rested. I figured I'd get an early jump on it."

"That's fine. We need to have a frank conversation and you can update him."

Luke wasn't sure what Captain Meadows had on his mind, but it was clear by his boss's expression that it was serious. "Are you concerned about the national rhetoric around the drowning cases?"

"Partly. I want you to listen to this. I got this message this morning." Captain Meadows leaned forward and hit the message button on his phone. After a second of static, the message played.

*"Captain Meadows, this is Retired Det. Ned Shaw. I saw on the news that you have a drowning case of another young man under mysterious circumstances. I want to offer my services. We believe there are multiple serial killers at work and the faster you have our information, the faster you can assign a detective to solve the case appropriately. We understand that your department has a high case closure rate, one of the best in the country. I believe we can effortlessly work together."*

The call ended with the man providing his contact information.

Captain Meadows sat back in his chair and pointed to the phone. "That is someone I don't want anywhere near this case. I don't want you to speak to him or let him near any evidence. I want you to warn the victim's friends and family not to have any contact with him. If we have to make a statement to the media that this conspiracy contingent is not at all involved in this, then that's what we will do. We will give this case every resource we have available no matter where it goes."

Luke had several thoughts but he agreed to everything that was asked of him. "I'll warn the family and friends, but you know I can't force them to do anything. If they choose to meet with him, they have every right. I'll caution them that it can impact the investigation."

"Assure them this case is a top priority for us and that we are going to do everything we can to come to a truthful and evidence-based outcome." Captain Meadows folded his thick arms across his chest. "I've been researching these cases since Cooper mentioned it earlier this year. When the drownings started in the south, I reached out to a few of the police departments who have handled what Shaw dubs the Cross Killings. I wanted to get an understanding about how Shaw mucked up the investigations."

It surprised Luke that Captain Meadows had the foresight to do that. Luke certainly hadn't given it that kind of thought. "What was the consensus?"

Captain Meadows held up two fingers. "First, Shaw wasn't involved in the initial investigations the way he and his colleagues are trying to be now. Most of the detectives had never heard of them until well after the cases were closed. The detectives in some cases did a more thorough job than others. I won't pass judgment on those cases but some left a lot to be desired. If I were one of the parents, I'd have questions too and maybe even look to fringe theories to find some justice."

Luke didn't want to make any judgments until he heard it all. "What's the second thing?"

"Not one police department I spoke to provided Shaw any access to case files or witness statements or reports from the medical examiners' offices. Shaw got most of the information from the parents and then went about interviewing other witnesses and drawing conclusions. Bottom line, Luke, they have an agenda."

That didn't surprise Luke, but he had no idea what the agenda might be. "I don't get it. Why would they want this case to be a serial killer or group of serial killers?"

"Fame and money," he said evenly. "My understanding is the logistics don't work for it being one serial killer, so Shaw is now focused on a group of serial killers playing a game with one another. They have said there is a website on the dark web where these individuals share information about victims and their next kills and the details of the murders. They have never, not once, put forth actual evidence of this. But the theory certainly is provocative. As you've seen, they get a bit of play in the media, on podcasts, and one of the cable channels even made a ten-part special on their theories. Shaw is paid a good deal of money to spew his nonsense, and he's more famous now than he ever was as a detective. That's the bottom line, Luke. He wants credit for solving these cases when other detectives can't. Except there is no national group of serial killers."

"Riley had one of these cases years ago when she was in New York," Luke said, not sure Captain Meadows had known. "She said it became a real mess."

"That's what I'm afraid of," Captain Meadows said with a deep sigh. "Listen, Luke, I can't control what happens in any of these other cities. You are to focus on the case here and only here unless the evidence brings you elsewhere. I'm clearing the rest of your cases and you and Tyler are to focus solely on Rob Hall. Is that understood?"

"Perfectly, sir." Luke sat there for a few beats and then said, "I have to say that the case is looking accidental right now. Are we going to have an issue if that's the outcome?" Luke didn't want to come right out and ask Captain Meadows if he expected him to rule the case a homicide if it wasn't. He had never known his boss to be anything but honest.

Captain Meadows shook his head. "Follow the evidence. Don't speak to the media about the case until I give the go-ahead. Do not even hint that the case is accidental right now. We keep everything close to the vest and we keep the family updated every step of the way. Purvis will ultimately make the ruling on his determination. Even if he rules it accidental, I still want you to go after every lead and prove the case beyond a reasonable doubt. We don't normally have to go this far, but this one calls for it. There can't be any lingering questions."

Luke took a breath, feeling the weight of responsibility. "I'll do my best."

A knock on the door halted the discussion. Captain Meadows yelled for the person to come in.

Det. Bill Tyler pushed open the door and had a thumb drive in his hand. "Before I came in, I called one of my city department contacts, woke him up on a Sunday, and got a copy of the video from last night. We can see the victim leaving the bar and heading toward the river. There's no one with him."

Captain Meadows gestured for him to give him the thumb drive. "Let's watch it right now." He put the drive into his laptop and then navigated to the file. Luke and Tyler came around to the back of the desk to watch the video with him.

A grainy black and white video jumped to life. It took Luke a moment to find Rob on the video among the crowd of people on the sidewalk. Luke noted the timestamp. It was just after midnight. Rob wasn't a small guy. He had a muscular build and stood just under six feet. Rob took a few steps out of the bar and then stumbled. Two guys passing by stopped to make sure he was okay. Rob shook them off and then continued down the road. He bumped into a group of women at the crosswalk and then crossed into oncoming traffic that had to stop to avoid hitting him. The traffic waited for him to pass to the other side and then he continued. For only a brief second, Rob was out of the frame with traffic passing. When he reappeared, he walked a few more feet toward the river and then was gone and the video ended.

Det. Tyler said, "It's clear he was drunk, but we don't know why he left his friends and headed toward the river. They were parked back behind the bar in one of the garages. We'll know more when we speak with the rest of his friends today."

Luke thanked him for picking up the security footage. "I want to see what was happening inside the bar before Rob left. The one friend I spoke to said Rob doesn't usually drink that much. He said him being that drunk was an oddity."

"Drugs?" Captain Meadows asked.

"Not that the friend admitted. It's possible and something that needs to be explored. Purvis will be able to tell us that once the toxicology comes back."

"That could take a few weeks," he countered.

Luke held his hand up to stop him. "It's one avenue. We will be exploring all of it when we speak to witnesses and we are going to ask to search the victim's residence too."

"Good." Captain Meadows dismissed them, handing the thumb drive back to Det. Tyler. "Luke, remember what I told you." His boss leveled a look at him that Luke couldn't shake.

It wasn't until they were seated at their desks that Det. Tyler turned around to face Luke. "What did he tell you?"

Luke recounted the message he heard. "Rob Hall is going to be our only focus until the case concludes. I hate to say it but I almost want this guy to have been murdered. If we find it was accidental, it's going to blow up in our faces."

# CHAPTER 3

After breakfast with Riley, Cooper headed back to his loft. There was a good deal of work he needed to clear off his plate before he could leave for New Orleans. He had spoken to his wife, Adele, about the plan before he talked to Riley about it. He had been concerned she might have a problem with him leaving, but she encouraged him to go. She was in the middle of a trial that was consuming all her time. Their new marriage could withstand a few weeks apart if Cooper promised he'd video chat with her in the evenings. He was more than happy to agree to those terms.

Cooper sat at the desk he had in his loft and made calls to a few clients to wrap up some older cases and then he called someone he knew from his early days as a detective with the Little Rock Police Department. Cooper had left police work to become a private investigator for the flexibility and to leave the politics of policing behind. Captain Meadows had more than once offered him his old job back. He was perfectly happy where he was and business was booming.

Former detectives sometimes made good private investigators. He knew his old friend recently retired and might want some work. The call went as Cooper expected and the man was more than happy to cover cases while they were out of town and extend that work as long as Cooper had cases available.

Cooper breathed a sigh of relief that everything was covered. He clicked open his email to start going through the files for the New Orleans cases when his phone chimed. It was a text from Captain Meadows asking for him and Riley to come down to the police station.

Cooper pulled back in surprise and read the simple text again, wondering what he had done wrong. He and Riley often threw their two cents into Luke's cases if it crossed something they were involved with already. In all his time working as a private investigator, he'd never been summoned to the police station by Captain Meadows. He texted back that they'd be there within the hour and then called Riley.

An hour later, Cooper and Riley sat at the conference room table, waiting for Captain Meadows.

Riley's eyes darted back and forth, looking around the room. "Why do you think he wanted us here? I'm kind of nervous and not sure why. It's like being called to the principal's office, only we don't work for the police department. We haven't had any active police cases in a while, right?"

Cooper shook his head. "Not that I can recall. It's mostly been child custody and cheating spouses. I had a couple of criminal defense cases for Adele that pled out. Did you ask Luke?"

"He's not answering."

They didn't have to wait too long because a few moments later, Captain Meadows opened the door and thanked them for coming so quickly. Cooper had expected Luke and Det. Tyler to be with him, but he came to the meeting alone. Captain Meadows took his normal seat at the head of the table. "I'm sure you're both wondering why I summoned you here. Cooper, you recently got a case that we need to discuss."

Cooper eyed his old boss. "With all due respect, you know I can't break a client's confidentiality."

"Of course not," he said and let the tension build. Then he locked his gaze on Cooper. "I'm the reason you got the case. I referred you."

Cooper furrowed his brow. "What case did you refer?"

"Two cases. The case in New Orleans and the one in Troy."

Riley looked over at Cooper. He shrugged. "Maybe you should explain. I haven't even had a chance to go through the case file or provide Riley with the information on the Troy case yet. We only both agreed to take the cases this morning."

"That's fine and it's good that we are meeting first," Captain Meadows assured them. He went on to explain that he had been calling police departments about the drowning cases and found that the detectives in New Orleans and Troy were both dissatisfied with the way the cases had been closed. Both felt they had enough to investigate the cases as homicides, but their captains had forced them to close the cases when the medical examiners ruled them accidental.

Captain Meadows rapped his knuckles in frustration against the table. "What happened was they received calls from Ned Shaw and dumped the cases before a publicity nightmare. There are families who might never have justice. I couldn't convince their captains to reopen the cases, but the detectives are willing to work with the pair of you."

"I spoke to the family of the victim in New Orleans. They didn't mention that about the detective," Cooper said, still confused.

Captain Meadows dismissed it. "I told the detectives to quietly pass your information to the families, and if they were open to hiring a private investigator, that's what they should do. I know with you two on the cases, the families will have resolution one way or the other. If the cases are homicides, the police departments will have no option but to reopen and arrest whoever you identify. If the cases are accidental drownings, then the families will be happy with the extra scrutiny. It's a win-win for everyone."

"I appreciate your faith in us," Cooper said, unsure of what else to say. There had been a whole backroom operation to get the cases to them that Cooper hadn't been aware of.

"Will we have law enforcement cooperation?" Riley asked what Cooper had been thinking.

"Quietly, but yes. Riley, you already know Det. Miles Ward from the Troy PD. He is willing to work with you on the case. He said he's willing to provide all the information you need, quietly of course."

Cooper locked his gaze on Riley. "That won't be a problem, will it?" He was sure Captain Meadows had no idea of the history between Riley and Miles. There had been a little too much flirting for Cooper's liking when they had worked a case together right before Riley got married.

Her back stiffened as Riley caught his meaning. She glared at him across the table. "It will be perfectly fine," she said through gritted teeth.

Captain Meadows tried not to smile. "I feel like I'm missing something here, but I'm not getting involved. Cooper, the New Orleans detective is Det. Clive Elio. He's been with the department for ten years. He's a good solid detective with good skills and instinct. He said to call him when you're in town and settled and he'll give you everything you need to get started."

Cooper added the detective's name and number in his phone and then raised his eyes. "Is there anything else we need to know?"

Captain Meadows folded his hands on the table. It was a gesture that Cooper knew meant he wasn't done. "I had a selfish motive for getting you these cases. These drownings are causing disruption across the south much in the way they have across the northeast for more than twenty years. I want these cases solved. I want definitive resolution locked down so tight that no one dare question them. If there is a serial killer in the south causing this recent rash of cases, then I know, you'll figure it out. If there's some serial killer still killing up there in the northeast, Riley, you'll figure it out. If they are all connected, then I can't think of a better trio to have on the cases. But you will find resolution – got it?"

For a brief second, Cooper forgot that Captain Meadows wasn't his boss. "You have my word that we will do our very best."

"You're going to need to do better than that," he said with a frown. "I have Ned Shaw already calling me and trying to get involved in the drowning that happened here last night. Riley, this morning Luke told me that you know Ned Shaw. What's your impression?"

"He's a menace," Riley said, shifting in her chair. "I worked on one of the older drowning cases several years ago when I first started as a private investigator. Ned Shaw and his team messed up that case, so I agree with everything you're saying. The only way to keep him out of the cases is if the families keep him out. We need to cut off all his access to case information. It's the families that are providing him with the case information – medical examiner reports and other documents that the family has requested from the detective. Sometimes they have even used Freedom of Information requests. Shaw takes these documents and then goes out to the crime scenes and looks for cross graffiti and creates a narrative – which doesn't seem to matter if it's based on fact or not."

Cooper had heard more than an earful about Ned Shaw after he had tried to convince Riley to take the drowning case in Chicago. She had convinced Cooper that it wasn't worth the grief that it would bring them. "What can we do to keep Shaw out of these investigations besides telling the families? I don't want to get to New Orleans and have to fight every step of the way during the investigation. I also don't want Det. Clive Elio to get annoyed and shut everything down."

"That won't happen," Captain Meadows assured him. "That's precisely why I gave him your information. Shaw had started to worm his way into the investigation and that's when it was closed.

The family is unhappy and Det. Elio explained that it was Shaw who caused the issue. You should be fine." Captain Meadows trained his focus on Riley. "Have you met Shaw in person?"

"Several times," Riley said with annoyance in her voice. "He harassed me for months to get me to share information with him, and when I wouldn't, he made sure to tell everyone who would listen that I wasn't competent. That the family should go with his theory and that I wasn't experienced enough or knew what I was doing. It was hard to debate because I was so new."

Cooper hadn't heard that it had gotten that bad. "What made him stop?"

Riley's face grew pained. "I hate to say it but another drowning case garnered more media attention. By that point, the father had gone too far down the rabbit hole of Shaw's theory and wouldn't hear evidence to the contrary. I had to walk away."

"That's exactly what we are going to prevent in these cases," Captain Meadows stressed and then dismissed them. "Please call and let me know if you need anything. It should go without saying that I expect you to loop Luke in on any evidence you find that may relate to the case here."

As Cooper left the office, he whispered to Riley, "I think I got us in over our heads."

"I wouldn't say we are in over our heads," she countered. "These are difficult cases with a good deal of emotion. I didn't fight hard enough to be heard back then."

"You shouldn't have to fight to be heard," Cooper reminded her. As they got to the top landing of the stairs, Luke and Det. Tyler were at the bottom speaking to someone. Cooper and Riley waited until they started ascending the stairs toward them.

"What are you doing here?" Luke asked, reaching the top and dropping a kiss on Riley's forehead. "I saw you called but haven't had a minute to call you back. I met with Purvis and was running down some leads on the drowning case."

"That's why we're here," Riley said and pointed to Captain Meadows's office. As the four of them walked to Luke's desk, Riley explained the meeting and that she was leaving for New York. She tugged on Luke's sleeve. "I had hoped to talk to you about this first before the decision was made, but it seems even if I don't want to go, Captain Meadows already promised that Cooper and I would take the cases."

Luke perched on the edge of his desk. "It might be good for you both to look into similar cases and catch if we miss anything. It will be good for the three of us to see what we find. If there are connections, there are, and if not, I'm perfectly fine saying that, too. We work them individually if or until a time comes that we need to connect them."

"Fresh eyes," Det. Tyler said and slapped Cooper on the back. "You going to be fine down in New Orleans on your own? It's a spooky city, especially this time of year. Don't get bit by a vampire."

Cooper laughed. With a catch in his voice, he said, "I'm sure I'll be fine. Besides, I don't believe in all of that."

"When are you both leaving?" Luke asked and reached for Riley's hand.

"I got a last-minute flight in the morning," she said and then looked at Cooper.

"In the morning," he echoed. "Did you get anything back yet on your case?"

Luke inched back farther on top of his desk until both legs dangled free. "Purvis didn't find any evidence of a homicide and wanted to rule it accidental. There was water in the lungs, so the victim drowned but no sign of foul play. He suspects Rob Hall stumbled into the water, was too drunk to swim, and drowned. The only saving grace for us is I asked him to rule it undetermined until the toxicology comes back. It buys us some time."

"Hopefully, time is all we need to solve these cases," Cooper said, feeling a sudden weight on his shoulders that hadn't been there earlier.

# CHAPTER 4

Luke and Det. Tyler spent the better part of the early morning making calls to every shop on President Clinton Avenue to hunt down surveillance footage along the path where Rob Hall had gone to a local bar and then disappeared.

President Clinton Avenue was the main road that ran through the River Market District. On a weekend, the area was filled with locals and tourists checking out Little Rock's nightlife. The whole area was a hub of activity with a mixture of restaurants, art galleries, entertainment venues, stores, and living loft spaces. The area was well-lit and had sidewalk benches, street trees, decorative lighting, and designed walkways. It was not a place people typically went missing.

Luke wasn't even sure he could consider Rob Hall *a missing person* when they knew exactly where he ended up. What was *missing* was nearly an hour of unaccounted for time. Unlike all the other cases of drowned young men causing a national stir, Rob wasn't missing for days, weeks, and even months in some cases before his body was found in the Arkansas River. It was a little over an hour between last sight and when Purvis called the time of death.

"Sixty-three minutes," Luke said, pinching the bridge of his nose. "We need to find out what happened in those sixty-three minutes. Rob left the bar, walked toward the trail on the river, and then is out of sight until his body is found floating in the river. The only witness we have is the homeless man who saw him around the statue garden heading west."

"Who initially called it in?" Det. Tyler asked, stretching back in his desk chair.

"Anonymous tip into 911. It was traced back to a cellphone but no one answers and it's one of those pre-paids we can't trace." That had been a worrisome development when Luke realized how the 911 had been called in. He also wondered how anyone could see a body that far into the river at that time of night. Rob's body might show that it was an accidental drowning, but there were definite indicators of suspicious activity that made Luke curious. He explained that to Det. Tyler and added, "This case is almost too neat – no evidence of foul play but almost no evidence at all. I don't understand how no one saw him fall in. Yet someone happened by and saw a body out in the water that time of night. It's too dark and doesn't make sense to me."

Tyler agreed. "I don't like an anonymous 911 call either."

"That's tripping me up, too." Luke checked his watch. Rob's friends would be there soon to be interviewed. Luke and Det. Tyler had spoken to Rob's parents that morning after running down surveillance leads. His parents didn't have much to add from when the death notification had been made. Their son had been out with friends and was drinking and listening to live music. He was doing what many other twenty-somethings were doing that night. No different.

Rob had no known drug use, no recent bad breakups, and no known enemies. There was no reason for Rob to have been murdered. While his parents would accept a finding of accidental, they had considered that just as unlikely. Rob wasn't known to be a heavy drinker and he was a strong swimmer. He had grown up in Little Rock and knew the River Market area well, so well that his parents couldn't think of any scenario in which he would have stumbled into the river.

Luke tried his best to keep his game face on during the interviews, not giving away that he was agreeing with them. The circumstances and the physical evidence simply didn't gel with one another. Luke wasn't sure of much, but he was certain Rob Hall's death was suspicious.

At five to noon, three young men made their way into the detective's bullpen to meet with Luke and Det. Tyler. They'd all be interviewed separately to not cross-contaminate their statements. Det. Tyler would take one, Captain Meadows another, and Luke would speak to Rob's best friend, Derek Vance.

When Luke saw them, he reminded Det. Tyler of the most pertinent questions then he went to greet them. After introducing himself and Det. Tyler, Luke pointed to a short hallway. "You'll each be in a separate interview room. We'll be conducting the interviews at the same time and then conferring with each other before wrapping up the last of our questions."

After the young men agreed, even as apprehension came over their faces, Luke directed Derek to the last interview room and told him to take a seat. He was a little taller than Luke and had a baseball cap turned backward with a tuft of brown hair that came through the front just above the snap. His eyes darted around the room and he appeared both uncomfortable and uncertain.

Luke sat and pulled in his chair. "Do you have any questions before we get started?"

Derek shifted his eyes to Luke. "Do I need a lawyer? My father said I shouldn't talk to you without a lawyer. I didn't do anything wrong so I'm not sure why I need one."

Luke rested his arms on the table, trying to hold back his annoyance. "If you didn't do anything wrong, then you shouldn't need a lawyer. You have the right to one if you'd like, but you're not a suspect. I'm not even sure a crime has been committed. I'm talking to you today to learn more about Rob's life and the events of last night."

Derek nodded and agreed to continue without an attorney. "When you say you're not sure a crime has been committed, do you mean that you're not sure that Rob was murdered?"

"That's correct. No one has said anything about a murder." Luke tried to read Derek's body language. He appeared nervous and closed off. "Rob's parents said you were Rob's best friend. How long have you known each other?"

"Since second grade. We went to high school together, played baseball together, and then went to college together. We shared an apartment and were both supposed to graduate next May."

Rob and Derek were already twenty-two so the math was a little off for Luke. "Did you start college late?"

"We both changed majors and had a little trouble with our grades as freshmen. Too much drinking and goofing off and we missed some classes. Both of us also had to work to pay for school, so it was hard to take extra classes or summer classes." Derek shrugged. "Better late than never."

"It wasn't a judgment," Luke assured him. "I wanted to make sure I had the right information. Sounds like you know Rob well then. Was he having trouble with anyone before last night?"

Derek shifted his eyes to the side. "What kind of trouble?"

"Anything. Fights with anyone. Girlfriend problems. Drugs. Gambling. It could be anything. I need to learn more about Rob's life to understand what might have happened to him." Luke leaned forward and said Derek's name to get his attention. Once the young man looked at him, Luke said, "I'm not reporting anything you tell me back to Rob's parents if that's your concern. This conversation is between you and me. I'm using the information to rule out murder. If it's an accident, then that's what it is. Otherwise, I need to know if anyone had a problem with Rob."

Derek remained quiet for a moment. His breathing was loud and uneven. "Rob had an issue with his girlfriend, Maggie. He recently found out that she was cheating on him." Derek shook his head and corrected himself. "That's not quite right. He found out that she had another boyfriend, so technically Maggie was cheating on the other guy with Rob."

"Do you know this other guy's name?"

"No. I'm not sure how Derek found out. He was upset one night and confided in me they had a huge fight about it. He didn't get into specifics because he was embarrassed by the whole thing. I guess he like, loved her or something. I have Maggie's information if you want it."

This was the first anyone mentioned that Rob had a girlfriend. It was something his parents didn't even know. "Did Rob's parents know about Maggie?"

"Probably not. They had only been dating a few months. Rob didn't share that kind of thing with them."

Luke noted that and looked back up at Derek. "What kind of relationship would you say Rob had with his family?"

"I don't want to say anything bad," Derek said, wincing. "You know how it can be with parents sometimes. They don't always understand that times have changed. Rob figured it was better to not tell them the things he was doing that might upset them." He realized then that he had opened a door. "Not that Rob was doing anything bad."

*Sure, he wasn't.* "What other kinds of things didn't Rob tell his parents?" Luke waited for the response, but Derek pulled back and seemed uncertain whether or not he should share. "Derek, I'm not here to ruin Rob's reputation or go back and tell his parents anything. I'm here because Rob drowned in the Arkansas River and his family and friends deserve to know if that was an accident or not. If it wasn't an accident, then Rob deserves justice and the perpetrator needs to be prosecuted and punished."

Derek gnawed at his bottom lip as he considered. "Rob was high last night. It was just a little weed, no big deal. The weed cookies had us all a little messed up."

"It was edibles?" Luke asked, making sure that's what Derek was saying.

"Yes. We made them back at the apartment earlier in the day and then ate them before we went out. We were in the bar for a while, had some dinner and drinks, and were hanging out listening to music. Right before he left the bar, Rob said he wasn't feeling all that great and wanted to get some fresh air. I figured he'd take a quick walk and be back. When he didn't answer his cellphone and never returned, we got worried. That's when we ran into you."

Luke did fast math in his head. "You couldn't have been too concerned. You waited a good while before searching for him."

"I feel terrible about it. I wasn't feeling that great either and I thought he was outside, sitting on a bench or something. I had no idea he went towards the river." Derek slumped forward and put his head in his hands. "I can't believe Rob is dead."

Derek cried softly, but it didn't tug at Luke's heartstrings, not even a little. Luke waited a moment for Derek to compose himself and then started again. "Run me through the events of the night starting back at your apartment. Why were you going to the bar last night?"

"It was a regular Saturday night out," Derek said, gesturing with his hands. "We didn't have much planned earlier in the day, but then another friend of ours wanted to see a girl who was going out with her friends, so he suggested we meet up with them."

Luke pointed toward the door. "Is this one of the friends who are being interviewed right now?"

Derek shook his head. "Some other guy we know."

"It was a last-minute plan then?"

"That's normally how it goes," Derek explained.

"How many of you ate the edibles?"

"Five of us but only four of us went to the bar. Our other friend, Erik, said he didn't feel like going out. He stayed back and watched a movie. He does that sometimes. He isn't much for getting high and then going to a bar."

"Was anyone sober to drive?"

"The edibles didn't kick in until later while we were down at the bar," Derek said, looking across the table like he assumed Luke didn't know how edibles worked.

Luke wasn't going to debate the point that one of them had ingested drugs and then drove. "Anything significant happen on the way to the bar?"

"No, we drove there and parked in the garage. Even at the bar, nothing significant happened. It was kind of a boring night. We grabbed a table in the back and hung out. The girls never showed up. We ordered food right before the kitchen closed for the night. Then sometime later, the band started to play and Rob said he wasn't feeling great. That's when he said he wanted some air. He hadn't even finished eating the burger he ordered."

"Was he using his phone or anything before leaving?"

It took Derek a moment to realize what Luke was asking. "I don't think so. He said he needed fresh air."

"Did anyone follow him out from your group?"

"No. We all stayed at the table together until we got concerned when Rob didn't come back. Then we split up and started looking for him. I ran into you and you told me what happened before I ever had the chance to call the cops." Derek rubbed his forehead. "I had no idea he was in trouble. I don't understand how it could have happened so quickly."

Luke didn't understand that either. He asked a series of questions, but Derek didn't have much else to add. For a young man who recently lost his best friend since second grade, he didn't ask any questions about Rob's death and didn't have much to offer, except the lead on the girlfriend.

# CHAPTER 5

Back in the conference room after Derek and Rob's other friends left, Luke met Det. Tyler and Captain Meadows to discuss. They had broken shortly during the interviews to confer if any follow-up questions needed to be asked immediately but there were none.

Luke pulled out the dry-erase board and set it up. He needed a visual timeline. He grabbed a blue marker and started with the boys back at their apartment and went right up to the point where Rob's body was found by the anonymous 911 call.

"Rob left the bar shortly before midnight," Luke said, mostly to himself as he stared up at the board. "Sixty-three minutes missing in the timeline. Is that enough time for a stranger to have killed him?" Neither Det. Tyler nor Captain Meadows responded, so Luke turned around to face them with his eyebrows raised. They were waiting for context to Luke's question.

Luke dropped the marker and pulled out the chair and sat so he was at eye level with them. "We can get into the interviews in a moment. I want us to think about this question. There are no bruises on the body, no defensive wounds. There was no struggle of any kind that we have evidence of so far. We have a young man, who eats some edibles, goes to a bar, orders dinner, drinks a few beers, and then leaves the bar, saying he needs some air. We know the direction he went and then sixty-three minutes later he's dead. Is that enough time for a stranger to kill him?"

"I assume you're asking about the serial killer theory?" Det. Tyler asked.

Luke wasn't sure he meant only that. "Sure, that's the most likely stranger murder. Otherwise, we'd be looking at a robbery or a fight and there's nothing to indicate either. I'd assume the serial killer would have had to be stalking Rob."

"That or the killer was stalking the area and chose the easiest victim," Captain Meadows suggested. "I know we don't want to leap to a serial killer because that's what Ned Shaw is doing, but let's cut through the chatter of all of that and think logically. We know how serial killers work. They have a method of killing they like and many have a preferred victim selection. Let's say we are dealing with someone who likes drowning his victims and is targeting young men. If that's the case, then an area like the River Market is the perfect hunting ground."

Det. Tyler picked up where Captain Meadows left off. "The killer is out there trolling the bars or waiting near the river, waiting for that one lone person so they can attack. In this case, Rob walked away from his group. In all the other cases in the south, the young men got separated from the group. None of them came back. All of them ended up in rivers."

Luke said, "The answer to my original question then is yes, a stranger could have had enough time to kill Rob."

"Enough time? Yes. But logistically, no," Captain Meadows countered. "He'd have to get Rob into the water without a fight and without leaving evidence of a struggle. I'm not seeing how that's possible. It's not like Rob was pushed off a bridge or a high cliff. He was parallel to the river and it appears he walked in and drowned." Almost as if reading Luke's mind, Captain Meadows added, "You need to go down to the river and walk through how to get a man into the water without struggle. See if that's possible."

Det. Tyler agreed that it was a good idea. "It might be easier because Rob was drunk, which will impact coordination and reaction time. What do you say, Luke? Can I try to drown you?"

"Later," Luke said dryly, wanting to stay on task. "I assume if we are looking outside of a serial killer, the likelihood of a stranger attack is nil?" Captain Meadows and Det. Tyler agreed with that. "Then, if we are looking at a homicide, then it's someone the victim knows who either followed him out that night or was waiting out there for him."

Det. Tyler leaned on the table. "Brian, the guy I interviewed, said Rob didn't feel well so he went outside to get some fresh air."

Captain Meadows added, "Same with Paul, the young man I interviewed."

Luke would watch the interviews back to see how they described the circumstances of the night. There was a chance that it was a story they had concocted before they came into the interviews. If that were the case, they'd all tell the story in similar language without corroborating details. "What do we think is the most likely thing to have happened?"

"Accident," Captain Meadows and Det. Tyler said at the same time. Then Captain Meadows turned his body to face Luke more squarely. "Unless you uncover some motive for someone who wanted Rob Hall dead, you have no evidence to say it's anything but that. It's not even twenty-four hours yet, so I say hit the field and see what you can find. You were right in asking Purvis to wait on ruling it an accident until the toxicology comes back. No point jumping the gun and giving Shaw any wriggle room in this case. Will you follow up with the family again?"

"I will when I have something to tell them. Did Paul and Brian confirm that they were in the bar all night long?"

"Brian confirmed it. He said that at one point he had to take a call and walked into a back hallway of the bar. He wasn't sure if Paul and

Derek remained at the table. He said he was gone maybe about twenty minutes, but he couldn't be sure," Det. Tyler explained.

"That must have been around the same time that Paul said he went to the bar to get everyone more beer. He said Derek was sitting at the table alone when he went to the bar and he thought Brian had taken a call," Captain Meadows said. "It sounded like Paul was a bit drunk, so I'm not going to give his timeline too much credibility. I think he was honest overall in the interview."

Det. Tyler and Luke thought the same about their interviews – although they both felt some emotion and depth were lacking. "It's nearing four, Luke. What do you want to do?"

Luke heard the question even though his mind was elsewhere. It took a beat to process it. He looked over at his partner. "We have a little time left in the day. I'm going back to the bar and interview the staff. I want to see what they can confirm and if there's any surveillance footage. You go get some rest and we can start fresh in the morning."

"Are you sure, Luke? I don't mind going with you."

"Go spend the rest of Sunday with your wife. I'm sure she cooked a nice Sunday dinner for you." Luke had felt bad dragging Det. Tyler in on a Sunday.

Det. Tyler patted his growing belly. "I need to start coming in early and hitting the gym with you."

Before they left, Captain Meadows pulled Luke aside. "I hope you don't mind that I had Cooper and Riley take those other cases. I figured if all three of you were on it we might get somewhere."

"I don't mind at all," Luke said, grabbing a pen off his desk and slipping his phone into his pocket. "It's a good excuse for Riley to go see her mom. I know she's been wanting to get up there. I'm only worried because of her involvement before. She's the only one of us that's had direct contact with Ned Shaw. I know she doesn't want that to happen again."

"How will she handle it if it happens?"

Luke laughed. "How do you think she is going to handle coming face to face with a man she can't stand who messed up a criminal case she had been working?"

"That well then," Captain Meadows said, sharing a laugh with Luke. "Let's hope their paths don't cross. You told Tyler to go home. You should do the same."

Luke checked the time again. "I'm just going to stop by the bar and then head home."

Captain Meadows slapped Luke on the back. "Don't work too late."

Luke gathered the rest of his things and left. He walked the few short blocks from the police station to the River Market District. Most of the bars were open and crowds of people swarmed around televisions watching Sunday football. Luke made his way to Coach's Bar, which sat in the middle of the first block. Luke tried to remember what the place had been called before, but he couldn't. It was one of those locations that changed ownership every few years. They couldn't seem to keep the current bar up and running and turning a profit. The next owner thought luck would be on their side, but it never seemed to work that way.

Luke pulled open the glass door and stepped inside. His shoes stuck to the black floor as he made his way up to the bar. He stepped around two guys arguing about the game and flashed his badge at the bartender. "I need a minute of your time."

The young guy pointed to the end of the bar. "Head in the back and talk to my boss. He's been waiting for you. He figured a detective would be in to speak to him about last night."

Luke liked that they were on the ball. He followed the bar to the end and then ducked behind the black curtain that separated the bar area from the staff. He found himself in a narrow hallway of several doors and wasn't sure where to go. "Hello, Little Rock Police Department," he called out hoping for a response.

Three doors down on the right, a man about Luke's age with blond hair and an average build popped his head out of the doorway. He extended his hand to Luke. "I'm JT Lamont, the general manager. I assume you're here about the murder that happened last night."

Luke walked toward him and shook his hand. "We don't know that it's a murder. That's what I'm here investigating. It might have been an accident."

"Oh," JT said surprised. "That's good then, better than thinking a murderer is running around." He ducked into the room and Luke followed. "I didn't mean that it was good it was an accident. I hate that anyone died. I hope you know what I mean."

It was clear to Luke that JT was a little nervous. "I knew what you meant. Do you have surveillance cameras inside the bar? Did any of your staff see Rob Hall and his friends last night?"

"We have surveillance video. I've not had a chance to go through any of it yet. I don't know what's on there. I can save all of last night to a removable drive if that would be helpful."

"Very." Luke sat and waited while JT went to work. "I don't normally find bar owners along this stretch so accommodating."

"I work hard to keep the drugs and riff-raff out of my bar, so there's nothing to hide from the cops." JT turned his back to Luke and clicked a few keys on his keyboard. "I asked my bartenders who were on last night if they saw anything. Rob's friends were looking for him so we were aware of what was going on. Then we saw on the news his body was found. I don't remember anyone hassling them if that's what you were asking about."

"There are a few things I'm looking for, but that answers one of my questions. For all we know, someone was watching them last night and followed Rob out. Then again, it could have been an accident. It's still important to see what was going on in the lead up."

"Certainly," JT said and then turned from his computer to Luke. "I've seen Rob and his friends here before. Good guys. Never cause any trouble. Rob was a quiet guy, more so than his friends. I was surprised when I heard the news." He turned back to the computer and finished up with the video. Then he turned and leaned over the desk, handing Luke the removable drive. "If there's anything you have questions about or need to speak with me further, please stop in. I wasn't here last night when Rob left, but I can put you in touch with the staff who were here all night. I had gone home by then."

Luke thanked him for the information, glad that the exchange was quick. He'd have time with Riley tonight before she left. He'd go through the footage tomorrow when he was well-rested.

# CHAPTER 6

Cooper woke on Monday morning to the smell of coffee brewing and bacon on the grill. Adele had told him the night before that court wasn't resuming until the afternoon so that gave them a little time together before Cooper left for New Orleans.

The total driving time was just shy of seven hours, but there were no last-minute flights to take. Besides, he'd rather have his truck with him. Cooper was able to book a room at the Hotel Provincial on Chartres Street. It was in the French Quarter and only a few blocks from the bar where the victim was last seen. He needed to hit the road to be there before nightfall. He wanted a chance to look around and get his bearings before meeting with Det. Clive Elio tomorrow morning. Cooper had wanted to meet with the detective that afternoon but scheduling wasn't possible.

That allowed Cooper to sleep in. He pushed himself up on his hands on the bed and adjusted the pillows behind him. "I think I pulled every muscle in my body last night," he called out to Adele.

Adele laughed. "You're exaggerating! But we did have fun." She came to the door dressed only in one of Cooper's tee-shirts and a pair of purple lace panties. Her black hair was braided and twisted around itself to make a neat knot on the top of her head. If he could have summoned up an ounce of energy, he would have dragged her back to bed.

She put a hand on her curvy hip. "Stop staring at me like a man who hasn't been fed."

Cooper ran a hand over his stomach. "I haven't been fed since dinner last night."

"That's not what I was talking about. Breakfast is nearly ready." Adele turned to walk away down the hall toward the kitchen but came back quickly. "What was the name of the hotel where you're staying?"

"Hotel Provincial. Why?"

Adele gave him a look he couldn't read. "I looked that up online this morning. Do you know that it's one of New Orleans' most haunted hotels?"

Cooper offered her a lazy grin. She was far more into ghosts and the paranormal than he was. Adele grew up in the deep south and she had recounted ghost stories to Cooper that she heard growing up. "You know I don't believe in ghosts."

"Well, it doesn't matter if you believe in them or not." Adele walked into the room and her expression was as serious as Cooper had ever seen. "Part of that hotel was a military hospital constructed in 1722. It was used during the Civil War for Confederate soldiers. Guests have reported seeing blood on the walls and hearing soldiers crying out in pain. There's also the ghost of a woman who was probably a nurse."

"I'm sure I'll be fine," he said dryly.

"You better get prepared, buddy," she said, playfully slapping his chest. "You can't shoot a ghost." She left looking over her shoulder at him and smiling. She was winding him up and she knew it.

Cooper wouldn't admit it but hearing the hotel was haunted gave him pause. He wasn't sure why, he didn't believe it. Still, he was investigating a murder that could be tied to a serial killer, and New Orleans, particularly the French Quarter, had a spooky enough vibe. He didn't need the added hocus pocus. He decided right then he'd stop by to see a friend on his way out of town.

Cooper pulled on a pair of shorts and a tee shirt and joined Adele in the kitchen. She was putting pancakes on plates that already had bacon and scrambled eggs. He pulled two mugs from the cabinet and fixed her coffee the way she liked it with a splash of sweet crème. He added a drop of milk and two sugars to his. He handed her the mug. "Tell me about your court case."

They carried their plates and mugs to the table and sat down to eat. In between bites, Adele said, "It's an assault case. A woman had broken up with her boyfriend and he showed up at her place and attacked her. She fought him off, breaking his nose and knocking two teeth out in the process."

"Tough woman," Cooper said, popping a piece of bacon in his mouth.

Adele shook her head. "Prepared woman. She saw the signs early on that he might get physical with her, so she broke it off. She said there was verbal and emotional abuse and she wanted out. But she didn't get an order of protection because she knew she didn't have enough evidence. Sure enough, he followed her home from work one night and confronted her in the driveway. He grabbed her by the hair and punched her, but she had taken a self-defense class and she fought back."

"I change my opinion then – smart woman. I'm surprised he didn't accept a plea bargain."

Adele pursed her lips. "No, sweet love of mine, she's the one who was arrested."

Cooper dropped his fork to the table, clanging it against the plate and scattering scrambled eggs across the table. "It's self-defense. Why would anyone arrest her?"

"Guy is friends with a few cops and he said she attacked him. She never reported the verbal and emotional abuse, not that the cops would have done anything with that. He was more beat up than she was in the attack, so the cops went after her." Adele sat back and smiled, proud of herself. "The prosecutor offered her a plea deal, which she refused. Why should she get probation and a criminal record for defending herself? What they don't know is that I have witnesses to the whole thing. The cops never asked the neighbors if they saw anything before arresting her."

Cooper hated that it had gotten that far in the criminal justice system. "Did you try to talk to Luke?"

"Different department and I didn't want him caught up in something. This is a winnable case, babe, no worries there. Besides, the prosecutor is up against me and she isn't going to know what hit her, pun intended."

Cooper was so proud of his wife that his heart swelled every time he looked at her. She had moved to Little Rock from Atlanta for him and her legal practice had taken off overnight. She had won every case she had so far and it was starting to gall the prosecutor's office. They had even offered her a job, which she flatly turned down. Who could blame her – the salary was terrible.

Adele reached for Cooper's hand. "Promise me we'll video chat at night. I love ending my day with you."

Cooper would keep that promise. They finished breakfast then got on with their day. Before leaving, they stood in the doorway kissing for longer than either intended. Cooper felt foolish that he was having trouble saying goodbye. He'd only be gone for a week or so. He shook off the feeling of missing Adele already as he watched her walk down the hall to the elevator. She waved to him as the doors closed.

It was close to eleven when Cooper stood outside a local shop – Hattie's Cauldron: Potions & Pastries. He looked up and down the street hoping no one he knew saw him going in. He had formed a fast and easy friendship with the owner, Hattie Beauregard on a previous case. She had been the victim of a burglary. It surprised Cooper how easily he had grown attached to her. Hattie chalked it up to him being motherless and told him that he was always welcome.

Cooper's mother died when he was a baby, and the series of stepmothers he had through the years couldn't have cared less about him. Now that his father had passed on, Cooper didn't have much family to speak of other than Luke, Riley, and Adele. Hattie was someone he trusted. In this case, she also probably knew more about ghosts than anyone. He didn't exactly believe she was psychic or could speak to the dead, but then again, he didn't *not* believe it either. Even though he had brushed it off, Adele had spooked him.

Cooper was lucky that Hattie's shop also had the best chocolate croissants and coffee in town. He got up the nerve, opened the door, and then stood silently at the entrance. Nearly all eyes turned to him, but that might just have been because he was the only man inside the shop.

"Cooper," Hattie called, waving to him. She stopped putting gemstones in small glass bowls and rushed over to him, wrapping him in a welcome hug. Hattie stepped back and patted him on the arm. "It's so good to see you. What brings you by?"

"I'm heading out of town on a case and thought I'd stop in and say goodbye," Cooper said awkwardly.

"Well, that's nice of you. We both know that's not why you're here." Hattie went behind the counter and grabbed him his favorite treat and poured coffee before gesturing to a nearby table. "Let's sit and talk before you go. I know you have a lot on your mind."

This was why Cooper liked her so much. All he had to do was show up and she offered him support. He thanked her for the coffee and treat. "I'm headed to New Orleans to work on an investigation. It may be an accident or a murder..." He stopped speaking when he saw Hattie's pained expression. "Is there something wrong?"

Hattie pulled out the chair across from him and sat. She pursed her lips. "I think it's best if I don't get into the details, but let's suffice it to say the last time I was in New Orleans it wasn't the best time for me. It's a strange city with an interesting vibe."

"That's what I heard." Cooper took a sip of coffee stalling for time.

"Are you worried about your case?"

"A lot is riding on it. It may or may not be connected to a drowning case here. That's part of what I'm trying to figure out, if it's a murder or not. Then if it is, is it connected to a few other drowning cases across the south."

"Do you want me to look at my cards for you?" Hattie offered, which she always did whenever Cooper had a question.

He declined as usual. "No, that's not why I stopped in." Cooper took another sip of his coffee. "Do you believe in ghosts?"

Hattie sat back, stifling a laugh. "Well, since I can see spirits, it's kind of hard *not* to believe in them. Do you have a ghost problem?"

The silliness of the question got Cooper to relax his shoulders and sit back. "I wouldn't say it's a problem," he said with a little grin. "You know I don't believe in all of that. Adele told me that the hotel I'll be staying at in New Orleans is haunted. I guess I got a little spooked," he admitted, blushing.

Hattie waited for him to continue.

"Given I'm going down there on a murder case, I don't need the extra complication, you know just in case all of this is real. If it were any other city, I wouldn't even be bringing this up. You know as well as I do, weird stuff happens in New Orleans and we are a few days away from Halloween."

Hattie squinted her eyes. With a teasing tone, she asked, "Does that mean you believe or not?"

Cooper raised his arms in a half-hearted shrug. "Let's say that I'm hedging my bets. If there was a ghost in my hotel room or roaming the streets of New Orleans, is there anything I can do to protect myself?"

"Cooper, Cooper, Cooper," Hattie said, holding back a laugh. "You're going to New Orleans to look for a murderer and you're worried about protecting yourself from a ghost. Is that correct?"

Cooper's cheeks flushed. "When you put it like that, it feels silly that I'm here."

"It's never silly to seek out a friend's help." Hattie patted his hand. "I'm glad you're here. Give me a moment and let me see what I can find for you." She got up from the table, leaving him there with his coffee and croissant.

The truth was Cooper didn't feel silly. Luke was remaining here with Det. Tyler to investigate his case and Riley was heading back to her hometown to investigate the case with Det. Miles Ward. Meanwhile, Cooper was heading out alone to a city he had only been to once and didn't know the lay of the land very well. He only hoped that Det. Elio was a decent detective and someone he could work with easily. Otherwise, he'd be on his own.

Cooper realized then that what he was feeling – his stomach churning and shoulders aching – wasn't about a ghost at all. It was a touch of anxiety about the case. Adele had so much on her plate that he hadn't wanted to burden her with it. The thing he hadn't acknowledged to anyone is how similar Cooper was in his youth to the victims. Had he been in his twenties still and drinking on the weekends, it could have easily been him. That just didn't sit right in his gut.

Hattie came back a moment later with a round black rock on a rope-style necklace. She handed it to Cooper. "You don't have to wear it but at least keep it in your pocket. I supercharged it with protective energy. This way you'll have a little bit of home with you."

Cooper pulled out his wallet to pay her for it and the treats. When Hattie refused, he dropped a few bills on the table. "You need to take my money. Donate it to charity if you want but take it. You've become like family to me."

Hattie beamed a smile at him. "You as well, Cooper, which is why I don't want your money. I'll tuck it away for someone in need. Now, you should get going before the rain starts. Those streets in New Orleans get easily flooded."

Cooper checked his watch. "I do need to get going, but there's no rain predicted."

Hattie winked. "Trust me. I know things. I have a feeling this is going to be a difficult case for you. Be careful who you trust."

Cooper wasn't psychic in the least, but he had the same feeling.

# CHAPTER 7

My morning flight to New York was uneventful. I was tired from the night before and slept part of the way. Luke had come home and talked with me briefly about the case before we made dinner and spent the night in bed making up for the time I'd be away. We were still floating in the honeymoon phase of our relationship. I was enjoying every minute of it.

Luke's shoulders had been tense, even when he was supposed to be relaxed. He hadn't come right out and said it, but I knew he was hoping Purvis would have found evidence of foul play in the Rob Hall murder – a bump on the head, signs of bruising from being pushed or held down in the water. Something to indicate it hadn't been an accident. I had never seen him want a case to be murder more.

I had planned to rent a car upon my arrival, but my mother insisted I use her SUV. She said that Jack, her new husband, was more than willing to drop her off for any nursing shifts she wanted to take or let her use his truck for errands and such.

For the most part, my mother had retired but still took a few jobs here and there to fill in while other nurses were on vacation or out sick. Mostly, I figured she wasn't ready to be completely out of the workforce. She had worked at the same hospital for more than thirty years, and since she crossed the threshold of sixty a couple of years ago, her knees couldn't keep up with the full-time work. Like many retirees, she was too antsy to sit still for too long.

The last time I was home, Jack Malone had proposed to my mother after a short courtship. They were hardly strangers having gone to the same church for most of their lives. Jack lost his wife several years ago and my mother had been divorced since I was a child. She had never dated after that until Jack swept her off her feet. I already loved Jack like a second father – my own being somewhat absent. Jack was a retired homicide detective with the Troy Police Department and worked as a part-time private investigator, taking only cases that interested him. Since I was no longer working in New York, I had a lot I could pass his way. He was choosey and I couldn't blame him. He spent most of his time doting on my mother, which they both seemed to enjoy.

I grabbed my luggage and then wheeled it to the front door of the small Albany International Airport. The brisk cold air walloped me in the face as soon as I stepped out of the double sliding doors. It felt like heaven after a long hot southern summer. I zipped up my hoodie and tugged my suitcase to the edge of the sidewalk. I glanced toward the oncoming traffic and waved when I saw Jack's truck approaching. He had said he'd be on time and he wasn't kidding.

Jack pulled to a stop and then got out to grab my suitcase and put it in the back for me. I slid in and got comfortable. "Thanks for the ride," I said when he got in and put the truck in drive.

"No problem. Your mom has lunch waiting. I scheduled a meeting at five with Miles once he's left work." Jack promised he'd help me work on the case with whatever I needed. He not only knew Det. Miles Ward, but he had trained him.

"Sounds good," I said too absently that Jack thought something was wrong.

He glanced over at me. "I can change it if that doesn't work for you, but I figured you'd want to jump in and get to work."

"No, it's great. I'm just a little tired."

Jack navigated out of the airport and then onto sideroads to head back home. I couldn't help but glance over and grin at him. There was a perfectly good highway that would have saved some time, but this is the route my mother would have driven. Why take a perfectly good highway when sideroads will do?

"Do you know much about the case?"

"Only what I heard on the news." Jack pulled to a stop at a red light. "The official story is Trevor Ellis went out drinking at the pub on River Street and fell into the Hudson River sometime that night. His time of death is around midnight. But he wasn't found until the following morning in the Hudson River near the Green Island Bridge." Jack gave me a knowing look.

The bridge was a stone's throw south from the back patio of the pub. Sitting on the back patio, cars could be seen going over the short expanse of the bridge. Patrons often walked across the bridge road to move farther south into downtown Troy. The official story didn't make any sense. "Wouldn't Trevor's body have moved farther given the current flow of the river?"

"That's exactly what Trevor's parents want to know. There are several inconsistencies and that's why Miles wanted to keep it an open and active investigation. As soon as the medical examiner's office ruled it accidental, Miles was pulled off the case and it was closed."

If I were a parent, I'd be frustrated, too. "Are there any leads to what happened?"

"Not much. The owner of the bar is pushing for the investigation. Trevor was a regular and was never known to drink much. He didn't appear drunk that night, but he was acting strangely. Like he was waiting for someone. The bartender said he seemed anxious, which wasn't his norm. He was seen talking to a guy outside of the bar around ten. It was a heated exchange and then the man left. Trevor was seen walking back to his car but the car never left the parking lot and he never made it home."

"Did he live in Troy?"

Jack nodded as he took a left. "Right out Spring Avenue about two miles from your mother's house. It was his roommate who reported him missing the following day."

"What night of the week did this happen?"

"Sunday of Labor Day weekend. He was working for a local tech firm while taking classes toward his master's at RPI."

RPI, or as it's known formally Rensselaer Polytechnic Institute, was among three colleges in Troy. For a city that only had fifty-thousand people, we were a college city. Many of the two and three-family homes that dotted the area around the college were filled with college students. Older students moved east to Troy's wealthier section with stately one-family homes and others that had long ago been broken into several family units. Crime had risen in Troy as it had with many cities, but without an apparent reason for Trevor ending up in the river, his death didn't make a lot of sense.

I considered the case as Jack drove the rest of the way. As we pulled into the driveway, guilt washed over me. "I didn't even ask you how you've been? The wedding pictures were lovely." My mother and Jack had snuck off to get married in the Bahamas without us. I can't say I blamed them. At their age, the last thing they wanted was a big wedding or even a small wedding. My mother had wanted a relaxed wedding and honeymoon and that's exactly what they had.

Jack parked and nodded up toward the house. "I couldn't be happier. Between you and me, I thought it would be weird with your sister moving back in. She keeps to herself and the house is too big for me and your mother. Your mother would never consider selling it."

My parents bought the five-bedroom Victorian with a wrap-around porch before I was born. When they divorced, she raised my sister,

Olivia, and me in this house. I couldn't imagine not having it here waiting for me to come home. "I was surprised when Liv moved back in. I knew she was a little lonely on her own."

"Those two are like peas in a pod. I'm lucky you left the dog here. Dusty and I are the only male energy in the place."

"I'm sure it can't be that bad." Then I remembered what it was like growing up there with the three of us. Karen and Liv were inseparable, even though I had been the oldest. My mother favored Liv because she was the easier one to control – not that my mother was controlling any more than most moms. Mine wanted things for me – marriage, kids, and a stable career – that didn't include crime fighting. Now that Luke and I were married, she was happier with my life choices. It's funny though, Liv didn't have a husband, kids, or a stable career, and my mother was fine with her life choices. I always chalked that up to the expectations for the oldest.

I turned to see Jack watching me. I threw my hands up and laughed. "Okay, it's probably that bad. I was remembering what it was like to be here with them. I hope they allowed you a man cave."

"Nope. It's why I work." He chuckled. "Come on. She'll be happy to see you." Jack got out of the truck and went to get my bag. I didn't feel any hesitation going into the house. I was, for the first time in a long time, happy to be back.

I walked up the porch steps but didn't even make it to the door. My mother pulled it open, and Dusty, my yellow lab, rushed me and knocked me back, jumping up to give me kisses. I squatted down to his level and rubbed him behind the ears. "You miss me. You're such a good boy," I cooed and then he calmed down and let me stand. When I left New York for Little Rock, I had intended to get settled and then bring Dusty down with me. He had grown so attached to my mother and she to him that I hadn't had the heart to separate them.

My mom held her arms open wide. "Do I rate a hug or is that

reserved for the dog?"

I moved in for a hug and squeezed her tight. Normally, she'd have something to say about my hair or my weight, but today, she just hugged me and told me how much she missed me. "We got our wedding photos back a few days ago. I can't wait to show you. Your room is all ready for you upstairs."

My bedroom hadn't changed since I left for college close to twenty years ago. "You should let Jack use my room as a man cave."

My mom patted my back. "Has he been filling your head with nonsense? He doesn't need a man cave."

"Your mother's right," Jack said as he followed up the porch behind me with my suitcase. He leaned in and planted a kiss on my mother's cheek. "I don't need a man cave. Maybe a shed out back."

"He wants to be able to smoke those stinky cigars," she said, rolling her eyes. "Not on my watch."

It was good to see my mother happy. It had been a long time since I saw her anything other than overworked and stressed trying to raise us alone. I went up to the second floor and doubled back down the hall toward the front of the house. Jack had already dropped my suitcase next to the bed. The room, as I suspected it would, looked the same as the last time I was home. I resisted the urge to lie down and close my eyes for a nap.

I took a quick check in the mirror and tucked my hair behind my ears and headed for the first floor. Walking down the front hallway, I stopped when I noticed my wedding photo hanging in the hall. Luke and I looked so happy. "Thanks for hanging my wedding photo up," I said to my mom as I crossed the threshold into the large eat-in kitchen.

My mother handed me a plate with a turkey and cheese sandwich on rye bread stuffed with lettuce and tomato and a pickle. She had added a handful of grapes and chips with it. It reminded me of summer lunches she'd make while we were playing in the backyard. "It's a lovely photo and a lovely wedding even if it was ruined by your father after the fact. Have you heard from him lately?"

I took my plate to the table and sat. "No. He's still wrapping up his old life. I'm sure he'll call when he can." My father, Patrick Sullivan, had a long history of government work, but he was retiring. I wasn't sure what kind of relationship we'd have when he was done. "Have you heard from him?"

My mother nodded and popped a pickle in her mouth while she carried her plate over. "Sully sent us a check for five grand after we got back from the wedding and honeymoon. I have no idea how he even knew we had gone away to get hitched."

Sully knew everything. "Don't question it. Just cash the check and enjoy it."

"That's exactly what I did." She laughed. "Liv said that she'd be home soon. She was there at the pub the night Trevor went missing. His parents go to Sacred Heart with me."

That surprised me and it didn't. Most of my drinking nights out included a stop at the pub. "Have they said much about what happened?"

"Only that they are angry the police aren't doing their jobs. It's why when I heard they wanted to hire out, I mentioned you."

I raised my head to look at her in surprise. "You mentioned me? Captain Meadows mentioned me, too. He was in contact with Miles who said he felt unsatisfied with the conclusion of the case."

"I know," she said as if she held some secret, which she did. After a beat, she laughed. "I talk to Miles sometimes. He asks about you, you know?"

"We worked well together on that previous case," I said, hoping I wasn't blushing. "When is Liv due home?"

My mother stared at me knowing I wasn't giving her the full truth. She thankfully didn't press the issue. "She'll be here at three, long before you need to leave." She took a bite of her sandwich and gave me a knowing motherly look. I had been warned.

# CHAPTER 8

Luke had spent the better part of the day following up on leads and going through the surveillance video from the bar. He had been sitting in the same position for so long that his back hurt and his elbow throbbed from leaning on it. Luke paused the video, stretched his arms overhead, and then took a sip from the soda can on his desk. He gagged and groaned. Not only had the soda gone flat, but it was warm. He chucked the can in the garbage and stretched again.

Luke had gone through all the footage but wanted to watch it a second time. He grabbed his notes from his interview with Derek and then played the footage again, slower this time, frame by frame. He knew he was missing something.

In the video, Rob swayed back and forth. He placed his hand on the tabletop for support. A moment later, he reached into his pants pocket, pulled out his phone, stared down at the screen, and then jammed it back into his pocket. He was annoyed about something. From the angle of the video, Luke wasn't able to see what was on Rob's phone. Roughly ten minutes after that, Rob spoke to Derek and then headed for the front door of the bar.

As Derek reported to Luke, he remained at the table. While he had said they were all there together, that wasn't true. One of the young men headed off with his phone in hand and the other went toward the bar. That matched their statements to Det. Tyler and Captain Meadows.

Luke hit stop on the video and backed up a few frames. This time, when he hit play, he scanned the crowd of people in the bar to see if anyone followed Rob out. Two minutes and twenty-one seconds after Rob left, a group of three women left the bar. At the three-minute mark, a man in the far corner of the frame downed a beer and then walked out of the bar, glancing once at Derek, who was sitting at the table alone. Luke hadn't noticed that the first few times he watched the video. He hit pause, backed up the video, and watched it again.

The man stood about six-one or two and had some bulk to him under his gray sweatshirt. He wasn't overweight but had broad shoulders and a thick chest and arms.

Luke wasn't sure if the glance over at Derek meant anything or not. The unknown man might have been looking at someone else and Derek was in his line of sight. Luke couldn't be sure. He marked down the time on the video, so he could later share it with Captain Meadows and Det. Tyler. Luke went back to watching the video and looking for more potential leads.

Close to twenty minutes later, Det. Tyler stood over Luke's desk and cleared his throat. He dropped a sheet of paper onto the desk. It floated down and landed right in front of Luke. It had a name on it – Maggie Hayden. Luke raised his eyes. "You found her? How?"

Det. Tyler put down a stack of pages on the desk. "I got access to Rob's cellphone records."

"The provider sent them that quickly?"

"No. Rob's mother had his password and gave me access to his online account. She printed me off a month's worth of information. I don't have text message content, but I have a record of the incoming and outgoing numbers."

Luke couldn't believe their luck. He figured they'd be waiting a week or more for the phone data. "Who was he texting right before he left the bar?"

"I found that number, Luke. It's not anywhere else in his records, just that night. It goes to a burner phone. We have no information on that. We won't know more until we get the content from the provider."

Luke figured as much. "Did you find anything about Maggie?"

Det. Tyler reached for his desk chair and positioned it in front of Luke's desk. "I scanned through the data until I found numbers that Rob texted and called and that called and texted him frequently. I ruled out his friends' phone numbers and then searched what was left. Maggie Hayden. She's a twenty-two-year-old nurse at the children's hospital. She graduated this past May and this is her first full-time nursing job. I haven't contacted her yet. I did a few online searches and dug up a little info. Want to pay her a visit?"

"Do you know her schedule?" Luke didn't want to have to pull her off her job at the hospital. Not only because she was a new employee and didn't want to cause friction at her first job, but interviews like that rarely gave him what he needed. No one wanted to be ambushed at work.

"I don't but I can call the hospital and check."

Luke shook his head. "Let's hold off on that. We don't know that Maggie did anything wrong. Let me call her and schedule something. We can always get her address and swing by her place."

"Fair enough," Det. Tyler said and then tapped on the back of Luke's laptop. "What about the surveillance footage? Find anything of value?"

Luke spun his laptop around so Det. Tyler could see the screen. He leaned over and hit play and pointed to the area of the video Luke wanted him to watch. The video played and then Luke hit stop. He sat back and folded his arms across his chest. "What do you think?"

"I'm not sure. The guy could have been looking over at Derek or he could have been looking past him or at the television near them. Is that the most significant thing you found?"

"Yeah," Luke said with a frustrated sigh. "The surveillance video didn't show much of anything. Derek said Maggie had been cheating on some other guy with Derek. He didn't know this other guy's name, so I'm wondering if that's the guy in the bar. Rob didn't seem to see the guy or make any contact with him while they were in the bar though."

"Then let's go talk to Maggie," Det. Tyler said. "We have no other leads right now."

Luke reached for the phone records and Det. Tyler pointed to the number. He jotted it down and then scanned through until he found a time stamp for when Rob had been in the bar. "Right here. There is an incoming text from Maggie about ten minutes before Rob walks outside. I wonder what that was about."

"I thought they had broken up," Det. Tyler said and tugged a page off the desk. He scanned down the page and then pointed out a section to Luke. "A week before Rob went missing, the contact between Maggie and Rob stopped. There are no calls or texts in the records. I didn't even notice the one the night he died."

"Derek said they had broken up because of the other guy. Only one way we are going to find out." Luke grabbed his desk phone and punched in Maggie's phone number. He was surprised when she answered. Luke introduced himself and told her that he needed to speak with her right away. He was even more surprised when she gave him her address and said she'd be there until seven that evening when she had to head into work for a twelve-hour night shift.

Luke hung up and stood. "Let's head there now."

Maggie's apartment community was out in West Little Rock off Chanel Parkway. It was one of the newer communities that Luke heard was raking in rents higher than most in the city. They found building four and then took the stairs up to the second floor. At Maggie's apartment, Luke knocked and stepped back.

A moment later, a short woman, no more than five-foot-three, with long dark hair answered the door wearing sweats and a tee-shirt. Luke introduced himself and confirmed she was Maggie. "As I said on the phone, we need to ask you a few questions about Rob Hall."

Maggie stepped aside and let them enter. "I wasn't in contact with Rob when he died. We had broken up about a week before his death."

Luke and Det. Tyler shared a look. "What about the night he died? My understanding is that there was some communication that night shortly before he left the bar."

Maggie closed the door. "I don't know when he left the bar, but I did text him that night. I never heard back, Det. Morgan. I felt bad about how things ended between us and I was hoping to speak to him. I texted and asked if he would call me. As I said, he didn't call and didn't text me back. I assumed he was still angry with me. I heard the next morning that he was dead." She gestured for them to sit down and then she sat on the edge of the couch.

Luke didn't sit, instead he chose to stand in the middle of the room, looking down at her. While her words said she was sorry, her body language betrayed her. She didn't seem sorry at all. "My understanding is that you and Rob broke up because he found out that you were already in a relationship with someone else."

Maggie winced. "That's not quite accurate. I had been in a long-term relationship for the past five years and I had broken that off. I'm only twenty-two and didn't want to be involved that seriously with anyone. I only finished nursing school in May. I wanted to focus on work and making new friends. A serious relationship seemed…constraining right now."

"What was Rob then?" Det. Tyler asked.

Maggie cast her glance towards him. "Fun. A little distraction. Rob said he didn't want anything serious and that was fine with me. He knew I work crazy hours and he was okay with that too. We met up when we could. Sometimes we'd meet for lunch when I worked nights. Other times, he'd meet me for breakfast or come over during the day. It's hard to find someone that accommodating."

"But you broke up with him?"

Maggie shook her head. "Rob broke up with me when he found out about my ex. Nolan was coming around a lot, causing trouble. There was one day when Nolan confronted Rob and they almost got into a fight. Rob said it was too much for something that was supposed to be casual and fun. I can't control Nolan and what he does. I couldn't even begin to try. I've been clear though that I'm not getting back together with him."

Luke asked, "Has he been harassing you?"

Maggie looked up at Luke. "Most would probably call it harassment. I started dating Nolan in high school and we were together through college. He was never violent or anything like that. He could be jealous and didn't like me around other guys. It was annoying enough that it drove Rob away, which I felt bad about. That's why I called him that night. I didn't like how we left things during our last conversation."

Luke believed she was telling him the truth. "Do you have a recent photo of Nolan?"

Maggie hesitated. "You don't think Nolan had anything to do with what happened to Rob, do you?"

"We don't know, but I'd like to see a photo of Nolan." Luke remained firm. It was clear Maggie still had feelings for Nolan. He even believed she might be downplaying their current relationship but sensed he wasn't going to get more from her in that line of questioning. When she walked out of the room, he turned to Det. Tyler. "What do you think?"

"Her explanation seems plausible. It sounds like Nolan is a bit hot-tempered and won't take no for an answer. I can see why if it was a casual fling Rob would walk away. Who wants to be harassed by someone's ex, especially if you're not serious about the relationship?" Det. Tyler then lamented the state of relationships today. He had been with his wife so long that even though he was only in his late forties, he often came across sounding like he was seventy.

Luke held back his commentary and let Det. Tyler bluster until Maggie returned with a photo. He was expecting one on her phone and was surprised that she had a framed photo of him. She handed it to Luke. "Is this recent?" he asked, taking the photo.

"It was taken about four months ago, not long before we broke up."

Luke glanced down at the photo, recognized the man as the one he had seen in the surveillance video, and then passed the photo to Det. Tyler. By the look on his partner's face, he recognized him too. Luke asked, "When was the last time you saw Rob?"

"About a week before his death. That's when we broke up." Maggie sat back down, seeming frustrated and tired of the questions. "Before you ask, I was at the hospital the night he died. I texted him while I was on a break. You can call the hospital if you'd like to check my alibi. I'd never hurt Rob."

Luke read off the unknown number that went to a burner phone. "Do you recognize that number?"

"No," Maggie said.

Luke asked, "What about Nolan? Would he hurt Rob?"

Maggie stared up at him and took an audible breath. She gave no response to the question other than a stare that told Luke all he needed to know – no answer was still an answer.

# CHAPTER 9

"Nolan Dunn," Luke said the young man's name as he typed it into the database he used to check for past criminal history. He added the birthdate and last known address, all information that Maggie had eventually relented and given to them. It turned out that Maggie and Nolan weren't the same age. She had been a sophomore when he was a senior. They had continued when he graduated and joined the Army and then was subsequently kicked out for drug use and a range of other poor behavior.

"It's hard to believe that a young woman like Maggie would date someone like Nolan," Det. Tyler said as they sat in the car. "She graduated and went right to college and now she has a good nursing job. I don't understand what she'd see in a guy like Nolan."

"They were young," Luke said absently as he waited for the full criminal history to load. "I'm sure he wasn't a criminal when they met or maybe he was and she liked bad boys. It's been known to happen."

"Maggie seemed too smart to fall for bad boys." Det. Tyler leaned over and looked at the laptop as the criminal history finally populated on the screen. He whistled loudly. "That's one long rap sheet. I can't see the particulars. What's the kid done?"

Det. Tyler wasn't exaggerating. The list of Nolan's arrests and convictions was as long as Luke's arm. There was everything from possession of drugs to theft and burglary charges, two drunk and disorderly charges, and even a physical assault charge from a bar fight. Luke read off the list to Det. Tyler. "This is all since he turned eighteen. We can't see his juvenile record. It would be sealed. I wonder why he's not done serious jail time."

"The criminal defense firm. I wonder if he's related."

Luke hadn't even thought of that. Dunn & Swartz was one of the oldest, most well-known, and respected law firms in Little Rock. Luke had gone up against their attorneys a time or two during a criminal prosecution. He hated being grilled on the stand by their attorneys because they were good, fought fair, but always brought their A-game. "I can't recall ever meeting the Dunn in the Dunn & Swartz law practice."

"I haven't met him either." Det. Tyler pointed to the rap sheet. "It's got to be his father. Otherwise, Nolan would have done some serious jail time by now."

Luke noted the most recent arrest. "He was arrested for assault not even three months ago. Looks like that case is still pending in the system. I bet it hasn't made it to the court calendar yet."

"Or his father is working out another plea deal," Det. Tyler countered. "Either way, let's go find this guy and bring him in for questioning."

Luke agreed but worried that as soon as they made contact, Nolan would lawyer up. If Luke had Dunn & Swartz in his corner, that's exactly what he'd do. "I have an address for him in Hillcrest. Check the law firm's website and get me a photo of Dunn. I want to see if they look similar."

Det. Tyler pulled up the law firm's website quickly on his phone and then went to the staff page. Luke could see it out of the corner of his eye while he was driving. He was anxious to hear the information.

Det. Tyler gave Luke the overview. "Larry Dunn went to Duke University for law school, clerked for the Manhattan prosecutor's office, then shifted to a well-known criminal law firm in Manhattan where he spent five years defending the mob. He returned to Arkansas armed with all that knowledge and opened his practice." Det. Tyler rattled off a few more details and then dropped his phone in his lap. "Sounds like Larry Dunn figured out how to be the big fish in a little pond. They are licensed to practice in six surrounding states and have offices in Atlanta and Nashville as well as here in Little Rock. Right now, they employ twenty-three criminal defense and personal injury attorneys in all."

Luke turned his head slightly to look at his partner while still paying attention to the flow of traffic. "Does Larry's bio say anything about having kids?"

"Seven." Det. Tyler whistled. "The man did all of that and had time to have seven kids."

"Does the bio name them?"

"Nope. Photo of him kind of looks like Nolan."

Luke navigated the winding streets of the Hillcrest neighborhood with ease. He had grown up on Overlook Road and his parents still lived in his childhood home. Later, he had an apartment a few streets over. Luke made a right and then a quick left and pulled in front of the last known address they had for Nolan. It wasn't the one in the database, but it was the one Maggie had provided to him. There was a black sporty BMW in the driveway.

"What do you want to bet his father bought him that car?" Det. Tyler said as he stepped out onto the pavement.

"We don't even know that it's his. There is no vehicle information listed for Nolan." Luke had been surprised about that. While there had been a few arrests for drugs, Nolan had no DUIs or anything that would warrant taking his license away. Based on his date of birth in the system, Nolan had recently celebrated his twenty-fifth birthday.

Unlike many of the houses in this section of Hillcrest, Nolan's house wasn't a duplex. It was listed as one family house. Luke didn't know if he still lived with his parents or possibly roommates. They'd know soon enough. Luke stepped up onto the porch and rapped his knuckles against the door.

A few moments later, a young man wearing a blue hoodie and gray sweats answered the door. His head had been shaved down and there were hints of tattoos poking out from under the sleeves of his hoodie.

"Nolan Dunn?" Luke asked, his voice commanding.

"Who wants to know?" He leaned casually against the doorjamb like he didn't have a care in the world.

Luke flashed his badge. Det. Tyler did the same. "We need to speak to you about an ongoing case."

Nolan righted himself and stepped back, grabbing hold of the door as if to close it. "I have an attorney for the assault case. You'll need to speak to him."

"That's not why we're here," Luke said, putting his foot up on the threshold of the doorway to prevent the door from being closed in his face. "We are here about a drowning death."

There was a flash of recognition in Nolan's eyes. "I should call my attorney."

"Have you done something wrong?" Det. Tyler asked. "You aren't a suspect. We aren't bringing you in for formal questioning. We just want to talk. We are trying to talk to most of the people in the bar that night," he lied with ease.

Luke couldn't deny him his attorney if that's what Nolan wanted. He knew as soon as the attorney got involved, there'd be no more questions. "Nolan, please reconsider. I don't even know if we are dealing with a homicide case. No victim equals no suspect. We are wrapping up some loose ends. That's all. We hoped you could help us. What do you say?"

Nolan considered for a moment and then gave in. As he stepped back from the doorway, he grunted, "I have the right to not answer your questions. I know what my rights are. If I tell you to leave, you have to leave."

Luke didn't even bother responding. He wasn't going to do anything to violate the kid's rights, but he was going to push him to answer questions as best he could. The house was tidy and the furniture new. There was a black leather sectional in the middle of the room positioned right in front of a massive television affixed to the wall. Someone had added curtains. Luke was sure that wasn't Nolan's doing.

"Do you live here with anyone?" Luke asked.

Det. Tyler pulled up the rear behind Nolan and stood on the edge of the doorway.

"Sometimes my sisters stay here when they are in Little Rock, but mostly, I'm here alone," Nolan said, sitting down on the couch. He waited for Luke and Det. Tyler to do the same. "I know what you're thinking. How do I afford such a nice house when I don't have a job? My father pays for it. He wanted me to move out of his house and so he put me here."

Det. Tyler glanced in his direction. "You're twenty-five and you don't have a job? What do you plan to do with your life?"

"I've worked," Nolan snapped, defensively. "Nothing seems to stick. That's not why you're here. What do you want?"

Luke didn't know how long Nolan would give them before he became completely uncooperative. "Can you tell me where you were this past Saturday night between the hours of ten and two in the morning?"

Nolan remained quiet for a moment, his eyes darting back and forth. "I didn't break into her apartment if that's why you're here. I was outside hoping to talk to her and when she told me to leave, I left."

Luke pulled back and tried not to act surprised. "Who asked you to leave?"

"My ex, Maggie. The only reason she broke up with me is because her parents don't like me. But we've been dating since high school. I'm sure we'll get back together."

Luke furrowed his brow at the information. "You saw Maggie on Saturday night?"

Nolan nodded. "Right around one in the morning. I went out drinking and then I went to her place. I wanted to talk but she didn't want any part of it. As I said, she asked me to leave, so I left."

Luke hadn't checked Maggie's alibi yet, but the young woman had claimed she was at work. "Where did you see her?"

"At her apartment where she lives."

"Did she come outside and speak to you?"

"No. She yelled it through the door."

Luke put that aside for now. "Tell me about the time before that. You said you were out drinking with friends. Where were you?"

"Downtown Little Rock. At Coach's. I got there right before ten and was there until after midnight."

"Were you alone?" Det. Tyler asked.

Nolan widened his feet and placed his hands on his knees. Luke expected him to end the interview but he didn't. "I was supposed to meet some friends, but they never showed. I saw other people I knew, talked to them for a while, and then left."

"Where'd you go after that?"

"I went for a walk," Nolan said and then stood. "What's this all about? I'm answering your questions but you haven't given me any information."

Luke stood as well but kept his body language open and relaxed. There was no point putting Nolan on edge. "Did you know Rob Hall? You might have seen on the news that he was found in the Arkansas River on Saturday night. We noticed on the surveillance video that you were in the bar at the same time as him. We thought you might have seen something suspicious."

Nolan's eyelids fluttered rapidly. "You knew I was in the bar but still asked me where I was? That's kind of messed up."

Det. Tyler said, "You didn't answer the question. Did you know Rob Hall?"

"Yeah, man, I knew him. So what? He died okay. He fell into the river and died. I don't see what that has to do with me." Nolan rocked back and forth on his feet. His cheeks flushed and his right hand clenched into a fist.

"Settle down, Nolan." Luke took a step toward him. "You're getting angry for no reason. It's how we interview people. We just need to know if you saw Rob in the bar that night?"

"Yeah, I saw him. I didn't talk to him or his punk friends. If you think someone killed Rob, you should ask Derek. Those two have been going at it for months."

Luke cocked his head to the side as if he hadn't heard that correctly. "Derek? As in Rob's best friend?"

"Derek was only pretending to still be Rob's friend. He told me himself." Nolan folded his meaty arms across his chest and stared at Luke as if daring him to argue. "Ask anyone who knew them. They hadn't been getting along in the last six months. Derek started selling and Rob didn't want any part of it. Rob threatened to kick him out if he didn't stop. There's bad blood between them, I'm telling you."

"What about the fight you had with Rob over Maggie?" Luke asked, his tone even and calm. Nolan was growing more agitated by the second.

"I hit the guy once, okay," Nolan admitted, jutting his chin forward. "He was screwing my girlfriend. He deserved it. I'd hit him again if I had the chance. Guess I won't get that chance now that someone killed him."

"We never said that someone killed Rob," Det. Tyler said, looking at

Nolan. "We don't know what happened."

Nolan shook his head, seeming confused, and then walked toward the door. "You need to go before I call my father. Don't come back. I didn't do anything to Rob. Even if you think I did, you can't prove it. I'm untouchable."

"I'll be back, Nolan," Luke said, heading toward the door. He wasn't sure that he'd get to interview him, but he knew this wasn't their last interaction on this case.

# CHAPTER 10

After lunch, when I couldn't keep my eyes open any longer, I went to my bedroom to take a quick nap. Dusty settled into my side, his tail thumping against me, and we both drifted off to sleep for one of my best naps in a long time.

I woke later to a knock on my door. "Mom said you need to wake up," Liv said before bouncing in and plopping down on my bed. "You two look cozy. He won't nap with me." She gave Dusty a good scratch behind the ears before he turned to me and I swear rolled his eyes before jumping off the bed and leaving us.

I sat up and crinkled my face in disgust. "Maybe he knows you're a cat person."

Liv grabbed one of my pillows and thumped me in the face with it. I returned fire and we tussled like that until both of us were winded and red-faced. Then she dove in for a hug. "I've missed you."

Our relationship hadn't always been this good. For most of our lives, I had been the one in charge when Mom was working. Liv resented me for that. She thought I was stuffy and boring, and I thought she was too wild and cavalier about her love life and lack of employment. Liv had worked for me when I was running the private investigation firm. Mostly, I paid her to take up space in my office where she read magazines and complained about my clothing choices. She was supposed to answer the phone but was terrible at taking messages.

Over the last few years, our relationship had become closer. I stopped feeling so resentful that she was closer to my mother and she seemed to stop caring what I wore or how boring I became as a married woman.

Liv pulled back from my hug and smoothed down her hair. "What do you think of the haircut?"

She had cut her shoulder-length hair into a blunt bob. "It looks amazing on you. I can't remember the last time you had short hair like that."

"Years ago." Liv sat back on the bed and crossed her legs under her. "I'm glad you're home. Mom said she told you I saw Trevor the night he went missing."

It was a quick mental switch from sister to investigator. "Who were you with at the pub?"

"I was on a blind date that didn't go well. He left after dinner and I went to the bar to hang out. I didn't feel like going home. You know you always run into people at the pub, so I figured there'd be someone to talk to."

I struggled to come up with the current name of the pub. Brown's Brewing, possibly. We always just referred to it as "the pub" and everyone knew what we were talking about, locals anyway. "Did you run into anyone you knew?"

Liv shook her head. "There were enough people in there to talk to so I had a couple of beers. I spoke to Trevor. He was there alone and sat a few barstools from me."

My ears perked up at that. "You spoke to him?"

"Not for long. I didn't learn much about him other than he was studying at RPI. I had asked where he was from, assuming out of state like most of them, but he was local." Liv looked across the room, her expression indicating she was trying to remember the details. When she looked back at me, she added, "He kept looking at his phone a lot and seemed annoyed. I jokingly asked if a girlfriend was checking up on him. He told me he wasn't seeing anyone. We talked probably another ten or fifteen minutes and then he paid his tab and left."

I recalled what Jack said about him arguing with someone outside in the parking lot. "Did you see Trevor arguing with anyone or talking to anyone at all?"

"I saw him talking to a couple of guys when he went to the bathroom. It didn't look like an argument to me. I figured it was people he knew. You know everyone kind of knows everyone in there."

That was true. Almost everyone I knew went to the pub on a somewhat regular basis. It wasn't the kind of bar you got drunk at. They had a great food selection and brewed their own beer. It wasn't uncommon to see kids in there with their parents or seniors out for dinner and everyone in between.

"Did it seem like Trevor was drunk?"

Liv said, "He only had two beers that I saw while we were talking. He was finishing up one and then had ordered another. He didn't finish the second. No slurred speech or stumbling when he walked – nothing to indicate that he might have been drunk or on drugs."

I considered what else I could ask her. "What did he say when he got up to leave?"

"He checked his phone again and said he had a few things to take care of. He said it was nice to meet me and he paid his tab and left." Liv took a breath. "The whole exchange was typical of the pub and pretty unremarkable. The only reason it even stuck out to me was the next day I saw on the news that he was missing and was last seen at the pub. Then shortly after that, someone found his body in the river."

So far, the story was the same as I had heard from Jack. "Did you call Det. Ward and let him know you had spoken to Trevor that night?"

Liv pulled back, concern on her face. "Should I have? I didn't see anything happen to him or have information to explain what happened to him. I didn't think I should get involved if I didn't have anything helpful to add."

I was surprised by how panicked she was acting. "It's okay, Liv. You're not in trouble or anything. I figured Det. Ward interviewed some of the people who were in the bar with Trevor that night."

Liv shifted her eyes away. "They did say on the news if you knew him or had seen him that night to come forward. I didn't think I had anything of value to add and didn't want to waste anyone's time."

I could have chastised her for that but figured it wouldn't help. She was telling me now. "What about when you left? Did you see Trevor outside or see anything that caused concern?"

"I was parked out front. I didn't see behind the building near the river."

"You probably didn't have anything to add to the case then."

Liv leaned back on her hands and eyed me. "You keep calling him Det. Ward like you didn't make out with him in high school. I see Miles from time to time when I'm out. Last I heard he was dating someone you went to high school with."

"Who?" I asked and then tried to brush it off like I didn't care. "Not that it matters who he's dating."

"You care," she laughed, teasing me. "It's okay to care even if you're married to Luke and aren't going to do anything about it. Miles is hot. If I didn't think you'd murder me in my sleep, I'd consider dating him."

"I'd probably murder you." I didn't want to have this conversation. Everyone was making a big deal out of my brief flirtation with Miles that happened during a case we were working on together. The truth was he was flirting because he remembered that we had shared a kiss our senior year of high school on a Memorial Day weekend trip. I hadn't even remembered it because he looks nothing like he did then. I'd be lying if I said I didn't have some lingering feelings that were completely harmless.

I side-eyed her. "Who is he dating?"

"Becky Palmer," Liv said with a grin. She knew that we hadn't gotten along in high school. That was close to twenty years ago now and I was over it for the most part. Becky had stolen my high school boyfriend right before prom and then made up a few lies about me.

"That's a poor choice. His to make," I said and scooted off the bed. I checked my phone and had missed a few texts from Luke updating me about his case. Cooper had also let me know he had arrived in New Orleans and was getting settled. "Speaking of Miles. I need to meet him in about thirty minutes. How is it living here with Jack?"

Liv made herself comfortable on my bed while I brushed my hair and put on a little makeup. "It's great. I've never seen Mom so happy. Plus, all those little things that go wrong with an older house are fixed immediately. Jack has a ton of projects going at once." She grew quiet for a moment and then said, "Sometimes I feel bad because I like Jack so much. I feel like I'm being disloyal to Sully."

I had the same feeling earlier today when Jack picked me up from the airport. I looked at Liv's reflection through the mirror. "Sully wasn't around when we were growing up. Jack is the first stable role model we've had as a father figure." I set my brush down and turned to face her. "We deserve a Jack in our lives."

"He doesn't even mind that I still live here." Liv hugged the pillow on my bed. "What do you think of me still living here?"

"The house is too big for Mom and Jack and they both like having you here. There's no point paying outrageous rent if you don't have to." I went over and hugged her before I left. "Don't bother saving dinner for me. I'm going to grab it at the pub."

"Good luck," Liv said, her voice sounding far off. Before I left the room, she had snuggled down into my bed. There was something wrong, but I wasn't sure what it was and I didn't have time right then to sort it out. I'd catch up with her later.

Jack and I arrived at the pub five minutes before our meeting time and found Miles already sitting at a table waiting for us. He stood from a booth and waved. His smile went from ear to ear. He wore crisp khakis and a blue sweater. His dark hair looked like it hadn't seen a brush all day. "I grabbed us a table so we could talk first," he called over the din of the conversations from other patrons.

We made our way to the table and Jack slid in next to Miles. He gave him a hearty handshake. "Are we ordering food because I'm starving?" he asked and rubbed his stomach for emphasis.

Once we had ordered, I made some pleasantries with Miles and then got down to work. "Jack gave me the overview of the case, but can you help me understand why it was classified as an accident? Also, what's bothering you about the case?"

The server brought our drinks and her presence gave Miles a minute to collect his thoughts. We took sips of our beer and then he explained, "At first, I figured it was an accident. Trevor had been drinking but not excessively. I assumed maybe he was walking too close to the river and fell in. Trevor's family and friends said he was a good swimmer, but the river current can be strong. The medical examiner ruled it an accident."

"Something didn't sit right with you though?"

Miles furrowed his brow. "I couldn't get past the fact that his body barely moved with the current. It didn't make a lot of sense to me. If his body went in around midnight and someone found him around eight that morning, why was his body in nearly the same place?"

It didn't make any sense to me either. "Why weren't you allowed to keep the case open if you still had questions?"

Miles started to speak but his attention was drawn to the front door of the pub. His eyes remained fixated. "Don't look now, but the reason I couldn't pursue the case just walked in."

I turned my head sharply around so I could see what Miles meant. There he was – the man I had hated for all these years. Ned Shaw. He stood about five-foot-ten and had a muscular build, not bad for a man in his fifties. At least, he had kept in shape. It did little to detract from his smug grin and a bad combover. "What's he doing here?"

"Causing trouble," Miles said, turning to look at me. "Riley, the less you engage with him and react, the better it will be."

That was going to be easier said than done – he had driven me off one case already. It wasn't going to happen again.

# CHAPTER 11

"Ned Shaw," I said my voice as tight as a growl. "What are you doing here?"

Shaw smirked down at me. In his thick New York City accent, he asked, "The question is…what are you doing here with Det. Ward?"

"That's none of your concern."

Jack put his hand out and introduced himself. When Shaw took his hand, he said, "I'm a retired Troy Police detective. I know you spent some time with the New York Police Department."

"I'm a retired homicide detective." He turned back to me, the same smirk on his face. "Which I'd say trumps Riley's little private investigator hobby." Shaw dared to gesture for me to shove farther into the booth so he could sit down with us. I wasn't moving an inch.

Jack, who could be as charming and diplomatic as a politician or as mean as a grizzly bear depending on the circumstance, wasn't having any of it. "Riley does what all great investigators do – she follows the evidence and doesn't manufacture it to fit an agenda." Jack raised his eyes and smiled. "Or her ego." His meaning couldn't have been clearer.

Miles had been quiet up until this point. "If you haven't gotten the hint, you aren't welcome here, Shaw. You say you want to help, but you're only helping yourself. A good detective puts his ego aside.

You're the reason these cases are being closed prematurely."

Shaw snickered. "You agree they are being closed prematurely."

Miles couldn't stand because he was blocked in the booth by Jack. He pounded his fist on the table for emphasis. "No, Shaw. I'm telling you, you're toxic to these investigations. No one wants you around."

"The families do. They want closure," Shaw countered. "And the public has a right to know what's happening. They have a right to know serial killers are targeting their sons." He pointed toward the back of the bar in the direction of the river. "Did you see the cross near the bridge? You have another Cross Killers murder on your hands and you're standing by doing nothing. Don't worry. My team will solve it."

I rolled my eyes. "The graffiti on that bridge looks like it's about ten years old. Cross graffiti is some of the most common. How did the killer know the body was going to end up under the bridge?"

Shaw had no answer, just like he never did when he was asked a logical question. Instead, he went on a tirade about how law enforcement wouldn't take him seriously because they were all hiding the truth. "You're one of the sheep, Det. Ward. Every bit of evidence I've brought forth has been dismissed by people like you."

"It's been dismissed because it's horse..." Jack didn't finish his sentence. He tugged at the collar of his shirt and made a guttural sound. He put his hands on the table as if to stand but simply turned his head to Shaw. "You aren't wanted here, Shaw. You're not wanted in this bar or this city. Just go away."

Shaw stepped back from the table. "I guess your local media doesn't feel the same way. I'm giving a press conference tonight about our findings in the case. You watch from the sidelines while the real detectives solve the case."

I turned and locked my gaze on Miles. This wouldn't be good for our investigations. It might be even worse for the Troy PD. I waited to see if either Jack or Miles would respond. When they didn't, I turned my head up. "I'm sure you'll do a good job showing off your enormous ego. I'm confident it won't do a thing to help solve this case."

"That's your opinion. We all know I ran you off the last case because you weren't smart enough to solve it. I'm sure I'll do it again on this case."

I stared at him but didn't say anything. He had run me off the case, not because I couldn't solve it, but because the father of the victim wouldn't hear anything I had to say to counter Shaw's theory.

Jack stood now and squared off with the man. "That's enough, Shaw. It's time for you to go. I've asked you nicely. If I have to remove you myself, I will."

Jack stood a few inches taller and was more muscle compared to Shaw's girth. Shaw's eyes darted around as if looking for someone to help him. No one at our table or nearby was coming to his rescue.

"Did you hear me?" Jack asked again, taking a step toward him.

Shaw held his hands up and stepped back. "I'm going but don't say I didn't warn you."

Once Shaw was gone, disappearing to the back of the bar, I rubbed my temples. "I hate that guy. What's a press conference going to do to the Troy PD, Miles? Are you worried?"

Before Miles could answer, Jack sat down. "It's all distraction, Riley. Don't get caught up with him. He's got nothing. There's been graffiti along the river and on all the bridges from here to New York City. It means nothing. His graffiti theory is garbage. He doesn't know where the body went in and no killer can predict where the body is going to be found after a body is placed in the water – certainly not a body of water with the currents of the Hudson River."

I wasn't sure if Jack was telling me or trying to convince himself. "Miles, does Shaw have anything on the case as far as real evidence? What has he had access to so far?"

"Nothing that I know of." Miles turned his head so he was looking back in the direction that Shaw went and then he turned back to me. "I don't know. Maybe the Ellis family spoke to him or some of Trevor's friends. The medical examiner wouldn't have given him anything and my department didn't.  I think Jack is right that it's all speculation. Who else is on Shaw's team?"

"Dr. Donald Humme is a forensic pathologist. His work has been largely shunned by most respectable pathologists.  He's known for being paid off by the defense for refuting the prosecutors' expert witnesses. He's a hack essentially. Then there is Rick Davis, another retired NYPD detective. Rick had several cases thrown out of court because he roughed up defendants and forced confessions. Let's just say he didn't retire willingly. He had his time in for retirement and his captain forced him out or he was going to be fired."

Jack eyed me. "What about Shaw's record?"

"Grandstander.  Always did things for show when he was on a case.  There are several old interviews he's done in past criminal investigations.  Even when he was asked by his department not to make a statement, he was front and center in front of the camera." I considered how Luke normally behaved during open investigations and compared it to Shaw and it was like night and day.

"All for the media attention?" Miles asked with hope in his voice.

I met his eyes and didn't look away. "You know how much you shy away from giving a statement to the media, particularly while in the middle of the case. You dig in, follow the evidence, and make an arrest. The media is usually more bothersome than helpful and even when you need them, it's on a need-to-know basis. Shaw thrived on media attention. He would often request the cases that would garner the most media attention. It was all about him and his ego. As a result, he didn't have the best closure rate. I heard his department was glad to be rid of him."

Miles nodded along as I spoke, confirming that's how he operated.

"I hated the media involved in my cases," Jack lamented and then moved us off that topic, for which I was thankful. "We've established what a piece of work Shaw and his so-called team are. Let's focus on what matters – the case." He turned to Miles. "The only way to keep Shaw at bay is solving the darn thing. Let's get back to where we were before. You were telling us that you were concerned because Trevor's body hadn't moved with the current."

"Right," Miles said, regrouping. "The medical examiner said that he died of drowning because there was water in his lungs and no other cause of death like a heart attack or drug overdose. But there is no way that he fell in around midnight and the current didn't drag his body down the river. I could understand if Trevor's body was caught on something or was half on land. Several scenarios could have made it possible that his body didn't move with the currents – I've ruled all of those out. It's simply impossible that he spent from midnight to eight in the morning in the water and didn't move with the current."

It was a morbid thought but needed to be asked. "Could his body have been kept someplace and then placed in the water later, closer to when it was found?"

"That's the only scenario I haven't ruled out yet. The medical examiner couldn't exclude that either. He said he wouldn't rule it in and say it was plausible, but he couldn't rule it out." Miles rubbed the spot on his forehead he always did when he was stressed. "Even that doesn't make a lot of sense to me."

It didn't make a lot of sense to me either because most people who killed someone didn't go through those kinds of theatrics. "Are you sure Trevor died in the river? Did the decomp match up?"

Miles sat back with his mouth set in a firm line. "That's what the medical examiner said. There were other wounds on the body that complicated that for me."

"Complicated how?" Jack asked.

"There were markings on his wrists like he'd been restrained and there was bruising on his face. The medical examiner didn't seem to take note of either as significant. Everyone we spoke to said that Trevor didn't have any kind of bruising like that, particularly on his face. It was noticeable. Maybe there was some kind of struggle before he went into the water. Maybe there was a struggle elsewhere and then his body was thrown into the river. That wouldn't account for the water in the lungs. He went into that river alive. I'm just not sure what to make of it all."

"Okay," Jack said slowly, dragging out the word as he processed what Miles told us. "That to me would indicate a homicide no matter how you look at it."

I sat up straighter and looked across the table toward the back of the bar. Not that I could see the patio or the river below it, but I knew the area like the back of my hand. "Are there cameras back there?"

Miles shook his head. "No. We don't have any down here. There are four bars in a row on this block and then not much else. Down farther are warehouse buildings that were long ago abandoned but have been bought up by developers who plan to turn them into loft-style apartments."

I wanted to bring up the fact that Liv had spoken to Trevor the night he went missing. I had been holding back waiting for a lull in conversation. This was the time. "I know that you interviewed several people who saw Trevor in the bar that night, but my sister, Liv, admitted to me that she was here in the pub and had spoken to Trevor. It sounded to me like she might have been one of the last people he spoke to before he left."

His head snapped up and Miles looked at me. "Why didn't she come forward sooner?"

It was a legitimate question. I felt protective of Liv even though

I had been annoyed with her earlier. "I asked that and she said she didn't feel like she knew anything of value. To be fair to her, she didn't know much. I interviewed her before I met with you today. Liv said that he was checking his phone a lot and seemed annoyed. She joked about him having a girlfriend who was checking up on him. He said he was single. They talked for maybe ten minutes more. He checked his phone again and said he had to leave." I went over the brief info they shared during the time they talked. "So, you see, she didn't know much. Liv did say he didn't seem impaired at all. Trevor had two drinks while she sat with him, but he didn't finish the second. He spoke to some guys near the bathroom and then he was gone."

"You're right, it wasn't much," Miles said, defeated. "It still would have been good to know while I was still on the case."

"You're still on the case," I countered, not sure what he meant. "You said you were going to help me, right?"

"I meant officially. I have to watch my back. I could get in serious trouble for continuing to investigate a case that my captain has already closed."

Jack put his arm around the back of the booth and squeezed Miles's shoulder in a reassuring fatherly way. "What do you want to do first?"

"Let's go walk the scene and see if you have any more questions. You'll need to come by my house at some point and take a look at copies of the statements I pulled."

I raised my eyes to him. "You have copies of the statements?"

"The whole file," Miles said and let that sit with us. He had broken protocol. He wanted this case solved as much as I did.

"We'll solve this, Miles. I promise you that," I said full of confidence.

# CHAPTER 12

Luke had stayed late at the office trying to run down a few more leads that got him nowhere. He sent Det. Tyler home at seven and stayed later going over the evidence they had so far. He had ordered a sandwich for dinner and ate it while he watched the bar's surveillance footage again. Now that he had identified Nolan, he wanted to keep his eye on him throughout the video footage.

The first time Nolan appeared on video was shortly after ten. He finished his beer and walked out of the front door of the bar a little after midnight – just like he had told Luke. The video footage of him on the street had Nolan walking down President Clinton Avenue in the opposite direction that Rob went. Nolan was out of the shot quickly after that. If Luke wanted to know where he went from there, he'd have to ask the city for additional video surveillance. What he was looking at now meant little to Luke. All up and down the street, there were access points to the river trail. Nolan could have gone one direction and then doubled back out of sight and Luke would never know it.

The first thing Luke had done when he got back to the office after interviewing Nolan was to check Maggie's alibi at the children's hospital. He confirmed with her supervisor that she had been working the hours she said – going in at seven that night and staying until seven that morning. The supervisor confirmed Maggie had been there the whole night. It meant there was no way Maggie had told Nolan to leave her alone at her apartment. Either Nolan had lied to them or Maggie had someone staying at her apartment with her. Luke had called Maggie and left a message to confirm. He was still waiting for her to return the call.

There was nothing left for Luke to do, so he leaned back and stretched his arms overhead. It had been a long day and it didn't feel like he had accomplished much.

The only light still on in the detective's bullpen was Captain Meadows. Luke couldn't remember the last time he had stayed this late. He closed the file in front of him and made his way over to the office door. He knocked once, waited to be told to enter, and then pushed the door open. "You're here late," Luke said, taking a seat without being asked.

Captain Meadows finished writing in a file and then closed it, tossing his pen down on the desk. "Going through performance evaluations. The city gave us the funding to add another two detectives. I'm trying to figure out if it's needed. Do you need another body?"

Luke shook his head. "We are staffed perfectly right now. Maybe check the gang task force. They are always in need of more detectives. They were scrambling a few weeks back trying to handle assaults and drug cases. They could probably use another undercover detective."

"You've got your finger on the pulse of this department, Luke. The other detectives respect you. That's important."

It was true that he was respected, and for the most part, Luke got along well with his co-workers. There was an undercurrent in Captain Meadows's tone that left Luke uncertain. "Something on your mind?"

"Perceptive, Luke." Captain Meadows sat back and folded his hands over his stomach, which had grown over the last year as he slowed down. "The fact of the matter is that I'm going to need to retire soon. The department wants younger blood in this position and there are only so many years I have left. You've been running the homicide division for several years, successfully I'd add. You'd be a natural fit if you're interested." He waited a beat and then raised his eyebrows. "That's the only question – would you be interested in my job?"

Luke started to speak and then stopped, unsure of what to say.

Captain Meadows shook his head. "This isn't a job offer yet, Luke. It's an inquiry about your level of interest. I'm not going anywhere right now. I'd like to retire later next year. We need time to get someone ready for this job and the brass wants someone from the inside. I can't think of anyone better than you."

For some reason, this didn't come as a surprise to Luke. There was a part of him that had known for a long time that he'd be having this conversation. In many ways, Captain Meadows had been grooming him for the job, giving him more and more responsibility.

"I don't know," Luke said honestly. "I like being in the field and investigating. I don't know that I'd want to sit behind a desk for the majority of my day. I know I'm supposed to want your job and to advance. I don't like the politics of your position."

"There is a lot of that," Captain Meadows said, his tone regretful. "I figured you'd say something like this. There's no reason you can't make this position your own, Luke. You could still take a few cases here and there. Your responsibilities would be greater and you'll be tied to the desk more, that is true. There is still investigative work to be done. You'll be taking more of a bird's eye view of the cases rather than being down in the weeds."

Luke tried to hide his smile. "I like being down in the weeds."

"I know," Captain Meadows said. "You're getting older, Luke, and you'll want to slow down eventually."

Luke didn't want to say that eventually for him was when he was sixty. "I'd have to think about it."

"Of course." Captain Meadows leaned forward on his desk and

changed the subject. "I'm sure you figured it out by now, but I got official confirmation that Nolan Dunn is Larry Dunn's son. The prosecutor's office has had its eye on the kid for a few years now. His crimes have escalated and they are tired of cutting deals. If he's good for this murder, they told me to go after him with everything we have."

Luke wasn't surprised by any of it. "Why go after him now and not before? I don't understand why they keep cutting deals with Larry Dunn."

"Politics and money. You prosecute Larry Dunn's kid and you can be sure that cash cow is cut off and one political party would be very unhappy."

It made Luke's job and the other detectives' that much harder. "That's something I will never understand."

Captain Meadows commiserated with him on that point. "Do you have anything right now tying Nolan Dunn to Rob Hall that night?"

"Nothing other than them being in the same bar and leaving a few minutes after the other. There is a prior altercation. We don't even have enough circumstantial evidence to build a case." Luke updated Captain Meadows about Nolan saying he went to Maggie's apartment later that night. "Either he's lying or she had someone else there. I should have that information confirmed tomorrow. It wasn't Maggie. That much I know for sure."

Captain Meadows encouraged him to keep going. "I want to run to ground every last lead we can find, even if it seems ridiculous. That's the only way we are going to be able to close the case without any questions. Have you heard from Riley or Cooper today?"

"Riley texted me that she landed this morning. Nothing from Cooper yet." Luke checked his watch and it was nearing eight. "We are supposed to video chat tonight around eight-thirty. If I find out anything from them, I'll update you."

Captain Meadows waved him off. "Update me tomorrow. No need to keep at it tonight."

Luke left the office and went back to his desk and gathered up his things to go home. He left Captain Meadows still sitting at his desk. Luke knew that the conversation about him being promoted to captain of the detective's bureau was only the start. There'd be more discussions to come. He'd have to talk it out with Riley and make some decisions about his future. The only thing Luke knew for sure was that he didn't want to deal with all the politics and sit behind a desk all day. He'd go stir crazy if that was the totality of his job, especially one he'd have for the foreseeable future.

Luke made it home in time to change into a tee shirt and shorts. He closed the back kitchen window he had left open earlier in the day and grabbed a beer from the fridge. He pulled his laptop off his desk upstairs and sat in the comfortable chair in the corner of the bedroom. Both Riley's and Cooper's names were lit up green and indicated they were on and available to chat.

He clicked the buttons and fired up the video chat. It took a moment for everyone's screens to jump to life. Luke smiled as soon as he saw Riley. She had her hair pulled up on top of her head and had already scrubbed her face free of makeup. She was in her bedroom at her mother's house. "I know it's not even been a full day yet, but I'm glad to see you both." Luke gave them the rundown of his case for the day and then asked if they had any updates.

"I didn't do much today," Cooper said from his hotel room. "Det. Clive Elio isn't available to meet until tomorrow. I don't have any case details yet. The parents didn't want to meet with me first. They said to speak to Det. Elio, and he's keeping everything close to the vest until he meets with me." Cooper glanced over his shoulder and then leaned toward his laptop, dropping his voice. "The hotel is kind of creepy. It's pouring out too, even though they said no rain."

Cooper moved his head to the side so Riley and Luke could check out his room. "Why is it creepy?" Luke asked and then added, "It looks nice to me."

Cooper shrugged. "Maybe it's just that it's old and this room feels like the front of a shop instead of a hotel room. It was the front of a shop back in the 1800s. It might be the rain too. It was pouring down so much I only made it about a block for dinner."

"It will seem better tomorrow," Riley said. "The rain can make anything creepy and it is New Orleans."

Luke looked at the square on his laptop that contained Riley's video feed. "What did you find out today?"

She tightened the ball of hair on the top of her head. "First off, Ned Shaw is here in Troy. He held a press conference today about the Trevor Ellis case, indicating they had evidence that the Troy PD is engaging in a coverup and withholding information that he believes will lead to a serial killer."

"Did the Troy PD have a response?" Luke asked.

Riley shook her head. "They can't be bothered with it. The family doesn't believe it, thankfully. Miles promised them no matter what happens he isn't dropping the case until they have some resolution. The family knows we are working together and Miles is doing this in his spare time."

"Is Shaw going to stay up there and focus on that case?" Cooper asked, looking relieved that he probably wouldn't have to deal with Shaw directly.

Luke felt the same relief but he didn't want Riley to have to deal with him either.

"I don't know his plan," Riley said. "He made sure to come over to the table when Miles, Jack, and I were meeting tonight and acted like a jerk. It was the first time Jack met him and there is already great disdain for Shaw. He's that kind of guy – he rubs people the wrong way because he's not good at what he does but thinks he is. There's no talking him out of his theory."

"What are we going to do if Shaw is right and there is a serial killer?" Cooper asked.

Riley wasn't convinced. "I'm sure if there is a serial killer or killers, it's not going to shake out like Shaw thinks it will. There are no Cross Killers. I don't think all these cases are connected." She sat back and sighed. "I'm not going to fight you both on it if we think that's where the evidence is going. I'm going to hate it if Shaw is right."

"I think we are all going to hate it if Shaw is right," Luke said, commiserating with her. "Is Miles giving you enough access to the case?" Luke tried not to have a hint of jealousy in his voice when he said the man's name. He didn't want Riley working with Miles but felt foolish for thinking Riley would break her marriage vows. He had to temper that jealous side.

"I have all the access I need. Jack said he'd help." Riley looked to the side and then back at the screen. She leaned down closer to her camera and lowered her voice. "Miles was able to copy the entire case file and has it at his house. I'm going over tomorrow to go through everything while he is at work. Hopefully, after that, we can get started."

"I'm glad you have access," Luke said, leaving out the part that he wasn't happy she was going to his house.

Cooper added, "I'm hoping to have similar access with Det. Clive Elio. I don't know much about him. He seems to know what he's talking about during the few interactions we've had." Cooper looked at his watch. "If there's nothing else, I need to give Adele a call."

After they said their goodbyes, the screen that had Cooper's video feed went black.

When they were alone, Luke asked, "How's it going being back?"

"It's good. You look like you've got something on your mind."

Luke wanted to share with her what Captain Meadows said about the possible promotion. It was too much to go into tonight. He smiled. "It's been a long day and I'm tired. I'm also missing you."

"Luke," Riley said slowly, dragging out his name. "Are you worried about me being here and working with Miles? My mother brought it up and so did Liv. You trust me, right? I know he and I had a mild flirtation before we got married but it was harmless. I don't want to do anything that would make you uncomfortable."

"You're not," he assured her. "Miles is a good detective. I'm sure you'll solve it quickly so you can get back home. Are you worried about Shaw being there?"

Riley didn't respond right away. She made herself more comfortable in the chair. "It would be easier if he wasn't here. I'll manage."

They talked for a few more minutes, said a few sweet things to each other, and then ended the chat with a promise to update each other the next day. Luke closed the laptop and went to bed. He only hoped tomorrow there'd be a bigger break in the case.

# CHAPTER 13

Cooper tossed and turned most of the night. As he told Luke and Riley, he had arrived right before a downpour of rain. The valet had taken his car while he checked into the hotel, which was a few distinct buildings around an inner courtyard. Walking down the cobblestone driveway, Cooper was effortlessly transported back in time.

His building was off to the left and faced Ursulines Avenue and the old Ursulines nuns' convent, which was now a museum. During its heyday, it was rumored that the nuns kept vampires locked away in the attic. Cooper learned that tidbit of information at check-in when an older man who frequented the hotel had regaled him with some unsolicited and terrifying history of the place.

It didn't help that Cooper's room was down a narrow alcove that dead-ended at a locked wrought iron gate. The room had once been a shop storefront and had two large double ceiling-to-floor doors that opened to the street. Standing in the open doorway, Cooper could see the small square windows of the convent's attic. He had shut and locked the doors and then for good measure shoved the back part of the desk chair under the doors wedging them closed.

Then he walked to get dinner and came back and talked to Luke and Riley and then Adele. After that he showered and crawled into bed, holding the necklace Hattie had given him in his hand. Cooper chastised himself for being so superstitious and silly. The fact was he could stop a serial killer with his Glock, but the gun did no good against a vampire or ghost – not that either was real.

After a fitful night of sleep, Cooper woke before sunrise and got himself ready for the day. He left the hotel and walked down Chartres heading toward the coffee shop where he was to meet Det. Elio at eight. The narrow streets of the French Quarter combined with the architecture left Cooper feeling he had gone back in time about two hundred years.

Cooper was twenty minutes early but was desperate for coffee and something to eat. He found the shop and stood in a line of people to place his order. All the pastries looked so decadent he had a hard time deciding. After he made his selection, paid, and was given his items, he found a two-seater in the back of the half-filled shop near the window. He hoped he'd be able to spot the detective as he approached. Cooper had no idea what the man looked like.

"Cooper Deagnan?" a man asked off to his left as Cooper took a sip of coffee.

He turned his head slightly to see a clean-shaven black man with a round face and easy smile. He was short but muscular and exactly how Cooper had pictured him. "Det. Elio, I was hoping to beat you here."

The detective held up his coffee. "I'm usually the first one in the shop when they open." He smiled and laughed to himself. "If I'm being totally honest with you, I wanted to scope you out before we met. I assume you were doing the same." Det. Elio stood and joined Cooper at his table. "Welcome to New Orleans," he said with an exaggerated local accent. "If you don't mind me saying it, you don't look like you slept well. Hotel okay?"

Cooper didn't want to start the conversation by admitting anything personal. "New place. You know how it is. The hotel is nice. I'll get settled soon."

"New Orleans has a weird vibe, Cooper. You never get used to it even if you live here your whole life." Det. Elio took a sip of his coffee. "Call me Clive by the way."

"Well. Clive. What have you got for me?" Cooper was itching to finally have the case details.

Clive sat back and gave Cooper the overview. He didn't read anything from a file and had committed the case to memory. "Danny Thibodeaux was a local kid attending Loyola University. His parents live in the Garden District in the same home where Danny grew up. He wasn't a kid who strayed too far from home. He was New Orleans through and through. Danny was supposed to be starting his senior year of college this semester. He had his whole life in front of him. He went out for his twenty-first birthday in August with friends before the semester started and died that night."

It was like a sucker punch to Cooper's gut. "Danny died on his birthday?"

"Yes," Clive said sadly. "Terrible thing when you think about it. Out for your twenty-first birthday on Bourbon Street and you never make it back home. He went missing during the celebration. There was a group of twenty of them who started at a bar called Prohibition and then the plan was to go on to other bars later in the evening. When it was time to leave Prohibition, one group went one way down Bourbon Street and the other group went the other way."

"Where did Danny go at that point?"

"Danny either got lost in the shuffle and was accidentally left behind or he headed off on his own." Clive took another sip of his coffee and waited for Cooper to ask a question. When he didn't have one, Clive continued. "Danny was last seen heading toward St. Louis Street on Bourbon Street. We believe he made the right onto St. Louis and headed toward the river. There is a witness who believes he saw

Danny on the corner of St. Louis and Decatur arguing with a man a few minutes after midnight. The witness didn't hear what they were saying, but the exchange looked heated. That's the last known sighting of him."

Cooper knew from studying a map of the French Quarter that there was a parking lot for the steamboat close to there and it was a stone's throw to the river. "How long was Danny missing?"

"He wasn't missing in the traditional sense. The missing person unit at the PD never got involved." Clive cradled the mug in his hands. "Because Danny's friends had split into two groups, both assumed Danny went with the other group. No one knew until morning that he was gone."

"That's a lot of time to be on his own," Cooper said, considering everything that could have happened to him before ending up in the river. "How long between Danny's friends going to different bars and the sighting of him down near the river?"

"Less than fifteen minutes," Clive said and leveled a look at Cooper. "I assume he walked from one bar to the other. I can walk it in less time, but if you factor in a crowded street or maybe he was drunk and stumbling. It's possible he stopped to check his phone. It just doesn't take that long. I've wondered if it was intentional."

"You think he went to the river to meet someone? When was his body found?" Cooper didn't mean to bark out his questions the way he did, his brain was trying to make sense of the night. There was still much he didn't know.

"I think he went to meet someone," Clive said. "Danny's body was found early the next morning in the river not far from where we assume he went in. Of course, we don't know the location for sure. The medical examiner said that Danny had a bump on the side of his head and there was water in his lungs. We know he was alive when he went into the Mississippi River. The question is how and why did he end up in there."

Cooper ripped off a piece of his croissant and offered some to Clive who declined. "Why did you think it wasn't an accident? If Danny was drunk and then was seen arguing with someone, he might have walked down by the river, fallen and hit his head, and stumbled in."

"That's what I considered at first. Then we got ahold of Danny's cellphone records."

Cooper hadn't heard anything about that. "What was in those?"

Clive leaned into the table, released his mug, and leaned on his arms. "It answered some questions I had and also led me to think this was not an accident. Someone had been texting Danny that night and asked him to meet down by the river. The texter said they wanted to talk but insisted they meet that night. I realized then that Danny probably broke away from his group on purpose to meet this person. Only Danny knows who he was going to meet."

Cooper didn't understand. "You couldn't get any cellphone data on the texter?"

Clive shook his head. "It's one of those throwaway phones. And even looking at the text exchange, it didn't tell me much other than the person wanted Danny to meet. I can't even tell you how Danny knew this person or the reason for the meeting."

"You ruled out robbery?" Cooper asked.

"Yeah. Danny was found with his cellphone in one pocket and his wallet in the other. He had a credit card, his driver's license, student identification, and two hundred dollars in cash in his wallet. No one robbed him."

Cooper took another sip of his coffee, running through all the normal scenarios in his head. "Drugs? Gambling?"

"No and no. His friends said that Danny drank his fair share but had never done drugs. He had been a high school athlete but was focused on his studies. He wanted to go to law school and didn't want anything to get in the way. His friends said Danny wanted to work in the prosecutor's office and worried that any kind of arrest would derail his career before it even got started. It kept him on the straight and narrow. It left me with few leads on the case."

"It sounds like Danny was a better kid than most. I wasn't thinking that rationally at twenty-one," Cooper said with a chuckle. "I can see why you wanted to investigate the case more. Why was it closed?"

"Ned Shaw," Clive said back and waited for Cooper to react. When he assured the detective he knew the name and all about him, Clive continued. "Then you know how toxic that guy can be to a case. When he called my captain and insisted it was a serial killer, the investigation was shut down that afternoon. The last thing anyone wanted to hear was that a serial killer was roaming the streets of New Orleans targeting young people drinking on Bourbon Street. If that happens, there goes tourism. But it ate at me. There's something about this case I'm missing."

Cooper had heard that before. "That's a common refrain from the handful of investigators across the country who have had these drowning cases of young men. The pieces don't always fit into a neat little package. Have you read much about the earlier cases Shaw has tied together?"

Clive nodded. "When I got assigned the case, my girlfriend mentioned them to me. She had seen a special on some cable channel that Ned Shaw put together. It was obvious there were many holes in their theories. She said that some of what they were saying didn't make any sense at all." Clive raised his shoulders to shrug but lowered them and shook his head. "It's a lot of dead kids with few answers. No matter how it shakes out, I didn't want this case to be among them. I wanted closure for the family and the whole city."

"That's a lot of pressure on your shoulders." Cooper assessed him. He got the feeling he was there more for Clive than the family. "Is that why you called me in?"

Clive took a beat and then admitted, "I'm officially not allowed to be working this case. My partner retired a few months back, and I haven't been assigned a new one yet. Most people know my obsession with this case and think I've lost my objectivity. As a result, my case assignments have been lowered even though I have one of the best solve rates in my unit. I don't want this to be a career wrecker for me. I'm not too proud to admit I need the help. I'm missing something but maybe fresh eyes won't. The family also wants closure. When Captain Meadows called and he suggested you, I jumped at the chance. Do you do this often? Investigate in other states?"

"Not really if I can help it." Cooper explained to Clive about Riley's case in New York and Luke's case in Little Rock. "With three of us on separate cases, the hope is either we will find a real connection or we will solve them separately and dispel the myth."

"New York isn't the south though. Shouldn't your friend have taken one of the cases in the south?" Clive asked.

Cooper hadn't considered that before. "We weren't asked to help on those other cases. The New York case happened in line with the more recent drownings. It's home for Riley. Maybe something she finds will help the older cases."

"You think they are all connected?"

"I don't think anything," Cooper said blowing out a frustrated sigh. "I'm a blank slate and open to wherever the evidence leads me. If there's a serial killer, I'm ready for it. If all the cases are accidental, then we need to figure out how to stop so many young men from ending up in rivers. If they are all individual homicides that aren't connected, then that's what we find." Cooper opened his arms out wide. "I'm going where the evidence leads."

"Good," Clive said and then stood. "Let's go start at Prohibition."

"Lead the way." Cooper drank the last of his coffee and finished his croissant. He was confident he was going to like working with Clive.

# CHAPTER 14

Cooper followed Clive from the Prohibition bar to the corner of St. Louis Street where they turned right and walked the same path Danny did the night he died. It was a straight shot down St. Louis to the corner of Decatur Street where Danny was last seen.

Cooper glanced around as they walked, taking in the shops and restaurants. He had never been in another city that had the same weird vibe that New Orleans had. Cooper couldn't even identify the feeling. It was a bit like stepping back in time and entering into a creepy horror movie. There was nothing on the surface that gave him chills up his spine. It was more an unidentifiable feeling. He also felt like he was being watched.

"Are you from New Orleans?" Cooper asked breaking the silence.

"Born and raised. I've never lived anywhere else." Clive looked over at Cooper and noted the strange look on his face. "It takes some getting used to. We get transfers with the police department all the time who get weirded out." Clive pointed to Cooper's pocket. "What's in your pocket that you keep reaching for?"

Cooper slowly pulled his hand out of his pocket as he felt his face flush. Reluctantly, he showed Clive the necklace that Hattie had given him. "I know it probably seems silly to you." Cooper told him about his relationship with Hattie and that she insisted he carry this with him on the trip.

"Not silly," Clive said, offering Cooper a smile. He tugged at a necklace around his neck and showed him a similar stone. "My aunt is a Voodoo Priestess. Voodoo runs deep in my family and protection from the spirits is everything. I'm not sure I believe but she tells me to wear it so I wear it."

Clive stopped in the middle of the sidewalk and then stepped toward the building out of the way of oncoming foot traffic.

"Is everything okay?" Cooper asked, stepping to the side with him. He glanced around but didn't see any reason for why they had stopped.

Clive waited until the people around them dissipated. "I wasn't going to mention this because I figured you'd think I'd lost my mind." Then he paused.

Cooper encouraged him to continue. "Go on, please. Whatever you feel like you need to say, tell me. I've had some weird cases and I'm pretty much open to anything at this point."

Clive didn't meet his eyes. "My aunt, the Voodoo Priestess. She threw the bones and saw that we are dealing with a serial killer or at least a killer who has done this sort of thing more than once. She said that we should expect the unexpected and trust no one."

Hattie had given Cooper a similar warning. "What does throwing the bones mean?"

Clive explained it was a form of divination often used in voodoo. Cooper assumed it was like Hattie reading her cards.

"Is that why you wanted to keep the case open?" Cooper asked without any judgment in his voice.

"Yes and no," Clive said dismissively. "My aunt is rarely wrong, but I also already knew we weren't dealing with an accident.Once I saw that Danny had been contacted that night with a request to meet, and a witness came forward to say he saw a man matching Danny's description arguing with someone down by the river, I knew the accident theory wasn't accurate. I had to continue the investigation."

Cooper was glad Clive had some logic to his reasoning. He wasn't going to dismiss Clive's aunt as nonsense, but he also wasn't going to hang an investigation on it either. "As I said at the start, I'll go wherever the evidence leads. I think Ned Shaw's Cross Killers theory is a bit off, but if there is a serial killer, I'm open to it."

"Good," Clive said, running a hand down his face. "I was worried that you might be shut down to the theory completely. I know Shaw has made a mess of everything and serial killer cases are rare."

Cooper knew it was possible. Luke's sister had been killed by a serial killer who targeted young women at college. He killed a victim once every fall and moved around the country to different schools. He told Clive about the case. When he finished, Cooper added, "That was about as far-fetched as you can get. I believe a killer may be targeting these young men."

"Let's go then." Clive started walking again. As they made their way down the street, he pointed out restaurants Cooper might like to try while he was in the city. Once they got to the corner of Decatur, Clive stopped. "This is it where Danny was last seen. Right there at the edge of the parking lot is where the witness saw Danny with a man. The area is somewhat dark at night. There are a few streetlights around but a lot of areas where you can step into the shadows and disappear. Where Danny was standing, the other person wasn't illuminated enough for them to get a good description. All we know is that it was a man."

While Cooper was glad that he was seeing the location, he'd walk the same path later that night to see it in the dark. It was one thing to be standing out there early in the day but quite different to follow the path at night. "What happened after?"

"We don't know. I assume either there was a struggle and Danny was hit in the head and dragged to the river or maybe one of them walked toward the river and the other followed and a fight ensued there. There was some kind of struggle."

"That's an assumption on your part," Cooper countered gently. When the detective glanced over at him, he added, "You know Danny had a bump on the head and ended up in the river and you know that he was arguing with someone that night, but you don't know that anything physical happened between them. The truth is you have no idea how Danny got the bump on his head."

Clive nodded his head. "You're right. It was an assumption on my part. We have to take some speculative leaps because of the lack of evidence."

"Excuse me," a soft voice said from behind them. Cooper and Clive turned to face a short woman with shoulder-length dark hair. She had her right eyebrow pierced and Cooper put her in her mid-twenties. She pointed to Clive's badge affixed to his belt. "Are you the detective on the Danny Thibodeaux case?"

"It's officially closed but I was."

"I called the police station shortly after it happened and left a message that I might know something about that night. No one ever called me back." The young woman extended her hand. "I'm Laura. I saw who I believed to be Danny arguing with a man and then walking away down toward the river."

Clive confirmed, "Yes, we had received a tip about that. We believe he might have gone into the river at that point."

Laura shook her head. "No. No. That's not what happened at all. Danny did walk toward the river and he was down there for maybe ten minutes. He was out of sight, so I don't know what happened down there. But that wasn't all. I saw him run across the parking lot toward Decatur in the direction of Jackson Square. One of my friends called to him to see if he was okay, but he never turned back around. He was running fast as if something spooked him. He didn't go into the river right then. That's what all of you got wrong."

Clive squinted his eyes. "Are you sure it was him?"

"If Danny was the guy that we saw arguing with someone at the corner of St. Louis and Decatur then it was the same guy running away from the river toward Jackson Square."

Cooper thought it was a promising lead. "Did you see anyone following him?"

"No. He looked back a few times like he was worried someone was following him. He was running fast, too, as if he thought someone might be chasing him."

"You didn't see anyone else around?" Clive asked, taking out his phone and pulling up a photo of Danny. He turned it to face Laura. "Is this who you saw?"

Laura leaned in and looked at the photo. "Yeah, it's him. There was no one else around. It's why we noticed him. We had seen him arguing with someone. One of my friends was worried it might turn into a fight, but they went their separate ways. The other guy walked off and Danny went toward the river. We were relieved at that point. But roughly ten minutes later, the same guy came running back up from the river. It freaked us out that night. We couldn't stop him and we didn't see anything from where we stood. None of us was willing to go down to the river though and see what he was running from. That's why when we saw Danny's body had been found in the river, I called the police station."

"Who did you talk to at the police station? The information was never provided to me." Clive shared a look with Cooper. It was obvious the detective hadn't been given the message.

"I didn't get to share the whole story with the guy who answered. He said he'd have the detective in charge call me back. I tried to call again about a week later and was told that the detective had the information and he'd call back if he wanted to speak to me. Otherwise, I should assume my information wasn't relevant."

Clive seemed caught off guard by that. "I'm sorry. I had no idea."

"It wasn't your fault then," Laura said, letting him off the hook. "I didn't know what else to do. I didn't think I could walk into the police station. I didn't even know your name."

"How'd you find me now?" Clive asked the question Cooper was wondering.

"I work just over there." Laura pointed to an H&M Clothing store across the street. "I saw you guys standing over here. Then I saw the gun on your hip and figured at least one of you had to be a cop. Since this is where I saw Danny, I hoped you were still looking into the case. I took a shot and here we are."

"Fortunate you were working today," Cooper said and then realized he hadn't introduced himself. He did so and then extended his hand to her. "Is there anything else you think we should know?"

"I don't know what happened to him down by the river, but Danny was freaked out. I've never seen someone behave like that. It scared us too and we went home shortly after." Laura told them the names of the people she had been with that night and provided phone numbers in case they wanted to verify any of the details. "Whatever happened wasn't an accident."

They watched Laura walk back to the store and then Clive turned to Cooper. "I can't believe I never got her messages. I've never had something like that happen."

"It happens," Cooper said and meant it. He was sure there were many cases he had worked where there were witnesses that he had never interviewed either because they hadn't come forward or there was miscommunication. Witness evidence was also some of the most unreliable. "At least we know now. If he ran going toward Jackson Square, where does that leave us?"

"I don't know." Clive turned in the direction where Danny was said to have run. "All we can do is walk it and see what we find. The one thing it does mean is that Danny went that direction only to be dragged back and thrown in the river north from here. It's how the Mississippi flows."

Cooper was a bit turned around on the city streets. It was hard from his vantage point to figure out north and south, so he took Clive's word for it until he could consult a map. "What's in that direction that would be open at that time of night?"

"Lots of bars. Too many to name and a handful of restaurants are open that late. There is also St. Louis Cathedral and Jackson Square. I'm not sure how long they keep the doors open." Clive ran a hand down his face and cursed. "He could have gone anywhere."

Cooper didn't have the same attachment to the case that Clive had. He wasn't emotionally invested yet, so the change didn't mean much to him. It didn't rock his view of it. "At least we have some evidence now. You believe Laura, right?"

Clive turned sharply back to Cooper. "Yes, I believe her. I wish I had the information sooner. Maybe my captain would have kept the case open. Let's walk and see what we find."

# CHAPTER 15

The next morning, I opened my eyes to Dusty licking my hand and tugging on my blanket to rouse me from sleep. I had expected to look at the bedside clock and see an ungodly early hour of the morning. I blinked twice not believing that it was after nine. I couldn't remember the last time I had slept so late. It must have been the comfort of my childhood bedroom.

I pushed myself up in bed and scratched Dusty behind the ears. "It's a good thing you woke me up. I have to meet Miles around noon." Miles figured he could sneak away from work for lunch and let me into his house. He said he was going to arrange the case file in a way that I could go through it with ease and without too many questions. I felt a bit weird going to his house, but I could understand why he didn't want to hand the case file over to me.

I reached for my phone that was sitting perched on the edge of the table. There were no texts or calls from Luke or Cooper. Miles had texted me a reminder message about twenty minutes ago. I texted back that I'd be there and to reach out if anything changed.

"Mom!" I called and my voice echoed through the house. I figured even if my mom wasn't there, Jack or Liv would respond. By the lack of response, I assumed I was alone. I looked down at Dusty who had taken his paw and was trying to drag my hand back to his chest for pets. "You never have enough, do you?"

I gave him a few more pets before I got up and got myself ready for the day. Dusty sat waiting outside of the bathroom door the entire time. I had asked if he wanted to go out and got no response. Normally, as soon as the word *outside* is said, he jumps around all excited if that's what he wants.

He followed me down the stairs and to the living room and then jumped up on the couch with me. "Are you allowed up here? When we lived together you weren't allowed on my couch." He glanced in my direction then turned around and snuggled his backside into me as if he didn't care whether he was allowed or not – he was staying.

I turned the television on to a local news station and saw a late-breaking report. Ned Shaw was giving another press conference claiming he had evidence in Trevor Ellis's death. The reporter asked a direct question and he bobbed and weaved around not giving a straight answer. For evidence-based questions, Shaw claimed he had it all and would only reveal it at the right time. He claimed again that there was a message board on the dark web where serial killers plotted how to drown young men. They traded stories about victims, trying to one-up each other.

When asked if he had handed that information over to law enforcement, Shaw said he had not. When pressed about sitting down with the FBI and handing over the evidence, Shaw outright refused, claiming the FBI didn't believe him. That much was true. Some years back they had looked into Shaw's so-called evidence and found nothing but speculation.

There were no cold hard facts to any Cross Killers conspiracy.

Now, I was watching Shaw do the same thing on my local news. I sighed loudly enough Dusty raised his head to check on me. We shared a look and he put his head back down. "I know. This guy is going to destroy everything."

I pushed myself off the couch, grabbed a quick bite to eat, forced

Dusty to take a tour of the backyard, and then let him back in before leaving my mother a note on the dry-erase board she's had in the kitchen for years. I didn't know exactly where the day would take me, so I wasn't sure I'd be home for dinner – which was the only thing my mother ever seemed to want to know. If only life was that simple.

I drove the short distance to Miles's house and was relieved to see his SUV in the driveway. He lived in a small Cape Cod-style house. It wasn't big by any stretch but it seemed to suit him. There was a tree in the front yard and two chairs on the porch. A porch swing sat on the left side of the front door.

Miles pulled open the front door before I had a chance to knock. "Have you seen the latest?" he asked, slightly out of breath. "My captain is flipping his lid that Shaw is still in town and talking about this case."

"It's what he does, Miles. I tried to warn you. You said to not let it bother me." I reminded him of our conversation the night before. "Now, I'm telling you the same thing. Don't give in to him and let's hope he goes away soon."

Miles glanced at me with a skeptical look. "You think that's how it's going to play out?"

"That's exactly how it will play out. It's what he does. He shows up in a city, stirs up everything, and then bails when the media gets tired of him not providing any real evidence. He goes from city to city doing this, whipping everyone up in a frenzy and never coming through."

Miles sat down on the edge of the couch. "Why does he do that?"

"Attention." I sat down in a chair across from him. "Figure it this way. If Shaw had real evidence, he'd be going after the guy himself for the fame of it, or he'd bring legitimate evidence to the cops, so he could stop them. Shaw isn't doing either of those things. He's dangling a carrot and letting the media jump on it. Eventually, they get bored of him and move on to another story. Meanwhile, he's given the family false hope and leaves the real investigators with an impossible job to do."

"He's sick," Miles said, shaking his head. "Has anyone checked where Shaw is while the murders are happening?"

I laughed. "You think he could be committing the drownings?"

"Maybe not the first ones, but after he got involved and couldn't solve them, maybe he decided he liked the attention too much and needed to keep it going. It's a way to keep the story going and his odd-shaped head in the spotlight."

I chuckled. "He does have kind of an odd-shaped head. A little eggish but with chubby cheeks like he's storing nuts for the winter."

We both laughed and then Miles looked at me with concern. "I can understand why he frustrates you so much. Ready to see the evidence?"

I followed him to the second floor and then turned right at the landing into one of the two bedrooms that made up the house's second floor. Miles had an entire bedroom as his office. "You carved a nice little space for yourself up here."

"Four-bedroom house and there's only one of me. I like working from home. It's quieter than the police station." Miles pointed to the box on the floor. "I only had a few days to investigate this case before my captain forced me to close it. Everything you need is in here – witnesses' statements, medical examiner's reports, photos of the body in the water, and even current reports of the river. I tried using those to prove there is no way Trevor's body could have been found where it was found."

There was something bothering me about that. "You said last night that Trevor's body had to move with the current of the river, right?"

"Exactly. There's no way it would end up where it did."

"What if he didn't go into the river behind the bar? It's an assumption because of where he was last seen, but if Trevor went into the river in a different place, then he might have ended up where he did."

Miles scrunched up his face. "What do you think happened then?"

"I don't know.  It's possible though and something we need to consider."

Miles looked like he was about to argue with me. "Trevor's truck was still in the pub's parking lot. If he went someplace else, then he went with someone."

"Then we are most likely looking at a homicide." I let that sit between us and then I explained my thinking. "Miles, you said the reason you thought this was a homicide was because where Trevor ended up the river didn't make sense to you. That's all I'm saying now."

"Trevor drowned, Riley," Miles argued. "Why would anyone move him to another location only to drown him in the river father up north? That doesn't make any sense."

An idea hit me all at once.  "Who said he drowned in the river? There was water in his lungs, but we don't know if it means river water. There are many ways he could have drowned."

That got his attention. Miles cocked his head to the side the way he did when he was processing information. "I'd have to reach out to the medical examiner to see if they can test the water. I don't know anything about that. Do you?"

"No idea.  I could do some research if you want to wait before reaching out. Do you think it will get back to your captain if you're asking questions?"

"It might..." Miles made a low guttural noise I took to mean frustration. "It's so aggravating to know this case is a homicide but not be able to do anything about it. I'm stuck."

I felt for him because I knew exactly what he was feeling. It had happened to me before on cases. I knew in my gut something wasn't right but didn't have the information or resources to prove it. "If it helps, I can talk to Luke. We have a good medical examiner in Little

Rock who I'm sure would be more than happy to review the report or answer questions for us. We might be able to video chat with him, too."

"That's good," Miles said relieved. "If I can put off calling the medical examiner here unless it's solid evidence, I'd rather wait. The last thing I want to do is stir up questions about why I'm still looking into this case."

"I can call Luke today and see what he says." It sounded like a solid first step to me and work that I'd start as soon as Miles left. I gestured toward the laptop on the desk. "Do you mind if I use your computer to research? I didn't bring mine. I can wait until I'm home if you'd rather."

Miles touched the keypad, and when the screen jumped to life, he typed in a six-digit keycode and then rattled off the numbers to me. "Use it for whatever you need."

"I appreciate that."

Miles turned from the computer and stepped toward me. We locked gazes on each other. He side-stepped awkwardly. "I need to get back to work. Help yourself to anything in the fridge if you're hungry. I have snacks in the cupboard too."

I thanked him and he headed for the door. He hesitated at the door and put his hand on the wall and then turned back. "You might have heard I was dating Becky Palmer. It didn't work out in case you're wondering. She's not going to show up here while you're here."

I wasn't sure why Miles felt the need to tell me that. "That's a name I haven't heard in a long time. I'm sorry it didn't work out."

"I'm not," Miles said with a laugh. "She's still terrible. When I told her that I had reconnected with you, she spent half a day telling me how awful she thought you were in high school and then trying to convince me that I shouldn't talk to you anymore out of loyalty to her."

A little surprised laugh escaped. "If you want to know the truth, Liv told me that you were dating her and I wondered why. I can't picture it. She sounds as bad as she did back then."

"She's worse than you can imagine. That's why I wanted to make sure you knew you'd be alone here all day and no one would bother you." Miles smiled over at me in the earnest and sincere way he did that caught my attention in high school. "Have a good day, Riley. Call me if you find anything."

I promised him I would. I stared around the space wondering where to start. I flipped the lid off the evidence box and peered down. There was less than I typically saw in a homicide investigation, but it was still a good deal of paperwork to go through for the afternoon.

I pulled my sweater over my head and tugged my tee shirt back down. I grabbed the medical examiner file first and got down to work.

# CHAPTER 16

The city officials in charge of the surveillance cameras in downtown Little Rock sent the files Luke requested two hours after the official ask. He hadn't been expecting them that quickly and was pleasantly surprised when the courier showed up with the drive containing all the footage.

Luke was finally able to see a broader picture of what Nolan did after leaving Coach's on the night in question. He had left the bar and walked in the opposite direction than Rob had gone. Luke thought for a moment when Nolan turned right at the next block that it was confirmation that he had told the truth and left the downtown area. Luke continued to watch, which was a good thing because he thought his eyes were deceiving him when Nolan looped around the block and came back down President Clinton Avenue not even ten minutes later.

Luke wondered if Nolan had simply walked to his car and then came back again. This time instead of turning into any of the bars or restaurants, he crossed the street and then ducked in between two buildings that led directly to the river. There were no cameras back there, so Luke had no idea where Nolan went. It was the same for Rob – he could only see him on the main street but once he headed toward the river, Luke was out of luck. But now he confirmed that Nolan had been in the vicinity at the time of Rob's death.

Luke hit the stop button on the video and then played it one more time. It annoyed Luke that the cameras only had one vantage point – pointing down President Clinton Avenue toward the William J. Clinton Library and Museum. The road didn't have other cameras that gave a view from different vantage points.

"What does he have in his hand?" Det. Tyler asked, suddenly standing behind Luke.

Luke angled his head to look up at him. "What do you mean?"

"Back up the video." Luke went back to the section where Nolan was still visible on the street. Det. Tyler got closer to the screen and pointed to Nolan's hand. "Right there. You can see something in his hand. It's not keys because he's got those hanging out of his pocket on this side. What is that?"

Luke hadn't seen it before and he didn't know. He inched closer to the screen and was surprised he had missed it. There was an unidentified object in Nolan's right hand. It wasn't flat like a cellphone, and as Det. Tyler noted it wasn't keys. It looked like the end of something – a hammer, no. Luke scanned the items on his desk for something that had a similar end but there was nothing. It had a flat end and then went into a slight curve.

Det. Tyler touched the screen again. "It looks like a knife to me. Go slower frame by frame and see if there's a better angle of it."

Luke did as Det. Tyler suggested and then clicked on the frame that gave the best angle of Nolan's hand. Then he enlarged the image until it was pixelated. He backed out slowly to get the largest image possible that was clear enough to see. Luke leaned down toward his laptop screen until his nose was inches from it. Det. Tyler was correct. "It is a knife with the handle facing away from his body and the blade facing him. That's the best position to strike. Where is he going?"

"Were there any other incidences of violence by the river that night?"

"Not that I know of," Luke said absently as he stared at the knife in Nolan's hand. The handle had an s-curve engraved at the butt of the handle. Luke was sure if he saw the knife again, he'd be able to recognize it. It didn't matter though – Rob wasn't stabbed. "Do you think Rob could have been forced into the water at knifepoint?"

Det. Tyler's expression gave away his answer. "Rob wasn't a small guy. I'd think if someone came at me with a knife, I'd run or fight. If Nolan had a gun, I could see Rob getting into the water, but his family and friends said he could swim. I know he might have been somewhat drunk and the water was cold, but I can't see it happening that way."

"Stranger things have happened," Luke countered without much conviction. He wasn't sure he was buying that scenario himself. "Let's take Nolan's photo and head down to the river. Maybe the homeless guy who said he saw Rob heading down there that night also saw Nolan. We might also find other witnesses who wouldn't speak to us the other night."

"I'm game for anything," Det. Tyler said, grabbing his keys and phone off his desk. When he was ready, he jutted his chin toward the door for Luke to lead and he followed right behind. When they were on the street, a ten-minute walk away to the River Market District, Det. Tyler asked, "Is there a reason Captain Meadows asked me if I thought you'd make a good captain?"

Luke hadn't planned on telling his partner anything about what Captain Meadows had said to him, certainly not before speaking to Riley and making a decision first. Luke got about a block away from the police station, letting the question hang in the air.

Then he stopped and turned to Det. Tyler. "I was going to tell you about the conversation. It only happened last night. It's not something I even discussed with Riley. Captain Meadows said he's getting closer to retirement and asked if I was interested in taking the job. It wasn't an offer. He was feeling me out to see if I had any interest."

Det. Tyler's expression was hard for Luke to read. "Do you have an interest?"

"I don't know," Luke said softly and honestly. "It's a promotion but not the kind of work that will keep me going for long. You know Captain Meadows is glued to his office, and when he's not there, he's in meetings with the brass and the mayor's office. Can you imagine that kind of life for me?"

Det. Tyler didn't hold back his chuckle. "No. That's why I thought it was odd Captain Meadows asked me the question. I don't want to hold you back, Luke. I'd sure miss you as a partner."

"I'm not going anywhere, at least not now." Luke chose his words carefully because he didn't want to make promises to anyone. "Captain Meadows isn't retiring well into next year and I need time to think about it. That's what I told him. I don't think it's for me."

"Consider it. You'd be good at his job."

They left it at that. Luke was glad Det. Tyler asked him. He didn't want to keep secrets from anyone. He just didn't know what he was going to do and didn't want to be pressured either way. He wasn't even sure how Riley would feel about it. It would be more money, but she cared more that he was happy.

They walked the few blocks to the River Market District and stood at the curb below the surveillance camera. They watched the foot and car traffic going up and down the street and then crossed when the light allowed, heading toward the river. There was a path that ran from the library out to West Little Rock. It was a good spot for bikers, runners, and families out for a stroll. At night, it was common that drug deals and other crime happened along the river. It was accessible but dark enough for those who didn't want their deeds to see the light of day.

Luke wasn't sure he was going to be able to find the same guy that he had spoken to on the night Rob's body was found. But there on the path, he sat with his sleeping bag and other belongings. Luke remembered the guy's name was Pete and he called out to him.

The man raised his head. "You're back again. No dead bodies today, Detective."

Seeing the man's bony frame, Luke chastised himself for not bringing the man coffee and something to eat. He'd rectify that. "Pete, I had a few more questions for you about the night we found the body." He waited to see if the man was okay being questioned again. Too many cops assumed just because a man was poor or down on his luck, his rights didn't matter. Luke didn't see things that way.

"Go ahead then. I'll tell you what I know."

Luke introduced Det. Tyler and then squatted down to Pete's level so the man didn't have to crane his neck to look up at them. "The night you saw Rob Hall, did you see anyone else down here with him?"

"No. I told you that the other night. He walked by me down that path alone and that was it. I didn't see him after that."

"Did anyone follow him down the path later?"

Pete squinted. "How later?"

Luke didn't know the timing of everything that happened. "Right after?"

Pete shook his head.

"What about within thirty minutes or an hour?"

"Yeah, there was one guy. He followed down the same path maybe fifteen or twenty minutes or so after. I didn't think much about him. He's not dead too, is he?"

"Nothing like that," Luke said and considered how much information he should share with Pete. In the end, he figured it couldn't hurt to say what he was thinking. Luke pulled out his phone and grabbed a recent photo of Nolan he had pulled off his social media page. He showed it to Pete. "This is the guy. I'm wondering if you saw him the night you saw Rob."

Pete leaned down getting his face close to Luke's phone. "I saw him, twice. I didn't think to say anything because it wasn't around the time that I saw the dead guy walk by. It was later. There was something weird about him."

"Weird, how?" Luke glanced up and noted how Det. Tyler was looking down at them. He was as curious as Luke. "Try to remember everything you can about that night. Even if it doesn't seem important, it might be."

"You only asked me about the dead guy before," Pete chastised. "I could have told you all this then."

Luke admitted, "It was the middle of the night. I didn't know what kind of case I was looking at then. I thought it was an accident."

"You don't think that now?"

There was something about the way Pete asked the question, his inquisitive and commanding tone, that caught Luke's attention. "What did you do before you became homeless?"

The corners of Pete's mouth turned up in a grin. "I was military police during Vietnam. I've done your job, son. You should have asked me all these questions the other night. You're falling behind and that's never good in a homicide."

"You think the case is a homicide?" Luke couldn't believe he was asking Pete that. But there he was moving from a squat to sitting in the dirt as Pete looked at him skeptically. "You were down here, Pete. You know what kind of evidence I need. If you think it's a homicide you must have a reason."

Pete raised his bushy eyebrows. "No reason for a healthy young man like that to drown in the river. He wasn't drunk enough by my assessment to have fallen in. Besides, there's nothing to fall into down here. It's a gradual slope and then you hit the water that isn't even deep until you wade out. If he wanted to kill himself, there are three bridges within walking distance. He looked like he was on a mission to meet someone. Then he's dead in the river not far from shore. It's curious to me. You had two guys walk the same way the dead guy went, but only one came running out of there like his pants were on fire. Only not on fire because he was wet."

"Excuse me?" Det. Tyler asked and they both looked up at him. "Did you say two guys and one of them was wet?"

"Up to his waist." Pete pointed over to Luke's phone. "It was that guy there. Ran like nobody's business back to the main street. He was running so fast he didn't even see me sitting here."

"Back up a little and help me understand," Luke said, confused by what Pete said.

"Okay," Pete said slowly, turning his face to Luke's. "Rob walked down the path alone. Then some other guy ten minutes later. He was on his phone and looked harmless enough like he was going to score some drugs. Then this guy you're showing me here. He went charging down the path and then came running back all wet."

"Would you testify to that in court, Pete?"

"I'll do whatever you need."

Luke stood and pulled out all the cash in his wallet and offered it to Pete who refused to take it.

He brushed Luke off. "It wouldn't look good you giving me cash after me giving you a statement. It could look like a bribe. Someone might say you paid me to say what I did. You'll blow your case before you even got one."

Luke thrust the cash toward him. "It's not a bribe and we both know that. Take it, Pete. Get yourself some dinner and a place to stay for the night. Do you have family or anyone I can call for you?"

Pete shook his head. "I have a daughter but she doesn't want to see me. I was messed up for too long – drugs, booze, you know the deal. I'm clean now, been clean for over a year."

"What about your military benefits?" Det. Tyler asked. "Is there a way we can help you access them?"

"Fellas," Pete laughed. "Don't stress about old Pete. I got a blanket, a bed of grass, and the stars overhead. If I wasn't out here, you wouldn't have a case. Let me be."

Luke handed him his business card and wouldn't let him refuse the money. He set the pile of bills down next to Pete. "Call me if you need anything. The police station is a few blocks back. If you need anything, tell them I sent you. Got it?"

Pete saluted him. "You're one of the good ones, Det. Morgan. Keep up the good work."

As Luke walked off, feeling guilty for leaving Pete there on the ground, he said to Det. Tyler, "I wish there was more I could do for him."

"He'll make a change when he's ready. I'll keep an eye on him." Det. Tyler shoved his hands in his pockets. "What's the plan now? If we try to bring Nolan in again, he's going to lawyer up."

Luke knew he was right about that. He needed to sit down and iron out the best plan of attack.

# CHAPTER 17

Det. Clive Elio was called away soon after learning that the victim, Danny, had not drowned in the river shortly after an argument with an unknown man. The witness had said he ran away from the river and down Decatur Street toward Jackson Square.

It left Cooper with the day in front of him and one lead to explore.

Clive had handed Cooper a key and told him that all the case files could be found at his house on the corner of Royal and St. Philip Streets. It turned out Clive lived right around the corner from Cooper's hotel. Before he left, Clive also sent Cooper a text with Danny's most recent photo and a promise to meet for dinner later that night.

Cooper thanked him for the information and then he was on his own. He made his way up Decatur looking at every shop and restaurant for some sign that it might have been a refuge for Danny that night. Of course, Cooper had no way of knowing where he ran. He walked up Decatur and stopped for coffee and beignets at Café Du Monde. He grabbed one of the tables out front and sat there considering the options while enjoying his snack. Cooper got so lost in thought he didn't hear the person sit down at the table next to him.

"Tourist?" the woman said loudly. When Cooper glanced in her direction, she laughed. "I asked you three times if you were a tourist.

You look like you're a mile away."

Cooper had been a mile away and even then, after she spoke, it was hard to focus on her. She had a tuft of short dark curly hair and green eyes. Cooper put her a little older than he was, given the lines around her eyes. He wasn't good at guessing anyone's age though. She had a line of freckles across her nose that softened her face. "I'm not exactly a tourist," he said and then wondered why he said that. He corrected himself. "I'm an investigator working on a case. Tourist adjacent."

She took a sip of her coffee and crossed her legs. "You had that look about you – overwhelmed and a little uncertain. That's why I asked. I was going to offer you directions or a recommendation, whichever you needed. What are you investigating?" She paused and then shook her head and smiled. "I'm Kathy, by the way. If I'm going to be nosey and ask you personal questions, I might as well introduce myself," she said with a laugh. "I grew up around here. I don't normally harass tourists though."

Cooper introduced himself and explained he was a private investigator. "There was a case back in August. Danny Thibodeaux. He ended up dead in the river. I'm here to see if it was an accident or if something else happened."

"Yeah, the cops closed that case too quickly. Everyone has been talking about it."

Cooper pulled back in surprise. "The community thought the cops rushed to judgment?"

"That's what everyone said. I didn't know much about the case. I recently read a few articles about it. There's a reporter who has been critical of the investigation from the start. If you want to know more, you should talk to George Benoit. He has mentioned a few theories about what could have happened and speculated he might have some evidence the cops don't have."

Kathy had Cooper's attention now. He hadn't even considered that other locals might have a different opinion on the case than the cops. It was short-sighted on his part. "What do you know about the case?"

Kathy gave him the overview of the official story the cops had told everyone including the fight that was speculated to have ended at the river and Danny falling in after the altercation. "People don't buy the official story, especially when the cops never found the guy who he had the disagreement with or what the altercation entailed. I heard that Danny didn't even go down to the river. That he left heading up Decatur Street. I also heard that it might have been a drug deal gone wrong."

"By all accounts, Danny didn't do drugs. He was heading to law school and didn't want to risk getting a record," Cooper countered. "He wanted to work at the prosecutor's office."

Kathy leveled a look at him. "I didn't say Danny was the one buying the drugs."

"Wouldn't selling be worse?"

"Not if it was a one-time thing, a favor for a friend."

"Were his friends into drugs or drug dealing?"

"That's some of the speculation, but also some of the questions the cops never answered. If Danny was meeting someone down near the river that night and got into a fight with them, what was it about? Why was he down there? It must have been something important to leave his friends on his birthday. What was it?"

Cooper had been pondering that very question when Kathy first spoke to him. He debated for a moment how much to share with her. Then went against his better judgment. "There might be a witness who saw Danny head to the river after the altercation but then came racing back to Decatur Street and head in this direction. The witness said he was running and seemed scared. Do you have any idea where he might have gone if he was headed in this direction?"

Kathy pointed back toward Jackson Square. "Check out St. Louis

Cathedral. Not only are there several places to hide, but it's always been a refuge for people in need. Speak to the priest. Father Francis Broussard. He goes by Fr. Frank and he should be able to tell you if anyone came in there that night. You could at the very least rule it out."

It was more of a tip than Cooper had when he sat down. "I appreciate the information. You've given me two names I didn't have when I sat down here."

Kathy stood and grabbed her coffee cup. "Always willing to help. I run a voodoo shop around the corner if you need more help. Stop in and I'll see what I can do."

"You're into voodoo?" Cooper asked, trying to cut the judgment from his tone. She didn't look like someone who'd be into voodoo and his shock was hard to contain. "I don't mean any judgment by that."

"Sure, you do," she laughed, "but it's okay. I run the shop my grandmother ran for years. I'm not a Voodoo Priestess or anything like that. I sell the supplies and I have someone who works for me that will create custom spells and such for those who need spiritual help. Try to keep an open mind as you're speaking to people here. Their beliefs are rooted deeper than you'd realize."

Cooper bit his lip. "I meant no disrespect. I just..."

"You don't believe." Kathy held up her hand to stop him. "It's okay, not everyone believes in it. I don't need you to believe. I'm simply letting you know that while you're in New Orleans if you need help with anything, you can stop by my shop. People talk to me and I know a lot of people in the community. We want to know what happened to Danny because no innocent life should be lost, but also let's be real, this could impact our bottom line."

*Tourism.* Cooper thanked her. "I appreciate all the information you provided. I'm going to chalk it up to fate that we ran into each other."

"The stars align sometimes," Kathy said smiling at him. She left and Cooper was alone again.

Cooper took another sip of his coffee and felt the heavy feeling of being watched hang over him again. He looked to the left and right and even turned all the way around but there was no one there except a few other people not paying any attention to him. Still, he couldn't shake the feeling.

Cooper finished his coffee while skimming a few of the articles George Benoit had written about the case. Then he sent off a quick email to the address in the article byline explaining who he was and asking to meet. Even if George didn't have cold hard facts, another perspective on the case wouldn't hurt, especially someone local who had been following since the beginning.

Cooper cleared his trash from the table and threw it in the nearby receptacle. He doubled back on Decatur toward Jackson Square. For a workday, Cooper was surprised by the heavy foot traffic. There was still a stream of tourists in the city even in October in the middle of the day. He dodged a few people taking photos and then slipped between the wrought-iron gates and found a quiet bench. He sat down, taking in the atmosphere of the park, and thought about what it probably looked like at night when Danny was running scared from the river.

Cooper assumed it was a desolate place at night. He took in his surroundings and noticed a sign that indicated when the park closed, which hadn't occurred to him before. It meant the park gates would have been locked at the time of night Danny was fleeing. He wouldn't have run through the center of the park but up the adjacent side street if the cathedral was his intended destination.

Cooper got up, pulled his phone from his pocket, and scrolled through to Danny's photo. He found an opening to the side street and then crossed to the only restaurant on that short block that would have been open that time of night. He entered the empty dining room and waited until a young woman approached.

"We aren't open yet. I can take a reservation."

Cooper held the photo out toward her. "I'm looking to see if anyone remembers this man coming in here on a Saturday night in August."

She didn't look down at the photo but glanced at Cooper skeptically. "Sir, we have thousands of people through this place. We barely notice one person from the next."

"Right, I know that. But this man would have been in distress. He would have been trying to hide out or have been upset. He might have stood out to someone." Cooper held the phone out to her. "Just take a look and if you don't recognize him, I can be on my way."

"Fine," she said with a tone that said she was humoring him. When she peered down at Cooper's phone, surprise and then recognition took hold. She raised her eyes to Cooper and then looked back down at the phone. She explained, "I remember him. He came in here one night about two months ago and tried to push past the hostess desk. We were near closing time and he was all wet. There was no way we were letting him in. He was also drunk and slurring his words."

"Do you remember what he said?"

"That someone was chasing him. We get homeless people and all sorts that try to get in here. I didn't think he was being serious. We kicked him out immediately." She shook her head like she wasn't sure why this mattered. "Who is he?"

"Danny Thibodeaux. His body was found in the river the morning after he was in here," Cooper said and watched as she pulled back in horror. "You didn't know then. I understand why you didn't let him in. I believe he was telling the truth that someone was chasing him. Did you see where he went after he left or did anyone come in after him looking around?"

"No one else came in. We locked the doors after he left. I know for a fact no one else came in. We finished serving the last few tables that were here and then let them out. We closed for the night without anything else happening."

Cooper pointed to the ceiling. "Do you have surveillance video?"

"We do but it runs on a week loop. Two months ago would probably be erased by now."

Cooper handed her a business card. "I'm investigating the case. Please have your manager give me a call if there is anything they can share."

Cooper left feeling like he had made some progress. His next step was checking out the church. Before he could reach the doors of the cathedral, his phone rang from a local number he didn't recognize. Cooper answered it.

"I'm glad someone is finally taking this seriously," George Benoit said, his tone indignant. "I can meet you right now. Name the place."

Cooper gave him the name of a café that he could see was open on the other side of Jackson Square. "I'm headed there right now," he said then hung up.

# CHAPTER 18

What surprised me most in the Trevor Ellis case was the utter lack of evidence that there had been a murder. The case on the outside, at least what Miles had gathered to date, suggested it was an accident. By the time two hours had passed, I had read everything there was to be read. At face value, looking at the evidence, I was convinced that it could have been an accident. The only thing holding me back was what had tripped up Miles – where his body had been found.

I pulled out a notebook and grabbed a pen and made a few notes. The three things I knew for sure were the location of Trevor's body, that he had been seen having a heated discussion with a man, and that his car was in the pub's parking lot.

I reached for the stack of witness statements, which were sparse in number. The statements from the patrons inside the bar corroborated what Liv had told me. Trevor was at the pub alone that Sunday. He ate dinner at the bar and then had a few drinks. There was mention in a couple of statements that he had been speaking briefly to a blonde at the bar. The description fit Liv. Others backed up Liv's statement that Trevor had been on and off his phone for most of the night and then he walked toward the back of the pub, spoke to a few people, and left out the back patio door.

Additional statements were provided by people who were on the patio or in the parking lot and saw Trevor arguing with a man. No one seemed to know what the argument had been about or even how it ended. It seemed after realizing it probably wasn't going to turn into a physical altercation people stopped paying attention. There were no statements to indicate they saw Trevor leave with anyone or fall into the river. Even the description of the man was spare and conflicting. I assume because the parking lot wasn't always well lit.

I flipped through the stack again searching for the piece of information that was nagging me. I couldn't quite remember what I had read that stuck out. It was a man who was in the bar, also not named. On the surface that didn't mean much to me. Not everyone knew everyone else.

It was the description of the man provided by two patrons that had caught my attention initially and then slipped my mind while I was looking for solid bits of evidence. I found the two statements and then read them back-to-back, focusing on the parts that I couldn't let go.

It was soon after Trevor had arrived at the bar and ordered dinner. He had been sitting there speaking to a man. The conversation seemed congenial at first but grew tense. The man paid his tab and left well before Trevor. Still, I couldn't help but wonder if that's who Trevor was arguing with outside later in the night. The description of the man wasn't unlike Ned Shaw. In truth though, it could have been anyone.

I grabbed my cellphone and called Luke. It rang a few times before he answered. After a few pleasantries and updates about our day, I got down to why I was calling in the middle of his workday. "I need to see if Purvis could review a medical examiner's report. I also had questions about water in the lungs."

"I'm sure Purvis would be happy to help," Luke said with hesitancy in his voice. "Is there a reason the medical examiner up there won't help out?"

"It's his report and I have questions about it. I'm looking for another opinion." I pulled the medical examiner's report from the file and opened it on my lap. "It has some conflicting information for me. Trevor has some bruising on his face and hands. He has some markings on his wrists too. The medical examiner seemed to brush all of that off though and claim it's inconclusive. More than that, I have questions about the water found in his lungs."

"What about the water?"

"I want to know if a medical examiner can tell what kind of water is in the lungs."

"Huh," Luke said and then murmured something to himself I couldn't understand.

"What?"

"Are you thinking the victim drowned someplace else and then was dumped in the river?"

That's exactly what I had been thinking. "My case is a little different from yours. Rob Hall walked down the river path and then was found close to where he went into the river. In my case, Trevor was found almost where he was last seen but the next morning. It's not possible with the river currents, so there's a discrepancy there I need to understand. I want to know if the water found in his lungs is the same river water. I was going to search online but figured I'd go right to the source."

"Sounds like a reasonable question," Luke said. "I'm sure Purvis would be happy to speak with you. I'll call him right now and see if he can connect with you. Find anything interesting to note yet?"

I hesitated, not sure that I wanted to tell Luke what I was thinking. He knew I didn't like Ned Shaw, but I had lingering questions. "This is going to sound out there..." I stopped and let my words hang.

"I've learned over the years that when you say *out there* it usually has merit." Luke shushed someone in the background, who I assumed was Det. Tyler.

I didn't know why I was nervous to speak my mind to Luke. If there was anyone that I should be able to be foolish in front of, it should be him. "Has anyone tracked Ned Shaw's movements related to these cases in the south?" I asked quickly and then asked him to wait to respond even though he wasn't trying to interject. "As I said, he's here in Troy right now and there are two witnesses who indicate Trevor was arguing with a man that night. The description could fit Ned Shaw."

That was met with deafening silence. I nearly started to take it back when Luke said, "Help me to understand your reasoning. It has to be more than a witness describing someone who might be Shaw. He's been all over these cities, people are bound to see him."

"But on the night of a drowning interacting with a victim before he dies?"

"I don't know, Riley," he said cautiously with a tone that indicated I was jumping to conclusions. "If you're asking me if you should speak to those witnesses again and show them a photo of Shaw, sure go ahead. If you're asking me if I think Shaw is a serial killer, you need to take a step back and consider why you'd jump to that conclusion. You don't like him, I get it. That doesn't mean he'd be responsible for something so heinous."

Luke was right. I conceded the point for now. "It's possible my objectivity is off because I don't like him. It's probably because Miles joked that maybe Shaw got frustrated that no one believed his theory about the initial drownings. They stopped for a few years and his publicity died down. Maybe he snapped and started killing young men to keep his conspiracy theory going and his face in the public eye." Now that I said it aloud, it seemed more than a little farfetched.

"That's a theory for sure," Luke said with more than a trace of disbelief in his voice. He didn't discourage me. "Go interview those witnesses again and show them a photo of Shaw. If you can't confirm who the mystery guy was in the bar that night talking to Trevor, then you have nothing to go on other than your imagination." Luke paused and then chuckled. "Which we all know can be overactive."

"You're in the doghouse for that," I teased. "Any progress on your end today?"

"Things I'm still exploring. Let me call Purvis for you and we can talk later." Before he ended the call, Luke told me how empty the house felt without me there. "Solve your case and come home to me soon."

"It's been a day. I'm sure you'll survive."

"It's not about surviving." Luke told me he loved me and then ended the call.

I went back to reviewing the statements and jotted down the names and contact information of the two witnesses who might have seen Shaw that night. I know what Luke said but that was how I was still thinking of it in my mind. The witnesses could prove to me it wasn't him.

As I put all the files and evidence back neatly in the box, my cellphone rang with an official Little Rock number. That's how the name read – Official Pulaski County – which I assumed was Purvis.

"Riley, Luke said you wanted me to call you," Purvis said instead of hello. "I hope you don't mind me calling right now. I've got three post-mortems to do and a report to write. I figured I'd call you now before I get busy."

I thanked him for taking the time. "I'll try to be quick. Are you open to me sending you a copy of a medical examiner's report? I just want another opinion on the findings."

"Email it to me if you can." He gave me his email address. "Luke said something about understanding water in the lungs. Is that what you want to know?"

I shifted in the seat and got comfortable, tucking my legs under me. "It's a little more complex than that. I want to understand if you can match a water sample with the water you find in the lungs. Are you able to tell what kind of water a person drowned in?"

"It's possible to an extent. The tests aren't normally done if we know where the body was found. There'd be no need for a test like that." Purvis gave me a website where I could read more in-depth. "There's a lot of science behind this. I'll bottom line it for you. Yes, we can tell whether it's fresh water or salt water by how it's broken down in the lungs and what we are seeing during an autopsy."

I hadn't even been thinking about salt water and wasn't sure whether what Purvis was describing would help me. "What about tap water versus river water?"

"You're getting down to a microbial level then. I'd need a tissue sample and water samples to run a comparison."

Trevor had already been cremated. I knew that wasn't going to be possible unless Miles could connect with the medical examiner and see if any tissue samples had been taken and preserved. I sighed as an avenue closed.

"What is it you're trying to prove, Riley? There might be an easier way."

I explained the situation to Purvis and my speculation that Trevor might have been killed someplace else. When I was done, he said, "Send me the report and let me see what I can figure out. The water sample is a good theory. It might not be that complicated. Let me see what we are working with first."

We ended the call with a promise that I'd send him the report. Miles would have to scan it and send it or he'd have to send me an electronic file. All in all, Purvis hadn't told me what I wanted to hear. I wanted him to tell me that he'd be able to figure out the water based on the current report. I hadn't considered before that I didn't have a lung sample to provide him.

I texted Miles the question about getting a lung sample and asked him to send the medical examiner's report to Purvis. I gave him the email address. Then I added that I wanted to go interview a few of the witnesses he had already spoken to. I got a quick reply a few minutes later to go do whatever I needed to do and he'd handle the medical examiner's report. He didn't mention the lung sample.

# CHAPTER 19

Luke sat back at his desk and considered what Riley had said about Ned Shaw. It was a wild theory but not one without merit. He hadn't wanted to tell her that and encourage her for nothing.

Captain Meadows had advised him to bring Nolan in however he needed even if the kid lawyered up. They had no choice but to try to interview him again. Luke wanted to speak to Pete one more time before that happened. While Det. Tyler was running down a few leads, Luke left the office to head back to the river.

On his walk there, he stopped at a local deli and grabbed two sandwiches, a couple of bags of chips, and a few different bottles of juice and soda. The clerk put it all in a bag for Luke and he was on his way. He had given Pete money and it had made the man visibly uncomfortable. Luke didn't see how he'd turn down food and drinks.

Luke rounded the bend in the trail and found Pete in the same place he had left him a couple of hours before. He held up the bag as he approached. "I thought you might be hungry."

Pete eyed him. "You're being awfully nice to me. I don't need your pity."

"Not pity," Luke said and sat down uninvited. The more Luke talked to the guy the more he genuinely liked him and hated that anyone was living on the street. Even if Luke couldn't force him to make a change, he could at least check in on him from time to time. "I had a break, realized I had a few more questions, and thought I'd grab you lunch. I don't normally have to keep going back to witnesses. I'm generally much more prepared than I seem to be now."

"I don't buy that for a second." Pete nudged the bag with his finger. "Is that all for me?"

"I didn't know what you liked. I figured you can have some now and then some later."

With a gruffness and uncertainty in his voice, Pete said thanks. He opened the bag and pulled out one of the sandwiches and unwrapped it. "I hope there's not any of that kale crap on here."

Luke laughed. "No, man. I don't eat that and wouldn't expect anyone else to either. One of them has turkey and cheese and the other is roast beef. There are some chips and drinks in there for you too."

"You're a good man, Det. Lucas Morgan."

Luke stared over at him. No one ever called him by his given name Lucas. He wasn't even sure that many people outside of his close friends and family knew that was his name. "Why'd you call me Lucas?"

"That's your name, isn't it?"

"It is but very few people know it."

Pete shrugged as if it wasn't an important detail. "I've been in this city a long time and you get to know people. Just because I don't live in a house like everyone else and hardly have any money doesn't mean I don't know what's going on. You have been one of the fastest-rising black detectives in the entire police department. Even putting race aside, you moved up the ranks faster than most. You have an exceptional closure rate, rarely blow a case, don't make stupid decisions, and have never once been tripped up on the stand by a defense attorney. You shy away from the media and are fair and balanced in your approach. The other detectives respect you and like you – a rare combination. Most leaders get one or the other but rarely both. You married a ball-busting firecracker from the northeast who rivals you in your detective skills. You like strong women and to be challenged. I've never seen you shy away from danger or a hard case or admitting you're wrong. You're a darn rockstar, kid."

Luke's mouth had fallen agape as Pete went on hitting every point about his life. "I didn't know anyone was paying that close attention."

Pete took a bite of his sandwich, told Luke how good it was, and then rested it in his lap. "I'm a forgotten person in this city, one of the unseen. There are many of us and that leaves me in the position of being able to watch - unbothered and unphased. No one notices me so I see a lot. I'm invisible to most and that has its advantages."

Luke had a feeling Pete knew more about him than he was saying. "That's why I'm here. I got back to the office and realized I keep doing this interview with you piecemeal and I usually don't do that."

Pete nodded and tore off another piece of sandwich and popped it in his mouth. "It's because this case isn't like any you've had before. You don't even know how the guy died. Sure, you know he drowned but you don't know how he got into the water – accident or murder. Usually, you've got that nailed down to start. Combine that with no suspects and any forensic evidence washed away by the water and you've got nothing to work with. Add in the media pressure and some nut trying to say it's a serial killer and you've got a cat-five twister coming toward you and no storm cellar to seek out for cover."

That about summed it up for Luke. "If you were me, what would you do?"

Pete didn't respond right away. He dug into the bag and pulled out a cold sweet tea. He turned the cap and chuckled at the *pop* it made. "I used to love that sound as a kid." He put it to his lips and tipped his head back taking a drink. "I'd clear the clutter out of the way. Forget the serial killer guy. Forget the media and focus on what you do best – plodding through the evidence with the methodical approach you've used to solve every case. Rule out what you can. You know it's not a suicide, you know it's not a robbery. What's the kid got going on in his background? Rule out all the obvious – partners, friends, and family – and see what you've got left. That's not the first thing I'd do though."

Luke imagined that Pete had to have been a solid investigator for the military in his day. "What is the first thing you'd do."

Pete didn't hold back the laugh. "Interview me thoroughly and correctly, so you don't have to keep coming back out here."

"What if I like coming out here?"

Pete glanced over at him and must have realized Luke was serious. "Then next time you come, we talk baseball or football or the weather."

"Fair enough." Luke leaned back on his hands. "Okay, let's start at the beginning. What did you see that night before you saw Rob Hall?"

Pete took one last bite of the sandwich and washed it down with tea. "It was a quiet night for the most part. Not your usual rowdy weekend. This path gets a lot of foot traffic. You know the deal – drugs, prostitution, and all sorts of other unsavory things in the dead of night. That night was quiet. I'd almost say unusually quiet, which is why I was paying attention. Rob headed down the path. He didn't smell like alcohol or anything. But there was something in his gait that told me he was angry or drunk or something was off. It was like a two-step forward, side-step kind of thing. Not any man's normal way of walking."

Luke knew Rob had been drinking. He'd seen him stumble on video. "Did he seem scared? Hesitant as if he didn't want to be walking down the path?"

"Possibly. That could be a fair assessment. Either way, he went down the path alone." Pete furrowed his brow. "What we can't know is if someone was down that path from the other direction. All I know is he was walking alone. Then as I said, about ten minutes later, some other guy walks in the same direction. He's on the phone – real casual-like. But he said something that stuck out to me. He said, 'I'm not sure where exactly I'm meeting him. I'm headed that way now.'"

"Was he talking about Rob?"

"No idea. I didn't think much of it at the time. I wasn't hearing the other end of the conversation and didn't hear anything else the guy said. He wasn't in a hurry or upset in any way. Like I said before, he looked like someone looking to score some drugs. The conversation I heard matched that."

It was only because Riley had raised the question earlier, Luke asked, "What about his voice? Anything distinctive?"

"Yeah," Pete said, nodding his head. "That stood out to me. It was deep and raspy. He wasn't from around here, or I should say he didn't grow up in Little Rock."

"Why do you say that?"

"Accent. New Jersey or New York City. Not snooty Manhattan but one of the boroughs."

Luke's gut dropped to his knees and he tried to remain calm as he pulled his phone from his pocket. He had to find a website for a photo. When he did, he turned the screen to face Pete. "Is that the guy?"

"Hard to tell. Could be him but maybe not. As I said, I only saw him in profile."

Luke wasn't giving up. He went to the search engine and did an image search and then found a photo of the man in profile. He showed his phone again to Pete. "What about now?"

Pete appraised the photo and hemmed and hawed, turning his head from one angle to the other. "That could be him. Hard to tell from the angle I was sitting and the way the light hit, I can't rule it out. It could be him. I can't say for certain." Pete looked over at Luke. "Is that who I think it is?"

"Ned Shaw."

"Well, that would be a bit of irony, wouldn't it? The man who is claiming serial killers are running around drowning young men is seen heading in the same direction of the victim right before it happened."

If it had been anyone else, Luke probably wouldn't have said, "It's not the first time he might have been with a victim before their death."

Pete looked at Luke, surprise on his face. "How's that?"

Luke recounted what Riley had told him on the phone earlier. "Nothing is confirmed. A witness gave a basic description as you gave. It could be anyone."

Pete held his hands up. "I can't say for certain it is him or not, but I'll tell you that I didn't see him again that night. He walked down that path like Rob did and I never saw him again. Only one of them ended up dead in the river."

Luke couldn't lose focus. "But you also said you saw Nolan going in that direction, too." Luke wanted them to refocus on the timeline and keep going.

"That's correct, about thirty minutes after Rob, so shortly after the other guy walked by me." Pete rubbed his forehead. "Did you know he had something in his hand? Did we cover that before? It was a knife, I think."

"He did have a knife. I'm able to see it in the surveillance video." Luke waited to see if Pete would add anything. When he didn't, Luke asked, "After all three of those men passed you, did you hear anything? A struggle? Conversation? Anything?"

Pete shook his head. "I can't say that I did." He pointed to a small radio in the mix with his sparse belongings. "I had the radio on for some time, not loudly, but it might have drowned out anything from far away. My hearing isn't great."

"Tell me again what happened when the young man with the knife came back."

Pete described what he had told him before, not verbatim like he was telling a story he had heard word-for-word, but in the way someone did when they were telling the truth. "I don't know what he got up to down there. Something scared him and he came running back all wet. He seemed terrified. I can't recall now if he still had the knife in his hand. Maybe he's not a suspect. Maybe he just saw something that spooked him that night."

Luke hadn't thought of that and it gave him the opening he needed to question Nolan without labeling him as a suspect. "Is there anything else you can think of about that night I should know?"

Pete patted Luke's leg in a fatherly way. "Good job this time. I think we covered it all."

Luke laughed and rolled his eyes. "Why didn't you tell me all of this before?"

Pete shrugged. "Maybe I wanted you to come back and talk to me or maybe it didn't seem important until you asked. Either way, you have everything now. I'll keep watch for you down here." He nudged the bag of food and drinks that Luke had given him. "You're a good man, Luke. Don't let anyone tell you differently."

# CHAPTER 20

Cooper waited anxiously at the café for George Benoit, who worked as a crime-beat reporter for *The Times-Picayune/The New Orleans Advocate*. Cooper felt lucky George was willing to meet right away. While he sat in the café waiting, Cooper had enough time to review the reporter's articles and credentials. George had some heavy hitters as sources for his stories.

Cooper had ordered another cup of coffee and a snack. It felt like all he was doing in New Orleans was moving from place to place eating. He had a flash of Brad Pitt in his mind from the movie where he ate all the way through it. Cooper chuckled to himself. On his best day, he was no Brad Pitt.

About five minutes after the meeting time, a man with short dark hair, dark-rimmed square glasses, and a look like he was staking out the place, entered. Cooper knew him from his newspaper photo. He waved. "George, I'm over here."

George hitched his chin toward him and then pointed to the counter. He disappeared into a sea of people and then returned minutes later with a cup of coffee and a bagel. George put the items down on the table. "I eat when I can because I don't always get the time." He extended a hand to Cooper. "I'm glad you're here. I didn't know if the police would ever take this case seriously. I even called the FBI who told me they had no jurisdiction. I'm in touch with Danny's parents and friends. All anyone wants is someone to do a thorough investigation."

Cooper felt a little protective of Clive. "The detective assigned to the case tried, but he was pulled off it before he could do much. He's been very helpful to me so far. I think he wants what you want but is constrained by the bureaucracy."

"I don't blame him," George said, sitting. "I've spoken to Det. Elio a few times on and off the record. He's been helpful but he hasn't been able to do his job. That's left us without much of anything. Now you show up. How'd you get involved?"

"Is this off the record for now?"

George nodded. "Off the record. This is an exchange of information. If you want to go on the record with something later, you tell me and I'll write it. For now, consider me a colleague. You can trust me. After more than twenty years as a reporter in this town, I wouldn't get anything done if I burned sources."

"Understood," Cooper said and reached for his coffee cup. He explained how he had been called to investigate the case and his connection with the Little Rock Police Department. "What's important to know is I'm not doing this in a vacuum." He explained Luke's case in Little Rock and Riley's case in Troy, leaving out any details they wouldn't want a reporter to know. "If this is a serial killer, then we have three cases we are looking at simultaneously. If there is a connection, we'll find it. If there's not, we can at least solve them individually."

George barely waited until Cooper finished. "I think there's a serial killer."

Cooper pulled back. "Why do you think that? It's not as common as you might think."

"I've been looking into all the recent drownings from August to this one in Little Rock. They all fit a pattern and all have more than one thing in common."

Cooper wouldn't pre-judge the information. "What do you have?"

George cut his bagel in half and smeared it with cream cheese. Then he pulled off a piece and ate it. George leaned his arms on the table and kept good eye contact with Cooper. "Not only is victim selection similar, but they were all at bars before being found in the river."

Cooper nodded. "We know that—"

George cut him off. "There's more. Each of them got a text about meeting someone and they stepped away purposefully from their group. I don't know the contents of these texts or who was contacting them and neither do their families or friends. That seems to be the mystery here. These kids don't seem like they were drugged or anything like that."

The texting certainly fit Danny's case.

George leveled a look at Cooper. "We have two possible suspects."

Cooper wasn't sure he had heard George correctly. "You have suspects?"

"I tried to give the cops this information and they didn't want it. I tried to give it to the local FBI office and they didn't want it either. They said they had investigated the other drowning cases and found no evidence of a serial killer. They said they had no jurisdiction on these most recent cases, as I said. The FBI wouldn't even look at what I had." George threw his hands up in frustration. "I've been sitting on the evidence for the past few weeks dumbfounded by everyone's unwillingness to even take a look at it."

"Have you told Det. Elio?"

"I tried. Got the runaround." George took another sip of coffee while Cooper waited for the full story because he couldn't believe that Clive had turned down legitimate evidence, especially when he had been so eager to bring Cooper in on the investigation. George righted himself in the chair. "First, when I called the police station, no one would put me through to him. I left a message that I know now he never received. Then, when I finally got a direct phone number for him, I left a couple of messages. He got back to me but asked me to hold off because he had another investigator coming and he officially couldn't do anything."

George leaned on his arms and stared at Cooper. "Do you have any idea how frustrating that is? Now, we have a new death in Little Rock. I honestly feel like we could have prevented that."

"If it's connected," Cooper said, not quick to buy into anything George was saying.

George caught the look on Cooper's face. "It's connected. I know you need hard evidence and I'm just a reporter."

"I'm not dismissing your information or ability," Cooper assured him. "These cases are hard, especially because a group of investigators got involved in other drowning cases and made such a mess of them. There's a stigma now that law enforcement agencies are up against. Even if there is a legitimate accident, families don't want to hear it. I hate to say it but going forward when young white men in their twenties drown after a night of drinking, there will forever be questions."

George brushed it off. "I get it, Cooper. I do but hear me out." He waited to see if Cooper would continue to argue and when he didn't, George went on. "We have eight drownings from mid-August to October. That's about a drowning a week. We found that in every case Ned Shaw immediately offered to help the investigation, and in fact, showed up in person to offer his help."

"I don't know if that's true for Little Rock," Cooper countered, wondering where he was going with this. "I'd have to call Captain Meadows with the Little Rock Police Department. I know a call was made but I don't know that there was an in-person meeting."

"I have a witness who saw him there," George said dismissively, seeming to grow frustrated with Cooper's interrupting. "There are two reasons this is significant. First, Shaw offered help before the case barely made the news. Secondly, in a few places, I have witnesses who saw Shaw the night of the murders. How did he know where to be if he wasn't somehow involved?"

Cooper cocked his head to the side in contemplation. He didn't trust that what George was saying was true. "How do you know this? I understand that you say you have a witness but how did you find that information out in other states? I realize here is easy enough but elsewhere?"

George sat back and folded his arms over his chest. "I don't want to go into my methods. But I know other reporters who were working on these cases and they have sources who were also willing to speak to me. Eventually, it all started to snowball and this is the result."

"You realize that if I were to believe you and take this to my other team members, we'd need to confirm the story and speak to the witnesses. We can't jump on a theory like this without seeing the cold hard facts for ourselves."

George nodded but didn't offer any other reassurance than that. "Our other suspect is more low-key. He's a technology sales guy who travels to universities and sells educational software. He's also been seen in the areas of each of the murders."

Cooper wanted to remind him that they didn't know if the drownings were murders. "How did you find him?"

"That was an accident. I was looking through photos of the crime scene here in New Orleans when the cops were pulling Danny's body out of the river. Then I happened to be speaking to a reporter in Atlanta and took a look at some of their crime scene photos and there was the same guy. I almost didn't notice him at first. He was wearing a Chicago Cubs hat and it stood out to me in the crowd. I'm a Cubs fan," George said with a shrug.

"Okay," Cooper said slowly, not understanding. "You've got the same guy at two scenes. That doesn't mean he's involved."

George waved him off. "Two you can dismiss, right? That might be an eerie coincidence. But you can't dismiss all of them." He paused for a moment and let what he said sink in. He added, "All of them, Cooper, except maybe for the most recent case in Little Rock. I don't know about that one yet because I haven't called any reporters there yet."

Cooper narrowed his focus on him. "Are you telling me this tech sales guy shows up in the scene photos of all the drowning cases other than Little Rock? Is he there when they find the body?"

"Every single time." George pulled his phone from his pocket and pulled up a photo and then enlarged it with his fingers. "Here he is. His name is Mark David Reed."

Cooper took the phone out of George's hand and peered down at the photo. It was a man who Cooper would guess would be in his mid to late thirties with dark hair under a Chicago Cubs hat. He had a strong jawline and dark eyes and a muscular build. He was the kind of guy you'd pass on the street and forget about a minute later. There wasn't anything particularly menacing about him or anything that would stand out.

Cooper scanned the photo of his face for any scars or distinguishing characteristics and found none. He was wearing a gray fitted tee-shirt with no logo or graphic and what looked like jeans. Cooper guessed the man spent some of his time off at the gym lifting weights. He might have even been a solid runner. Cooper would need to see far more evidence than this to suspect the guy or Shaw.

He handed the phone back to George. "What else do you have on the guy other than showing up at the scenes?"

George stared at him blankly. "Isn't that your job? I can't do all the work."

Cooper tried to control the sarcastic tone he knew would come through. "I was merely asking if you found anything about his background that made you suspicious or if it was just showing up at the scenes that put him on your suspect list. For instance, did you find any connections between him and the victims?"

"No. I didn't get that far." George sat back and stared across the table. "Are you going to tell me that I don't have enough? You're kind of my last hope here. I've gone as far as I can go as a reporter and need to know that I'm handing this off to someone competent enough to do something with this."

Cooper could understand why the FBI and the local cops weren't going to run with it. That said, George had found a few weird things that Cooper believed warranted exploring. "I'll look into this more. How did you find out Mark Reed's name from a photo in the paper?"

George rolled his eyes. "The first thing you're going to need to do is to get his name right. There are about a hundred thousand Mark Reeds out there. It's Mark David Reed. That's what he goes by on his LinkedIn profile."

"How did you find out his name?" Cooper asked again, growing tired of George.

"He was interviewed briefly in the case in Atlanta and his name was under one photo. We got lucky there. Then I searched him online." George stood, grabbed the rest of his muffin, and folded it up in a napkin to take with him. He grabbed his to-go coffee cup. "If there is anything else you need, call me. I'll see if I can arrange meetings with those witnesses about Shaw. You should have enough to at least start on that."

Cooper thanked him for the information, feeling slightly disappointed by the meeting. He wasn't sure why but he had been expecting more. It sounded to him that George, like Shaw, had speculation and wild conjecture based on flimsy evidence more than solid leads.

Cooper hoped his next stop would prove more fruitful.

# CHAPTER 21

The entrance to St. Louis Cathedral was mere steps away from the café where Cooper met George Benoit. On his way, Cooper passed by artists showing their paintings and photographs and a few card readers offering predictions. Hattie flashed in his mind and he reached into his pocket to wrap his fingers around the necklace she had given him. Maybe if not protection, it might afford him some good luck on the case. He ran his finger over the tiny stone as he walked into the church.

A blast of cold air and the smell of burning candles hit him as he entered. Two things one would think would be in direct opposition. The stillness washed over him and his eyes darted back and forth taking it all in.

Cooper walked from the vestibule into the main area of the cathedral. His breath caught in awe at the beauty of the architecture. Cooper wasn't particularly religious. His father hadn't raised him in any religion and Cooper never felt the need or desire to seek one out either. It didn't mean he didn't feel an overwhelming sense of connection to…he wasn't sure. He didn't have a name for it. The feeling lingered for a moment and Cooper contemplated sitting down in peaceful quiet, but movement on the other side of the church caught his eye. It was a man dressed in a black short-sleeve shirt and black pants. It was only when the man turned his head slightly that Cooper noticed the white collar. He assumed it was Fr. Frank.

Cooper sidestepped a woman who had been standing next to him. She had been so quiet and unassuming that she took Cooper by surprise. He apologized for nearly bumping into her and then made his way through the pews to the man.

"Fr. Frank?" Cooper called, too loudly for the quiet space. He ducked his head when the man turned his head to him. More quietly, Cooper apologized. "I didn't mean to be so loud. There's an echo in here I hadn't anticipated. Are you Fr. Frank?" Cooper extended his hand to the man.

Fr. Frank appeared to be in his late forties or early fifties. He had fine lines around his eyes and some thinning dark hair on top. He was fit though and gripped Cooper's hand with the strength of a man much younger. "Yes, can I help you?"

Cooper introduced himself. "I'm not sure if you can help me. I'm here investigating the death of Danny Thibodeaux. I'm wondering if you know much about the case."

Fr. Frank frowned. "I knew Danny well. He was a member of our church and went through his confirmation only a few years back. I knew him for many years and presided over his funeral mass."

"Oh, I'm sorry," Cooper said, feeling foolish for not having known that even though there was no reason he would have. "I had no idea. Did you happen to see him the night he died?"

Fr. Frank's eyes grew wide. "Should I have?"

"As you know his body was pulled from the river not far from here, only a few blocks. The detective on the case suspected Danny had a fight with someone and fell into the river and drowned."

"Yes, that's the official story. Is that not what happened?" Fr. Frank's tone indicated that he might have suspected something different all along.

Cooper glanced over his shoulder at a group of women who entered.

"Do you have an office or someplace more private that we could speak?" He turned back to Fr. Frank. "I need to ask you a few questions. I could use some help."

Fr. Frank ushered Cooper through the church and past the altar through double doors that had been propped open. They went down a narrow hall and into an office. Fr. Frank closed the door behind them and then they sat at a small table.

Fr. Frank started. "I don't believe the official story about what happened to Danny. I don't believe that he got so drunk he fell into the river. I also don't believe he got into a fight with someone. I've known that young man for many years and it wasn't his personality to fight with someone."

"It wasn't a physical altercation," Cooper corrected for him and the priest nodded and seemed satisfied with that. "Danny was seen having a heated discussion with someone that night. Someone we think he might have gone to meet, for reasons still unknown. A witness has come forward and said that she saw Danny walk down toward the river but then came back running in this direction. A hostess at a restaurant on Jackson Square said Danny tried to get into the restaurant that night. He was wet and distressed but they didn't let him in. He fled in this direction. I thought he might have been seeking shelter at the church."

Fr. Frank had grown considerably pale. "I'd feel terrible if I missed an opportunity to have helped him that night. I wasn't here the weekend Danny died. I was in another part of Louisiana ministering to sick people in two hospitals. The assistant pastor was here that night but certainly wouldn't be in the church that late."

"Would the doors have been unlocked?" Cooper asked.

"Depending on the time. We usually try to lock up by eleven but other times it's much later. We try to be a welcoming place for the community and we aren't always here hovering around people as they come in and pray and such. That time of night though…"

"Criminal activity and vandalism," Cooper said finishing what Fr. Frank hadn't said. The priest nodded. "I understand the need to lock up. Do you happen to know why Danny might have been coming to the church if that's where he was headed after the restaurant?"

"I assume to see me or to seek shelter if someone was after him." Fr. Frank sat back and folded his hands on the table. He had a pensive look on his face and Cooper didn't try to push him for more. He had an air about him like he was trying to remember something or decide if it was worth telling Cooper.

After a few moments of silence when Cooper was sure the priest wasn't going to say anything else, he pushed. "Fr. Frank, if you know something, it doesn't matter how small or insignificant, please tell me. I barely have any leads on this case. We don't know what will lead to the thread that unravels the whole thing."

Fr. Frank got up from the table and went to his desk. He pulled out one of the drawers and lifted out a thick black book. "My calendar," he said when Cooper eyed him. He carried it over to the table and dropped it with a thud. Then Fr. Frank flipped through several pages until he landed on a date. "A week before Danny died, he came to me to ask my opinion about something he was considering. We spoke at length about it, but he left without any resolution. He was quite confused by the request and what he wanted to do."

The priest was talking in code and Cooper had no idea what he was referencing. "You're going to have to be a bit clearer, Fr. Frank. I have no idea what you're talking about." The priest still didn't seem moved by Cooper's plea. "Father, Danny is dead. There's nothing to protect him from anymore. If you know something that can help the investigation, we might have a shot to bring his killer to justice."

"You think he was murdered?" There was no surprise in his voice.

"It's looking more and more likely."

Fr. Frank sighed. "I'm not even sure I can explain it. Danny came to me because he was contacted by Ned Shaw, that detective who thinks there's a serial killer. He said he heard that Danny was an excellent student on his way to law school and then hopefully the prosecutor's office. He said he had a project for him that would look great on his résumé. Shaw wouldn't discuss the details over email but said he'd text him and set up a time to meet. Danny wasn't sure what to tell him. How would a young kid not even out of college yet know how to help on a murder investigation? The request made little sense."

That was the second time Shaw's name had come up in a sketchy way in less than an hour. "You said Shaw initially contacted Danny through email. Did they ever speak on the phone?"

"Not that I'm aware of. Danny might not have told me that. He knew who Shaw was as he'd seen him on television. Danny knew young men like him were drowning and there was a part of him that felt compelled to help Shaw figure out what was happening. There was another, I'd say more rational, side to Danny that knew he didn't have the experience or knowledge to take on something that big. What conflicted him the most was that he didn't like Shaw personally and didn't want anything to do with it."

Cooper focused on Fr. Frank. "Do you know if Danny and Shaw had met before?"

"I asked him the same thing and Danny said no, it was just his impression of him on television." Fr. Frank closed his calendar. "Do you think that's who Danny met that night down by the river? Was it Shaw he was arguing with? Danny said that in the email Shaw hadn't asked to meet but rather said he'd be in touch about meeting like it was a foregone conclusion. Danny said Shaw was being pushy with him. That's why he was having trouble responding to the request. He felt backed into a corner like he couldn't say no."

Cooper didn't know what to make of the information. "Did you see the email or have Danny's email address?" Cooper wanted to read the email from the source.

Fr. Frank shook his head. "I don't and until you came in today, I hadn't thought much of the conversation, only that Danny had died the same way."

"You didn't find it odd?" Cooper asked, wondering how the priest had brushed off the similarity so easily. Cooper was feeling more than a little creeped out by it.

Fr. Frank clasped his hands together on the table and closed his eyes briefly. When he opened them, he said, "Of course it crossed my mind. I didn't think Danny had met with Shaw yet. He said he'd tell me when he did and what he would ultimately decide to do. Given the number of drownings similar to Danny's, I didn't believe his death was an accident. Then again, what else were we supposed to believe? Shaw's theory about a serial killer was farfetched. Crosses? That's the graffiti he thinks the killer is using? You see crosses everywhere. If there was a serial killer there had to be more evidence."

"I thought you didn't know much about the cases?" Cooper asked, feeling like he was missing something.

"After Danny told me, I went back and watched the online special about the cases. I was hoping to understand it better to give Danny more advice. I had told him to do what he thought was best. Yes, while it was a noble pursuit, he was probably right that he wouldn't be able to help. Plus, his focus should be on finishing school, not helping a detective go on a wild goose chase. So, after the conversation, I wanted to make sure that's what it was."

"What did you think of Shaw's information?"

Fr. Frank frowned again and shook his head. "If I had seen the documentary first, I would have told Danny to run and stay as far away from Shaw as possible. This theory is nonsense and a distraction from the real investigation." Fr. Frank raised his fist and brought it down on the table so hard that Cooper jerked forward. "Shaw should be ashamed of himself," the priest snarled.

Cooper swallowed hard, caught off guard by Fr. Frank's anger. He waited a few beats to let the tension dissipate. "Do you think Danny would have met with Shaw?"

Fr. Frank collected himself, and then with his voice calm again, said, "If the man requested a meeting, Danny would have gone to tell him he wasn't going to help him. Danny wasn't one to be dismissive of someone's request for help. He wouldn't have ignored him if the man had wanted to meet. Do you think Danny met Shaw that night?"

"I don't know that the meeting ever took place," Cooper said honestly. "Is there anything else you can think to tell me about Danny's life that might have made him a target if this was murder?"

"No. The thing with Shaw was the only thing that had been troubling him recently – that I was privy to anyway." Fr. Frank stood and pushed his chair back. "I need to head out and meet one of my parishioners. Is there anything else you need?"

Cooper realized he was being dismissed. He stood and extended his hand to Fr. Frank who tentatively took it this time. "I appreciate your time and the information."

As Fr. Frank led Cooper down the narrow hall back into the church, he stopped and turned to Cooper. "Now that you're bringing this to my attention, it does seem odd that Danny would die in the same way as those other boys so soon after he was contacted about the murders. I don't have an explanation for why I didn't consider it sooner."

"It's okay," Cooper assured him, his smile stiff. "Sometimes we don't want to think the worst in people."

"Yes, that must be it."

Cooper thanked him again and then made his way out of the church, trying to process everything that had occurred with Fr. Frank. There was something about the interview that was troubling for Cooper.

He didn't want to accuse a priest of lying, but he got the sense Fr. Frank hadn't been honest with him. Cooper kept turning to look over his shoulder as he left the cathedral. When he reached the last pew, Cooper turned one more time. It was then he spotted Fr. Frank standing at the side of the altar, watching him.

# CHAPTER 22

After spending time trying to track down the witnesses that had spoken to Miles and failing to reach anyone, I turned to easier pursuits. I sat in my mother's car in the parking lot of the pub where they had found Trevor's car. I could see the back patio of the bar as the late afternoon crowd of young professionals had started to gather for happy hour. I was about to interview Chris, the pub owner, when my cellphone rang.

"Cooper," I said as I answered. "How's New Orleans?"

"It's creepy," he said with a tension-filled laugh. "I have a crazy theory I want to run by you. Do you have a minute?"

Cooper never had crazy theories, so this should be good. "I'm about to interview the owner of the bar. We don't have a scheduled time to meet, so I have all the time you need. What's on your mind?"

"Is Shaw up there with you still?"

"I assume so. Why?"

"You know him better than I do. I've never even met the man. Do you think there is any way that Shaw could be involved in these murders?" Before I could rein in my shock and collect myself enough to respond, Cooper chastised himself. "I know it's a stupid theory. I don't even have much to go on. I was just speaking to this priest and he said Shaw wanted to meet the victim. I don't know, Riley. There isn't a lot about this case that makes much sense. There's this reporter too—"

"Cooper, slow down," I said, interrupting him. "I don't think Shaw is an out-there idea. I said the same thing to Luke earlier today. He cautioned me that I was being swayed by my hatred for the guy. No matter what Luke said, I still think there's something to it. What do you mean Shaw wanted to meet with the victim before he died?"

Cooper went into detail about the conversation with Fr. Frank, stopping every so often to see if I was still following along. When he finished, Cooper provided me with the details of his meeting with George Benoit, the reporter. The information George had gathered sounded more thorough than anything we had so far. To be fair, George had been involved longer than any of us.

When Cooper finished, he said, "There's something off with Shaw. I'm sure you've noticed it. More than wanting fame or fortune. He's speculating about these cases and calling it fact. Do you think he believes the things he says?"

"I don't know," I said evenly. "How did Shaw even know about Danny? Was he an exceptional student? Been involved in projects like these before? I don't understand the connection. Did Shaw just pluck a random kid out of obscurity?"

"All unknown at this time. I only just found out the information. I left St. Louis Cathedral, found a park bench, and called you. I had to talk through it with someone." Cooper dropped his voice low. "What if Shaw is the serial killer? He could be stalking out areas like New Orleans and then luring the boys to a meet place. Then he strikes."

I didn't want to sound as skeptical as Luke. "It's a theory. Shaw has certainly shown himself to be a liar and a narcissist. I don't know what he's capable of doing."

"We have to explore it then. I had been expecting you to tell me that I was talking nonsense. If both of us believe it's possible, then we have to consider it." Cooper's voice got quiet again. "Don't judge me for asking this, but why are priests so weird?"

"Weird, how?" Having grown up Catholic and gone to Catholic schools for all of grade school and high school, I had interacted with many priests. Some of them very weird.

"While Fr. Frank was pointing the finger at Shaw, it made me suspicious about his involvement with Danny and this case. I think he lied to me. He acted like he hadn't thought about Danny dying in the same way as the other young men – the very thing that Shaw wanted him to help investigate."

That seemed strange to me too. "He might feel bad or he might be second-guessing himself. Where was he the weekend Danny died?"

"Fr. Frank said he was out of town at hospitals ministering to the sick. That's a thing priests do, right?"

"That is a thing priests do," I said and tried not to snicker. Cooper had no experience with priests. Not that I could blame him, most people didn't. "I don't know why he'd be lying to you. I wouldn't worry about it. I think you need to tell Det. Elio what you found and see if there is any way you can get into Danny's email. You said he got a text to meet that night, right?"

"Yes, and we haven't confirmed who sent that text. From what I hear, we aren't going to be able to confirm it either. It's suspicious though. Shaw tells Danny he will reach out to meet and then someone reaches out to meet and the next thing we know Danny is dead."

"I have the same suspicions. Keep running it to ground and tell me what you find." I didn't like lying to Luke but sometimes to avoid an argument, I kept things from him. "Luke isn't so keen on the idea that Shaw might be in the mix of this. I'd keep it to yourself for now. What about this other suspect? The one showing up to the scenes. Mark David Reed? Do you know much about him?"

"I will research him later today. I'm going to text you the link to his professional profile. Take a look. See if you can get your hands on any photos from the scene when the body was found. If you can, look in the crowd and see if he's there. You can also ask around and see if anyone knows him."

"I'll do what I can. Is that the only thing you have on him? He showed up to a few scenes."

Cooper confirmed. "I'm not saying this is a great lead. One or two scenes I could understand, but all of them? That's according to George. We need to independently verify all of this."

We talked for a few more minutes and then ended the call. I didn't want to make Chris wait any longer. I glanced at the link Cooper sent with a photo of Mark David Reed and then stuffed my phone back into my pocket. I made my way across the parking lot and up the steep back steps to the patio. I nearly bumped right into Chris as I hit the landing.

"Riley," he said, putting his hands on my arms to steady me. "I was just heading down to the storeroom if you want to join me."

Chris and I had a little history, if I could even consider it that. It was mostly a lot of flirting that led nowhere back when I was going to bars. We hadn't had much conversation in the years following, and I thought it might be weird interviewing him. It didn't seem to be weird for him, so I wasn't going to let it be weird for me. I followed him back down the stairs.

"I was told you wanted to hire a private investigator. That you were the driving force for me being here. Is there a reason you did that?"

Chris unlocked the storeroom door and pushed it open. He flipped on the light and turned back to me. "I felt horrible for what happened. Trevor was last seen here and his body was found in the river practically right behind my pub. As you know the cops said it was an accident, but no one believes that."

"You were here that night?"

Chris raked a hand through his blond hair that hadn't thinned with age. "I was in and out of the bar area and my office upstairs. I saw

Trevor and spoke to him briefly. The place had a weird vibe that night, Riley." He sighed and put his hands on his hips. "You know it's never a weird vibe, but we had a strange mix of people in there. Liv was there. Have you asked her?"

I explained that she had given me a statement without going into too much detail. "Who else was in there that night?"

"There were only a handful of regulars." He shrugged and said, "It was a mismatched group."

"Was there anyone there that I'd know?"

"Fr. Michael from Sacred Heart was there. He was down having a few beers with a priest from out of town. They had dinner and then made their way over to the bar area and were watching football. There were a handful of guys you'd probably know from high school and just Troy regulars and then a few strangers I don't know that well. It was just an odd mix of people. Trevor isn't normally alone either. He has a group of friends or his roommate. When he came in that night, he was alone. He said he was meeting someone but then sat at the bar alone."

"I heard he had an argument or disagreement with a guy at the bar. Do you know about that?"

Chris laughed. "That was probably Bobby. He was arguing about football with anyone who'd engage him. He's harmless."

"Did Trevor leave the bar with anyone?"

"No. He left out the back door to the patio. I'm sure you heard he was arguing with a guy out back. We've never been able to identify him."

"It wasn't Bobby? Maybe the argument carried over?"

Chris shook his head. "Bobby was still in here at closing time." He gestured with his hand toward the river. "Riley, we get our share of robbery and gun violence in the city, like any city. We even have a bit of a gang issue on the rise, but this..."

I knew what he was saying. This wasn't normal here. I had been to the pub countless times and walked to my car in the dark after a night out with friends. "I think what you're trying to say is if someone killed Trevor, it wasn't random."

Chris blinked rapidly a few times and then nodded. "It wasn't random. I also can't imagine who'd want to kill him. He was a nice guy, Riley. He wasn't a big drinker. Not into drugs or gambling. I never knew him to start a fight or even have a bad word to say to anyone."

I figured I could test some theories out on Chris and see if anything matched. Even though the person Trevor argued with at the bar had been identified, I still had Shaw in the forefront of my mind, especially given what Cooper had told me. I pulled out my phone. "I'm not saying any of these people are suspects. I just want to know if you saw any of them in the bar that night." I turned my phone to him and showed him a photo of Ned Shaw.

"Yeah, he was in here that night. Then he's shown up here several times since, saying he's heading up an investigation." Chris pointed to an area between me and the river. "He held a press conference out here the other night."

I thrust the phone toward him as my heart raced. "You saw Ned Shaw here the night Trevor was in here? Was he with anyone?"

Chris shook his head. "No, he was drinking whiskey down at the end of the bar alone. I recognized him from television right away. I even went up and said hello. I asked him what he was doing in Troy and he said he was meeting with someone."

"Was he still at the bar when Trevor was here?"

"No. He left maybe twenty minutes or so before Trevor arrived. Shaw wasn't here long."

I flipped through my photo reel. "What about this guy? Did you see him in here that night?"

Chris bent over to look at my phone again. "Yeah, actually he was. I got into a brief conversation with him because he was wearing a Chicago Cubs hat. You don't see that much around here. We had a brief conversation. He said he was a tech sales guy and had a few meetings with the local colleges."

My hand was shaking as I asked, "You're sure he was in here the night Trevor went missing?"

"Yeah, Riley. What's the big deal? He had meetings with a few of the local colleges. He was a nice enough guy – quiet, stuck to himself." He stared down at me waiting for me to explain my reaction, but my heart thumped loudly in my ears and I couldn't explain even if I wanted to.

Just because I didn't think this could be any weirder, I pulled up the St. Louis Cathedral website and found a photo of Fr. Frank. I showed the photo to Chris. "Is this the priest with Fr. Michael?"

Chris glanced down. "It could be. I didn't pay much attention. I waved to Fr. Michael but didn't go over to his table that night. Please tell me you're not about to accuse Fr. Michael of killing Trevor."

I laughed even though none of it was funny. "No. I don't think Fr. Michael had anything to do with it. I don't even think the other priest did. I was just curious about the other priest. My investigative partner just met a priest down in New Orleans possibly related to another drowning case. Cooper said the priest was a bit strange."

"The whole case is strange, Riley." He hitched his chin forward. "Why'd you ask me about Mark?"

I wasn't sure if I should share with him what Cooper told me. Chris was looking at me with such curiosity and since he was the reason for me being there, I caved. "A reporter came forward in New Orleans and said that Mark has shown up in several scene photos when bodies have been found. That's all we have. I didn't expect you to have seen this guy, let alone know him. It took me a bit off guard. Given he was here that night, I have to question him. Do you know how I can reach him?"

"He was still in the bar when Trevor left, Riley. He's not involved."

"Let me worry about that. Do you have a way to reach him?"

"I don't. It's not like we're friends. He was a customer I had a few minutes conversation with about baseball."

Everything seemed to be a dead end. "Is there anything else you think I should know?"

"No. I just hope you find out who did this."

"Me too," I said quietly and thanked him for his time. I headed off toward my car while I stared off at the abandoned buildings nearby. I wasn't sure what was calling me to them. They'd need to be searched.

# CHAPTER 23

L uke sat in his living room at close to nine dumbfounded by what Riley was saying. "Riley, you can't be serious," he said but had no choice but to believe her. She had found solid evidence and a witness who was willing to go on record.

Riley was going to make him believe her. She stressed, "I'm telling you that three people connected to the New Orleans case and potentially other cases were all in the pub on the night Trevor died."

"All three?" Luke asked, running a hand down his stubbled face.

"All three. After I met with Chris, I called Fr. Michael and asked about the priest who had visited in August. There are so many visiting priests he had to go check his calendar for me. Sure enough, it was Fr. Frank from New Orleans."

"What does that mean, Riley? I'm not sure I understand." Luke sank back into the couch and lowered the volume on the television. He reached for his beer that was sitting on a coaster on the end table and took a sip.

"I don't know that it means anything. Priests often visit other parishes. I just thought it was a bit odd that he was there the night Trevor went missing and also knew the victim in New Orleans. Cooper spoke to him earlier today and said he was weird. I didn't think much of it. I almost didn't even bring it up to Chris, but he mentioned Fr. Michael being there that night. I thought, what are the odds, so I asked."

Luke wasn't sure he could take a priest as a suspect seriously right now. Sure, there were scandals of sexual abuse across Catholic parishes around the globe, but a serial killer priest? No, his mind simply couldn't go there with minimal evidence. "What about Mark David Reed? He sounds like more of a viable suspect to me." He was holding back his information about Ned Shaw because he knew Riley would run with it.

"There's not much to tell. We are going to need to get Cooper on the call for that. All I know is that some reporter gave Cooper the tip on Mark and said he was in scene photos. Chris said that Mark was there that night and wearing a Chicago Cubs hat. Sure enough, Luke, I called the Troy Record and asked for photos from the scenes. Guess who I saw wearing the same Chicago Cubs hat?"

"Mark David Reed," Luke said, excited that Riley might have a viable suspect.

"The only thing is that Chris didn't think Mark left the bar before Trevor or followed him out." Riley sighed loudly and then murmured to herself something Luke couldn't hear. "I don't know how I feel about this guy as a suspect. If you can find him in scene photos in Little Rock too, maybe I'll take this seriously. Otherwise, we are going on the word of this reporter. It's suspicious Mark was in Troy. It's hardly a solid slam dunk on the case."

"Does Cooper have the photos or did the reporter just tell Cooper they exist?"

"We'd have to check with him. Where is he?"

Luke had texted Cooper earlier and asked if he wanted to check in, but he said that he was meeting with Det. Elio to go over witness statements and wouldn't be available. Luke told Riley that and added, "It sounds like he's doing the best he can right now. So far, he's the one getting most of the evidence. Not that I haven't had a few leads."

Luke waited for Riley's reaction. She had been gunning for Shaw and he didn't want her to have tunnel vision.

But Riley didn't jump. Instead, she said, "I'm glad you're getting leads. I haven't had much of anything here other than today when Chris said all three of those people were in the pub that night. That was as surprising as it was confusing."

Luke kicked his feet up on the ottoman. "You don't want to know what I found?"

"You can tell me if you want." Riley yawned loudly. "I'm exhausted and feel like I haven't stopped since I arrived."

It was no fun when he couldn't get a rise out of her, teasing her with information. Luke told her about Shaw. "I have to admit that when I found out Shaw was there that night, I was kicking myself for not listening to you. It's from a credible source." Luke waited for Riley to have the reaction he assumed she'd have, but he was disappointed again.

She merely grunted an *I told you so* and then added, "We have to consider him a suspect. The reporter Cooper spoke to identified Shaw as a suspect. We have all the locations zeroed in on him. There's something at play here that we are missing."

"Let me run it down since you have some history with him."

"I'm not going to argue with you there. I think Shaw might still be up here. Does that mean you'll come up here to interview him?"

Luke wasn't sure if that was going to be necessary. He still had some other leads to run down. He had yet to follow up with Nolan. "Let me speak to Captain Meadows and see what I can do. In the meantime, we need more information about Mark David Reed. We can't assume the cases are connected until we have a common denominator that we can prove. Speculation by a reporter doesn't do much for me. He has to turn over everything he has to Cooper if we are going to do anything with it."

"Agreed." Riley grew quiet and Luke thought she might tell him she wanted to hang up, but instead, she said, "You said the witness who saw Shaw in Little Rock is credible. Who is he?"

Luke gave Riley the rundown about Pete including having to go back three times to interview the guy. "I'm embarrassed to say that I didn't do a good job the first two times."

"You have a lot on your plate, Luke. We all do."

There was something in Riley's tone, more than tired, that caught Luke's attention. "Are you okay?"

"Yeah, I'm fine. I'm just feeling like I did when I had that previous drowning case. I forgot how hard these cases are to prove. The water gets rid of most of the evidence and it's almost impossible to tell how someone ended up in the water unless there is a direct witness, which we don't have."

"All circumstantial."

"Right," Riley sighed again, "and you know cases like that don't go anywhere, sometimes even when you do solve them." Luke was about to give her a pep talk, but then Riley added, "You know the reporter mentioned one thing to Cooper that I thought was interesting. He said that all the victims had been texted about meeting someone. It's what led Danny away from his group. Trevor told Chris that he was meeting someone and Liv said he kept checking his phone all night."

"Do you think the killer was luring them out?"

"I do," Riley said evenly. "You have the most open and recent investigation. See if you can get some phone records for Rob Hall. Maybe we can find a number that's been contacting them. Cooper also said Shaw had reached out to Danny by email, so he was going to see if he could access that too. I don't have any confirmation right now that Shaw interacted with Trevor in the pub that night, just that they were there at the same time."

Luke was starting to believe that wasn't a coincidence. Still, he wanted to temper Riley's excitement. He assured her, "Det. Tyler already has the phone records. We'll go over them again."

They talked for a few minutes more and then they said goodnight and hung up. Luke figured he'd watch television a little while longer and then go to bed and start early the next morning. He got about thirty minutes into a thriller movie on Netflix when something rattled the back kitchen door.

Luke lowered the sound on the television, not sure he had heard correctly. He pushed himself upright and sat perched on the edge of the couch, waiting to hear it again. The rattle happened seconds later and then again. Luke took the stairs two at a time to grab his Glock off the dresser. He checked the clip and then came back down the stairs and went directly through the living room into the kitchen.

"Who's there?" he shouted as he positioned himself with the gun pointed toward the door. The rattle happened again as Luke watched the doorknob turn. The locked deadbolt stopped the person from entering. "I'm not going to ask again. Who are you? I'm a Little Rock Police Detective and I'm armed."

"Don't shoot," a muffled voice shrieked out. "I only want to talk."

The voice wasn't unfamiliar to Luke, but he couldn't quite place it. Luke walked toward the door with his gun in his right hand still pointed at the door. He flipped the back porch light on, undid the bolt lock, and then tugged the door open.

Nolan stood on the other side with his hands shoved in his pockets.

"Let me see your hands," Luke instructed with his voice firm and commanding.

Nolan removed his hands slowly from his pockets and raised them. "I swear I only want to talk. I shouldn't have tried to open the door. No one can know that I'm here. My father told me not to talk to you. But I'm in trouble and don't know who can help."

Luke didn't trust him no matter what he was saying. He didn't lower his gun as he stepped outside and instructed Nolan to take a seat in one of the patio chairs. "You shouldn't have come to my home. How'd you get my home address?"

Nolan didn't meet Luke's eyes. "My father's computer. He has all kinds of records on people." He raised his head. "Look. I know I shouldn't be here. I didn't know what else to do. I tried to talk to my father. He told me to shut up and not tell anyone what I know. I'm in danger."

Luke eyed him suspiciously. "Danger from who?"

"The guy who killed Rob."

Luke lowered his gun but kept it by his side as he sat down. "What do you mean the guy who killed Rob? You told me that you thought it was his friends. You're scared of them?"

Nolan shook his head. "I lied about that. They weren't selling drugs and Derek wasn't angry with him. I saw the killer."

"You saw him?" Luke asked with disbelief in his voice. Nolan had lied too much, it was hard to believe anything.

Nolan shook his head. "I didn't see his face. I was trying to find Rob that night. He said he was going to get some air down near the river. I left the bar a few minutes after him. I couldn't find him at first. Then I heard struggling in the water – splashing around and voices. I couldn't make out what was being said. It was grunts more than anything. I didn't know what to do. I thought someone was drowning so I called out and then I went into the water to help the person. That's when I saw Rob face down in the water. I flipped him over thinking maybe I could save him but he was already dead. I panicked and didn't know what to do. That's when I heard other movements in the water and I got out of there as fast as I could."

Luke tried not to show any emotion on his face. That was normally easy for him. This time it was hard to hold back the shock at what he was hearing. Luke challenged him. "We have you on video surveillance leaving the bar and heading around the corner. You come back with what looks like a knife in your hand. What were you doing with that?"

Nolan swallowed hard. "You saw that?"

"I saw that, Nolan. If you want me to believe you, you better start telling me the truth."

Nolan took a few seconds and then admitted, "I was going to confront Rob. I figured we might get into a fight and wanted to protect myself." He waited for Luke to respond and when he didn't, he begged, "Listen, you have to believe me. I wasn't going to hurt him. Rob didn't have any stab wounds, did he? Someone was out there in the water with him, drowning him. He must have swum off as I went into the water. I didn't even know it was Rob out there. I thought I could help someone. When I rolled the guy over and realized it was Rob and that he wasn't breathing, I didn't know what to do. I panicked and got out of there."

"You didn't think to call the police?"

"People knew of my history with Rob. I figured they'd think I did it. With my record and the number of times I'd been in trouble, I was scared." Nolan threw his hands up in the air frustrated. "You found me anyway."

"Where's the knife?"

"What?" Nolan asked as if he hadn't heard. Luke asked the question again. "I don't know. I dropped it when I went into the water. I forgot all about it when I thought someone was drowning. I swear to you, I went into the water thinking I might prevent someone from drowning. I didn't do this."

Luke locked his gaze on him and Nolan looked away. "Look at me, Nolan. Why didn't you tell me this when we spoke earlier?"

Nolan took a breath and finally made eye contact with Luke. "I wanted to speak to my father first. He advised me not to speak to the cops. He said that if I admitted to being there, no matter what the truth was, they'd pin it on me." He had fear in his eyes. "Is that what you're going to do? Arrest me for something I didn't do?"

Luke didn't know what he was going to do with the information. He wasn't making that decision tonight. "You'll need to come into the station tomorrow and make a statement. If you want me to help you, you need to go on the record and make a formal statement."

Nolan shook his head furiously. "I can't do that. I really can't."

"You don't have a choice." Luke stood and headed for his back gate, opening it for Nolan to leave. The last thing he was going to do was argue with him. "You need to go home and don't ever come here again. I'll call you in the morning to figure this out. If you want to clear yourself as a suspect, you'll come in and give a statement. Otherwise…well, I don't think you'll like the consequences." Luke let the veiled threat linger until Nolan nodded and walked out the gate promising to call him tomorrow.

# CHAPTER 24

ooper made it back to his hotel just before eleven that night. He had spent the evening with Clive going over all the witness statements and evidence the detective had collected. After they were done, Clive took him to one of his favorite restaurants and they shared war stories of police work until they finished their dinners and had a few beers.

Cooper didn't realize until he was leaving the restaurant that he'd be walking back alone on the darkened streets of the French Quarter. He encountered a few drunks and some groups of people. The closer he got to his hotel, the quieter the streets became. The moon was nearly full overhead and each alleyway hinted at something menacing. Cooper quickened his pace and only relaxed once he reached the entrance to his hotel.

He walked down the cobblestone path past the first building and then cut left through the small courtyard toward his room. The lone orange bulb over his doorway in the tiny alcove cast shadows that only amplified Cooper's paranoia. He had not been able to shake the feeling of being watched.

Cooper's paranoia turned out to be warranted. As he reached for the keys in his pocket, Cooper noticed the slip of paper on the ground near his door with a remnant of tape still sticking from the top. He assumed it must have once been tacked to his door but had fallen to the ground. He looked around to make sure he was alone and then bent to pick it up.

*Meet me in Jackson Square at midnight. I know who killed Danny. Don't involve the police.*

Even with the seriousness of the message, Cooper couldn't help but chuckle at the note. It was cliché like something in a movie. Cooper didn't relish the idea of going back to Jackson Square that late, especially alone. He was armed and wanted information. What bothered him the most was that someone knew where he was staying – not just his hotel but his room. Someone had been watching him.

If Cooper felt any fear for his life it hadn't settled into him yet.

That didn't mean he wasn't cautious as he unlocked the hotel room door. Cooper stood at the threshold with one foot in the room and the other still outside. He scanned the room looking for anomalies but found none. There was nothing disturbed that he could see.

After a quick sweep of the bathroom, behind the shower curtain, in the small closet, and under the bed, he sat back in the only chair in the room. He contemplated texting Luke but decided it was too late. He considered calling Clive next but figured the detective would want to go with him to Jackson Square. For whatever reason, the person who wanted to meet didn't want to speak to the cops and there was no point in scaring them off.

Cooper couldn't help but think that Danny had been summoned like this on the night he died. No one had texted Cooper and he wasn't a twenty-one-year-old unarmed kid. Cooper was on the doorstep of forty and was more than capable of handling himself.

He clicked on the television and watched the local news broadcast for a short period before gathering his things and heading back out. Cooper was surprised to find the front iron gate that ran across the driveway entrance to the hotel closed and locked. He didn't remember seeing anything about a curfew. He stood there in the middle of the road staring at the gate before remembering the hotel clerk had mentioned a side gate that was through the courtyard on the other side of the building. His room key could be used to unlock it.

Cooper doubled-back and instead of taking a left made a sharp right, cut through the courtyard near the pool, and found the side gate. Cooper turned back and faced the far building of the hotel. That was building five, the one that had been a hospital during the Civil War. It was known to be the most haunted building in the hotel. He shuddered and then kept moving, not wanting to linger too long on those thoughts.

Cooper didn't like New Orleans alone at night. If it wasn't for rowdy drunks and partygoers, the streets were barren. He walked the few blocks as quickly as he could, and as he had anticipated, found the gate to Jackson Square locked. From Chartres Street, he cut down St. Ann's, made a right on Decatur, and started back up St. Peter toward Chartres. He made it about halfway up the block, just passing the restaurant where Danny had sought help, when he noticed a man standing near the park gate in the shadows.

Cooper put his hand on the top of his gun, reassuring himself it was still securely on his hip, and then made his way toward the man. As he approached, Cooper said, "You wanted to meet me?"

"Quiet," said the man who stood about five-foot-ten and had dark hair combed to the side. He had on jeans and a polo shirt. "I don't have much time."

Cooper leaned against the fence to the park. "Who are you?"

"Fr. John Lundy. I'm the associate pastor at St. Louis Cathedral."

Cooper had no reason not to believe the man, but he didn't look like any priest he'd ever seen. He guessed Fr. Lundy was at least ten years younger than him, putting him right around thirty. "Is there a reason you called me out here? You said you know who killed Danny."

Fr. Lundy glanced back at the church and then stepped closer to

Cooper. He dropped his voice low. "I think it's Fr. Frank." When he saw the look on Cooper's face, he added, "Let me explain."

"I think you'd better because accusing a priest isn't something that strikes me as something one should do casually or without a good deal of evidence."

Fr. Lundy gnawed at his lower lip. "He has a temper that most people don't see. He is quite the violent man. I've seen him throw things in the rectory where we live. I've heard him scream at people on the phone when he thinks no one is listening. I'm telling you this because you have to know the mild-mannered way Fr. Frank presents is not who he is."

"I'm listening," Cooper said. He had a weird vibe from Fr. Frank, but he hadn't been expecting this. It occurred to Cooper that Fr. Lundy was who Fr. Frank said was at the church the night Danny was in the area seeking help. "Did you see Danny the night he died?"

"I did but only for a moment. I was locking up the church for the night when I saw Danny in the street. He looked frantic and scared. I called out to him and he started to run toward St. Ann Street. I stepped out in front of the church and called him again. He stopped and looked at me and called out for Fr. Frank. I told him that Fr. Frank was out of town." Fr. Lundy was shaking his head in disbelief. "You have to understand I was so confused. I had no idea what was happening. I tried to stop him from running but he took off. I don't know him well, only from seeing him at mass. I thought the kid was drunk."

Cooper had read all the statements Clive had taken after they found Danny's body and no one at the time had admitted to seeing Danny after he left his group at the bar. Fr. Lundy hadn't come forward with the information. The hostess at the bar hadn't been identified then. Cooper said sternly, "Calling out Fr. Frank's name doesn't mean he did anything to Danny. They were close, according to what Fr. Frank told me. Why didn't you come forward with this information about seeing Danny when the police were investigating the case?"

"As I said I didn't think anything of it at the time even when Danny was found in the river. He was impaired that night and the cops said it was an accident. I saw him behaving strangely but as you said that's no reason to bring Fr. Frank into it. It was a ludicrous thought at the time." Fr. Lundy was watching Cooper for a reaction, maybe validation he had made the right decision.

Cooper wasn't quite sure what to say. There was logic in Fr. Lundy's excuse he couldn't deny. "I assume something changed?"

Fr. Lundy dropped his voice even lower. "I started seeing news reports about the other drowning cases that followed. Fr. Frank was out of town for every one of those cases. A few times he had told me he was in the same city."

"Coincidence?" Cooper asked, raising an eyebrow.

"I thought so at first. I kept remembering what Danny said about Fr. Frank being after him that night." Fr. Lundy expelled a loud breath. "I hate to admit to doing this. I went through Fr. Frank's calendar and called the parish where he was supposed to be the weekend Danny died. He said he was going there to help the priest at the local hospital. Only, he never went. They had no record of him being there. I had to pretend that I was confused and got the wrong dates. You should have heard me on the phone. I was practically incoherent stumbling over my mistake. But the fact remains, Fr. Frank lied about where he went."

"Is it possible that he went someplace else?" Cooper figured there had to be a logical answer.

Fr. Lundy shook his head. "He came back full of stories from that weekend. It wasn't just a one-off lie. It was a whole story that he fabricated. There were details to make it seem real. I believed him at the time only to find out later it was all made up."

Everything about Fr. Lundy's body language told Cooper he was telling the truth. "Is there any reason that Fr. Frank would be harassing Danny or try to hurt him?" Cooper immediately thought of the church's sex abuse scandals and wondered if something like that had happened. Was it possible that Danny was about to tell someone? Cooper realized he was so lost in his thoughts he wasn't listening to Fr. Lundy. "I'm sorry, what were you saying?"

Frustrated, Fr. Lundy said, "I said that, no, I don't know of any reason Fr. Frank would hurt Danny. They were friendly with each other. Fr. Frank had even given him advice more than a handful of times."

"There is the sex abuse scandal. Do you think…" Cooper wasn't even able to get the full question out before Fr. Lundy objected.

"There is no way that was happening."

"How do you know for sure?"

"I just know." Fr. Lundy had grown agitated by the mere suggestion of it. He wouldn't discuss it further and Cooper didn't press the issue. "There's something else you should know. Fr. Frank's nephew drowned fifteen years ago. It was one of the first cases that Ned Shaw said was connected to the Cross Killers. Shaw inserted himself into the investigation and the cops closed it without any real resolution. Forget about justice, there's never even been a reasonable explanation for why the drowning happened. Fr. Frank has been enraged about it to this day. He hasn't been able to let it go."

With a confused expression on his face, Cooper asked, "Then why would Fr. Frank help to perpetuate the myth of a serial killer by becoming a serial killer? That doesn't make any sense to me. And if he's so friendly to Danny, why would he choose him as the victim?"

"All things I've questioned myself," Fr. Lundy said with a hint of sadness in his voice.

"Did you come up with any answers?"

"I don't know why Fr. Frank would do it. Anger and grief can do strange things to a person. As to why Danny – his parents are wealthy and well-connected. Danny is a sympathetic victim. He was well-liked and an upstanding member of the community. Maybe Fr. Frank thought it would pull in a lot of public sympathies."

"Does he want to be found out? Because Danny's parents are the reason I'm here." Cooper looked down at the man, his expression stern. "I don't walk away from cases until I solve them. So, if this is Fr. Frank, he just bought himself a ticket to prison. Is there anything else?"

"No. I just couldn't hold this in any longer. It was weighing on my conscience."

Cooper understood that even if the information turned out to be nothing. He was still having trouble wrapping his head around a motive and how a priest could be so mired down in guilt and anger that he'd do something so heinous. Cooper asked Fr. Lundy if he could get a copy of Fr. Frank's calendar so he could cross-reference his trips out of town with the drownings and follow up on alibis. Cooper didn't want to sound the alarm and embarrass a well-known and respected priest in New Orleans unless he had to. Fr. Lundy promised he'd try to get the information.

Before they parted, Cooper asked a question. "How did you know where I was staying?"

"Fr. Frank mentioned it to me in passing. He told me that you were at the church today. I assumed you told him."

Cooper had not told Fr. Frank the hotel and certainly not his room number. As Fr. Lundy turned to leave, Cooper called him back. "Make sure to let me know if Fr. Frank leaves town."

Fr. Lundy nodded in understanding and walked off into the night, leaving Cooper standing next to Jackson Square feeling the weight of the man's confession nearly knock him to his knees.

# CHAPTER 25

"That is beyond creepy," I squealed as I crossed my legs under me after Cooper told us Fr. Frank knew where he was staying. I steadied my laptop on my knees and waited for Cooper to respond. Luke had texted us both that morning and asked if we could check-in. Their investigations, it seemed, were moving at a pace mine wasn't.

Cooper had just explained to us about his late-night meeting with Fr. Lundy and the information he provided. He was surprised when I told him that Fr. Frank had been spotted in the pub the night of Trevor's murder. We now had him connected to two cases.

Captain Meadows had been able to make some calls and confirm that Ned Shaw was connected to all eight cases, at least in the immediate days after. Luke had been able to confirm that Shaw had tried to have an in-person meeting with Captain Meadows a few hours after Rob's body had been found in the river. Pete, his witness, had identified him from that night on the river.

I hadn't found much on Mark David Reed other than that his work credentials checked out and that he travels extensively for work. I had checked with the Troy Record and did confirm that there was a photo of Mark in the paper in the crowd when Trevor's body was found. We didn't have the rest of the evidence that the reporter said he had. Cooper was still working on that.

The information about Fr. Frank made me shudder.

"It is creepy," Cooper agreed. "I'm not sure what I can do about it right now.  I hate to say it, but I'm not coming up with any reasonable explanation for how Danny died. Det. Elio did a good job of getting statements and checking the alibis of people who knew Danny. Everything is above board. There are no other suspects – not even the hint of one. We know for sure it's not a robbery, and given the circumstances, I think I can rule out an accident.  I'm left with no suspect and no motive. Danny was running from someone that night and it appears they caught him and killed him. According to Fr. Lundy, when he was running he called out Fr. Frank's name. I don't know if he was asking for Fr. Frank or saying he was running from Fr. Frank. It makes no sense to me. If he was running from Fr. Frank, why would he run toward the church?"

"Is it possible Fr. Lundy misunderstood Danny that night?" I asked. "Maybe that's not even what he yelled."

"He seemed confident enough.  It's what made him start asking questions about Fr.  Frank," Cooper said and threw his hands up. "What do you have, Luke?"

"I'm in the process of ruling out the only suspect I had," Luke said with frustration in his voice. He had told us about Nolan's late-night visit and that he was sitting at the office now waiting for him to come in and make a formal statement. "If he shows up and is willing to put on record what he saw, then his story tracks with the witness we have. Pete saw Nolan running scared and wet."

"You don't think he attacked Rob?" Cooper asked before I could.

Luke shook his head. "Maybe I'm being stupid, but I don't think he's good for this one.  He's got a criminal record and he had been in a fight with Rob previously. If Rob had been stabbed or had there been defensive wounds on Rob's body, I might think it was Nolan. It sounds like Rob was ambushed, dragged into the water, and drowned.

Nolan was a witness to some of that. By the time he got to Rob, he was already dead. Det. Tyler suggested there might be a charge given he didn't call 911 and we can't be sure that Rob might not have been saved with CPR. I don't think going after Nolan right now is going to help anything."

I agreed with that. I had to accept Luke's theory, as he knew far more about his case than I did. "Who are you thinking is responsible?"

Luke sat back in his chair with a defeated look on his face. "I hate to say it, but Shaw is my lead suspect. Have we figured out if he's still in Troy?"

I had swallowed my pride and a whole heap of annoyance and called Shaw this morning for Luke. The goal was to try to get him to meet. Shaw had surprised me by answering, but he didn't give the answer I had been hoping for regarding his location. "This is probably more manageable for you, Luke, but he's headed back down to New Orleans. He said he has more work to do on the case there. That means he's going to be crossing paths with you, Cooper. Be on the lookout for him."

"Did he say where he was staying?" Luke asked.

"I didn't think to ask him that. I don't know if he would have told me. He was pretty smug when I asked for a meeting and flat out refused to share evidence with me, not that I think he has any."

Luke didn't look surprised. "You're sure he's going to New Orleans? I don't want to go all the way down there for nothing."

"Positive." I wasn't sure why Luke was avoiding the obvious. "Luke, call him and see if you can set up a meeting. I'm sure if you acted like you wanted his help on the case, you'll get in front of him. Then you can interrogate him."

"That's what I'm going to have to do. I wanted to be in the same city to make it harder for him to refuse and then find him immediately if he denied me."

Cooper gestured with his hand like he wanted to interrupt. "Luke, you can crash here with me."

"Let me finish up a few things and then I'll call Shaw and confirm he's down there." Luke called out to Det. Tyler that he was nearly done and then he focused his attention back on us. "What's the consensus? Can we say yet that these are all connected?"

I looked at Cooper and he looked back at me, both of us uncertain. I said, "I think we can say that the cases seem to have a few of the same players. You still need to confirm that Mark David Reed was in Little Rock at the time of the murder and Fr. Frank as well. Those two and Shaw seem to be our best suspects so far. I don't feel like I can say anything for certain."

Cooper was nodding his head. "I agree with Riley. Can we say with certainty that all the cases are murders and not accidents?" Luke and I nodded and Cooper continued, "That's more than we had a few days ago. Riley, did you ever get anywhere with the lung sample from the medical examiner's office?"

"That looks like a dead end. For us to get it at this point, the family is going to need to convince the medical examiner to release the evidence and Miles doesn't think that will happen. He's already angry that he's been second-guessed in this case after calling it an accident."

Cooper asked, "What's your next move?"

I checked the time on my phone. "In about two hours, I'm meeting up with Jack and Miles and we are going to search some of the abandoned buildings near the pub. Trevor was taken someplace the night he died. This case is different than yours in that regard. Luke, you know that Rob was killed that night right away and was found soon after. Cooper, you know that Danny was seen running from the river and was found the next day. Trevor was moved either before or after death before going in the river and I need to figure out where that is."

"Your case may not be connected then," Luke said.

I didn't agree with that. "If Fr. Frank and Mark David Reed weren't known to be here along with Shaw then I might agree with you. The fact that I have Chris, the bar owner, who saw all of them in the bar the night Trevor died tells me it's connected even if it looks different. There's no way that's a coincidence."

"I'll concede that point," Luke said. He stretched his arms overhead and asked if we wanted to discuss anything else. When Cooper and I said we'd check in later, Luke clicked off, leaving Cooper and me still online.

"How are you really doing down there?" I asked Cooper before we left the chat.

"I'm fine. Going out last night alone without backup could have been a disaster. I did what I had to do though." He sat back and stared at me. "What do you think, Riley? Do you think Fr. Frank might be capable of these murders? He's young enough and seems strong enough."

"Serial killers do often start with someone they know and branch out. Danny's was the first in this series of drownings. It's not impossible to believe. I think what confuses me is how Fr. Frank might come in contact with the other victims. Trevor was waiting for someone that night, but Fr. Frank was already in the bar. I don't know how he'd get away from Fr. Michael, who he was there with, to kidnap Trevor and then kill him. If you knew Fr. Michael, you'd think that's about the most asinine thing you'd ever heard. I'm not saying a priest can't be a killer, but he's at the bottom of my suspect list. Plus, we don't even know if he was in those other locations. All you know right now is that he wasn't in New Orleans when the other murders occurred."

"That's true," Cooper said, conceding the point. He reached up to click off the chat and told me to be safe before saying goodbye. I was worried about him because I knew there was something he wasn't telling me. I got the feeling he wasn't comfortable in New Orleans alone. He'd been eager to have Luke there.

If I had a weird priest, who I considered a suspect and somehow knew where I was staying, I'd be a little freaked out too. I closed my laptop, got out of bed, and got myself ready for the day. I heard my mother and Jack in the kitchen below and felt a pang of guilt for not spending more time with them while I was in town.

Close to an hour later, I joined them in the kitchen. My mother had made a fresh pot of coffee and there were bagels from my favorite shop in a bag on the counter. "Thanks for picking these up. I can't get bagels like this in Little Rock."

"You could always move back," my mother said, sipping her coffee while sitting at the kitchen table. She was smiling behind her coffee cup. She knew it wasn't even open for discussion but that didn't stop her from teasing me about it.

"You have your hands full with Liv here," I said and looked toward the kitchen door. "Then again, she's hardly home. Where is she?"

My mother shook her head. "Maybe she started seeing someone she's keeping a secret from us. You know she was dating a lot and said she gave up. Maybe she was trying to throw us off her tracks."

"Leave her be," Jack cautioned with a teasing tone. "Liv will tell us if and when she's ready."

I spread chive cream cheese over my bagel, dropped the knife in the sink, carried my plate and a cup of coffee over to the table, and sat down with them. "If Liv's dating anyone, she hid it from me, too. Jack is right though. She'll tell us when she's ready."

Jack saw an opening to change the subject and jumped on it. "Making any headway on the case? I heard you up there and assumed you were talking to Cooper and Luke."

I took a bite of the bagel. "We have a few potential suspects but nothing locked down yet. We agreed this morning that the cases were murders." I wanted to ask Jack if he thought Shaw could be involved but didn't want to do that in front of my mother. She saw firsthand my frustration with Shaw years ago.

"Where are you two headed today?" she asked.

"The abandoned buildings near the pub," Jack said. "I called the developer and asked if we could take a walk-through and he gave permission. He didn't think we'd find anything since they were long ago abandoned. He can't do any work on them until the city approves their plans and gives him the permits."

My mother finished her coffee and went to the sink to rinse her cup. "I'm off to see Fr. Michael about an upcoming fundraiser at the church."

I bit my lip as I looked up at her, debating whether she could do some digging for me. "I might be able to use your help." I gave her the rundown on Fr. Frank and the fact that he was seen in the pub with Fr. Michael that night. "Could you see if Fr. Michael remembers anything about that visit that stands out? Don't tell him we are investigating Fr. Frank but kind of feel him out to see how the visit went."

My mother seemed almost giddy by the idea of doing a little undercover work. She clapped her hands together. "This could be fun."

"Don't go overboard," I cautioned her, already regretting asking. "Just be casual about it."

My mother planted a kiss on the top of my head. "Don't worry. I have it all under control." Then she kissed Jack goodbye and left.

When she was gone and the front door was firmly closed, Jack socked me gently in the arm. "You created a monster in one request. She's been asking me if she can go out on cases with me."

I laughed. "I didn't know that. I figured she might be gentler in speaking to him than I would be. If I did it, he'd know something was up. The last thing we want to do right now is go public that a priest might be a serial killer."

Jack winced at the sound of that. "Maybe you made the right choice." He checked his watch. "Miles is going to meet us there in fifteen minutes. You ready?"

I scooted back my chair and finished off my bagel. I grabbed a to-go coffee cup with a lid from the cabinet and poured myself more. I wasn't sure why but I already felt like it was going to be a long day.

# CHAPTER 26

We relied on flashlights to lead the way. The first building we entered from the back and realized quickly that the structure might not even be sound enough for us to search the top floors. The wood floors had been ripped up in spots showing the subflooring that had been rotted away years ago. Some of the walls had holes. In other places, entire areas of sheetrock had been removed and the piping, probably copper, had been ripped out. Electrical wires were left dangling, so it was good that the place didn't have power. It would have been a fire hazard.

Jack put a hand on my shoulder. "Riley, why don't you search down here and Miles and I will attempt the upper floors."

"Fine by me. If you don't think it's safe, don't go. No point risking our safety when we don't even know if anything is in here." Before they left, I turned to Miles. "I can't remember now if you said you searched these buildings after Trevor's body was found."

"It was a cursory search," Miles explained. "We hadn't had permission at the time to enter the buildings to search and there was no cause for a search warrant."

"Got it." I let them head to the rickety staircase that I was glad I wasn't climbing and went room to room searching for anything to indicate that Trevor might have been there.

Miles and Jack made it to the fourth floor of the building but came back down about thirty minutes later defeated. There hadn't been anything found other than mice. The inside of the building didn't even have graffiti or trash like kids had been exploring or the homeless had been camped out – that was a testament to the poor condition of the building. It appeared ready to fall at any moment.

We decided to move on to the next building and then the next. It wasn't until we were in the fourth building farthest from the pub's parking lot that we found what could be considered a suspicious scene.

We went in through the back door of the building and it was in the second room from the front that we found a chair, cut zip ties, and a bucket. I spun around the room. "Is the water still on in here?"

"No, that can't be possible," Jack said, not sounding convincing at all. He left the room with Miles right behind him. The room was darker than most because the windows had been boarded up. The plywood was flimsy and starting to rot. I assumed it had been up there for some time. The windows had probably been broken or removed and that was put up in its place.

I used my flashlight to do a grid search of the room looking for more evidence. I didn't want to jump to conclusions about the chair, zip ties, and bucket, but it wasn't too far of a leap to think that Trevor had been there. Given the set-up, it wasn't a stretch to imagine Trevor being held down face first in the bucket, which would have been large enough for that purpose, or even water boarded. I shuddered at the thought of either.

I kept my search on the floor as I waited for Jack and Miles to return. I flashed the light from one corner to the next in a sweeping motion, taking small steps back after each area was covered. When I was done with the room, I did it again. It was on my second sweep that I saw the faint outline of gouge lines in the wood near the chair.

I set the flashlight on the floor and got down on my hands and knees to get close enough to see it. Even then, I had to brush away some dirt.

The lines weren't too deep and looked like they had been made with a small sharp object, keys even. I sat back on my heels and focused the beam of light right on the area. *It started in New Orleans Shaw*

I had to read it a few times to see if that's what it said. The 'O' was clear but the rest of the letters were barely visible. 'Shaw' was positioned a little farther away from the rest not quite forming a full sentence. When I was confident in what it said, I nearly fell over.

"Jack! Miles!" I called out, pushing myself to a standing position. "Jack! Miles!" I called out again. I didn't want to leave the spot, fearful I might not be able to find it again.

A moment later, their heavy footsteps echoed through the building. Jack reached me first. He shone the light right on my face and I shielded my eyes from the blinding light. "Are you okay?" Jack asked, lowering the light and stepping closer to me.

I pointed my flashlight beam at the area. "There is a message on the floor. I want you to read it and tell me what you think it says." I stepped back out of the way while Jack did what I had done, getting down on the floor on his hands and knees to get a close-up view of it.

Miles came in a moment later. "Did you scream? I was outside. There is a water source and the electricity in this building is on. I don't want to turn on any of the lights for fear of sparking old wires. I'm surprised any utilities are running to this place." It took him a moment to realize Jack was on the floor. He stepped closer. "What's going on? What did you find?"

"Riley found an odd message on the floor," Jack said, standing. "Take a look and tell me what you see."

Miles replaced Jack on the floor. "It's hard to read but there is writing here." He brushed his hand over the area again and focused his flashlight and then said aloud the same thing I had read.

"That's what I saw too," Jack said, looking over at me. "What do you think it means?"

"We know that the first in the southern murders started back in August in New Orleans. From there, there were several more across the south, then up here in New York, and then more in the south. The last in Little Rock. At least, that's what we assume is the last." I paused to process my thoughts. "There was some question if this one in New York was connected because we aren't in the south and this murder looked different than the others. We don't have to question that anymore. This is connected. Why was Trevor killed here and not in the river like the others?"

Miles locked his gaze on me. "You assume he was killed here."

I gestured toward the scene in front of me. "I'd say it's a pretty good guess that he was here being held for some time. You found a water source and the bucket is big enough to hold someone's head in. What more proof do you need? He even named his killer."

Jack looked over at Miles. "I'd have to agree with Riley. The scene is convincing. If he was killed here and his body placed in the river later, that would answer why he didn't move far with the current. The biggest question I'm left with is what Riley said – why kill him this way? I think you're going to have to talk to the medical examiner, Miles, and see if he ran any tests on the kind of water found in Trevor's lungs. I have no idea if that's routine or not."

Miles had an uncertain look on his face. "Jack, do you think Trevor was killed here?"

"I do," he said with a little more force in his tone than he normally used. "I know you're probably second-guessing your investigation. But remember, Miles, you said yourself that this was a murder. You're the reason Riley is here."

"Yeah." Miles stepped back. "I should have searched the inside of these buildings. I don't normally make mistakes like this."

That's when it hit me that Miles wasn't resistant to the idea that Trevor was killed here, he was questioning whether he could have solved his murder sooner. "Miles, you would have had to track down the owner of the building like Jack did or get a search warrant. There was no reason to do that at the time. This was a hunch on my part."

Miles offered me a sad smile. "Are you saying that to make me feel better?"

I shook my head. "I don't do that in investigations. If anything, I'm going to try to make you feel worse," I teased him. "I'm serious, Miles. Blame Shaw for killing him and then calling the police department to insert himself in the investigation. He had to have known by history that as soon as he did the investigation would be closed. You were the one who pushed to continue the investigation. Your instincts were right. Don't beat yourself up."

"I appreciate that," he said softly and then headed out of the room. When I asked where he was going, Miles called over his shoulder. "I'm going to call the medical examiner and my captain. I'm going to try to officially reopen this case even if I have to take it to the press to do so."

"Is he going to be okay?" I asked Jack.

"He'll be fine.  Give him some space and let him work.  In the meantime, what do you want to do?"

"If this is Shaw and all the cases are connected, then let's let Luke go after him since Little Rock is the most recent case. He seems convinced now that Shaw should be a person of interest. As for here," I took a breath and let it out slowly, "I want to go interview Trevor's roommate to see if there's something we're missing. I also need to check with Miles about Trevor's emails to see if he received anything similar to Danny.  I know he got his texts but the messages were vague.  The one phone number of interest was tied back to a burner phone. We're missing something."

"I agree with that." Jack checked his watch. "Do you want me to go with you?"

"I'd rather go alone. I know you have another case to work on this evening. If you take me back home, I can grab Mom's car."

"You sure you'll be fine going alone?"

"I'm sure." I was sure because I firmly believed now that Shaw was the killer. The way he inserted himself in the investigations, guiding everyone including the parents with speculation and fake evidence, was a sure way to corrupt the cases and make sure justice was never served while gaining him national fame. Of course, no one would suspect the man desperately trying to solve the cases was actually the one committing them.

We found Miles outside and I explained where I was headed. Miles said he'd call me if he got any update from the medical examiner. Then he left and Jack and I made our way back to my mother's house. I was surprised to see her SUV in the driveway. I hadn't realized our search would take as long as it had.

Before I was even able to get in the door, my mother rushed me. She put her hands on my arms and squeezed in excitement. "I have information for you!" She pulled me by the arm into the living room and sat me down on the couch with her. "I wasn't sure that I was going to be able to do what you wanted me to do. But I did it. I pretended like I knew Fr. Frank and said I had heard he'd been here recently. I asked how the visit went."

My eyes got wide. "You lied to your parish priest?"

My mother waved me off. "I'll just admit lying in confession next time."

"In confession to the priest you just lied to?" I was trying to hold back a laugh. I hadn't been to confession since I was in high school and forced to go. My mother, however, was a much better Catholic.

"Riley, don't be so difficult. Do you want the information or not?" When I nodded my head, she went on. "Fr. Michael said that Fr. Frank didn't stay at the rectory that night. He left right after they got back from dinner. He thought that was weird since Fr. Frank was supposed to stay the night and attend a meeting with him in the morning. It was the reason he was here in Troy. Fr. Frank never came back for that meeting, and Fr. Michael didn't see him again. Fr. Frank later apologized for leaving like that. He said he wasn't feeling well and had to return home, but Fr. Michael had called New Orleans and they hadn't seen him either."

That was a lot to take in. "What did he think happened?"

"Fr. Michael wasn't sure. But this is good, right? I did a good job helping you."

My mother was so excited that I hugged her. "You did a great job, Mom." I leaned in and whispered, "Jack still isn't going to let you go on cases with him."

She leaned back and eyed me, knowing Jack had told me. "Then I might have to be just like you and start my own private investigation firm."

I knew she was kidding but after the number of years she had chastised me for my work, I wasn't sure what to make of the woman my mother was quickly becoming. One thing for sure was that it was a welcome change.

# CHAPTER 27

Nolan had come into the police station near the end of the day and given the statement Luke hoped he'd make. At the end, when Luke had what he needed, he thanked Nolan and told him he'd be in touch. The young man expected to be arrested and was surprised when Luke let him leave.

If Rob had defensive wounds on his body or had been stabbed, it would be a different outcome for Nolan. Right now, Luke had no reason to hold him. He was fine with that decision even if Det. Tyler had looked at him skeptically.

"I believe him," Luke said, avoiding his partner's glare as he sat down at his desk after the interview.

"You think that's wise?"

Luke didn't want to get into a debate about this. He rarely disagreed with Det. Tyler. "I know it seems like I'm making a mistake, but I don't have a legal reason to hold him. He admitted to being there and gave me a statement about what he saw. He's the one who came to me and admitted to being there. We have no physical evidence of him hurting Rob that night. We also have a witness who saw him approaching the area and then fleeing, which tracks with Nolan's story. Pete said it seemed like Nolan was afraid and kind of freaked out."

"Wet," Det. Tyler said with emphasis. He sat down at his desk and then spun the chair around to face Luke. "I assume if Nolan had committed his first murder, he might have the same reaction."

Luke raised his eyes but didn't say anything. Det. Tyler wasn't wrong. If Luke had wanted to make a murder charge stick, he could have. The prosecutor's office also had enough circumstantial evidence that they probably could have made a case. None of it sat right with Luke. That was the hardest of all to explain. "There are other avenues to explore," he said and hoped that would be that. But it wasn't.

Det. Tyler tapped on Luke's desk. "Are you sure you haven't gotten caught up in Riley's hatred of Shaw?"

Luke sighed loudly. It was akin to releasing all his frustration in one long breath. "Cut me some slack on this one and let's see where this goes. If I find more evidence to pin this on Nolan, then I'll circle back to him. Right now, I have him on record, even against his father's wishes."

"You're the boss," Det. Tyler said and then swiveled back to face his desk.

With that done, Luke checked his cellphone and saw that Riley had called while he was taking Nolan's statement. He listened to the message, his face registering surprise. When he ended the message, he called out to Det. Tyler, who turned to face Luke again.

He explained what Riley told him. "Riley found what she thinks is the place where Trevor Ellis was killed. There is a message gouged into the floor that all of this started in New Orleans and then Shaw's name. Nolan may have a motive for Rob's murder, but I can't see him committing the others. Feel free to run down his alibi for the other dates if you still have concerns." There was no sarcasm in Luke's tone even though he knew his words might imply it. He assured Det. Tyler that he hadn't meant it that way.

"I know you're frustrated," Det. Tyler assured him. "What are you going to do now?"

"I'm going to check at the newspaper for photos that were taken at the scene and then head to New Orleans to interview Shaw."

"Do you want me to go with you?" Det. Tyler asked, even though his face registered displeasure at the idea.

"No. You stay here and continue to work other angles in case Shaw doesn't pan out. No reason to put all our eggs in one basket." Luke stood from his desk. "I didn't mean to get frustrated with you. I'm having trouble explaining why I'm sure Nolan didn't kill Rob. You have every right to question me on it and push. If you still want to go after him and see if more solid evidence exists, please go ahead. Pete also saw Shaw down there that night and he never came back the way Nolan did. Nolan said the person who drowned Rob swam off. We know there are countless ways on and off that path. I want to rule Shaw out as much as I want him to be guilty of this."

Det. Tyler gave a curt nod and then smiled. "This is why you'll make a good captain."

"Thanks. We aren't there yet." Luke had pushed that internal debate to the side and hadn't wanted to consider or think about it until he had spoken to Riley, which wasn't going to happen until this case was over. "If you need anything, don't hesitate to call me."

As Luke headed toward Captain Meadows's office, Det. Tyler called after him. "Be safe down there in New Orleans."

Luke waved his hand overhead but didn't turn back. He knocked once on the door, heard Captain Meadows yell for him to enter, and then Luke nudged the door open wider. He came in and took a seat and gave Captain Meadows the overview of the case and his plan to go to New Orleans. "Det. Tyler will stay here and follow any additional leads that might arise."

Captain Meadows agreed. "You're right to go after him. Shaw's action might be giving him some cover. He's created a bit of mystique over the years that has probably shielded him from speculation."

Luke went over the other two suspects Riley was considering – Fr.

Francis Broussard and Mark David Reed. "We don't have much of anything on either one of them. I've not even been able to verify that they were here in Little Rock when Rob was killed. Riley said Mark has been showing up at the scene when the body was found. I'm heading to the newspaper now."

"Let me make some calls about the priest. I've got some inroads into the handful of Catholic churches in the area. I assume he'd maybe check in with one of them if he were in town." Captain Meadows made a note and then raised his eyes to Luke. "You need anything before going to New Orleans? You should call the police department down there and let them know you're tracking someone. You don't have any jurisdiction down there."

"I made the call this morning and let them know. I reached out to Det. Elio who Cooper is working with. He said he'd tuck the info away for now because the less his boss knows the better." Luke hadn't been sure he liked working that way, but Det. Elio insisted. He and Captain Meadows spoke for a few more minutes and then Luke left for the newspaper office.

*The Democrat-Gazette* was the last remaining print newspaper in the city. There was a society magazine and alternative paper but only one with a crime beat that would have covered the scene. Luke was grateful for that. He had already placed a call to the three local news stations and asked for their footage so they could check for Mark David Reed. It seemed like such a long shot to Luke.

The newspaper office was a few blocks away from the police station heading away from the river and farther into the city. He walked instead of driving because parking would be a nightmare mid-day. At the front desk, Luke flashed his badge and was told that the man he was looking for, Jeb Turner, was on the third floor and the last office on the left. He'd have all the photographs of the scene.

Luke found the office and knocked once. A muffled voice yelled back to enter. Luke found a young guy in his twenties with a mouthful of chocolate and a mess of wrappers across his desk. "Jeb Turner?"

The young man, with blond hair that didn't seem to want to stay in one place, waved Luke in. He pulled a can of soda off his desk, drank a long gulp, and then laughed self-consciously. "I'm hungover and in desperate need of a sugar rush."

Luke gestured toward the desk. "I'd say you're headed for a sugar overdose." Luke remembered those days, but his go-to was never sugar. It was strong coffee and pancakes from a local diner near his college.

Jeb rubbed his head. "I'm feeling about as good as I'm going to get. You said when you called you wanted to see photos of the scene when the body was found in the river last weekend, right?"

Luke had called ahead, hoping everything would be ready for him to go through. "That's correct. I'm looking for one individual in particular in the crowd. I don't know that he'll be there, so it might be looking for a needle in a haystack. I've requested footage from the local news station that we'll comb through at the station later."

"That's good," Jeb said absently as he clicked his fingers across the keyboard. "I have an entire file right here for you. I can spin my laptop around for you or you can drag that chair over here and we can go through it together."

Luke opted for going on Jeb's side of the desk for easier access. When he sat down, he asked, "How many photos do you have?"

"About fifty," Jeb said, moving over and pulling the laptop closer so Luke would have a better view. He brought up the first in the series of photos. "It was so late that night and dark that there weren't that many people around. The ones who were milling around were fairly drunk and didn't seem to care what was going on. It wasn't much of a scene. Also, no one knew what was happening only that there was a body in the water. At that point, even that was speculation. I don't want to say people didn't care…but they didn't care." He added a shrug for good measure.

Luke reached for his phone and showed Jeb the photo of Mark David Reed. "This is the guy we are looking for. It might be hard to spot him in the crowd. I've heard at other scenes that he wore a Chicago Cubs hat."

Jeb snapped his fingers. "That guy is here, man. I saw him." He started advancing through the photos so quickly that it was starting to make Luke dizzy. "I have a hat just like it that's why I noticed it. It's even got that same worn tired look as my hat. It's my favorite though and no way I'm getting rid of it."

While he was scrolling, there was a flash of a person Luke wanted to see. "Stop scrolling and go back a few photos."

"It's not him," Jeb insisted but scrolled back a few photos until Luke told him to stop. "See, he's not there."

"No," Luke said and indeed Jeb was right. The photo didn't show Mark David Reed, but it did show Ned Shaw standing in the back of the crowd looking on. His features were tight and he seemed concerned about what was happening. Luke couldn't see what Shaw was looking at, but whatever it was had him worried or scared. Luke didn't know the man well enough to read everything on his face. What the photo showed more than anything was that Shaw was there that night, confirming Pete's statement and Riley's suspicion. "I'll need you to print me that photo."

"Is that who I think it is?" Jeb asked, leaning toward the laptop.

Luke pointed to the man. "Ned Shaw. He's the detective who is claiming all the drownings are connected to someone he calls the Cross Killers. He said that either where the bodies go in the water or where they are found, there is cross graffiti. That's what connects the cases."

"I know who he is." Jeb stared over at him. "Are they connected?

That seems like a big leap, but I just take photos. I don't solve crimes."

"That's what we are trying to find out." Luke gestured toward the laptop screen. "Advance to the photo you said is the Cubs hat guy."

Jeb did as Luke asked even though he appeared to have many more questions. When he got to the photo, Jeb pointed to the computer screen. "Right here. That's him." He advanced through four more photos. "He was there a while looking on. Then this last photo shows him walking away." When he got to the end, Jeb scrolled back to the beginning of that series of photos.

Luke glanced down at the photo of Mark David Reed on his phone and then back up at the laptop. It was indeed him. "Print those for me, too."

Jeb brought up each photo and then hit print, sending the photo file to a large color printer sitting on a table across the room. While he went through each of the photos, he didn't stop talking. Most of what he was saying – Cubs stats, the weather, hangover cures – Luke didn't care about. When he mentioned Shaw, Luke paid attention.

Jeb glanced over at Luke. "You know a friend of mine had some contact with Shaw about a month ago. He got this weird email from him, asking for his help on the drowning cases. I only found this out after they found Rob's body. My friend thought it was a scam so he didn't respond."

Luke remembered what Cooper had told him about the victim in New Orleans. "What does your friend do?"

"He graduated from law school last year but hasn't found his groove yet in a law firm. He's had two jobs and quit both. He's been tending bar most nights."

The hairs on Luke's arm stood on end and he fought the shiver that ran up his spine. "Does he still have the email?"

"No. He thought it was a scam. What does he know about solving a murder? He deleted it and then ignored the next two that came in."

"There was more than one?"

Jeb nodded. "Shaw was persistent, but he didn't account for my friend's utter laziness and lack of desire to work a criminal case." He got up and gathered up the photos from the printer and handed them to Luke.

Luke thanked him for the information and said, "Tell your friend to call me. He made a good choice not responding to that email. It's probably why he's still alive today."

He left Jeb standing there with his mouth agape and a confused expression on his face.

# CHAPTER 28

Even though Luke and Cooper were thousands of miles away from me, it still felt like we were working the cases together. We had a way to share information and leads and then use them to connect the cases. Luke left Little Rock knowing that both Shaw and Mark David Reed were in Little Rock at the time of Rob's murder.

On his drive to New Orleans, Captain Meadows had called with the surprising news that Fr. Frank had been in Little Rock the previous weekend. He had been visiting a local Catholic parish but was notably absent for most of the weekend. He had shown up at the rectory for dinner on Friday night. Then left and wasn't seen or heard from again for the rest of the weekend, even when the local priest had tried to contact him. As Luke recounted the details to me, I was reminded of the eerily similar story my mother had told me about Fr. Frank's visit to Troy.

We now had solid confirmation that all three men were in New Orleans, Troy, and Little Rock at the time of the murders. We had no information connecting them to each other and flimsy evidence connecting them directly to the victims. We knew for sure that Danny knew Fr. Frank and we had confirmation that Shaw had been contacting the victims and meeting with them before the murders. We also knew Trevor had written Shaw's name on the floor before he was murdered.

Based on information Luke received at the newspaper office about Jeb's friend being contacted by Shaw via email, we were going to unspool that thread until we unraveled the whole sweater. That was our only working theory based on what we knew right now.

Miles was still in the process of trying to convince the medical examiner to change his findings, so he could convince his captain to formally reopen the case. By five, when he finished work for the day, he still hadn't made much progress.

I was on my way to Trevor's apartment to meet with his former roommate, Evan, to ask some questions. Unfortunately, no one seemed to know where Trevor's laptop had gone. Miles said he hadn't taken it as evidence and his parents didn't have it. I had been hoping to go through it to search for emails and saved documents that might connect him to Shaw. That would have to wait for now.

I found Trevor's apartment with relative ease. It was a three-family house common for Troy. I double-checked the address Miles had provided me and noted Trevor had lived in the first-floor flat. I had called Evan ahead of time to make sure that he'd be home this evening. He said he'd be there any time after five and it was nearing six. I wanted to give him enough time to get home and comfortable.

I walked up the few steps to the porch and knocked on the first-floor screen door. The main door was slightly ajar but the screen was locked. A dog barked loudly and someone inside told him to quiet down. A moment later, a young man in his early twenties came to the door with a gray and white boxer right behind him. The dog stared up at me the way dogs do, assessing if I was a friend or foe. When his tail started whipping back and forth, I knew I had passed the test.

I introduced myself and then asked, "Is he friendly?"

"Very. I'm Evan." He unlocked the screen door and held it open for me before I could respond. "Bruno will jump on you if you let him.

Just nudge him with your knee and he'll stop."

I stepped into his flat and Bruno jumped as high as he could to reach me. I didn't have the heart to make him stop. I scratched him behind the ears while I told him what a good boy he was. Eventually, he found his way back to putting all four paws on the floor and let me pass into the house.

As I entered a small room with a chair and bookshelf and desk in the corner, I turned back to Evan. "Thanks for meeting with me. I only have a few questions and won't take up too much of your time."

"It's okay." He gestured toward the front of the flat. "Let's sit in the living room and we can talk. I don't know what I can tell you that I haven't already told Det. Ward. Trevor and I were best friends for years. I wish I had gone to the bar with him that night, but I was at work."

"What do you do?" I asked as I sat down on a well-worn couch. Bruno rested his head on my leg. I petted him as we talked.

"I work for a company doing some computer programming. That's what Trevor was studying to do as well. I finished my master's a couple of years ago and Trevor was in the same program when he died."

I went through the normal questions – enemies, friends, threats, and such. Nothing seemed out of the ordinary or any different than what Evan had told Miles earlier. Evan seemed relaxed and comfortable, not like he was holding anything back or lying. There was no reason to. Miles had already confirmed that Evan was working that night and his alibi was rock solid. He wasn't under any suspicion and had cooperated with the investigation.

When it came to the real reason for my visit, I sat up straighter and locked my gaze on him. "Do you know anything about emails Trevor may have received leading up to his death?"

Evan raised his eyebrows. "Could you be more specific?"

I could but I didn't want to. I wanted the information unprompted and didn't want to lead him into telling me what I wanted to hear. "Before Trevor's death, did he say anything to you about strange emails he might have received? Anything at all, even if it doesn't seem particularly relevant to the situation?"

Evan pinched the bridge of his nose and he looked poised to ask me another question. I didn't think that he was being difficult or evasive. The look on his face told me he was trying to do the mental math of what I was asking – how what he knew might factor into my investigation. Finally, he leaned forward slightly. "Trevor had been contacted about a job that he didn't want."

Now it was my turn. "What does that mean?"

"Someone had contacted him about doing some computer work and he wasn't interested. There was a part of him that felt compelled to help." Evan sat back and watched me absorb the information.

I wasn't done with my questions so easily. "Was that computer work legal?"

"That was a question Trevor asked me." He raised his shoulders as if to shrug but he remained frozen like that for a moment. "I thought it was odd he asked *me*."

"Why was that?" I asked.

"Because the man who asked him for the favor was a cop or used to be. If anyone would have known the legality, it should have been him." Before I could respond, Evan got up and went to the back of the flat out of sight. I sat with Bruno and waited. Evan came back carrying a slip of paper. He handed it to me and sat down. "Read that and tell me what you think."

I lowered my eyes and read an email from Ned Shaw, who had used a free email provider and his name as the address. In the body of the email, he introduced himself and explained an overview of his Cross Killers case. He asked Trevor for help analyzing some chat room conversations. Shaw noted that he had heard Trevor was good at that kind of thing, and it was crucial to his investigation. Several lines were intended to guilt trip Trevor for not helping. The communication said that Shaw would pay for Trevor's time and that he'd be in touch to arrange a meeting.

When I was done reading, I rested the page on my lap and looked up at Evan. "Did Trevor meet with him?"

Evan shook his head. "We didn't believe Shaw had sent this. We knew who Shaw was because I had seen the television special about the Cross Killers. If you've seen Shaw in action, you know he's cocky as all get out. There was no way he was asking some lowly grad student for his help to solve the case, particularly given that he was a detective and had real experts that could help. How did he even find Trevor? He's listed on his work website, but he's never been a hacker or someone who did that kind of work. It didn't make sense to either of us."

I had been so focused on why and how Shaw was guilty that I had overlooked that part of his personality. He wouldn't readily admit that he needed help from anyone. Sure, he could use this method to seek out victims, but wouldn't there be an easier way for him? That was the question that needed to be considered.

Evan was staring at me waiting for a response.

"What did Trevor do with the email?"

"We wrote back and pretended to be interested." Evan's face transitioned from fully confident to a bit unsure. "We wanted to see who was emailing him, so we said that we'd meet. The plan was for both of us to be at the location, but Trevor got a text that night when I was at work and he ended up going alone. I didn't realize that's what had happened until a few weeks after he was found in the river."

I didn't understand. "Wouldn't you have thought of that right away?"

Evan shook his head. "That night Trevor told me that he was going to the pub to watch football. It hadn't even occurred to me that he'd try to meet this guy alone. After we responded to the email, we never heard back again in email or text. We had given the person Trevor's phone number, but we never heard from him. We both brushed it off thinking it had been a prank. Trevor never told me that the guy contacted him."

"You now think that's what happened? You think Trevor went to the pub to meet the guy that night?"

"I do." The corners of Evan's eyes grew watery and it was clear he was carrying guilt about what had happened to his friend. "He shouldn't have gone alone. That wasn't the plan. Maybe he did it to protect me. I feel terrible that I wasn't there."

I glanced down at the email again. "How do you know that's what Trevor did? He could have gone to watch football as he said."

"I don't think so. Another friend of ours was going to another bar and Trevor didn't want to go with him. He said he was meeting someone. I know everyone Trevor knows and no one was meeting him that night. Who else could it have been?"

My heart rate quickened. "Did Det. Ward know about this email?"

"I tried to tell him. He didn't want to hear it at the time. The case was already closed. He said he'd be in touch but that never happened."

I held out the page with the email. "Am I the first person who knows about this email?"

"That can do anything about it. As I said, I tried to tell Det. Ward. He wouldn't listen." Evan had uncertainty on his face as if he was remembering something. "I don't know if this matters, but we told our friends about the email. Trevor and I talked about it one night at the pub. We joked that if Shaw thought Trevor could trace some messages in a chat room then he was smart enough to trace the email. We mentioned to our friends that we were sure it wasn't Shaw sending those messages and we were going to find out who was really the sender."

"How long was this before Trevor died?"

"Thursday night right before it happened."

Hearing that, it fell into place for me. All the unanswered questions about why Trevor hadn't been killed right away. The reason he had been held and tortured, unlike every other case. "You threatened the killer," I said softly, the words escaping my mouth before I realized it.

There was a flash of recognition on Evan's face. "You think that conversation got Trevor killed?"

I shook my head. "I think his email was intended to lure Trevor to the pub and he would have been killed if he showed up. Whoever agreed to help the killer would have been killed. I'm talking about why Trevor was held before he was killed."

There was a flash of fear on Evan's face. "What do you mean held?"

Our find earlier that day hadn't made the news yet. I explained to Evan what we found in the abandoned building. "There was always a question why Trevor's body hadn't moved at all with the flow of the river if he drowned around midnight. It hadn't made sense to Det. Ward. That's ultimately what brought me here to investigate. Now we know that he had been taken to a building and was possibly killed there." I still didn't know that for sure, but it was a solid assumption that Evan didn't need to know right now. Not until it was confirmed.

"Do you think the killer overheard our conversation that night?" Evan didn't wait for me to respond. He continued almost as if talking to himself about the mistake they had made. "We were loud about it, not worried who was hearing us. We thought it was a prank. Trevor wanted to talk about it thinking it was one of our other friends who was pranking him. It's why he made the joke about tracing the email back to the sender."

"Were you planning to do that?"

"We tried and it came back to a coffee shop in downtown Troy. They have free Wi-Fi. The sender could have been anyone."

I reached for my phone, knocking Bruno's head off my lap. He stared up at me with sad dark eyes and then lay on the floor. "Sorry, buddy," I murmured as I scrolled through my phone. I stood and walked across the room and showed Evan two photos. "The night you were discussing the email in the bar, did you see either of these two people?"

Evan glanced down at the phone but shook his head. "I don't know them. I know Shaw wasn't in the bar that night. I would have recognized him. We would have just walked up and asked if he had sent the email."

That's what I suspected. I slid my phone back into my pocket and asked if I could keep the email. "I promise I'll return it."

"Do whatever you have to do," Evan assured me. "I have other copies if I need them."

I asked him for copies of other communication with Shaw and he provided me what he had. I thanked him and left, feeling a tiny bit closer to knowing the truth, with an obvious glaring fact – I still didn't know who had killed Trevor.

# CHAPTER 29

ooper sat at the bar in a French Quarter restaurant sipping beer and eating the best gumbo he'd ever tasted. The day hadn't gone quite as planned. He hadn't seen Clive since the night before when Cooper went over the evidence file. Clive had landed another homicide investigation, unrelated to their case, and he was hard at work on that. He wasn't going to be able to have much more time to help Cooper. It seemed he was on his own until Luke arrived, which would only be in a few hours. Luke hadn't made it out of Little Rock quite as early as he had planned. Nearing midnight was his estimated time of arrival, so that left Cooper with the night on his own. He planned to eat dinner and then head down to the area where Danny was seen arguing with the man to get a sense of it in the dark.

Cooper had spent the day tracking down the handful of witnesses Clive had interviewed right after Danny's body had been found. He also met with Danny's parents. None of the meetings yielded further information. Cooper didn't know any more than he had the night before after speaking with Fr. Lundy.

Danny was last seen on St. Ann Street on the eastern side of St. Louis Cathedral running back toward the river. That was it, the last known sighting Cooper could find. He had spent the day canvassing all the businesses in that area to see if anyone had seen Danny that night. Nothing. Not one credible sighting. But Cooper knew Danny had ended up back toward the river and was murdered.

After three phone calls and nearly begging the man, George had finally provided all the evidence the newspaper had collected on Shaw and Mark David Reed. Even though George had told Cooper he had the evidence, he was still surprised to see each of the scene photos with Mark in them wearing the same Chicago Cubs hat. Cooper was fairly certain that had Mark not worn the cap in every photo, he might not have been so easily recognizable.

Cooper was left with one main question. *Did he want to be seen?*

Mark might have thought the hat would shield him and provide him some anonymity. In the end, it made him stand out more.

Cooper had left messages for all of George's sources who had information on Shaw. Not one person had answered or called him back yet. He wasn't sure they ever would. It hadn't stopped the case from progressing though.

After Luke had gathered the photos from the *Democrat-Gazette*, he had gone back to his office and ran a background check on Reed. The man had no priors and not even so much as a speeding ticket. The only question Luke had was the man's photo in the system didn't look exactly like the professional photo on LinkedIn. It wasn't too dissimilar, but it had given Luke pause. Cooper chalked it up to an old license photo and one that was done professionally.

Cooper knew Mark's presence at each of the drownings couldn't have been a coincidence. One or two and maybe even three he could twist himself into believing was a coincidence. Definitely not all eight even if he had a legitimate reason for being in each of those cities at the time. While it looked compelling, Cooper knew it was a flimsy case against the man.

As he ate, Cooper's thoughts drifted back to Shaw. The evidence had mounted against the man enough that Luke was coming to New Orleans to interview him. Riley might have been right about him all along.

"We need to talk," a male voice said, drawing Cooper's attention to his left. Fr. Frank pulled out the bar stool and sat down without being invited. He ordered a stout from the bartender and threw a five-dollar bill down on the bar. "You've been asking about me."

There had been an obvious demeanor shift in the man. He was no longer dressed in a black shirt and pants and he had no white collar at the neck. He had on a basic blue button-down shirt with the sleeves rolled up and a pair of faded jeans. If Cooper hadn't met him previously, he'd have no idea he was a priest.

"How'd you find me?" he asked, tension rising in his voice. Cooper was tired of the priest tracking his every move. First his hotel room and now the restaurant.

Fr. Frank didn't respond. Instead, he demanded, "Why are you asking about me? There are things at play here you don't understand."

Cooper turned his head back to his beer and took a sip, purposefully slowing the conversation down. If the priest was going to stalk him, things were going to go at Cooper's pace. "Enlighten me then, Fr. Frank. I'd think given your relationship with Danny that you'd want to know who killed him. Unless…" Cooper didn't finish the sentence. He just let the words hang.

Fr. Frank didn't deny the unspoken accusation nor did he confirm it. "As I said, there are bigger things at play here and you're in the way. I'd watch your back if I were you."

Cooper bent forward and scooped gumbo into his mouth. "Have you had their gumbo? It's the best I've had."

Fr. Frank crashed his fist into the bar top, startling other patrons. He lowered his voice to a low growl. "Go back to Little Rock and let me handle things."

Cooper finally turned his head to look him square in the face. "What exactly are you *handling*? You were in each of the cities when there was a drowning." He watched the priest's face register a moment of shock before returning to normal. "That's right. I know your secret. I have confirmation that you were there in Little Rock and unaccounted for. The same in Troy and the other cities."

That wasn't technically true. Cooper hadn't been able to confirm Fr. Frank was in the other cities other than Troy and Little Rock. He couldn't even confirm that Fr. Frank was in New Orleans the night Danny died. All Cooper knew for sure was that Fr. Frank had lied about where he was going. For now, Cooper would bluff his way through.

"You're in over your head. I'm not going to warn you again – stay out of my way." Fr. Frank downed half the beer in one gulp and then slammed the glass into the bar top with such force that Cooper was surprised the glass hadn't shattered. Fr. Frank jabbed an index finger toward him as he growled one last warning. "I don't want to hurt you, but I will if you get in my way. Tell me right now you're leaving New Orleans."

"I won't lie to a priest," Cooper said evenly, trying to show no reaction. "It must be hard to deal with these drownings after what happened to your nephew."

Fr. Frank got up from the bar stool, his anger simmering near the surface. For a moment, Cooper thought Fr. Frank might hit him. He didn't. Instead, he got low to Cooper's ear and growled a final warning. "Then your fate is sealed." Fr. Frank strode out of the bar as quickly as he had arrived, leaving Cooper stunned and confused.

"Did you skip mass last weekend?" the bartender joked with him as he grabbed the cash and the half-empty glass. "What did you do?"

Cooper expelled a breath. "I'm not sure." It took him a few moments to compose himself as he sat there with his beer and food still in front of him. Someone had told Fr. Frank that he'd been asking about him. It could have been Fr. Lundy who told him that they had met the night before. It felt like games were being played and Cooper hadn't been given the rulebook.

Cooper waited until the bartender walked back toward him. "Do you know much about Fr. Frank?"

The bartender leaned back against the counter and tossed a dishtowel over his shoulder. "I was an altar boy. I've known him for a long time. That flare of temper you just witnessed is something I've seen more than a few times."

Cooper had been directly threatened. "Have you ever seen Fr. Frank hurt anyone?"

"With words, yes. I've seen several kids cry with one of his verbal dressing downs. His secretary has been known to shed a few tears. For a while, the church went through a new secretary every six months because of Fr. Frank's behavior. This one has stuck it out the longest." The bartender shifted against the counter and folded his arms. "I've never really seen Fr. Frank physically hurt anyone before. I was a kid when Fr. Frank was a young associate priest here. He grabbed one of my friends by the arm and dragged him out of the church for screwing up something during mass. I don't even remember what it was now, so it couldn't have been that important. Nothing more than that though."

Cooper took in all the information, trying to process it. Fear crept in around him and he felt like his thoughts were veering to the irrational.

The bartender pushed forward from the bar and stood upright. "Do you think Fr. Frank hurt someone?"

"I don't know," Cooper responded. He had no proof. Cooper took a moment to explain why he was there and the case he was investigating. "Fr. Frank is giving me some strange vibes. That's all I can say. You saw him react in here tonight. There's more than I know going on. His demeanor was completely different than it was yesterday."

The man nodded his head. "That's that Jekyll and Hyde thing he does.

It took my parents a while to see it when I was younger. Once they did, they stopped me from being an altar boy and switched churches."

Cooper didn't want to mince words. "Do you think he's capable of killing someone?"

"Aren't we all capable of killing someone under the right circumstance?" he asked and let the question linger. Then he went on. "Fr. Frank is stronger than he looks and he's got a temper. There's no saying what he could do if he snapped while he was alone with someone. Under the right circumstance, I'd say anything is possible."

That's what Cooper had thought. He pulled out his wallet, put enough money down to cover the tab and a generous tip, and thanked him for the information. He headed toward the door but stopped at the threshold, waiting for a moment before stepping outside. Cooper had several blocks to walk back to his hotel and a sense of concern hung heavy over him.

He patted the gun at his hip tucked slightly under his long Henley shirt. Someone paying attention would notice the gun, but most on the streets wouldn't notice at all. The scene was loud as if life exploded before his eyes. Music filled the streets and people milled about in groups holding plastic cups branded with local establishments. The smell was a cologne of booze, body heat, and the desperation of bad decisions.

Cooper waited until a group of young boys, probably not older than Danny and his friends, moved past and then he stepped out onto the sidewalk. He didn't make it far when a group of three young women blocked his path. The middle woman, who Cooper didn't think was even drinking age, smiled up at him and swayed. She reached a hand out to touch his chest. He stepped back in time, just out of reach.

She pouted. "Where are you going all alone?" she asked, her words a jumble. "Come and party with us. We'll have a good time. I promise!" Then she and her friends broke into a fit of drunken giggles.

Cooper didn't bother responding, he kept it moving. The sooner he could make it back to the hotel the better he'd feel. He wasn't even going to walk down toward the river where Danny had died. Not tonight and not alone.

As another group of young women approached, Cooper moved off the sidewalk onto the road to give them a wide berth. With his head lowered to look at the ground and make sure he didn't trip, he smacked square into a man about his height. Cooper reached out to steady himself, grabbing the man's canvas jacket.

"Sorry," he said as he stepped to the right so the man could maneuver around him.

The man sidestepped, mumbling, "No problem." Then hurried on his way, keeping his head bent low. Cooper thought it odd to be wearing a jacket this time of year. His light shirt was warm enough for the late October evening.

Cooper started to walk off but a flash of memory made him stop. It wasn't the man's jacket that made Cooper stop. It was the man's hat – faded Chicago Cubs.

At that moment, Cooper was sure it was Mark David Reed. He hesitated in the street as people brushed past him. Cooper raised up on his toes, trying to get a line of sight above the crowd to see in which direction Mark went. Cooper couldn't see him, but he wasn't going to give up that easily.

He stepped around a group of people and moved through the crowd in pursuit, dodging and weaving as he went. Everything got quiet for Cooper, the sound of the streets dulled in comparison to his thoughts of finding and trailing the man.

Up ahead, he caught a flash of the cap and kept his eyes focused on the top of the man's head as he turned to the right, heading down a side street. Cooper looked behind him but didn't see anyone following him. There was still the looming threat of Fr. Frank. Not seeing anyone,

Cooper quickened his pace pushing his way through the crowd of people. At the street where Mark turned, Cooper was hot on his heels. He kept groups of people between them as a buffer but followed through several turns and down streets and across others.

Cooper wasn't sure where the man was headed. He didn't stop at any bars or restaurants. He didn't interact with any people. He kept his head low, the hat pulled down over his forehead, and his hands shoved into the pockets of his jacket.

Cooper kept his pursuit at a safe distance until all at once he lost sight of the man in the crowd. It was like he vanished right in front of him. Cooper walked a few more feet and then stopped. He turned right and then left but no one. He jogged past the place where Mark was last seen and then stopped and spun around in a full circle, not believing he could have lost him as people continued to brush past him.

Cooper expelled a frustrated breath and reached for his phone. It was then the dread loomed over him. He knew he'd made a grave mistake. The blade of the knife cut through the fabric of his shirt with ease, piercing the skin of his abdomen. He lurched forward as the blade was removed and plunged back in again.

Cooper grabbed for his assailant and raked a finger down his hand. As Cooper fell to the ground, he clutched the blood gushing from his middle, unnoticed by those around him. He raised his head and met the coldest eyes Cooper had ever seen. He tried to fight against the searing pain to stand back up but more blood gushed from him, rendering him immobile.

Mark leaned down, putting his face inches from Cooper. "You've been warned," was all he said before righting himself and fleeing into the crowd of people.

# CHAPTER 30

After meeting with Evan, I went directly to Miles's house to tell him about the interview and question him about the information I received. I found him in the kitchen making himself a late dinner. He had no idea about the email and I believed him.

"I swear, Riley. I didn't know anything about this. I would have followed up. I know Evan said he had more information for me right as the case closed and he said he'd call me. When he didn't call, I assumed he had changed his mind." Miles sat hunched over his plate at a small kitchen table and read the email again. "What do you think this means?"

I jabbed a finger down on the page. "I believe this is how the killer is choosing his victims. I spoke to Luke and he heard something similar from the photographer at the newspaper. He told him that a friend also received an email like this but ignored it. I have a feeling the killer is using this ruse to target young men in the area. If someone bites, then he gets their phone number and lures them out."

"How many emails do you think he's sending in one location? How's he finding them?"

"I don't know," I said honestly. I didn't have all the answers. I hadn't even been convinced of anything until Luke said he had heard something similar. Then I knew this had to be it. "Enough that he gets a bite. That says to me he's scouting the locations ahead of time. He's maybe in the area long before the murder and knows the river areas. Luke said Rob was dragged into the water and drowned. We know Trevor had a different experience. Did you hear anything from the medical examiner?"

Miles dropped the slip of paper to the table. "I spoke to him right before I left for the day. If it hadn't been so late, I would have called you. He luckily still had a sample from Trevor's lungs. He found it's not water from the Hudson River."

"How can he tell?" I still didn't understand the science behind it.

"Minerals and bacteria and such that's commonly found in the water sources. He tested a sample of river water against what was in Trevor's lungs and it didn't match." Miles sat back and looked over at me, his eyes tired. "He said it's not routine to do that test. I don't know if I believe him or not. They wanted this case closed as an accident from the start."

"It seems that way with all of them."

Miles yawned and covered his mouth. "You were right, Riley. He was killed elsewhere. Most likely in the abandoned building. I got the crime scene techs out there as soon as I got permission. I'm sure they will be working well into the night. I only came home to take a break and eat. I might go back to the site."

"What about Trevor's cellphone records? Was someone asking him to meet that night?"

"We only got phone numbers and not the text content. I would have requested that information had the case not been closed. I can't do it now unless they reopen the case." Miles sat back, frustrated with himself.

"You need some sleep." I wanted to leave so he could do that.

He asked, "Do you think it's Shaw? Would he be dumb enough to leave a trail of evidence like that?"

"I don't know what to think. Evan made a good point that Shaw wouldn't ask for help – real help or even pretend. His ego wouldn't allow it. I tend to agree with that. If Shaw wanted to dupe someone, there are easier ways without leaving an email evidence trail. He had to know the cops would find it."

Miles opened his eyes wide. "We didn't find it. You did. If you hadn't gotten involved, we wouldn't have known. Maybe Shaw was counting on that. He knows these drowning cases are dead in the water, no pun intended, once he gets involved. That might be his cover."

"It's possible…" I trailed off because I didn't know if that was probable. I had only ever argued with Shaw. We had butted heads the moment we met. I had never given the man a chance to sit down and talk rationally. For as much as I knew about him, there was a lot more I didn't.

I stood and pushed in my chair. "Get some sleep and check in with the crime scene techs in the morning. You need rest more than you need to go to the scene and hover."

Miles chuckled and ran a hand through his hair. "You're right about that." He got up to let me out. At the door, he lingered for a moment. "I appreciate you coming up here to help with this case. I didn't realize the evidence was right under our noses."

"Sometimes it happens that way. Fresh eyes can do wonders for a case. Hopefully, we can get it solved now." The heat of the chemistry we once shared still lingered between us. I stepped back unsure of what to do. "Have a good night," I said awkwardly and then turned to leave. As I walked to my car, I looked back to see Miles still standing there. He waved once and then closed the door when I was safely in my car.

I sat outside his house for a few moments, not feeling ready to go home. I texted Liv who hadn't made it back home for dinner that night. She responded almost immediately and asked me to meet her at the pub for a beer. That I could do.

Twenty minutes later, we sat at a booth in the front dining section of the pub with a cherry raspberry ale in front of each of us. "What has you so busy? You're never home."

"Real estate." Liv smiled above the rim of her glass as she took a sip. "I know that sounds completely boring and not something you'd ever imagine me doing, but I got my real estate license. I've been selling houses for a few months. I didn't even tell Mom and Jack what I'm doing. I wanted to make sure I liked it and would be successful at it before I told anyone. I didn't want it to be one more thing I tried and failed." She giggled to herself as she said it, but there was sadness in her voice.

"No one thinks you're a failure," I told her with sincerity. "It takes some people longer than others to figure out their passion. If you found it, I'm happy for you."

Liv raised her glass and toasted us. She took a sip and set her glass down on the table. "How's married life?"

"Fabulous. We both work a lot right now, but we enjoy our time together."

"Any kids in your future?"

I nodded even though I wasn't sure. Luke wanted children more than I did. I wasn't opposed, but it was taking me longer to come around to the idea. "What about you?"

Liv looked off to the side and then leaned into the table. "I froze some eggs just in case."

"I assume Mom doesn't know." I couldn't believe my sister had made such a grown-up decision without talking to me. There was a time when Liv and I told each other everything.

"She doesn't know. I didn't want her to talk me out of it or be involved." Liv chewed on her bottom lip. "It doesn't mean I'm going to do anything about it. Insurance policy, I guess."

"Be proud of your decision, Liv. Who cares what Mom thinks? She can't live your life for you. If you want kids now or later, it's important to take the right steps and it seems like you are."

Liv stared past me. I couldn't quite read the expression on her face. At first, I thought she was lost in thought about having to tell our mother she had frozen some eggs. Quickly, I realized that wasn't it. She pointed over my shoulder toward the window that looked out onto the sidewalk.

"Isn't that Ned Shaw?"

"I doubt it. He told me he's in New Orleans." Liv urged me to turn around. There he was pacing a path in front of the pub. I cursed under my breath. I turned back to my sister. "I need to go talk to him."

"Hurry back," she called as I got up from the table and marched toward the door.

I stepped out into the cold night air, my temper burning. "What are you doing here? You said you were in New Orleans."

Shaw took a few steps toward me and looked into the window at my sister. He grabbed me by my upper arm. I jerked back out of his grip. "Riley, I need to talk to you. That's why I'm here. I never made it to New Orleans."

"Were you ever planning to go or was that a lie to throw me off your track?"

Shaw stared down at me with his beady eyes. "We need to get out of here. I need your help."

I wasn't going anywhere with him. "You need my help like you needed Trevor's help and all those other young men you drowned?"

Shaw stepped back, seeming confused by what I said. He shook his head in disbelief. "I didn't drown anyone. What do you mean like I needed their help?" When I didn't say anything, Shaw balled his hands into fists and cursed at me. "I don't have time to play around with you. We don't like each other, fine. Someone is trying to set me up. You need to tell me what you know."

I held firm because I knew he was lying. He knew more than he was saying. "I'm not sharing any information with you."

He wasn't deterred. Shaw pointed toward the abandoned buildings where there was a line of police vehicles still parked out front. "You can start with what they are doing."

"That's police business and not something I'm at liberty to share with you."

Shaw lunged for me and grabbed me by the arm – hard enough to leave a bruise. "You need to come with me to New Orleans." He started to pull me toward the parking lot.

I wrenched my arm free of him. "Don't ever grab me like that again!" I yelled so loudly other people on the street turned to look at us. I turned back to see Liv grab Chris and head toward the door. "My sister is coming with the bar owner. You need to tell me what is going on before I report you." It was a veiled threat. He hadn't done anything more than grab me. No cop in the world would take that report. I stood my ground even when Liv and Chris stepped out onto the sidewalk.

"Riley, are you okay?" he asked, looking between Shaw and me. "Come inside with me. Shaw, you need to calm down and take a walk."

Shaw was right on the edge of talking. I could feel it. "Shaw, if you want to speak to me like a rational person, then let's go inside the bar and we can talk. Liv can go hang out at the bar and wait for me."

"You can use the upstairs if you want," Chris offered. "That area of the dining room is closed tonight. You'll have all the privacy you need." He went back inside with Liv and let us continue our conversation. Chris remained in the front window watching us.

Shaw's face contorted not in anger but fear. I saw it clearly now – he was afraid of something. "I don't know that I can help you, but I'm willing to try. Let's go in and talk."

Shaw seemed to debate with himself for several moments. Then he gave up, and without saying a word, moved past me and went into the pub. I followed right behind him and thanked Chris as we walked past. Shaw headed right past the empty hostess desk and up the flight of stairs.

Once we were up there, he grabbed a chair, spun it around, and straddled it, resting his arms on the back. "You tell me what you know and then I'll tell you what I know."

I sat at a chair across the table from him. Even scared he was going to play hardball. "It looks like you're drowning these young men. You are in these cities when they get separated from their friends and drown. Before it even makes the news, you're calling local law enforcement and offering help – which you know by now only shuts down the investigations."

"Do you have evidence of this?"

I wasn't giving more away. "We have enough evidence to make you a person of interest."

He nodded his head. "You're not going to believe me."

"Try me."

Shaw tapped his hand against the back of the chair. Almost too casually, he said, "I'm being set up." He might have thought I'd have an immediate response because he paused for a long time. When I said nothing, he went on. "These young men contacted me and told me they had information about the Cross Killers cases. When I was finally able to get their phone numbers after going back and forth in email, I agreed to meet them in person because that's the only way they'd meet. None of them ever showed, but…"

"Let me guess, it was on the nights they died."

Shaw blinked rapidly at me. "How'd you know?"

"Because the killer is luring them the same way." I explained to Shaw about the emails the young men were receiving. "Trevor assumed it wasn't you but was determined to figure out who it was. I assume the killer is using several burner phones and email addresses to pull off the ruse." There was something I didn't understand. "Why keep trying to meet when you knew they were dying when you were in the city?"

"After the second time, I knew I was communicating with the killer. I knew I was being set up and I was trying to figure out who he was. He never gave me enough information about the victims to find them and warn them. I've been trying to stop it."

"Why didn't you tell the cops?" I asked the question and he didn't respond. I knew why. It was twofold – he wanted to be the one to catch the killer and he was afraid they'd arrest him if they found out the truth. It disgusted me. "Why were you trying to get me to New Orleans?"

"I believe that's where he lives." When I pressed for information about what he knew, Shaw said nothing. He stood from the chair suddenly. "Will you come with me?"

"I don't know that we will get a flight that easily and it's a long drive." That was the least of my concern. Luke and Cooper would object to me going anywhere with Shaw. Not to mention, I still didn't trust him and didn't *want* to go anywhere with Shaw.

"I have access to a private plane," he said not missing a beat.

Against my better judgment and instinct, I stood from my chair. "I'll meet you in the morning at the airport at six."

# CHAPTER 31

Luke had just passed a sign that said ten miles to the French Quarter when his dash lit up to alert him that there was an incoming call. The ringing overtook the soft rock he had playing in the background. He glanced over at a number he did not recognize and clicked the button to engage.

"Det. Luke Morgan?" a woman asked.

"Yes. Can I help you?"

She said her name but Luke forgot it seconds later. "I'm a nurse with University Medical Center in New Orleans. We have Cooper Deagnan here and he listed you as his emergency contact. He wanted us to call you."

Luke's heart slammed into his chest. "Is everything okay?" he asked while trying to keep his eyes focused on the road. There was no place for him to pull over or he would have.

"Cooper was stabbed in the abdomen in the French Quarter tonight and brought in by ambulance roughly two hours ago. He's resting comfortably now but his wounds required surgery and a blood transfusion."

"I don't understand. How was he stabbed?" Luke had trouble keeping the SUV in his lane. This wasn't a call he should be multitasking while driving at night on unfamiliar roads.

"I'm not at liberty to discuss that with you. Cooper will be awake in the morning and can tell you everything. I know that the police have already been here about the incident."

Luke gripped the steering wheel tighter and cursed softly under his breath. He apologized. "What's your address? What room is he in?"

She tsked. "You can't see him tonight. I said he's resting. You'll be able to see him in the morning." Her tone was curt and unwavering.

That didn't sit well enough with Luke. He knew from dealing with other hospital staff that there was no point in arguing. He wouldn't get anywhere on the phone. "Thank you. I appreciate the information. I'll be there bright and early in the morning."

"We don't allow visitors before eight," she said and then ended the call without saying goodbye.

After she ended the call, Luke slammed the palm of his hand into the steering wheel and cursed, again and again, each time louder and with more force. He needed to find a place to pull over.

Luke navigated the interstate to the exit for the French Quarter. The off-ramp dumped him onto a road that had several shops and gas stations. He pulled over at the first one and found a place to park. He kept the engine running to use the car's Bluetooth and made sure the doors of the SUV were locked. He scrolled through his phone until he found the number for Det. Clive Elio. It was nearing midnight and he didn't care if he woke him.

"Hello," Det. Elio said as if he was sitting by the phone waiting for him. "I was going to call you. I'm just getting in. I assume you know about Cooper?"

"I got a call from the hospital. What happened?"

"It's a mess," Det. Elio said, not hiding his frustration. "He was stabbed on the street. With the crowd of people out tonight, it took some time before anyone realized he wasn't just another drunk lying on the ground. A bystander called the police and other officers showed up as well as the ambulance. I wasn't notified until Cooper asked for me. I didn't get there before they took him in to emergency surgery. I saw him in recovery, but he was out cold. I'll speak to him in the morning. The doctor said the two stab wounds didn't hit any major organs. He's lucky because it could have been much worse."

"He was stabbed twice? Who would do something like that?" Luke knew the French Quarter could be dangerous. Cooper was never off his game though.

Det. Elio explained, "Cooper told one of the officers at the scene it was Mark David Reed. Cooper bumped into him on the street and then followed him for several blocks, thinking he was keeping a safe distance back. He lost him or at least that's what he thought. I don't know if Mark bumped into him on purpose, knowing Cooper would follow, or if it was all some strange coincidence. Either way, Mark got the jump on him. He got away and then once Cooper's defenses were down, he pounced. Stabbed him twice with a utility knife. Cooper said it looked like something someone in the military or law enforcement would carry."

Luke didn't know what to say. He sat there stunned by the information. "Did he tell the officer anything else?"

"Cooper said to tell us that he thinks Mark must have some specialized training. That he had to have used some tactical training to shake his tail and then attack at the right time."

"I'd say so. I can't remember the last time someone got the jump on Cooper like that." Luke reflected on what Nolan had told him about what happened to Rob. "If Mark is the killer, he's got some strong skills in the water, too. I believe the killer probably came up behind the victim in Little Rock and dragged him back into the water before he could respond and drowned him. It was a swift and accurate attack. The victim had no time to fight him off and had no defensive wounds."

"Sounds like something special forces would do." Det. Elio paused for a moment and then added, "Cooper wouldn't let them take him into surgery until they took a sample from his fingernails. He insisted that he had scratched Mark David Reed. If he's military or law enforcement, we'll get a hit."

Luke had already searched. "I searched for Mark David Reed and came back with nothing."

"Maybe that's not his name," Det. Elio countered.

"I did have questions about the photo I found in the database."

"We'll know for sure soon." Det. Elio grew quiet and then said, "This might sound out there, so take it for what it's worth. As Cooper was being wheeled away into surgery, he told a nurse that Fr. Frank was there that night and threatened him right before he was attacked. Cooper was under some heavy drugs at that point and wasn't making a lot of sense."

Luke figured it would all get sorted in the morning. "The nurse said I can't see Cooper tonight. If I go to the hospital anyway, will they let me see him?"

"Not a chance. I live right near Cooper's hotel. If you can get here, I have a key for you. We can meet up in the morning and go see Cooper."

Luke got some basic directions and then ended the call. He made his way over to the hotel and found the outer gate to the driveway entrance locked. It felt like it took him longer than his drive there to find street parking and then he walked back on foot. He got the key from Det. Elio and was finally able to reach Cooper's hotel room from a side gate the detective showed him.

Once inside the room, Luke collapsed back against the door, emotions flooding him. Cooper had been all alone on the streets of an unfamiliar city. He had no real backup or partner with him as he and Riley did. Luke wasn't sure how he could have been so stupid to think coming to New Orleans was a good idea. He had let Cooper down.

Luke took three long, slow deep breaths, trying to get his head right.

He had a call to make.

The phone rang four times before a sleepy Adele answered. "Luke, what's happened?"

"Cooper is okay. Let me start there," Luke said rushing his words to make sure she knew that much. Then he explained what Det. Elio had told him. "I don't know anything more right now. The hospital won't let me in to see him. He's sleeping comfortably and I'll go over in the morning."

Adele was silent as she absorbed the information. "I'm in the middle of the trial. I can't just leave. I need to speak to the judge."

Luke assumed she'd want to be by Cooper's side. He wasn't sure that was the best idea. "I'm hoping once I speak to Cooper, I can convince him to go back to Little Rock. If he's not cleared to drive, I'll buy his flight back and we can worry about his car later."

"He's not going to come back. You know that as much as I do. He's not going to get blindsided like that and not redeem himself."

"There's nothing to redeem. This could have happened to any of us," Luke argued as he finally moved farther into the hotel room. He tossed his suitcase on the floor near the dresser and sat down on the bed.

"You and I know there's nothing for him to redeem. You know how Cooper thinks. He's going to be in this to the end," Adele said more calmly than Luke would have been if Riley was in the hospital. Luke knew her ability to be calm during a crisis was like a superpower for her.

Luke envied that. "I still don't think you should ask for a continuance and come down here," he pressed. "I can't tell you what to do, so I apologize if I'm coming across that way. Why don't you call him in the morning before court and see what Cooper wants you to do."

"You're as hard-headed as he is, Luke. But you're right. The judge will toss my butt out of court if I ask for a delay." They talked for a few more minutes, Adele asking more questions about the attack than Luke had answers. Then she said she was going to check on Cooper's status at the hospital and try to get some sleep.

When they hung up, Luke flopped back on the bed and closed his eyes, trying to shut out the guilt that had crept over him. It wasn't his fault. Intellectually, he knew that. It didn't mean the feelings weren't still valid. He pushed himself upright as his phone rang.

He reached for it thinking Adele was calling back with an update. Luke was surprised to see it was Riley. He hadn't called her about Cooper and there was no way Adele had enough time to tell her. "You're up late," he said.

"I have something to tell you and don't want you to get upset," Riley said, her voice rushed. "Did you make it to New Orleans? Cooper should probably be on the call too, but his phone goes right to voicemail."

Luke didn't want to drag it out. He told her about Cooper and assured her that he was going to be okay as she sucked in deep breaths of concern. "He's going to be fine," he said again. "I'll know more in the morning and call you with an update."

"That's what I wanted to tell you. I'll be there in New Orleans in the morning and you can tell me then." When Luke asked why she was coming, she hesitated.

"I've had enough for one night, Riley. Just say it." Luke didn't mean to snap at her. He was tired to his bones and still concerned about Cooper. It was too much for one night.

"I'll be flying down to New Orleans tomorrow morning on Ned Shaw's private plane."

Luke's throat went dry. His first instinct was to yell and tell her that she had to stay away from him. He quelled his first instinct and simply asked her why. "I thought he was already in New Orleans."

Riley explained her meeting with him earlier that night and that

Shaw was claiming he was set up. "It sounds to me like the killer set up both Shaw and the victims. Got them to the same place and then made it look like Shaw was responsible."

"Why would someone do that?" Even though Luke knew it was Mark David Reed who had stabbed Cooper, he didn't trust Shaw any more than he had earlier that day. He was there to interview him as a person of interest. The last thing he wanted was Riley going anywhere with him.

"I don't know why. I have a lot more questions than answers right now. Jack offered to come with me, but he has cases he needs to work on here in Troy," Riley said, her voice trailing off. "I told him that you were in New Orleans waiting for him and he agreed to meet, so I hardly think he's going to do something to me between now and then. I told him that several people know about the trip."

That made Luke feel a little better. "Do you want me to meet you at the airport?"

"Given what you told me about Cooper, go straight to the hospital and I'll meet you there without Shaw. Then we can figure out the plan of action." Riley grew quiet for a moment. "At least, we will all be in the same city."

Luke laughed lightly. "Don't get me wrong, I'm glad you'll be here. I don't trust Shaw."

"If it makes you feel better, I'll be on guard because I don't trust him either."

That did make Luke feel better, enough that he'd sleep tonight. He hung up with Riley and then took a hot shower. The windows in the room were practically right on the sidewalk. He could hear people's conversations as they walked by. He clicked off all the lights and pulled back the curtain on the double floor-to-ceiling doors and stared out. He wondered if everyone would look so joyful and full of fun if they knew a killer walked among them.

# CHAPTER 32

Cooper opened one eye and then the other. The harsh light made him wince them shut. Pain seared his side and he reached his hand to hold himself. He had bits and pieces of memories from the night before. One flittered in and then was replaced by another, giving him a kaleidoscope of images that didn't make much sense.

"Cooper," Luke said his name quietly and then stood by his bed. Cooper could feel a hand on his leg. "I'm here. Do you want some water or more pain medication?"

"Pain medication," Cooper tried to say but the words caught in his throat, which was the driest it'd ever felt. He tried to sit up as the pain shot through him. He groaned and laid back against the pillows. He opened his eyes again and squinted at Luke. "Could you close the blinds? The sun is too much for me."

Luke did as Cooper asked and then headed toward the door. "I'm going to get the nurse to tell her you're awake."

The messy images in his brain began to form a fuller picture. He'd been stabbed the night before by Mark David Reed. He had collapsed to the ground, people still moving by him, not noticing that he was hurt. One woman thought he was drunk, another thought he was faking. No one paid any attention until a woman saw the blood and screamed her foolish head off for someone to call 911.

One idiot stood there using his phone to film Cooper writhing on the ground. He assumed that footage was now blasted all over social media. It was good Cooper didn't have a presence on any of it. He didn't need to see his humiliation in a full color video. There were still gaps in his memory. Things that hadn't quite come into focus yet. Cooper closed his eyes again, letting the memories come forward on their own.

Cooper assumed he passed out at some point because the only thing he remembered after that was the medics trying to get his name and loading him onto a stretcher. He tried to stay as conscious as possible after that to make sure he told someone what happened.

At the hospital, there were bits and pieces of memories stringing themselves together. He remembered telling a uniformed cop what had happened. Although now, he couldn't remember what he said. He remembered saying Adele's name and then Luke's, hoping someone would contact his only family. Then he was wheeled into surgery and his memory became a black wall of nothingness until now. Someone had reached Luke because he was there. Cooper was grateful to have not woken up alone in a strange hospital.

The nurse came in moments later with a cup of water and a syringe she put into his IV. "For the pain," she explained as she worked. Then she checked his vitals and fixed his pillows. She pulled back his covers and lifted the side of his hospital gown to check the incisions. She told him all looked good and then covered him again. "You'll feel better in a few minutes. It might make you sleep some more, which is what you need."

Cooper was grateful for the shot for now. "Can you get the doctor to prescribe me something else? I have work to do and need to be clear-headed. When can I leave?"

The nurse shifted her eyes to Luke and offered him a sympathetic smile. "You rest, Cooper. That's your only job right now." She patted

Luke on the arm as she left.

Cooper rolled gently from side to side to get comfortable. When he was finally in a position that was bearable enough, he raised his eyes to Luke. "Is there something you're not telling me? Am I dying?"

Luke shook his head and sat down in the chair by the bed. "You're not dying. You are seriously injured and it's going to take some time before you're back out there solving cases."

"I know that," Cooper said even though it pained him as much as the stab wounds to admit. "I can't lay in this hospital bed and do nothing while the guy who put me here kills someone else. I can't do what I normally do, but you have to let me be productive." Cooper said that and knew within the next twenty minutes he'd be asleep from the pain meds the nurse had given him. They knocked him out completely, which was nice for the pain, but it took a toll on his mental faculties.

Luke looked like he wanted to say something that Cooper knew he wouldn't like. After taking longer than Cooper would have liked, he finally said it. "I called Adele and we both think you should go back to Little Rock when you're well enough. Riley is on her way here and we can handle it together."

Cooper ignored what Luke said because he wasn't going to do it even if it was the best thing for him. He assumed someone had called Adele. As much as he wanted to talk to his wife, he wasn't ready for a battle with her about coming home. "Why is Riley on her way here? Because of me?"

"No," Luke said, an edge of frustration in his voice. "She has a theory about Shaw and she's traveling with him." He must have seen the shock on Cooper's face. "I know. It's one of those crazy things she does where she thinks she's being rational. I didn't even try to talk her out of it. Riley will be safe. Jack was taking her to the airport and waiting for the flight to leave and then she said she would come right here." Luke checked his watch. "She should be here soon."

"What's her theory?" Cooper asked, his voice cracking.

"Riley thinks Shaw is being set up. To be fair, it's Shaw who told her he's being set up. While she doesn't trust him, Riley believes there could be merit to it. He came to her with a story that sounded eerily familiar to what the victim's friend told her. It relates to your case, too."

Cooper wasn't sure he understood. "What part of it? Danny had no connections to upstate New York as far as I know."

Luke shook his head. "You told us Danny received an email from Shaw asking for his help and then he was texting with someone he needed to meet the night he died, right?"

"Yes. When Danny graduated in May, he was headed to law school to become a prosecutor and Shaw offered him an internship of sorts. Clive said that the phone number was traced back to a burner phone, so it didn't help to identify the person. I haven't been able to get my hands on the email to confirm."

"Well, according to Riley, Shaw got the same kind of emails from the victims claiming they had information about the murder cases. He texted back to the numbers they provided and arranged a time to meet. My guess is he was also texting a burner. The killer handled communications with both and made sure Shaw was in the area when the murders happened, thereby making him look like the guilty party."

Confused and thinking it might be his brain on pain meds, Cooper told Luke he didn't understand. "Shaw just kept letting it happen? I'm sure he figured out after the first that the same kid he was there to meet ended up dead. Why did Shaw continue?"

Luke held up his hand to stop him. "Let's wait until Riley gets here to figure it out. I don't know all of it. She told me last night after I found out what happened to you." Luke pulled something from his pocket and handed it to Cooper. "I found this at the hotel last night on the sink counter in the bathroom. I thought you might want it with you." Luke opened his hand to reveal the gemstone necklace Hattie had given Cooper for protection in Little Rock.

Cooper reached out and plucked it from his hand. "I stopped by Hattie's shop and she gave me this for protection. I guess it only works if you have it on you."

Luke nodded but a smile slowly spread across his face. "I didn't realize you were among the superstitious now."

Cooper wasn't going to discuss it. He was just glad to have it with him again. He wasn't sure why but holding on to it made him feel calmer and more at peace. It was probably the mere suggestion that's what it was going to do. Whatever it was, he was going to take it.

As Cooper's eyes drifted shut a man's voice outside the door caught his attention. "Could you go see who's out there?" he asked, opening his eyes, not sure he had heard correctly.

Luke got up from where he was sitting and went to the door. A moment later, the door was closed and Luke was gone. Cooper could still hear the angry voices from the hallway. Luke's voice was raised and stern. "I don't think that's a good idea. Cooper's resting and shouldn't have visitors right now. He's been through an ordeal and the person responsible is still out there."

Luke raised his voice again for the man not to enter. The door was pulled open and Cooper was expecting to see Luke at the end of his bed. It was Fr. Frank with Luke and the nurse coming in right behind him. Luke's features were tight and his anger was on full display.

"What's going on?" Cooper asked, his voice growing weak from the medication. He struggled to get himself more upright but failed. "I don't want you in here. You threatened me last night and then I got stabbed."

"You're alive," Fr. Frank said with disbelief. "I warned you to be careful. You didn't listen." Fr. Frank tried to walk around the side of Cooper's bed, but Luke grabbed the man's arm and pulled him back.

Fr. Frank angrily shook him off. Luke wasn't having it and stepped around in front of the priest putting himself between Fr. Frank and Cooper. Luke put his hands on the man's chest and pushed him back. "You got around me to get into this room, but you're not going anywhere near Cooper. He said he doesn't want you here, so you need to go before I call security or remove you myself."

Fr. Frank snarled, "Who do you think you are?"

Luke kept one hand on the man's chest and pulled his badge from his pocket. He flashed it in Fr. Frank's face. "Little Rock police department detective. Det. Clive Elio is investigating what happened to Cooper. I'd be more than happy to call him. But the only way you're getting to Cooper is through me."

"Enough!" the nurse yelled but even her shrill voice was no match for the standoff between Luke and Fr. Frank.

"You shouldn't have come here, Cooper," Fr. Frank said, still trying to push past Luke. When he realized that Luke wasn't budging, he backed off holding his hands up in defeat. He looked over at Cooper. "I warned you."

"Was this your doing?" Cooper asked, mustering up the last of his remaining strength "I didn't back off so you sent some muscle to take me out."

Fr. Frank dared to chuckle. "You have an overactive imagination, Cooper. I didn't do this to you. For your sake, I hope you heal quickly and then go back home. You don't belong here." He stepped back a few feet and then turned and left without saying anything else.

The nurse didn't know what to make of the interaction. She asked Cooper if he was okay and then left when he told her he was fine. It wasn't until they were alone that Cooper admitted, "I think Fr. Frank had something to do with me getting stabbed last night."

Luke went over to the door and closed it. "No one will bother us now," he said returning to the chair where he had been sitting. "I don't know a lot of priests. I've never met one like him. He's stronger than he looks."

"That's the second time I've heard that," Cooper said and recounted what the bartender had told him the night before about Fr. Frank. "Something is going on with him. I'm not sure how he fits into this case."

Luke looked over at him. "Do you *really* think he's responsible for what happened last night?"

"He threatened me the way he did here now. As soon as I left the bar last night, I bumped into Mark David Reed. I don't think that was an accident. I assume Fr. Frank sent him after me."

It was clear by Luke's expression that he wasn't so sure. "Let's take our time with this. You need some rest and then once Riley is here, we can go over everything." Luke pointed to the corner of the room. "They even left us a tiny dry-erase board so we can take notes."

Cooper laughed even though it hurt. "I don't think the nurse wants our case notes up there." He wanted to say something else but the medication finally took hold and dragged Cooper under. He drifted off to a dreamless sleep.

Cooper woke sometime later to the sounds of Luke and Clive talking. Cooper couldn't quite make out what they were saying. He wanted to open his eyes and push himself upright. In his mind, he did it. In reality, he got one eye open and mumbled enough to get their attention.

"Are you feeling okay?" Luke asked, coming to his bedside with concern.

"Fine," Cooper struggled to say and then tried to push himself up.

Luke helped him and then hit the button to raise his head on the bed. "Clive came by because he has some evidence. Actually, you got the evidence last night when you were stabbed."

Cooper had no idea what he was talking about.

Clive stepped forward toward the end of Cooper's bed. "You scratched Mark David Reed after he stabbed you. You were adamant last night when you came into the hospital that we take a sample from under your fingernails. You were sure you had his DNA." Clive patted Cooper's foot under the cover. "You did it, Cooper. We know who he is now."

"What do you mean? Mark David Reed. We know who he is," Cooper said, struggling to make sense of his actions.

Clive shook his head. "No, Cooper. You were sure that Mark David Reed wasn't his real name and you were right. His real name is Austin Chalek and he was special forces with the Army."

"I don't understand." Cooper was trying to put all the pieces together and came up short.

Clive offered him a sympathetic smile. "Given this guy's record, you're lucky to be alive."

Cooper shook his head. "No. If a guy like that wanted me dead, I'd be dead."

# CHAPTER 33

It was cliché to think that the tension in the room was so thick I could cut it with a knife, but that's exactly what it was as I entered Cooper's hospital room. Luke stood at the end of Cooper's bed next to a man I assumed was Det. Clive Elio. Their faces were contorted in emotions I couldn't read. For half a second, I worried that something more had happened to Cooper. Then I heard his voice and what he said about being dead and dread washed over me.

"Luke," I said tentatively, closing the door behind me. As soon as he saw me, he rushed over and wrapped me in a hug.

"Did everything go okay?" he whispered in my ear.

"It was fine," I assured him, pulling back from the embrace. I stood on tiptoes and kissed him hello. "I got us a room at the hotel where Cooper is staying to make it convenient. Shaw said for us to take our time and he'd meet with you later. He's staying at another hotel."

"Shaw?" Det. Elio asked, his voice raised an octave.

Luke then introduced me to Det. Clive Elio who told me to call him Clive. I shook his hand. "You didn't look like a doctor," I said and he chuckled. He had a warmth about him that I liked immediately. I would explain about Shaw in a moment. First, I needed to attend to Cooper.

I went over to his bed and tried to give him a sort of side-armed hug as best as we both could manage. He winced and I apologized. I opted for pecking him on the forehead in quite a sisterly way. "Are you okay? I was talking to Adele downstairs on the phone before I came up. She said she knows you are avoiding her. That's why she hasn't tried your cellphone this morning. She's been checking in with your nurses every hour." I nudged his arm. "Stop avoiding your wife."

Cooper shifted his eyes away from me. "I'll call her soon. I figured she'd lecture me about going back to Little Rock."

"She knows you better than that." It pained me to see Cooper lying in a hospital bed with an IV in his hand and his face the palest I'd seen. "Was it a vampire who got you? I heard the story about the convent when I checked into the hotel."

Clive laughed and we all turned to him. "Cooper might have been luckier if it had been a vampire. I was telling Luke and Cooper as you came in that we were able to identify the man. Austin Chalek. He left the military three years ago and the trail runs dry. He has a Wisconsin driver's license but no criminal history. I can't find a job for him either."

"What about the LinkedIn page we found for Mark David Reed? It said he was working for a software tech company that was selling tech to colleges."

"Company exists," Clive said and then looked over at Cooper. "Mark David Reed's page was hacked and his photo was replaced with one of Austin. A call to the company's human resources confirms that Mark David Reed is not the man in that photo, although they look similar. The company sent me a photo of the real Mark David Reed."

Clive pulled an image of the real Mark David Reed out of the folder and passed it to Luke first who held it up to show Cooper and me. The resemblance was uncanny and they could have passed for brothers.

Cooper started to ask a question but the words caught in his throat. He reached for his cup of water and drank a little. "Didn't the real Mark know that his profile got hacked?"

"He's been dealing with it for the last few months," Clive explained. "Human resources was aware. Of course, they had no idea who the man in the photo was or why he had hacked the page. It seems Austin set himself up an alibi or at least a reason why he'd be traveling from state to state. If anyone recognized him, they'd be searching for Mark David Reed, not Austin Chalek."

"That's exactly what we did," Luke confirmed. "I knew the photo in the database was different. I figured it was an old photo. Without the DNA confirmation that they are two different men, we might never have known."

"Austin doesn't have a criminal record either," Clive explained to Luke. "If you had his real name, you would have come back with his military record, which would have been helpful to know. We would have been on higher alert. No one could have suspected that a software tech sales rep would have skills like that." He looked over at Cooper and grimaced. "You're probably right. If he had wanted you dead, you'd be dead."

I stepped toward Luke. "Where does that leave us? Do we know why he went after Cooper? There was no indication that he was getting close to Mark. How did he even know that we were looking at him? You hadn't called his employer yet. Had you, Luke?"

He shook his head. "I didn't do anything other than run his name through the database. I didn't get any criminal history."

"Is Cooper's case yours?" I asked Clive.

"Yes, thankfully. That will free me up and give me some time to work with all of you."

Cooper groaned. "While I lie near death in a hospital bed."

"Don't be dramatic," I teased and then blew out a loud breath. "Back to my original question. Why did he go after Cooper?"

All eyes turned to him. His eyes moved to look at each of us. "I think it has something to do with Fr. Frank. They are connected somehow—"

Clive interrupted, "That's a major accusation. You have to be sure."

"I'm sure," Cooper said with as much oomph as he could muster. "Fr. Frank knew where I was last night. He also knew where I'd been staying. He had been in the restaurant not long before I left, maybe thirty minutes at most. He threatened me as he did here earlier today. Luke, you heard him." Cooper looked at his best friend with pleading eyes.

"I did hear him and he behaved unlike any priest I'd ever encountered," Luke said, confirming. He turned to Clive. "We have to explore the connection. I can't stand here right now and say there is a connection or there isn't. We need to start there and see what Austin's connection is to these cases and New Orleans. Why did he start here? If Austin is the one killing these young men, is he responsible for all the other ones Shaw has connected?"

"I wouldn't think so," Clive said. "I'd assume he would have been deployed for many of them."

I raised my hand slightly to get their attention. "Austin is from Wisconsin where there were a few drowning cases. Maybe he knew someone who drowned. If Shaw is telling the truth, then he was set up. Austin knows enough to steal someone's online identity; he could create the kind of situation that would bring Shaw near the victims."

Clive tossed Austin's folder down on the end of Cooper's bed. "We still don't have a why though. Why kill those young men and then go after Cooper? Someone had to have tipped him off that Cooper was looking into him."

"The reporter is the only person who knew," Cooper said low enough he could have been talking to himself. He raised his eyes to me. "I need someone to speak to George Benoit. I wouldn't have known about the guy without George. He's the one who brought him to my attention. George also told me he had called around to the other cities and had spoken to reporters who pulled photos from the scene."

"How did George identify him at the start?" I asked, not sure how a reporter could make an early connection like that. "Someone had to have tipped him off."

Cooper closed his eyes. "A reporter saw the name under the photo. But how they spotted him at the start, I just can't remember, Riley. Sorry. These drugs are messing with my head. Also, George was annoyed and angry that no one would take him seriously. He kind of threw the evidence at me. I barely had time to ask him anything."

I could tell Cooper was frustrated with himself. I looked over at Luke and pointed toward the door. We let Cooper rest and walked out into the hallway. Once I closed the door, I said, "We need to let him sleep. He's struggling to keep up right now. Luke, you know he's going to push himself beyond the point of healthy. If he won't stop, we have to make sure we make him stop and get rest. How long did they say he'd have to stay in the hospital?"

"A few days if everything goes okay. Do you think it's okay to leave him here? I want to interview Shaw."

"I'll stay a little while longer and then head out to speak to George." I pulled out my cellphone and read off Shaw's number to Luke. "Shaw said he'd be at the hotel. I'm not sure he'll stay there though."

Clive raised his perfectly arched dark eyebrows. "Do you believe him?"

"I spent an entire flight with him in a small airplane while he went over the details time and again. I don't think he was lying. It wouldn't surprise me if he wants to get the credit for solving it on his own." I turned and locked my gaze on Luke. "I don't think he has any idea who is doing this to him. It's why it's gone on for so long. I assumed he had to be fairly desperate to ask me for help."

"Or he thought we were closing in on him and preempted it," Clive offered.

I couldn't disagree with him. "If you know Shaw, you know he's manipulative and out for his own gain. No one can deny that. I wouldn't put anything past him. Luke, interrogate him and figure out what more he knows. If he told me the truth, you should be able to confirm the facts. Shaw wanted to show me his email and phone. I didn't want to get into all of that with him. He told me enough that I figured it was best to let law enforcement handle it from here. As a private investigator there's not much that I can do with it." I shrugged and smiled. "I'm also completely biased and would find any reason to see Shaw behind bars. That's why I think he's telling the truth. I'm not someone he'd come to for help if he had other resources."

"I'll take care of it," Luke assured me.

"I'll dig more into Austin's background," Clive suggested and then offered Luke a room at the police station to interview Shaw.

Luke declined. "I don't want to give the appearance that we are arresting him. I want the conversation to be more casual. If I need to bring him in, I will."

I agreed with that approach because I didn't think there was any way Luke was going to get Shaw to go into the police station for formal questioning. Armed with our plans for the day, Clive left ahead of Luke.

Once he was gone, Luke stepped to the side of the hallway and pulled me into his arms. He kissed my forehead and breathed me in. "I want you to be careful talking to George Benoit today. He might be a reporter, but he's the one who connected Cooper to Austin. There are too many things we are missing. I don't want you to put yourself at risk."

"I'll be careful. I want to spend some time doing a little research before I head out. I brought my laptop. It's in my rental car. Shaw wanted me to drive with him, but I insisted on getting a rental. We can return it later if we don't need it."

"That's good," he said, tucking some stray strands behind my ears. "Is there anything I should know about Shaw before I interview him?"

I gave Luke an overview of the man's toxic personality. "Don't try to be the big man. Let him think he's in control and smarter than you and it will be easier. Shaw is great at walking himself into corners. When he does, he'll get silent and have this far-off look on his face. Then he will immediately get defensive and try to prove his point."

"Helpful," Luke said, kissing me goodbye. "Let's meet for dinner tonight and compare notes. I'll call you when I'm done."

I walked with Luke down the hall before heading back to Cooper's room. I found him awake and staring over at the door. "I figured you need the rest," I said as I entered.

"I do. I need to call Adele but first I need your help."

"With what?"

"Fr. Frank," Cooper said and waited for my reaction. When I didn't have one other than sitting down by his bedside, he went on. "Riley, I know he's involved or knows something more. Luke and Clive think I've lost it or have it out for Fr. Frank the way you had it out for Shaw. Trust me on this, there's something off with him. Will you figure it out?"

I did the only thing I could for my partner – I agreed to look into it.

# CHAPTER 34

"Riley tells me that you believe you're being framed," Luke said, sitting down at a table in the back of a café near Shaw's hotel. Luke had met Shaw outside and they walked a few blocks until they found a quiet café to grab some coffee and talk. Luke didn't waste any time getting down to business. He understood why Riley didn't like the man. Shaw carried himself in a way that made him come across like he was looking down at everyone. Luke wouldn't be intimidated, but he would follow Riley's suggestion and allow Shaw to think he was in control.

Shaw took a sip of his coffee and relaxed back in his chair, crossing his legs at the ankle. "I don't *believe* I'm being framed. I *know* I'm being framed. I'm not drowning those young men. I'd never do something like that. I've been the only one championing for the cases to be reopened and changed from accidents to homicides. You do know my work, right?"

The way he said it left little for Luke to say. He didn't want to bolster the man's ego any more than it was and he couldn't be contentious. "I've heard about your investigation. I've also heard that law enforcement agencies close cases fast when they see you coming. Why is that?"

Shaw turned his head away in disgust. "That's the speculation. They don't want me to show them up."

Luke considered how to phrase the questions he had. There was no way to ask them without ruffling the man's delicate feathers. "Have you shown any of the detectives your evidence? That usually will turn heads fairly quickly. I know if someone came to me and showed me evidence of a homicide on a case I closed as an accident, I'd consider it."

Shaw snickered. "Then you're not like any detective I've ever known. It's territorial work, Luke. You have to know that."

"I know it," Luke conceded because Shaw wasn't wrong. "I also know that if you have the right approach you can get further." Luke took a sip of his coffee, waiting for Shaw to snap back. When he didn't, Luke went on. "If I go in thinking I know more than them and try to put them down or make them feel stupid for what they might have missed, I'm met with resistance. If I bring them solid evidence and do it collaboratively, I'm usually met with at least professional courtesy."

Shaw stared over with skepticism on his face. "Does it ever change their minds?"

"Sometimes it does."

"I've never found that to be true." Shaw turned from Luke and looked over at the white tables and chairs placed in neat rows across the café. "I never thought I'd be targeted like this. I'm honestly trying to do something good. I believe those young men were murdered and I believe I have solid evidence to prove it."

"Have you ever shared that evidence?"

Shaw drew back in surprise. "I'm not just going to hand it over."

"That's part of the problem then," Luke said, gesturing with his coffee cup in hand. "What do you expect them to do if you refuse to show it?" Shaw didn't bite on the question. Luke turned his body to fully face the table and locked his gaze on Shaw. "Listen, you were a detective with the NYPD. If someone came to you and told you that you messed up one of your cases and that you were denying justice to a family, you probably wouldn't even hear them out. On the off chance you did, the first thing you'd ask is for their evidence. If they couldn't or wouldn't provide it, then what are you supposed to do?"

"Point taken." Shaw also turned himself so he was looking at Luke. "I'll let you in on a little secret. When I first started, I tried to show them my evidence, which they said was all circumstantial. Others said the evidence didn't make any sense. I concede that the Cross Killers theory probably didn't do me any favors. It was what we were seeing out near the rivers either where the bodies were found or where they went in."

"You don't know where the bodies went in," Luke argued. "That really can't be determined with total certainty unless it's captured on video or you have some other evidence to back it up. There are too many variables with water flow and what's in the water slowing down the body." Luke paused. "It's speculative at best. As detectives, you and I both know we don't deal in speculation to solve cases. Sure, something can start with speculation, but we need cold hard facts to back it up. I don't see that you have it."

"What about the evidence I found online about a gang of serial killers targeting young men?"

"I'd say turn that over to the FBI and let them handle it. They have far more advanced tech skills than most local departments. If it's real, they probably already have their eyes on it. If it's not, they will tell you."

Shaw eyed him. "They told me it wasn't real."

"Then stop talking about it because it makes you look like you're not credible."

"It gets me in the news and even got me a television show. I bet you can't say that for yourself," Shaw said with a smirk that Luke wanted to knock off his face.

"I don't want to be on television or get glory or fame for the work that I do. The look on a parent's face when I tell them I solved their daughter's murder and we can bring a killer to justice is enough for me." Luke made direct eye contact with Shaw then. "That should be enough for you, too."

Shaw looked away. "Keeping the story in the news is all that's important now. It's putting pressure on law enforcement agencies to do something about it. To do that, I have to give the people a good story."

"You have to make up evidence and sensationalize the circumstantial evidence you have," Luke said aloud what Shaw wasn't saying.

He seemed to have no shame about doing it.

Shaw dropped his shoulders dismissively. "If that's what I have to do to keep the media's focus, that's what I'll do."

Disgusted, Luke pulled back from the table. He wanted to tell Shaw it was that attitude that kept the cases from ever seeing justice. "Let's talk about why we are here. You believe you are being framed. I have a witness who saw you on the walking path near the Arkansas River in the same vicinity as the victim that night. Why were you in Little Rock?"

Shaw seemed to have no reaction that a witness identified him. "I told Riley that the victim, Rob, I believe his name was, contacted me to share information he said he had about a drowning case in Michigan. He emailed the address that's on my website for tips. In the email, he left a phone number. I tried to call him back, but it rang and rang. There was no voicemail set up. You know kids these days, no one wants to talk on the phone, so I texted the number and he responded within the hour. He said he was too nervous to text the info and didn't want to email it. He asked if there was any way I could meet in person. I said yes and we set up a time and place to meet. When the time came, I couldn't find him. He had stopped texting me that day and I hadn't heard from him. I went to the meet-up location but no one was there.

I kept walking down the trail and eventually ended up about a mile from where I started."

Luke didn't know what to make of that. "You never saw him?"

"I never saw anyone who identified themselves as Rob Hall, no. There was a man who passed me going in the opposite direction, back toward the way I had come. I asked if his name was Rob. He shook his head and kept going."

That had Luke's attention. "Could you identify the man who passed you?"

Shaw considered for a moment. "He was probably close to six-foot, medium build. It was hard to tell though as he had on a windbreaker. He had a bag thrown over his shoulder and a hat pulled low on his head."

"Do you remember the team logo?"

Shaw narrowed his eyes at Luke. "Pardon?"

"The team logo on the hat. Do you remember it?"

Shaw looked like he didn't want to answer. "Chicago Cubs," he said slowly. "Is there a reason that's important?"

"No reason. Just other leads we are running down."

"Care to share?"

"No," Luke said firmly and redirected. What Luke hadn't said was that he knew from Rob's cellphone records that he hadn't been texting with Shaw on that night. That alone indicated that Shaw might be telling the truth. "If my count is correct, Little Rock is the eighth time this would have happened to you – being contacted like that. Why keep going? Why not contact the Little Rock Police Department immediately and let them know that we were looking at a potential drowning murder happening in our area? You knew the kid's first name and the night of the meeting. If you were set up, you knew by then what was going to happen."

Shaw looked right at Luke. "I didn't think anyone would believe me.

I was trying to catch the guy myself. He was toying with me. Setting me up to take the fall. My team knew and even they didn't want to be involved."

"The other detective and your medical examiner?" Luke asked, finding that noteworthy.

"Yes. I figured out what was happening after the second time. I told them and they told me to go to the cops." Shaw laughed and shook his head. "With my reputation, do you think anyone would believe me? No. I'd go down for the drowning. I was there and probably saw both the victims and the killer on those nights. Here in New Orleans, I interacted with the victim."

Luke sat up straighter. "What do you mean you interacted with the victim?"

"Down near the river. I interacted with the victim – Danny Thibodeaux. I had come to New Orleans and we met at the meeting point, only Danny said that he was there because I had contacted him about an internship. I thought he was pulling some kind of sick prank. We argued, and eventually, I walked off angry about the whole interaction. Danny left too and walked toward the river. I saw later that his body had been pulled from the river. That was my first indication that something was wrong. Then I got the next email."

Luke asked a few questions about his interaction with Danny that night that didn't yield much information at all. They both showed up at the meeting place and insisted the other had initiated the contact. They grew frustrated with each other and then Danny left. He hadn't seemed drunk or scared, just annoyed that he thought he was doing this good thing by offering his help only to have been duped on his birthday.

Luke remembered something Riley had told him about the night Trevor had gone missing. "Did you interact with the victim in Troy?"

Shaw nodded. "I spoke to Trevor outside the pub and the same kind of interaction I had with Danny ensued. Trevor wasn't as angry as Danny. He was confused. Strangely, he hadn't believed that I was contacting him. Neither one of us had additional information to share and we went our separate ways. Trevor walked back toward the pub and I left. My other investigator was with me that night."

"Is he willing to corroborate that?" When Shaw said yes, Luke jotted down his contact information to provide to Riley. Luke would check with her before making a call on her case. "Did you have contact with any of the other victims?"

Shaw shook his head. "And before you ask, no, I haven't figured out who is doing this to me. I have a feeling he's connected to New Orleans. I ran an IP trace on a few of the emails and they come back to shops with free Wi-Fi in the French Quarter. There are other cities, but the majority are here in New Orleans. That's why I wanted to come back here. It was the murder here that started it and where I believe this killer is living."

"Why would someone do this to you?" Luke had his ideas but was curious about what Shaw thought.

"Maybe they feel threatened by me. I considered for a while it might be someone in law enforcement. If they set me up, I might have to back off the other cases."

"Does this mean you think these cases are separate from the other drowning cases you investigated?"

"Without question. In those instances, the victims were drunk and possibly drugged, although we haven't been able to prove it yet. In these cases, here in the south and the one in Troy, the victims were lured away to a meeting spot. It's a completely different set-up and different killer."

Luke couldn't argue with that. "I'd ask if you have any enemies…"

Shaw interrupted with a laugh. "The list is longer than your arm. I don't know who it is. Probably someone looking for their fifteen minutes of fame."

Luke could say the same thing about Shaw. He asked a few more questions. Shaw seemed open and honest with Luke and he hated to say it, but he believed him. He didn't get the sense that Shaw was holding anything back. "What do you plan to do now that you're in New Orleans?"

"I don't know. I don't have many leads to go on. I know a few of the shops that he emailed from. I was going to see if they keep a surveillance record and try to sort it out. I was going to try to interview Danny's friends and see if they could provide me any information."

"That's what Cooper was doing and he didn't get far."

"I might be better than Cooper."

"Doubtful," Luke said, anger finally slipping through his voice. "I'd tell you to let us handle it. I'm sure you won't back off though, so I won't waste my breath."

They locked eyes on each other and neither made a move. They remained there for several moments until Shaw relented. "I'll stay out of your way if you stay out of mine."

"I might need to formally question you," Luke said, standing. "I'll have Riley call your partner and confirm your story. You're not off the hook yet, Shaw. But as you know, I don't have enough to bring you in."

"And you never will." Shaw stood and extended his hand.

Luke waited at the table and watched Shaw leave. When he was gone, Luke sat back down and called the hospital to check on Cooper.

# CHAPTER 35

George Benoit would not meet me at the newspaper office. He insisted that we meet at a local restaurant in the Garden District on Magazine Street. I took the streetcar to get a feel for the flavor of the city. It was my first time in New Orleans.

Adele texted me on the way to the meeting to assure me that Cooper had called her. She was going to remain in Little Rock and handle her trial. The judge was not willing to give her a continuance, so she didn't have much of a choice. I assured her that I'd drive Cooper's car back to Little Rock from New Orleans and bring him back home safely as soon as he was released from the hospital. Ending my call with Adele left me feeling significantly lighter. That was handled and I could focus on the investigation.

As soon as the hostess led me to a table in the back of the restaurant, Luke texted me an update about the interview with Shaw. He also provided me with contact information for Shaw's partner. I wasn't surprised that it was Shaw who was seen speaking with Trevor that night in the parking lot. It did little to remove my suspicion of the man.

Shaw might very well be telling the truth that he'd been set up. He had certainly tried to convince me on the long flight to New Orleans. At the very least, he was guilty of letting the drownings continue by not telling law enforcement. Even if he hadn't wanted to go to the cops, with the media hanging on his every word, he could have used them to issue a warning that he'd never reach out via email asking for help. He chose neither option. Instead, he allowed innocent victims to be led to their deaths while he tried to figure it out. I wasn't sure what crime he could be convicted of or if he'd ever be charged. That was for someone else to decide. Set up or not, his actions didn't let him off the hook in my mind.

I took a few deep breaths, letting the stress go, so I could focus on the meeting at hand. I glanced up from my menu to see a man fitting George's description at the hostess stand. I waved and he marched toward the table, all business. We introduced ourselves and then the server was there taking our order before George even looked at the menu. He explained that he was a regular at the restaurant.

In a clipped tone, George said, "I've already spoken to your investigative partner. I'm not sure how I can be of more help."

There was no point in hiding anything, so I laid my cards on the table. I provided George with all the gory details of what happened to Cooper as I watched the man's face contort in terror. "I'm taking over where Cooper left off. We have to find the man you identified as Mark David Reed."

George shook his head in disbelief. "I had no idea that something like that would happen. I mean I know investigations can be dangerous. Is it the stabbing that occurred in the French Quarter last night?" he asked, his voice coming out in short breaths of air. When I confirmed that it was, he went on. "Another reporter is covering that story. I've only heard bits and pieces of what happened and no names involved. The victim's name was withheld in the story."

"I believe that was Det. Clive Elio's request given the investigation."

"That normally doesn't occur. He must have had some pull. Is Cooper going to be okay?" The server dropped off our drinks and food, halting our conversation for a moment.

When she was gone, I explained, "He'll live but his recovery will take some time. The stab wounds were not as deep as they could have been." I leaned on the table and dropped my voice low, making sure no one around me could hear. "I wanted to meet with you in person because I need to understand how you came to suspect Mark."

I wasn't ready to tell him Mark's real name yet.

George grabbed his glass and took a sip. "We had a tip at the newspaper after we released the story about Danny and a few photos from the scene. We received mail with one of the photos cut out of the newspaper. Mark's face was circled and there was a note that he was at all the crime scenes. The tipster didn't say that he was the killer. Just that he was at the crime scenes."

"Did the tipster give you the name Mark David Reed?"

"No," George said shaking his head. "As I told Cooper, his name appeared with the photo in one of the newspapers. Then I did a basic search online and found his LinkedIn profile. It took some time to connect with other reporters in those other cities and confirm what the tipster said."

"And you still have no idea who sent that to you?" When George shook his head, I asked, "Did you contact law enforcement?"

"Of course," he said dramatically. "I tried every jurisdiction where there had been drowning cases, but no one wanted to see my evidence or believed anything I had to say. Cooper was the first investigator willing to sit down with me and hear me out. We are on eight murders now and counting. This has to stop."

There was something I didn't understand. "When did the tipster send you this information? New Orleans was the first drowning. How would they have known about the others?"

"It wasn't right away," George explained, sipping from his water. "The tipster sent the information around the halfway mark. Five of the drownings had already occurred."

"How would they have known he was at every scene? It seems like the tipster would have needed some inside information. There was nothing to indicate the identity of the tipster?"

"We don't go after our tipsters like that," he said dismissively. "We allow people to send information to the newspaper anonymously. That's how people break stories all the time."

"I understand that," I said. "I just would have thought with a case like this where everyone thinks it's murder, you'd want to know who was handing you a suspect – even for your own curiosity."

George said nothing for a few beats. Then he shrugged. "I was more than curious, of course. Even if I had wanted to find the person, there was no return address or name."

"Postmark?"

"New Orleans, which doesn't exactly narrow it down." George sat back. "Did they ever confirm that Mark was at the scene in Little Rock? That's the only one we hadn't confirmed by the time I gave the information to Cooper."

"He was there," I said. "Det. Luke Morgan confirmed it."

"Then there you have it," George said, righteous indignation in his voice. "You have the killer and you can stop him. Are we done with the work talk now? I'd like to enjoy my lunch for a change."

If only it were that easy.  "Does the name Austin Chalek mean anything to you?"

George shook his head and took a sip of water. While still holding the glass, he asked, "Should it? That's not someone we have covered in the newspaper related to these cases. I'm telling you, Mark David Reed or Ned Shaw. That's who you need to be looking at."

I studied George, wanting to trust him. "I want to tell you something, but it must remain completely off the record. This information cannot get out there. Can I trust you?"

"Completely," George assured.  "I want the cases solved.  I'm not looking to do anything that could disrupt that. I've grown somewhat attached to these cases. It's probably unhealthy but it's kind of stuck with me in a way other cases haven't."

I understood what he meant. "You were right about Mark David Reed, but there's a catch. Cooper identified Mark as his attacker last night. He scratched him during the struggle and the cops ran his DNA. We found out that Mark David Reed is actually Austin Chalek."

George didn't understand. "How is that possible? What about the profile I saw?"

"Austin hacked Mark's LinkedIn profile and changed the photos so that it appeared online as if Austin was Mark. I don't know why he did that. The assumption is that if anyone searched his photo, as you did, you'd come back with Mark David Reed rather than Austin Chalek. It was a rudimentary way to shield his identity if someone noticed him at the scenes. It was easy enough to look him up and find that he was a tech sales rep for colleges. Maybe he thought people would assume it would be natural to see him in those states. It's certainly suspicious even if he was supposed to be there. I can't understand his thinking. If he didn't want to be spotted then just don't go to the scenes. Something compelled him to be there. At the same time, he wanted some cover."

"You know who he is now," he said, making a sweeping motion with his hand as if to say I had all I needed to know. He looked at me with skepticism on his face. "Can't you just go and get him?"

"It's not that easy. He has a Wisconsin driver's license. He doesn't have a local address that I'm aware of or any known ties to New Orleans. We know he was here last night because he stabbed Cooper. He could be long gone by now. Det. Elio is doing some background and has all the appropriate alerts out on the man. They have even set up checkpoints out of the city. The only thing we haven't done yet is go to the media."

"Then maybe that's what you need to do." George saw the look of concern on my face. He reassured, "I'm not going to announce anything before you're ready. What I'm saying is if this guy has left town and gotten past those checkpoints, then blasting his face all over the national media might prevent another death. Everyone will be on high alert and looking for him."

It may come to that. I countered, "It may run him underground never to be caught. Austin was Army special forces. If he wants to hide, he has the skills to do that. He could disappear and we'd never catch him."

"Or you may prevent another *death*," George said, stressing the word. He knew he was pushing and he figured out quickly that I wasn't budging. He sat back and held his hands up. "I'm not going to do anything, I swear. But consider it. That's all I'm saying. I can make the connection for you to a local news station and you can hold a press conference."

"I'm sure the New Orleans Police Department has a solid public affairs office to handle that."

George smirked at me. "If you think the police department is going to do that, then you haven't been paying attention. They closed the case. It's done and nothing is going to make them reopen it. I'm here when you need resources."

He was probably right and I tucked the information away for later. I redirected the conversation. "Do you happen to have a copy of the photo that was sent to you with the note? I'd like to be able to read it myself."

George pulled out his phone. "The original is locked away in my desk drawer. I do have a photo of it." He fiddled with his phone and then passed it to me. "You'll see the newspaper cut out and then the writing right across the page. I should have been clearer. There was no attached note. The tipster wrote right on the newspaper."

I glanced down at the photo from the newspaper. Austin stood in the front row of onlookers with his head down and ballcap pulled low on his head. There was no question it was him. His face was circled in red ink and the words – *He's been at every crime scene* – were scrawled above his photo. The writing was a blend of cursive and print, which wasn't unlike my own. I can't remember the last time I wrote fully in cursive or handwrote anything at all. The "b" in *been* was distinct with the rounded part not closing the letter but rather dipping below the line leaving the circle open.

"Can you send me this?" I asked, still holding onto the phone. I wasn't going to leave without a means to take it with me. Even if I had to take a photo of a photo with my phone.

"Sure, I'll text it to you." I handed the phone back to him and reached for mine. A moment later, I received a text of the photo. George raised his eyes to meet mine. "Is that all? I need to eat and then get back to work."

I had forgotten my salmon salad was in front of me. The interview was done for now. I couldn't help but wonder if there was anything else George knew that he wasn't saying. My general mistrust had started to seep through the whole investigation.

# CHAPTER 36

Late that afternoon, Luke found himself back in the hospital sitting in the chair near the bed while Cooper napped. The doctor had come in earlier to update them that Cooper's condition was improving but that he wasn't out of the woods yet. The doctor wanted to keep him in the hospital for a couple more days to watch the incisions and make sure no infection occurred.

Luke agreed even if Cooper did not. Luke didn't think Cooper was in any condition to travel. The hospital keeping watch rather than Cooper being alone at the hotel sounded preferable. Luke also didn't trust that Austin wouldn't find Cooper at the hotel and finish off the job. Cooper had already said that Fr. Frank had been watching him.

That didn't mean Luke wanted to be far away from the hospital for too long. He had made himself a comfortable spot in the chair and was going over notes on his laptop from his interview with Shaw. He had called and updated Captain Meadows and Det. Tyler about the case. They were both concerned about Cooper and told Luke to remain in New Orleans as long as he felt he needed. They offered help in any way they could. There wasn't much Luke needed right now. There were still leads to be run down, but he was sure that with Riley and Clive's help, they'd figure it out.

Luke kept running the interview with Shaw over in his mind. He understood now how the young men had been lured to locations where the killer would have access to them near the rivers. Luke also believed that if Austin was indeed the killer, he could with relative ease attack the men on dry land, incapacitate them, and drag them into the water, drowning them before anyone had any idea what was happening. It was something Luke was sure special forces were trained to do. It also explained the lack of defensive wounds on all the victims other than Trevor.

Luke read through the newspaper articles about all the recent drownings and studied the victim profiles. They were all young men who would be no match for a killer like Austin.

As a show of good faith, Shaw had forwarded several emails from the killer that read exactly as he had said they would. Shaw had even provided him with the results of the IP address search. Luke had been surprised Shaw had followed through and was hard-pressed looking at the evidence not to believe him.

Luke had no trouble believing Shaw could be so easily lured to another city to speak to a potential witness who claimed they had evidence to support his wild theory. Shaw had one motivation in life and that was to keep the Cross Killers case in the news. All the killer had to do was dangle the opportunity for potential evidence in his face and he came running. But, to his credit, it hadn't taken Shaw long to figure out what was happening.

It also didn't surprise Luke that Shaw was now trying to go after the killer on his own and had not warned law enforcement in the cities he knew the killer was lurking. Shaw knew that as soon as he received an email with the first name of a new victim and where they wanted to meet that another murder would happen. Shaw kept that information to himself to go after the killer alone. The result was unconscionable as far as Luke was concerned.

There was a soft knock on Cooper's hospital door and Luke leaned to the side expecting a nurse or doctor to enter. It was neither. Clive opened the door partway and gestured for Luke to come out into the hall. Luke glanced at Cooper, who was still asleep. He stood and set his laptop on the chair and then followed Clive into the hallway.

Luke pointed to the end of the hall. "There's a family room where we can talk privately."

"How's Cooper?" Clive asked, walking in step with Luke.

"Asleep. The doctor won't release him for a couple of days. To be honest with you, I'm glad. If he went home now, he'd never sit still. I'm sure he'd end up ripping his stitches or something much worse. This is the best place for him until he's healed."

"I still can't believe that happened." Clive grimaced and then apologized to Luke. "I had another case that I had been assigned to, so I wasn't able to be with him."

Luke opened the door to the small family room the nurse had told him about earlier. "No one is blaming you for this. Please don't blame yourself. We've all been injured during cases. It comes with the territory. Cooper was armed but Austin got the jump on him. Even if you were there, you wouldn't have been able to stop it."

"I could have gone after him," Clive said regretfully and then let the subject drop. He handed Luke the file he was carrying. "I was able to get more background on Austin. The one thing I can say with certainty is that he's not responsible for the Cross Killers drownings that Shaw is so focused on. He was in the military for almost all of them including several deployments. His little brother, Nick, was one of the victims."

Luke's eyes got wide. "How did you figure that out?"

"Chalek isn't that common of a name. I pulled all the records that I could on Austin through official means. You'll see part of his military record there." Clive ran a hand down his face and gave Luke a knowing look. "The part that's not been classified, that is. It doesn't surprise me that he set up this whole thing and was able to kill the victims as he did."

"I had been thinking about the same thing. His background explains a lot – makes the impossible look possible."

Clive nodded. "It also makes sense why Riley saw signs of torture on her case. Austin was skilled enough to pull that off. I assume he wanted to know what Trevor knew. Then he killed him and made it look like the other drownings."

Luke whistled softly. "All that to target Shaw. I can't imagine how much he hates the man. He could have just killed him. He's destroying his reputation instead."

"He's humiliating him and showing him for the fool he is," Clive stressed, driving home the point. "Shaw was dumb enough to be lured into Austin's game in the first place. Now, he's trapped. Austin used Shaw's hubris against him. I can understand Austin's frustration and anger at Shaw. What I can't understand is killing innocent kids to make his point. He's putting other families through what he went through. It's sick and cruel."

"It's sacrifice," Luke said, his voice low. "He's trying to take down Shaw and, in the process, if other people have to be sacrificed to accomplish his mission, so be it. I'm assuming he's got that military mission mindset. I'm not saying it's right, but he's committed no matter the cost."

"That's a sick mentality," Clive said and Luke agreed. "We've had two sightings of him in the French Quarter earlier today. As you can guess, he slipped away from officers both times. I would suspect he knows we are on to him. We have eyes on the airports and roadways. He's not getting out of New Orleans."

Luke took a seat near one of the windows and flipped through the file. He didn't think Austin would be easily contained. If he wanted to get out of New Orleans, he'd find a way. It wasn't that New Orleans Police Department wasn't any good. Austin was better.

Maybe he'd go after Shaw more directly now. It was the first time Luke considered that Shaw's life might be in danger. If Luke admitted it to himself, he didn't care. He rubbed his forehead, disgusted with himself. Shaw was a fellow detective, even if a despicable one.

Luke read over Austin's file and noted the many skills the man had on water and land. He was also a highly trained sniper. As Luke read the file over, he paused to consider what had happened to Cooper. *Why injure him and not kill him? What was the point of that?*

Injured, Cooper could report to the cops who had stabbed him. If the point of the attack was for Cooper to stop investigating and back off, why add more fuel to the fire? That act alone was what turned them on to Austin. If Cooper had never scratched the man, they wouldn't have even known his real name. *Did he want to get caught?*

Looking at the file, Luke had more questions than answers. He closed the file and glanced up at Clive. "Do we have any known address or associates for him here in New Orleans?"

"None that we could find."

Luke considered it for a moment. "Have you put out any kind of alert to local hotels to see if he or someone registered as Mark David Reed is a guest, particularly in the French Quarter?"

"We haven't gone that route yet," Clive said, hesitation in his voice. "We can go public with Austin's name and photo. We were hesitant to do that though. News travels fast in the French Quarter and we'd never be able to keep the investigation under wraps."

Luke agreed they didn't want the media involved yet. The plan might also be impractical. There would be no way to contact every hotel in New Orleans, but they could start with the French Quarter. He considered it and then quickly dismissed the idea, never having spoken it aloud. "He might not even be staying at a hotel. Maybe he has an apartment or house rental."

"That's what I assume. Given the nature of why he's here, he'd want more privacy."

"Why here?" Luke asked and then added, "The victim in Troy wrote on the floor that it all started in New Orleans. He identified Shaw too and now we know why. But why New Orleans?"

"I honestly don't know," Clive said and sat down near Luke. He sighed in frustration. "There's a lot we don't understand about this case still. Are we positive now that it's Austin?"

All the pieces fit, even with all the questions that remained. "I'm positive. With the way Rob was attacked, it had to have been someone with skills like Austin. Anyone could have come up with a scheme to trick Shaw. He's completely ego driven. It takes skill to attack someone on land, drag them into the water, and drown them." Luke gestured with the file folder in hand. "Austin is the only person of interest we have identified that has that level of skill. Shaw couldn't pull that off. Neither could Fr. Frank."

Clive didn't disagree. "What do you make of Cooper's suspicion of Fr. Frank?"

Luke wasn't sure. "I can understand it. He threatened Cooper right before he was attacked. His behavior coming to the hospital to see Cooper was out of control." Luke paused as the implications of what he said and something Clive said earlier hit him all at once. "How did Fr. Frank even know Cooper was in the hospital? You said you left Cooper's name out of the newspaper."

Clive remained quiet for a moment and then shook his head. "I have no idea. Maybe Fr. Frank was still in the French Quarter and saw what happened that night."

"Maybe Fr. Frank was involved," Luke said quietly almost to himself. He checked his phone. "Riley was going to speak to Fr. Frank on Cooper's behalf. When we left earlier today, Cooper asked her to investigate Fr. Frank. I know that you've never worked with Cooper before, but he's not one to make wild accusations. If he believes there's something off about Fr. Frank, then there's something off."

"Do you think Riley will be able to get that information?"

"She might. She's Catholic and went to Catholic schools until college. She might have a way of talking to him or understanding him that we don't."

Clive looked over at Luke. "What do you want to do at this point?"

Luke kept his eyes focused on the file folder. "What are we missing? There's something big. Why New Orleans? I keep coming back to that. Did you find any connection between Austin and Fr. Frank?"

Clive stood and shoved his hands in his pockets, his frustration growing. "None that I'm aware of. Cooper did mention that Fr. Frank's nephew was also a victim of the Cross Killers and was angry that Shaw had used crosses in his theory. He and Austin were both family members of the victims. I have no idea if they ever met or knew that about the other."

It took Luke a moment to process what Clive said. He hadn't remembered Cooper telling him about Fr. Frank's nephew. "Did the families on those other cases ever get together?"

Clive shook his head. "I don't know anything about the older cases. Who would?"

Luke stood now, that feeling of getting close to something important growing in his gut. "Shaw and Riley. She's been out of the loop for a while. Shaw would know unless they purposefully held that information from him. Riley worked previously with one of the victim's families. She might know how to still reach them. She should be on her way to speak to Fr. Frank. How far is the church from here?"

"It's in the French Quarter so about twenty minutes with traffic. Do you need a ride?"

"No. I drove. You're welcome to join me."

"I'm in," Clive said and they left the hospital together. Luke resisted the urge to run but sent a text to Riley while he was in the elevator, warning her about his suspicions.

# CHAPTER 37

I had been in and out of Catholic churches for most of my life. I had never seen one like St. Louis Cathedral with its triple steeple and white façade. The grandness of it stopped me just outside the door. I took a moment to look up and take it all in. Then I pulled open the heavy wooden door and stepped inside. Three older women stood together near rows of candles. They turned in my direction as I entered and I smiled and nodded my head greeting them. I moved off to the left to other candles and dropped in a dollar and lit one. I said a silent prayer for Cooper and also that Fr. Frank didn't kill me right there in the church – a prayer I never thought I'd have to pray before meeting a priest.

I had spent enough time in churches growing up. I didn't want to die in one at the hands of a deranged priest.

My phone chimed, the noise echoing in the quiet space. I apologized to no one in particular and turned it on mute before I read the message from Luke. He was on his way to the church with Clive and warned me to be careful. He also asked if I knew how to contact the father of the victim from the case that I had worked on years ago. I knew his phone number by heart. That was how many times I had called him during my short investigation. Luke had one very specific question he wanted me to ask the father of the victim.

I checked the time and was glad to see I had a few minutes before

I was scheduled to meet Fr. Frank. I had called and asked to meet under somewhat false pretenses. I had claimed I needed some spiritual guidance about my marriage. I had also used a fake name. I assumed he wouldn't have met with me otherwise.

I turned from the candles and noticed the women staring at me. "You don't use your phone in church," one of them snarled. "Don't you have any manners?"

I lowered my head so I was looking straight at my feet and made my way out of the church. All I had done was text Luke letting him know I'd ask the father. It had been a long time since I'd been scolded for bad behavior.

Once on the street, I stepped to the side of the doors and made a quick phone call. The phone rang and rang and I worried his number had changed or he just wouldn't want to speak to me. He answered though on the sixth ring.

"Philip, this is Riley Sullivan," I said when he answered.

"It's been years, Riley. There's been another drowning, you know?" His tone was filled with righteous indignation. Our last meeting years ago had not gone well. When I wouldn't buy into Shaw's serial killer theory, Philip called me stupid and said I was useless to him. He had lost his son and I hadn't found the killer. I had given him a break then. Pain could do unimaginable things to good people.

I cleared my throat. "I know about the case. I'm actually in New Orleans working on one of them. I had a question for you. I'm hoping you can help."

"Go on then. I'm not sure that I know much about these recent drownings."

"Have all the families from the older drowning cases, the ones Shaw connected, met as a big group recently? If not, are all of you in touch with each other?"

Philip let out a sound. I wasn't sure if it was a groan or a word.

"Why would you need to know that?" he said slowly. It was clear the question itself aroused his suspicions, which answered the question for me.

"That meeting may be related to the current drowning cases."

After a few beats, he said, "We met recently in New Orleans."

The answer knocked me back. "While you were in New Orleans did you meet Fr. Frank at St. Louis Cathedral?"

"Fr. Frank hosted all of us in the church. That's where the meeting was held."  Philip sighed loudly the way he used to when he was frustrated with me. "What's this about, Riley? It was a perfectly nice meeting and great support to the families. It was something we should have done years ago."

I ignored his questions for now. "When you were in New Orleans, did you meet Austin Chalek?"

"Yes.  His brother, Nick, drowned while he was in college in Michigan. Austin was deployed when it happened and he has been as frustrated as the rest of us in trying to get some justice for our boys."

There were so many questions flooding my mind. "What was the outcome of the meeting?" When Philip didn't respond, instead letting the silence hang over us, I pressed, "This is important, Philip. I know I wasn't able to solve your son's case. Likely, many of those drownings will never be solved and my heart breaks for all of you. But now, we have all these new cases in the south and the one in Troy. I can tell you they are connected and we believe these are murders. I need your help. You might be able to help other families."

Philip relented with a grunt. "If you want to know, the truth is you were right. We decided that our best bet would be to move away from Ned Shaw and go in another direction. All the families decided his theory was unfounded since he refused to show us any evidence. Some of the families decided to accept the cops' and medical examiners' findings that the victims died by accidental drowning.

Others decided we should start bringing awareness to the risk of drowning for college students drinking at bars near rivers. Still, others are convinced their loved one was murdered and are going to work with local investigators."

I held my breath as I asked the question. "What did you decide to do?"

"I haven't decided. I know you thought it was connected to his friends and I haven't ruled that out yet. If the time comes and I hire someone, would you be willing to speak with them?"

"Of course," I said, glad that he wasn't asking me to get involved again. "What was your interaction with Austin? How was he at the meeting?"

The anger that Philip had been directing at me early in the call seemed to dissipate. "Austin was angry like the rest of us. A lot of his anger was directed at Shaw. He felt, like many of us, that Shaw had done more harm than good for the cases."

This was one of those times I hated being right. "Did Shaw know about the meeting?"

"No."

"Was someone tasked with telling Shaw the outcome? He was only getting information from the families and this decision would cut off that pipeline."

"That was me. I took responsibility for that," Philip responded. "I told him, but it went in one ear and out the other. Shaw said that he was going to continue and no one could stop him."

"Did you tell the other families about that?"

"Yes, I reported back."

"How did Austin handle Shaw's response?"

"Anger like the rest of us." Philip grew quiet again and then softened his tone. "Austin was a nice man, but he was deeply hurt that his brother drowned and that no one was trying to figure out why. He was convinced that Nick had been murdered. He had anger at the cops and Shaw."

"That's certainly understandable."

Philip paused and then said, "Riley, I'm not saying this right. Austin had more than anger. It was..."

"Rage," I said, finishing his sentence for him.

"I was afraid for him. Has Austin done something, Riley?" He asked the question, but his tone told me he wouldn't be surprised if I said yes.

I couldn't go into the details with him right now. "We believe Austin might be responsible for stabbing my investigative partner. We are here in New Orleans investigating the drownings and Cooper was stabbed last night."

"That doesn't surprise me," Philip said evenly. "All that rage had to go someplace. I suggested counseling but Austin laughed off the idea. He said that's not how he handled things. I was worried if I'm being honest."

It seemed Philip had every reason to be worried. "How long ago was this meeting?"

"Hold on and let me get the dates for you." Sounds of movement echoed through the phone. "Right here," he said absently and then his voice became louder. "It was July fifteenth through the seventeenth. I flew back to New York that Monday morning as did most of the families."

"What about Austin? Did he leave for Wisconsin?"

"No. He was staying in New Orleans. I'm not sure if he lives there now or was staying with someone. I asked about work and he said that he wasn't working, that he had a place to stay, and he was figuring things out, whatever that meant."

"Did he say anything else?"

"Austin didn't disclose much about himself to any of us. He stayed in the back of the church and remained quiet for most of it. There were a few outbursts of anger, but that was common among us. It was during some one-on-one time with him that he expressed most of the rage."

"What about Fr. Frank? Did he talk to Austin much?"

"Hmm….I wouldn't say he spoke to him any more than to any of us. You know Fr. Frank's nephew drowned. His was one of the cases Shaw had lumped in with the rest. Fr. Frank had a vested interest in all of this. He wasn't just doing something nice for the families. He was tired of Shaw as well."

"But you don't know if he had any personal ties to Austin or any kind of relationship with him?"

"I don't have any idea, Riley. You can't possibly have concerns about Fr. Frank." He had a chastising tone in his voice that I ignored.

"We are exploring many avenues related to the drowning case here." I considered what else I might need to know right now. There was nothing else pressing and I needed to get inside to meet Fr. Frank. I thanked him for his time.

"I'm here if you have more questions." Before hanging up, he had a warning for me. "Riley, be careful. I'm sure you know that Austin was in the military. He's highly skilled and full of rage. I had no reason to believe he'd do anything violent or stupid. I would have tried to stop him. But don't underestimate him."

I believed Philip meant it when he said he would have tried to stop Austin had he known. We ended the call and I searched the crowd for Luke and Clive, hoping they'd be here before I went to speak to Fr. Frank. I wanted to do that alone, especially now that I had a little more information. I sent Luke a quick text asking him to wait outside for me and then I went back into the church.

I found Fr. Frank sitting in one of the pews midway up the aisle. I couldn't help but turn to face the altar, genuflect, and bless myself before moving into the pew with him.

"Old habits die hard," he said glancing over at me.

"How do you know that it's an old habit?" I asked, sitting down next to him. It surprised me how much smaller the pews felt as a grown adult compared to when I was a kid. It had been that long since I'd been in church – outside of the occasional wedding or funeral.

Fr. Frank reached over and clasped my hand in his. "Because I know who you are, Riley."

"I didn't even give you my real name over the phone. How could you know?"

Fr. Frank sat still for several moments. He glanced up at the altar and let out a soft long sigh as if his whole body deflated. When he did, his body slumped back into the pew and his grip on my hand released. "I did some research on Cooper after he came to visit me."

"You were willing to meet with me?" I asked, surprised at his admission and that he was sitting here, seemingly much calmer than in all his interactions with Cooper.

"Your friend is hard-headed. I tried to warn him and now look what happened." For the first time, Fr. Frank shifted his body to look over at me. "I prayed for Cooper. How is he doing?"

"He'll survive. His recovery will take a while and that will cause him stress. He's not used to being injured like that. He hurt his knee a few years back and that was too much immobility for him and recovery was only a month or so long. This will be much worse for him."

"But he'll live," Fr. Frank said matter-of-factly. "I'll pray for his recovery."

I stared at the grand altar, so different from my Catholic church growing up, which was plain and sparse in comparison. "Cooper didn't understand your warning. He suspects that you're involved in the drownings. I know you've been in each of the cities and unaccounted for during the drownings."

"Is that so," he said and sat with that revelation for a moment. He shifted his body again, nearly turning all the way sideways, so his knee rested on the bench, to face me. "Then maybe it's good that you're here. I might have a confession to make."

I turned to face him surprised by his words. "I'm listening whenever you're ready."

# CHAPTER 38

After Fr. Frank said that he had a confession of his own, he sat there quiet for an inordinately long time without speaking. I grew more uncomfortable by the second, waiting for him to say what he was going to say. I considered getting up and giving him some space but didn't want to break the tension in the air between us. I remained quiet for fear that I might say the wrong thing and have him change his mind. All I could do was sit with him and listen to the pounding of my heartbeat in my ears as my palms grew moist with anticipation.

Finally, he bowed his head, whispered what I thought was a prayer, and then reached for my hand again. He raised his eyes to mine. "I thought that I could break my vows but I cannot."

"So, you don't have a confession to make?" I asked, not hiding the disappointment in my voice.

"I do not in the way you believe."

I pulled my hand back out of reach from him. "That's a riddle, Fr. Frank. Young men are dying and we don't have time for games. Either you know something you can tell me or you don't. You showing up in each of the cities on the nights the young men are murdered doesn't look good for you."

"I didn't kill anyone, Riley," Fr. Frank said, his voice strong and clear. "I had my reasons for being there just like I had my reasons for warning Cooper."

"What are those reasons?"

"I cannot tell you. As much as I want to be able to tell you, I cannot." Fr. Frank breathed heavily. "You are Catholic, yes?"

"Yes. I grew up Catholic. Went to Catholic schools and mass every weekend. I'm not that practicing right now."

He laughed at that. "I hear that from many. You know then the Catholic laws I must abide by."

There were so many things at the tip of my tongue I wanted to say, particularly about the church's ongoing child sexual abuse scandal. He was taking a moral high ground I wasn't going to give him. "I know what's right and wrong, Fr. Frank. I'm asking you to do what's right. If you can stop people from getting hurt, then that's what you must do. Forget the rest."

Fr. Frank lowered his head. "Riley, I cannot just forget Catholic law. I will be excommunicated as soon as the words leave my lips."

I turned my head sharply to him then, the meaning finally hitting me all at once. "Austin confessed to you. He told you what he was going to do, didn't he?" I asked, my words rushing. I knew he couldn't answer me. Not just wouldn't answer me but couldn't. There was a picture forming in my mind. It was pure speculation. "After the family meeting, which you organized, it was decided that Shaw was out. You weren't going to deal with him anymore. You all knew he wasn't going to give up that easily, so Austin decided to do something about it. He was going to frame him for the murders. Was it just recent ones or all of them?"

Fr. Frank shifted his eyes toward me but remained tightlipped.

"It couldn't have been all," I said, realizing that would be impossible to pull off. "But the speculation would hang over him, right? People would question it even if he was never arrested for the drownings. People would wonder and his reputation would be destroyed. Did you help plan this?"

"No, Riley, never," Fr. Frank said with anger in his voice. "I would never harm an innocent person like that. My family has been through so much with the drowning death of my nephew and then to have Ned Shaw get involved and just destroy..." Fr. Frank sucked in a sharp breath. "You have no idea the destruction he caused when he decided that my nephew's case was part of this broader conspiracy of cases. It was devastating to our family. He keeps dangling the idea that he has all this evidence. We hoped for a while that we might get justice. My brother and his wife had the money to pay a local private investigator but witnesses were burned by Shaw. The conspiracies and wild speculation. It was too much. After a while, it was like these cases became a parody. No one wanted to touch them and no one took Shaw seriously. Do you know how many times I wanted to say to him put up or shut up?"

"I've said that to Shaw several times," I commiserated with him. "I know what your family went through. Years ago, I worked for Philip on his son's case. I just got off the phone with him. That's how I knew about the family meeting. Why did you host the families here?"

"It's been too many years, Riley. Too many drowned young men," Fr. Frank said, gesturing with his hands. He shook his head as he spoke, his voice filled with regret. "I thought if I could get all the families together in one place, we might be able to develop some consensus about how to move forward. I brought in counselors and had other resources available. Mostly, it was good to hear all the families speak about how frustrated they were with Shaw and how he wasn't helping anything. In truth, his involvement sealed the deal that none of these families would get justice."

I started to say that I understood, but Fr. Frank went on, growing angrier by the second. "Shaw billed it as law enforcement not listening to him. The FBI not listening to him. He had all the answers. He alone could solve the cases. At the end of the day though, he had never put forth one solid bit of evidence. The Cross Killers theory was asinine. There are crosses all over the place in graffiti. I could walk down the river today and point out fifty to you. It doesn't mean they connect to a murder. It galled me that he chose something so common to fit his narrative. As a priest, it went a whole other level. He didn't know where those bodies went into the water and the killer would have no idea where the body would be found. It defies any logic."

Beads of sweat had formed on Fr. Frank's hairline and brow. His beet-red face pulsed and he pounded one fisted hand into his other palm.

I still wondered if Austin had confessed his crimes to Fr. Frank. I'd never get him to admit that or tell me what Austin told him, so I had to find a workaround. "When I spoke to Philip, he told me Austin was full of rage. I'm sure he had a lot of guilt that he wasn't able to protect his brother."

"He wasn't able to protect his family from Shaw either," Fr. Frank said, giving me a knowing look. "Many of us felt that way. Those of us a little removed from the immediate family struggled with the death and then watched Shaw destroy these families. I tried in the early days to talk my brother out of giving Shaw access to information. I couldn't stop it. I prayed about it and hosting the family meeting seemed right. Now, I'm not so sure."

"That was the beginning of the end," I said and looked at Fr. Frank. He didn't nod exactly, but his head movement was an acknowledgment that I was on the right track. "Austin knew Shaw couldn't be stopped. Why not just kill him?"

"Some would say that killing him would just drive the conspiracy." Fr. Frank sat back and folded his hands in his lap. "I don't know if you realize, but these cases are talked about online quite a bit. There are whole chat room threads dedicated to these cases with people who believe Shaw. It's taken on a life of its own. If something happened to Shaw then it might fuel the conspiracy that he was getting too close to the truth."

I hadn't thought of it that way. "Are you saying that framing Shaw and ruining his reputation was the only way to stop him?"

Fr. Frank said nothing. I was too close to what Austin had told him in the confessional. Fr. Frank didn't need to say anything at this point. His denial and silence said it all.

"I don't understand how Austin could put other families through what he went through to stop Shaw." I meant that honestly. I had no idea how he could do it. "Austin certainly knew how to kill people; his military training gave him that. The way he set it up was good but not genius. And in some ways, he made the murders too clean. They were all closed as accidents."

"Drowning cases are the hardest to prove as homicides," Fr. Frank said, still not giving anything away. "I can't say more, Riley. I'm going to tell you the same thing I told Cooper. You should get your husband and go back to Little Rock and leave this alone. You're only going to get hurt."

"No, Fr. Frank. Someone has to stop Austin. We cannot leave here until we do that, so if you know where he lives or he's hiding out, you need to tell us."

Fr. Frank met my eyes then. "I don't know where he lives."

"Have *you* tried to stop him?" Fr. Frank remained quiet because any answer would admit to me that he knew Austin was the killer. I've never understood why a crime admitted in confession can never be disclosed, especially if someone admits they are going to do something rather than have already done it. We sat there in quiet for a few more moments as I tried to formulate questions I could ask.

Fr. Frank stood suddenly. "You should go home, Riley. If there is any situation to deal with, let me do it."

I glanced up at him, unsure of what he meant. "You haven't been able to stop him so far."

"Please, go."

I stood and turned to him, something occurring to me then. "Was it you who tipped off the newspaper? Someone sent in the photo of Austin and noted he was at every scene. That wouldn't have been breaking your vows if you had seen the newspaper. That would merely be an observation."

Fr. Frank's eyebrows lifted a fraction of an inch as his eyes met mine. "I'll pray for you, Riley. I do wish you'd leave. I'd hate to see anything else happen to you and your friends."

It was my cue to leave. I extended my hand and shook his and thanked him for his time. I didn't bother asking him to call me if he knew anything else. Fr. Frank wasn't going to break religious law for anything – not even to save young men from being murdered. I don't know how the man slept at night. "I'll pray for you, Fr. Frank. Living with this on your conscience must be difficult." I turned and left, knowing that my guilt trip wasn't going to do anything. I had said it though and meant it.

I walked down the center aisle and didn't look back at Fr. Frank. I made it to the back of the church and noticed a small bulletin board off to the side of the door. I don't know what made me stop and look. But I was glad I did. There on the board was a handwritten note asking for new altar boys. The writing contained the same style of letters as used on the newspaper clipping. Someone in that church knew about Austin and was trying to stop him. I resisted the urge to tug the page off the board. I settled for snapping a photo of it.

All I wanted was to talk all this over with Luke. Something big was coming and I felt entirely impotent to stop it. I breathed a sigh of relief to see Luke and Clive sitting on a bench near the entrance to Jackson Square Park directly across the street. I waved as I exited the church and they both stood and walked over to me.

"Anything?" Luke asked, squeezing my shoulder.

"Nothing confirmed through words." I looked back at the church and then at Luke. "I believe that Austin confessed the murders to Fr. Frank before they happened. Maybe that's why Fr. Frank is going to the locations, trying to prevent the murders or stop him."

Luke looked to Clive. "Can you arrest him or bring him in and make him talk?"

Clive didn't respond to Luke. He looked at me. "Did Austin tell him during confession?"

"Yeah, that's the problem."

"What does that mean?" Luke asked, his voice full of frustration, not understanding.

Clive explained, "A priest cannot disclose what he's heard during confession even if it's a confession of murder or a crime about to be committed. The priest will be excommunicated and, no, he cannot be arrested for it. It's speculation. Good speculation but we don't have anything."

I showed them both the photo of the newspaper clipping and the note on the bulletin board in church. "Someone in that church knows and is trying to stop him. We just need to find Austin."

Luke sighed loudly. "Let's go get dinner and discuss how."

I looped my hand in his. "We'll stop him, Luke." I wasn't sure I believed my own words.

# CHAPTER 39

Cooper sensed the person at the side of his bed before he saw them.

Earlier that night, he had finally eaten a substantial meal, albeit hospital food, and was starting to feel a little more alive. Around nine, the pain had intensified and he asked for more medication, even though he hated taking it. The doctor had told him that sleeping off his misery would only do him good. Cooper relented and fell asleep shortly after the nurse gave him the medication. She promised him she'd be quiet when she did her nightly vitals check.

Cooper wasn't surprised now that he had heard her. "I'm still alive," he joked, turning his head slowly to the side and opening his eyes. He was surprised the nurse hadn't joked back. They had developed a good rapport.

Cooper blinked several times, trying to focus but his vision remained blurred. That happened with the pain medication. He raised a hand to wipe the sleep from his eyes in the hopes of seeing better. The room was bathed in darkness with only the lights of his monitors giving off a greenish hue. The nurse bumped his bed and the whole thing jostled. There was no apology.

Before Cooper could say anything else, a man with a cap pulled low over his forehead leaned over the bed, his face inches away. "Scream and I'll put a bullet in you faster than you can blink."

Cooper closed his eyes in disgust. "You really like that hat, don't you? For a special forces guy, you forgot the one rule of flying under the radar. You never wear the same thing twice – let alone all the time. It's what gave you away."

Cooper had been wanting to tell Austin that since he stabbed him. The guy might have been special forces and able to shoot someone from a distance, but he was lacking in basic undercover skills.

Cooper pushed himself into a sitting position as best he could. "What are you doing here, Austin? Came back to finish the job?"

Austin glared down at Cooper. "How'd you figure it out?"

"I scratched you, on purpose, after you stabbed me," Cooper said, letting that little bit of information land. "I figured the best way to confirm your identity was to run a DNA match. I had my suspicions about a tech sales rep who just happened to be in each of the cities where a drowning happened."

"I need a way out of New Orleans." Austin fixed his eyes on Cooper's. "You got me into this and you're going to get me out."

"I got you into this?" Cooper fished around under his blanket for the call button for the nurse, but all he found were the cool sheets and his phone. He slipped the phone into the pocket of his flannel pajama bottoms and kept his breathing even, trying to keep himself calm. "You got yourself into this mess when you decided to start killing young men like Nick."

Austin reeled back at Cooper's words. "How did you know about Nick?" Austin stopped himself then. "We don't have time for this. Get out of bed. You're coming with me." He turned around and shut off the machine that was monitoring Cooper's blood pressure and other vitals. He pulled the oxygen sensor from Cooper's finger and attempted to rip the IV out of his arm.

Cooper stopped him, shoving his hand away with as much energy as he could muster. "I'll do it myself. I don't know how far you think you're going with me. I've made it to the bathroom across the room by myself and up and down the hallway once. I'm in no condition for distance because of your actions."

Austin pulled a gun from the waistband of his jeans and pointed it at Cooper. "You're either going to help me or you're going to die right here."

"Okay," Cooper said, hoping to slow him down until a nurse figured out what was happening. He didn't want to get someone else killed though. Cooper winced as he reached for his IV, undid the protective tape, and slid the needle out, covering it to stop any bleeding. The nurse earlier had helped him into regular pajamas instead of the stupid hospital gown he had grown tired of wearing. "I don't have pants or anything. Just my pajamas. I have a pair of sneakers in the closet. You'll need to get them for me."

When Austin turned his back, Cooper wondered if he could hit him with something or attack him in some way. It was going to be an effort to get up off the bed. Austin brought over the sneakers, helped Cooper into them, and then pulled his arm to help him off the bed.

Once in a standing position, Cooper asked, "How do you expect we are getting out of here?"

Austin pointed to a lab coat thrown over a wheelchair at the end of the bed. "Follow my lead and you might make it out alive. Don't do anything stupid either. I have no problem killing anyone in our way. I need to get to a house outside of New Orleans and then I'll let you go."

Cooper doubted that very much but didn't have much of a choice other than to do what Austin asked. Austin helped him into the wheelchair, then put on the lab coat, which had a hospital badge attached to it, and wheeled Cooper out of the room, looking left and then right as they went.

The halls were eerily silent at that time of night. They didn't see a soul until they got out of the elevator on the first floor. There was a man with an older woman walking out of the hospital. Then a handful of nurses came from a long hallway and one lone security guard sat at the front desk. The nurses were caught up in conversation and didn't notice them. The security guard didn't even look up from whatever had his focus.

They broke free of the front door of the hospital and Austin rushed them toward a small tan SUV. At the driver's side door, Austin dropped keys into Cooper's lap. "You need to drive because when we go through the checkpoint, you need to talk us through it."

Austin would hide under a tarp in the back of the SUV. He assumed that as soon as Cooper identified himself as one of the investigators working the case, he'd be let through. It was the half-baked plan of a desperate man. Cooper had to give it to him though, it had worked so far. They were out of the hospital with no one in pursuit. Cooper wondered how long it would be until the nurse noticed.

Austin helped Cooper into the SUV and then they were on the road. Cooper held his side and drove with one hand, his side burning with all the movement. Austin barked directions from the back. At the checkpoint, Cooper braked the SUV. The cops flashed his flashlight into Cooper's face and then asked him where he was heading. Cooper wondered if the man knew about the stabbing. *Would he know and try to rescue Cooper? Would he understand Cooper was in danger?*

The cop didn't recognize Cooper or react when he said his name. Cooper explained that he was meeting Det. Clive Elio about a recent development in the case. The cop simply nodded his head, walked around the SUV once, and then let him pass.

"We are through the checkpoint, Austin. Where are we headed?" Cooper asked, keeping one hand on the steering wheel and using the other to raise the hem of his shirt to check his wound. The bandage was still clean with no blood seeping through. He took that as a good sign.

Austin barked directions from the back of the SUV as Cooper navigated the dark roads, which only grew darker the more off the beaten path they traveled. The interstate led them to a four-lane road, which after a few turns led them to a two-lane road, and then eventually, to a single-lane dirt road with no street signs. Austin told him to take the road until it dead-ended at a driveway and then to follow that to the house.

Cooper did as he was told. The wheels kicked up dust and rocks as Cooper pulled up the driveway to a large house with columns that ran from the second-floor porch to the first. In front of the house stood a large weeping willow with branches that hung to the ground. There was a single light on in the downstairs room.

"We're here," Cooper said, putting the car in park. "Can I go now?"

Austin opened the back hatch and climbed out. He came around to the driver's side door and opened it. "You're coming inside with me. I promised I'd let you go and I will, but not now."

"You know the longer you keep me, the higher the risk of you getting caught. I'm sure they are looking for me already," Cooper said, turning his body to get out of the SUV and wincing in pain. "Why didn't you kill me in the street?"

Austin grabbed Cooper under the arm to help him walk. He wasn't as rough as he could have been and the support was annoyingly helpful. "My fight isn't with you, but you wouldn't stop pursuing me. I needed to get you off my trail. I still have work to do."

"I hate to tell you," Cooper said with a laugh, "but I wasn't on to you. I was focused on Fr. Frank. I thought he was responsible. I didn't focus on you until after you stabbed me."

Austin stopped walking. "Are you telling me the truth?"

"No reason to lie. Why?"

"Fr. Frank said you were closing in on me, but that you hadn't told anyone else yet. He said I needed to stop you."

Cooper glanced over at Austin, and in the dark of night, met his stare. "I hate to say it but you were deceived by a priest. Fr. Frank found me that night and warned me to give up my investigation. I was focused on him at that point. You were nothing more than another avenue left unexplored."

Austin didn't seem to know what to make of that. He gripped Cooper's arm tighter, offering more support, and walked the rest of the way to the house in silence.

Before getting his last dose of pain medication, Riley had texted and gave him an overview of her meeting with Fr. Frank. What she said made sense. Cooper had assumed then that Fr. Frank had warned him because he knew what Austin was doing and how dangerous he was.

Now, knowing that Fr. Frank had lied to Austin about Cooper closing in on him was like throwing out pieces of a puzzle that had finally been laid in place. It just didn't add up.

"Who lives here?" Cooper asked as Austin pulled out a set of keys and unlocked the front door.

"I know the owner. That's all you need to know. I have the place to myself and have been staying here for a few months until I suddenly couldn't get out of New Orleans." Austin opened the door and nudged Cooper through. "Go sit in the living room while I make a phone call. Someone is meeting me here. We are going to straighten out a few things and then I'll let you go."

Austin kept repeating that – that he'd let Cooper go – but Cooper wasn't so sure that was going to happen. He did what Austin told him and made his way into a large living room off the main foyer. It had a threadbare couch and chair that looked older than Cooper. The furniture was placed on top of a throw rug that covered wood flooring that needed refurbishment. The house could have been spectacular but looked like it hadn't been in loving hands in a long time.

Cooper was able to get himself down in the chair and was thankful for the rest. The driving and short walk to the house from the car had taken all the energy Cooper had. He fought a yawn and closed his eyes.

He must have dozed off because sometime later he woke to the sounds of men yelling. Three distinct voices – all vaguely familiar to Cooper. None of them someone he considered to be an ally.

"What am I doing here?" Shaw asked, his voice gruff and angry.

Cooper turned his head toward the doorway in enough time to see Shaw being shoved into the living room by Austin with Fr. Frank standing right behind him. Austin had his gun aimed at Shaw, whose face was contorted in fear. No one had seemed to notice Cooper.

"What's happening?" Cooper asked, finally drawing their attention.

Fr. Frank turned to Austin. "What's he doing here? You told me that you weren't going to involve any of those investigators."

Frustrated, Austin barked, "I had to get out of New Orleans and this was the only way."

"He can't be a witness to this." Fr. Frank marched across the room and tried to jerk Cooper up by the arm, making it feel like every stitch ruptured.

Cooper wrenched his arm free from the priest and slid back into the chair. "If I'm going, I need the keys to the SUV. Austin took them away from me."

Fr. Frank turned and demanded, "Give him the keys."

"You can't leave me here alone with them!" Shaw yelled at Cooper with fear in his voice.

Austin fired off a shot toward the far wall over Shaw's head. "No one is leaving!"

"I think Austin is right," Cooper said too calmly. "Let's sit down and talk this through." There was no way Cooper was getting out of there on his own. The only tool in his arsenal was remaining calm and keeping them talking.

# CHAPTER 40

Luke woke to phones ringing. First, it was his cellphone. Before he could answer, the phone on the bedside table rang. He grabbed the phone as quickly as he could, sitting straight up in bed. Riley roused next to him.

Luke listened but struggled to comprehend what Clive told him. "What do you mean Cooper is missing?" he asked with disbelief in his voice. "How could he be missing? He's in the hospital."

"Austin got to him," Clive responded, his tone tight. "The nurse went to check on him during her rounds and found Cooper gone. She called hospital security and they checked the video. Austin, wearing a lab coat and hospital badge, wheeled Cooper right out the front door. I'm sorry, Luke, we should have had a cop sitting outside of his room."

Luke flipped the light switch on the bedside table and glanced down at the clock. The red lights said four-twenty-seven. Riley sat up in bed next to him. "He's been gone about two hours," Luke said to her and then focused on the conversation with Clive. "Do we have any idea where they might have gone?"

"We know which direction," Clive said, bringing Luke some relief. "Cooper used his head. I assume Austin snatched him to get out of the city. We have all those checkpoints set up. Cooper was driving the SUV, and when he was stopped, he told the cop who he was and that he was working with me. That's pretty memorable. As soon as it went out over the radio that Cooper was missing, we got word back that they had been spotted. They were headed west out of New Orleans." Clive rattled off the road they had been on and the mile marker where the checkpoint stopped them. He didn't know the area well enough for it to have any meaning.

Luke's pulse thumped in his wrist as he considered the options. Riley nudged him in the side, drawing his attention. He asked Clive to hold. "Cooper went missing from—"

Riley interrupted, "If Cooper has his phone with him, I can track him on the app. We set it up on our last surveillance case. We were worried we'd lose each other during mobile surveillance. It's for safety too. Cooper didn't like that I was going out alone. He insisted we share our locations, so he could track me. We can track him now." Riley threw back the covers and darted across the room to where her phone was charging on the desk.

"Does Cooper have his phone with him?" Luke asked Clive, his voice coming out rushed as he got out of the bed in search of clothes. He explained what Riley said about tracking the phone.

"I have no idea. I wasn't in his hospital room. I can call over there."

"I have him!" Riley shouted, showing Luke the phone as she came closer to him. "He's along Route 18 near the Mississippi River. It's about thirty minutes from here." Riley tossed the phone to Luke and then scurried off to the bathroom after grabbing clothes from her suitcase.

Luke didn't have to think about whether he wanted her to come with him or not. All he could think about was Cooper's safety. He looked at the map on Riley's phone and then took a photo of it with his cellphone. He explained to Clive what was happening then texted him the photo of the map. "That's Cooper's location. We need to get over there."

"The area is old homes and several historic plantations," Clive explained. "It's heavily wooded and swamp land. I'm going to call in SWAT. What do you think Austin will do?"

Luke pushed himself off the bed, his mind a swirl of thoughts and plans. "I don't know but we should go in quietly. Maybe if I can go in there alone, I can get Cooper out."

"He's dangerous, Luke. We don't even know if Cooper is still..." Clive trailed off not wanting to say what Luke had already considered.

"He's still alive. Cooper is smart and he's been in situations like this before. He'll keep his head about him." Luke made a plan to meet Clive about a mile from the location on the map and formalized a plan of action. They discussed calling Cooper's cellphone and then thought better of it in case Cooper had the ringer on. They didn't want to alert Austin that Cooper had his phone.

Riley came out of the bathroom as Luke finished dressing. "I'm going with you, Luke. I know you don't want me to, but I'm not letting you go alone. I'll stand back and let you and Clive handle everything. I just need to be there."

In the end, Luke was glad she was going. He reached for her and pulled her into a hug. "I wouldn't have it any other way." He asked Riley to call Adele when they figured out what was going on and keep her up to date on the news. Luke had considered for a moment not waking Adele with the news until Cooper was safe, but he'd never forgive the person who held back information had it been Riley.

Forty minutes later, they pulled to a stop on the side of the road behind a long line of police vehicles. Clive stood with a group of SWAT officers. As Luke's headlights dimmed, Clive left the group and made his way to Luke's SUV.

"All I know is that there are two cars in the driveway. We haven't been able to get eyes inside yet, but there is a light on downstairs. The rest of the house is dark," Clive said, his hands on his hips. "I explained to SWAT that you want to go in alone. The hostage negotiator said it's up to you. While you go in, they will find positions around the property to see if they can get a clean shot."

"Give me time," Luke said, grabbing a vest from the back of the SUV and putting it on. He had his gun on his hip and cellphone in his hand. He called Clive, whose phone rang in his pocket. Luke explained while Clive answered the call. "I'll keep this in my pocket so you can hear what's going on. You'll need to give me some time to assess and see if it's possible to get Cooper out of there."

Clive agreed and assured him that he would be the go-between for Luke and SWAT. "Are you sure you don't want me to go in there with you?"

Luke shook his head. He knew he was putting himself in considerable danger and didn't want to have to worry about anyone else. Luke assured him he was fine. Then he turned and wrapped Riley in another hug and kissed her on the lips, not letting the kiss linger before getting back in his SUV. He didn't look back as he drove the distance to Cooper's location.

When Luke was in situations like this, lingering goodbyes with Riley were too much emotion for him. The uncertainty of possibly never seeing each other again hung too heavy over them. They had spoken about moments like this and both agreed if they treated it like any other day, it was the only way they'd both get through it.

Luke set all thoughts of Riley aside and focused on the mission at hand. Luke had no idea what he was walking into. He pulled his car over a few feet from the driveway, double-checked the map, secured his vest and gun, then exited the car. He climbed the driveway on foot, staying low near the tree line, his gun drawn, and ready to act if needed. As soon as he got to the edge of the porch, movement between the open slats of the green shutters caught his attention.

Luke tested one porch step, assuming it would creak under his weight. He was surprised when it didn't, so he took them slowly and cautiously to the top. He peeked between the slats. Cooper sat slumped in a chair on the far side of the room. He looked tired and in pain but otherwise okay. Luke breathed a sigh of relief and then spotted Shaw sitting on the floor not far from Cooper.

Fr. Frank and Austin stood in the middle of the room arguing.

Luke stepped back and stood in between the windows, straining to hear the conversation inside and watching between the slats.

"I didn't sign up for this, Austin. You promised me if I brought Shaw here this would end. Say what you need to say to the man and then you need to disappear and leave for good," Fr. Frank barked, annoyance tinging his voice.

"He's not leaving here alive," Austin said and then pointed his gun. He aimed but didn't pull the trigger.

Shaw sat there defenseless but still arrogant. "If you're going to kill me, do it, and get it over with. You've been threatening to kill me for as long as I've been here." When Austin didn't respond, Shaw barked, "You killed all those kids, Austin. Surely you can kill me. I'm the reason you're doing all of this, right?"

Austin shoved a chair out of his way and walked right up to Shaw and pressed the barrel of the gun to his forehead. "You deserve to die. You have screwed up the system so badly that the cops assumed the drownings were accidents even when I *tried* to leave evidence. Because of you, they closed the cases right away. They didn't even suspect you!"

Shaw laughed at that and it disgusted Luke. "You killed that many because you couldn't frame me on the first try? You're pathetic, Austin. Absolutely pathetic."

Austin looked back at Fr. Frank who hovered over them without speaking. For a moment, Luke wondered which one of them was really in control.

Cooper said, "Austin, you don't have to do this. Shaw is finished.

No one will ever believe him again. He might even go to prison for what he's done."

Shaw glanced in Cooper's direction but said nothing. It was clear though that Shaw believed him and he was weighing if death or prison was preferable. He had the good sense to keep his mouth shut.

Luke heard SWAT moving in all around him. Their footfalls were quiet but the leaves on the ground crunched and the branches of nearby shrubs rustled in the night. Up until that point, the darkness had been silent except for the occasional chorus of frogs in the distance. Luke suspected that Fr. Frank had heard the movement outside, too, because he turned sharply to the window and then rushed over and looked out. Luke inched back and put his back flat against the house.

"Austin, if you're going to do this, let's get on with it," Fr. Frank said. "You'll have to take care of Cooper now that you've told him so much. I didn't plan for all of this."

Luke couldn't believe what he was hearing. He had been expecting Fr. Frank to talk Austin out of shooting Shaw, but the priest was rushing Austin and including Cooper.

Luke had heard enough. He slid along the house until he reached the door. He tried the handle and found it unlocked. He pushed it open, not caring if he made a sound, and rushed in with the gun in front of him ready to shoot if he had to. "Put the gun down, Austin, and step away from Shaw!" Luke shouted, drawing all eyes to him.

Cooper's head snapped up in surprise. Fr. Frank stumbled back.

Austin swung his body toward Luke, aiming the gun right at him. "I don't want to kill a cop, man. You're not supposed to be here."

"Shaw was a cop. Cooper, too. You didn't have a problem hurting them."

"It's different," Austin said, stumbling over his words, uncharacteristically rattled.

"Come on, Austin, no one else has to die." Luke started to take a step into the room. Shaw moved faster, leaping up from his position and tackling Austin now that he was distracted. The gun went off in the process, the bullet missing Luke by a hair. As Luke crashed to the ground on his side, he glanced up and couldn't believe what he was witnessing. He took it all in as though it was slow motion.

Shaw slammed Austin to the floor and the gun skirted across the floor as the two tussled. Fr. Frank picked it up and aimed it at Austin and Shaw. Before Luke could react, the priest fired off a volley of shots at the two rolling around on the ground, striking each of them several times.

Luke had no choice. He rolled to his stomach, the easiest position he could get in, and fired off two shots at Fr. Frank, striking him in the leg. It was enough that the priest dropped the gun and slumped to the ground. He looked in Luke's direction with horror on his face as SWAT advanced on the house, coming in the door and surrounding the scene.

All Luke cared about was getting to Cooper.

As Luke pushed himself off the floor and ran across the room to Cooper, he realized both Austin and Shaw were moving around and moaning in pain. Although both had been shot, the wounds looked mostly in their limbs.

It turned out Fr. Frank wasn't a very good shot even standing that close.

SWAT radioed for medics for all three of them while Luke checked on Cooper, who was slumped in the chair with his eyes closed. Luke put his hand on his shoulder.

Cooper opened his eyes and offered a weak smile. "If you thought you were going to heaven, I think you just lost your chance by shooting a priest."

Luke couldn't help but laugh. "I have a feeling I'll be forgiven. Are you okay?"

Cooper gestured to the scene in front of them. "I'm better than them."

That was all Luke could hope for at that moment. "Come on. Let's get you out of here and back to the hospital."

# Epilogue

A few days later, Luke and I sat in Cooper and Adele's living room after dinner. It was the first time after leaving New Orleans that we were all together. We had forgone cooking and ordered take-out from a new restaurant that had opened on the first floor of their loft building. I was envious of how much they had within walking distance. Not that Cooper was going to be doing a lot of walking anytime soon.

Being kidnapped by Austin had worn him out, and by the time he and Luke made it back to the hospital, Cooper was all too willing to take whatever medication the doctor wanted him to take and go to sleep. They had kept him for two more days, which was fine given everything Luke needed to sort out in New Orleans. Then I drove Cooper back to Little Rock and got him upstairs to his loft. That's where he'd stayed under the care of his local doctor.

"How's the trial coming along?" I asked, helping Adele clear the table.

Adele took the plates from me and set them on the counter. "I'll rest my case tomorrow and anticipate closing arguments will be in a few days. I'm confident the jury is on my side." She turned her head to look out into the living room area where Cooper was sitting in the recliner. "He's not talking much. How do you think he's doing?"

I glanced over at Cooper and then shifted back to Adele. "As well as can be expected. You know he's not good at staying still. He's taken a confidence hit that will probably take more recovery time than his physical injury. He'll be fine in time. You know as well as I do that he's going to push himself too hard and then have to rest and he'll get frustrated by the whole process."

Adele smiled and hugged me. "It's helpful to have you and Luke around because you know him so well. It's like a cheat sheet."

"Cooper isn't complicated," I started to say and then stopped myself. We were all a little bit complicated and Cooper could be moody. "Feed him, love him, and tell him about your cases so he feels like he's staying busy. That's all you can really do."

"What are you two talking about?" Cooper asked, looking over at us.

"How difficult you can be," I teased as Adele and I walked back into the living room. I sat down on the couch next to Luke and Adele sat next to me. "If you have to be that nosey…"

"It's my house," he said with a grin.

"I was telling Adele that you'll be grouchy over the next few weeks, but you'll be fine." He smiled and I returned the gesture. "I was also telling Adele how you were the only one who saw Fr. Frank for what he was. None of us believed that he was involved. I missed it when I interviewed him. I truly believed that Austin had told him what he was doing in confession. I believed Fr. Frank when he said he was trying to stop Austin. I couldn't believe that a priest was directing the murders and using Austin in that way."

Adele's eyes got wide. "Is that what he was doing?"

Luke nodded and turned to look over at her. He recounted the information about the family meeting in New Orleans. "It was the first time Austin and Fr. Frank met. Everyone could see how full of rage Austin was and the unresolved trauma he was dealing with – post-traumatic stress from his deployments and survivor's guilt over his brother. Fr. Frank exploited that for his sick purposes. That house Austin took Cooper to belonged to Fr. Frank and he let Austin stay there. He said he could rest and regroup. All the while Fr. Frank was filling his head about how Shaw needed to be stopped and Austin was the only one brave and strong enough to do it. He told him that it would atone for not being able to save his brother."

I asked, "Did you ever figure out why Danny called out for Fr. Frank at the church?"

"Austin told me that Fr. Frank was down by the river with him that night. It was the first murder and they were still working out how to go about it. Danny got spooked by Fr. Frank telling him that he had to make a sacrifice and took off. Austin had to chase him down and then drag him back to the river and kill him."

"That's so sick," Adele said and we all agreed.

"It was Fr. Lundy, the associate priest, who sent the photo to the newspaper and then told Cooper about Fr. Frank. He didn't know the whole story, but he knew enough to be rightly suspicious," I explained. Fr. Lundy came forward after Fr. Frank was arrested and told us his role in the whole thing.

Adele asked, "Did Austin confess to everything?"

Luke confirmed, "As the medics came to work on the three of them, Austin told me everything. He said he wanted to stop but he was so confused and conflicted. It was Fr. Frank who sent him after Cooper. Once he attacked Cooper like that, Austin said something snapped for him. It was like he woke up and realized all the damage he was doing wasn't going to bring back his brother. Hurting Shaw wasn't going to accomplish anything."

I still didn't understand how that happened. "How did Fr. Frank get Shaw there?"

"Fr. Frank used Shaw's ego against him," Luke said, offering a wry laugh. "It was rather simple really. Fr. Frank told him he knew where

Austin was and this was Shaw's opportunity to bring him in. Shaw jumped at the chance and went there willingly. Once he got there, he realized what he had walked into. Fr. Frank wanted Austin to kill Shaw since he hadn't been arrested for the other murders. Austin didn't want to do it. He figured if Cooper was there, there'd be a witness to what Fr. Frank was doing."

"Austin wanted to get caught," Cooper said, drawing our attention. "Whether he consciously was doing things to get caught or it was all subconscious, he didn't want to continue. He had to know if he kept showing up at the scenes and being photographed that someone would start to put the pieces together. He wanted to be stopped."

Adele stared over at him. "It sounds like you forgive him for what he did to you."

"I don't know if forgiveness is what I feel. He was a troubled man who had suffered a great loss. Someone he should have been able to trust exploited that." Cooper shrugged dismissively. "I feel bad for him in a lot of ways."

Adele smiled over at him lovingly and then turned her head to Luke. "What's going to happen to all of them?"

"New Orleans will have the first crack at prosecution. I'm working with Clive to connect all the other locations. You wouldn't believe how many other jurisdictions still didn't believe their cases were murders even with Austin's confession. After New Orleans, we will extradite him to Little Rock and then up to Troy. Those are the three of the eight right now on board."

"What about Fr. Frank?" I asked, still annoyed that I hadn't seen through his lies.

"He'll be prosecuted in New Orleans for conspiracy to commit murder and shooting Austin and Shaw. He's sitting in a prison hospital right now healing from the gunshot wounds."

"Why didn't you kill him?" Adele asked. "You had every justification to. No one would have blamed you."

Luke sat there for a moment not saying anything. Finally, he said simply, "I honestly don't know. I think a part of me wanted him to pay for his crimes and killing him was an easy out for him. I could neutralize him without killing him, so I did. I'd like to think I'd do that even if he wasn't a priest, which he isn't anymore. The diocese defrocked him immediately."

There was still something that was bothering me. I had heard all the information through Luke and hadn't been involved in any interrogation by him or Clive. "Why did Austin go all the way up to Troy? Why choose that location?"

"Austin got frustrated and thought that if they went back to the northeast, similar to the older cases, then someone might connect Shaw. He knew a previous case had happened there." Luke raised his eyebrows. "Austin got more than he bargained for with Trevor. He had overheard them talking in the pub about not believing it was Shaw sending the emails. Austin assumed they had figured it out. He was afraid they were going to tell someone. You were right that Austin killed him in that warehouse trying to get information out of him. Then when he died, Austin waited until morning and threw his body in the river. That's why Trevor didn't move with the current. He'd only been in the water a short time."

Adele sighed. "It was all so pointless. All those deaths for nothing. Will Shaw face any jail time?"

I knew this was the most frustrating part for all of us. "We don't know. New Orleans can't prosecute him because it was the first case and he didn't know in advance. The Little Rock prosecutor's office said they'd consider it. Troy has declined to prosecute him for lack of evidence. As Luke said, the other jurisdictions are hesitant to even listen to Austin's confession." There was only one bit of good news I had to share. "Shaw was freaked out enough by the whole thing that he's promised to let the Cross Killers theory go. He's going to make a public announcement and then retire."

"It's already out there," Cooper said. "The damage is done. There are online forums full of people who believe the Cross Killers theory is real. There's no walking that back. Consider what the families have gone through."

I recalled what Philip said to me on our call. "Those families are working together to get the closure they need."

"That's important," Adele said. "Cooper, what's the plan for your cases now that you're going to be out of commission for a few months?"

"Weeks," Cooper corrected, holding back a smile. "I hired some help."

My phone rang as Cooper gave the highlights about the new investigators. I excused myself so I could answer my mother's call in the other room. The one regret I had about the case was that I hadn't been able to stay in Troy long enough to spend some quality time with her and my sister. Before I could even say hello my mother blurted out the news.

"Tim Rattan was released from prison after eighteen years for the murder of Alex McCormick. His case was overturned on an appeal and the prosecutor's office is considering retrying him. He called the house looking for you. I took a message but told him I couldn't give out your cellphone number. What do you want me to do?"

"Why would he call me?" I asked, wondering how he'd get my mother's number.

"You all went to college together. I assume he knows you're an investigator. He said he needs your help because he didn't kill Alex and can prove it." My mother remained quiet for several moments. "Jack thinks you should take the case."

Alex had been murdered in our college apartment during our senior year of college. We had been good friends at the time and she had been dating Tim. Everyone assumed he killed her. I had my doubts even then. Tim and I had several classes together and he didn't seem like that kind of guy. But I was young and assumed the cops knew more than me.

I didn't take long to consider it. "Tell Jack I'll be up in a few days."

I hung up and walked back into the living room. They were talking about the latest binge on a streaming channel. All eyes turned to me. "Is everything okay?" Luke asked.

"It's fine," I said, not wanting to tell Luke or Cooper right now that I was leaving. I wanted to just let things be calm for one more night.

When Adele and Cooper were focused on each other, Luke leaned into me and said, "When we get home, I want to talk to you about a promotion Captain Meadows offered."

I smiled, happy for him. I squeezed his arm. "That sounds exciting. I need to talk to you too, about my mother's call." We left it at that and enjoyed the rest of our evening.

It sounded like changes were on the horizon.

# About the Author

Stacy M. Jones was born and raised in Troy, New York, and currently lives in Little Rock, Arkansas. She is a full-time writer and holds masters' degrees in journalism and in forensic psychology. She currently has three series available for readers: paranormal women's fiction/cozy mystery Harper & Hattie Magical Mystery Series, the hard-boiled PI Riley Sullivan Mystery Series and the FBI Agent Kate Walsh Thriller Series. To access Stacy's Mystery Readers Club with three free novellas, one for each series, visit StacyMJones.com.

**You can connect with me on:**
- http://www.stacymjones.com
- https://twitter.com/SMJonesWriter
- https://www.facebook.com/StacyMJonesWriter
- https://www.bookbub.com/profile/stacy-m-jones
- https://www.goodreads.com/StacyMJonesWriter

# Also by Stacy M. Jones

Read Book #9 WHAT HE SAW in the PI Riley Sullivan Mystery Series

**Access the Free Mystery Readers' Club Starter Library**
PI Riley Sullivan Mystery Series novella "The 1922 Club Murder"
FBI Agent Kate Walsh Thriller Series novella "The Curators"
Harper & Hattie Mystery Series novella "Harper's Folly"

Sign up for the starter library along with launch-day pricing, special behind-the-scenes access, and extra content not available anywhere else. Hit subscribe at
http://www.stacymjones.com/

**Please leave a review for The Drowned Boys. Reviews help more readers find my books. Thank you!**

**Other books by Stacy M. Jones by series and order to date:**

**FBI Agent Kate Walsh Thriller Series**
The Curators
The Founders
Miami Ripper
Mad Jack
The Fuse
Dead Senate

**PI Riley Sullivan Mystery Series**
The 1922 Club Murder
Deadly Sins

The Bone Harvest
Missing Time Murders
We Last Saw Jane
Boston Underground
The Night Game
Harbor Cove Murders
The Drowned Boys
What He Saw

**Harper & Hattie Magical Mystery Series**
Harper's Folly
Saints & Sinners Ball
Secrets to Tell
Rule of Three
The Forever Curse
The Witches Code
The Sinister Sisters
Scandal Knocks Twice

**WHAT HE SAW**

Two cases with unreliable witnesses. One cold case in a sleepy college town. The other the victims have a strange carving on their backs.

Eyewitness testimony is often unreliable. PI Riley Sullivan knows this and when she's asked to investigate the case of her murdered college roommate and the only witness is the man convicted of the crime, she doesn't have a lot to go on. She is drawn back to her college days and must for the first time confront the murder and all the people she once called friends. Along the way, she wonders if she knew them at all. Can she uncover long-buried secrets to find the killer?

Meanwhile, Det. Luke Morgan and Riley's partner, Cooper Deagnan, are faced with challenging cases of their own. Cooper witnesses what he believes is a murder and the cops are hard-pressed to take him seriously – at first. Once the body is found, what Cooper witnessed conflicts with the evidence at hand. When a cryptic carving on the victim's back ties to another case, it's apparent something sinister is lurking. The pair must confront the seedy underbelly of the city to find and stop a killer.

www.ingramcontent.com/pod-product-compliance
Lightning Source LLC
Chambersburg PA
CBHW021227310726
48971CB00006B/1716